RED BUOYS,
BLUE DOLPHINS

RED BUOYS, BLUE DOLPHINS

America's Homeland Security under Threat

RALPH E. DANBERT

iUniverse, Inc.
Bloomington

Red Buoys, Blue Dolphins
America's Homeland Security under Threat

iUniverse books may be ordered through booksellers or by contacting:

iUniverse
1663 Liberty Drive
Bloomington, IN 47403
www.iuniverse.com
1-800-Authors (1-800-288-4677)

ISBN: 978-1-4759-9352-3 (sc)
ISBN: 978-1-4759-9354-7 (hc)
ISBN: 978-1-4759-9353-0 (ebk)

Library of Congress Control Number: 2013910173

Printed in the United States of America

iUniverse rev. date: 06/06/2013

Dedicated to
BARBARA LYNN

CHAPTER 1

Saturday, Day 1, 11:00 hours.

Nothing exciting ever happens on the Olympic Peninsula, yet Matt and Doc had gone only a short distance on their stroll on the Olympic Discovery Trail when a loud explosion rattled the air. It came from the beach area ahead of them.

"It's along the water, come on. Let's get up there." Matt took off at a run.

Sprinting around a clump of trees on the point, they could see the remains of a van, burning furiously on the beach. The van was about fifty feet from the trail and thirty feet above high-water mark. Scattered flotsam and debris dotted the sand. Heat from the fire reached them as they approached. They even felt it radiating from the sand as they ran toward the spectacle. Spiral fingers of flame sent billowing black smoke, mostly from the tires, clawing the air for altitude, creating a leaf shaking wind. Matt tried to take it all in as they got near.

Three young boys, riding their bikes along the trail were already at the scene, standing watching the van burn. They were unaware of two bodies lying in the sand about thirty feet away.

Doc was the first to spot the downed men. "Look over there Matt, between those two big logs." he called, pointing at the still bodies on the beach. Shredded clothing, exposed and torn flesh were evident. Blood escaped from puncture wounds covering their bodies, as if they had been perforated with a shotgun. Matt knelt beside one man, Doc took the other.

"This one's alive." Matt shouted.

Doc scrambled over, while Matt gently rolled the body onto its back, he asked, "Find any vitals?" Not waiting for an answer, Doc felt the carotid artery in the man's neck. "Weak, but it's there." He pulled the eyelids back. "Pupils dilated. Get someone to go for the ambulance"

Matt, thinking ahead, ran over toward the boys. People were gathering now to see what had happened. They were crowding around the burning van. Matt yelled, "Get back. The whole thing could blow. Move away."

People scattered. "You boys." He took the arm of the closest one. "You, get on your bikes and go to a phone and hurry. Call an ambulance, fire department and police." The boys wheeled away and lit out to complete their tasks. Not only would that get the help needed, it would also remove the boys from danger.

Walking back to help Doc, Matt couldn't believe the damage spread out in the sand. The sand, still smoking was strewn with various debris. A little up the beach the Chevy van was ripped apart. One side was torn off and thrown along the beach with the remaining carcass, half filled with firewood, still flaming. It was now a pile of twisted, burning metal.

A rectangular depression in the sand between the van and the water's edge was close to five feet long and, Matt guessed, a foot deep. It looked newly dug. Logs and sawdust were strewn away from this depression in a radial pattern. What could have caused this carnage? Matt considered the van's gas tank, if it still held fuel, this was no place for a crowd of curious spectators. He began clearing them away, a task made easier by the intense heat from the fiery van. Matt kept at them and had moved most of them back to a safe distance as the police arrived. Once he saw them, he headed up the beach to help Doc.

"How is the survivor?"

"Not quite dead. Severe lacerations and he's losing a lot of blood. There are some bones broken and I'm sure he's torn up pretty badly inside. That must have been some explosion. It really beat these guys up." Two different siren sounds neared as they were bent over the bodies.

"Here's the ambulance now," someone in the crowd yelled.

"Matt, I'll leave you to get this man to the hospital. I'm going on ahead to prepare the equipment and support staff I'll need. Don't waste any time getting him moved. He may not last long!"

The fire truck arrived at almost the same time as the ambulance. Matt directed paramedics to the injured man and passed on Doc's instructions. He walked back to the still burning van where the firefighters were spraying carbon dioxide.

Scanning the area, he could see some logs had been cut into short, wood-stove lengths with chain saws. Seeing wood half filling the van, he felt confident assuming the men really were wood cutters. That explained what they were doing on the beach, Matt thought, but what could have caused the explosion? He scanned for some clue. He looked particularly for a fuel can which could have held chain saw gasoline. The saws themselves should be here someplace, too.

With siren wailing, the ambulance took off at high speed. Totally engrossed in the destruction, Matt hadn't even noticed the stretcher being carried past.

Matt deduced, a spark from the chain saws could have ignited the gasoline in a fuel can. This, in turn, likely set off the fuel in the van's tank. If his deduction was right, there should be some remains of the saws or gas cans. There were none to be found.

The crowd of curious began leaving and the police, busy until now with crowd control, were trying to find out who the downed men were and what they were doing on the beach. Moving around among people left, they questioned anyone with information to offer. One approached Matt.

"I'm Deputy Petrie," he stated, "Aaron Petrie. I've talked to some of the people here. I understand you were one of the first to arrive."

Matt said, "I'm Commander Mathew Reynolds with the Coast Guard." He told the deputy what he knew.

An older couple came over to the deputy. "We were walking by just minutes before it happened," the man said. "These two men were on the beach cutting up logs with chain saws."

"Noisy chain saws." the woman with him injected.

"I thought they might have been parks board workers," the man continued. "It looked like they were cleaning up the beach area, what with all the garbage that floats in and ruins what could be a fine beach."

"There ought to be a law," the woman added, "about when they're allowed to make all that noise, I mean the quiet of the seashore and all."

"Yes, Ma'am, I understand," the deputy said. "Did you see anything out of the ordinary? Were there any cars going by or parked on the road?"

"No!" said the woman, "That's what was so nice, there was no other noise at all except waves lapping on the shore, then those saws . . . , they make so much noise."

"Yes, Ma'am. Did you notice anything, sir? Where there any boats close to shore?"

"No, not that I can recall. It was quiet."

"Thank you both." The deputy closed that line of questioning and walked back toward Matt.

"Well, deputy, I guess you have the beach under control now, so if you need me, you can catch me at the Coast Guard base. Doc Johnson is at the hospital with the other man. You can catch him there. Looks like the fire department has the blaze under control."

"Thank you, Commander. We'll likely give you both a call later."

Matt went back to get his car. Walking along the beach he and Doc had walked not more than half an hour ago, he tried to fit pieces of the puzzle together. They were there, but he couldn't make a clear picture.

Well, today was a workday and Matt had a patrol to complete. He headed back to the base to take his cutter out into the Strait to start his daily patrol sweep.

The Coast Guards obligation to protect the country never escaped Matt. That was one of the reasons he enlisted at an early age. The sea figured largely during his youth and he felt comfortable near it. Matt's base is located in the Strait of Juan de Fuca at Port Angeles on the Northwest corner of America and it's a huge area. His base responsibility covered safety and security of the entire ocean from Tacoma and Seattle in Puget Sound, north and west along the Olympic Peninsula to the open sea at Cape Flattery. The base was built on Ediz Hook, a long spit on the shore of Port Angeles, reaching in a narrow arc two miles into the Strait.

Matt stood, feet astride on the bridge of the cutter Confidence, looking out of the encircling bridge windows, binoculars scanning the water ahead. Cumulus clouds dotted the sky like big cotton puffs while up ahead, scattered herring gulls screamed, wheeling lazily in the light breeze. The bright glistening sun bounced off the shining white paint of Confidence as the ship sliced easily through the water. Green waves lapping at her hull formed a long, frothy tail of white foam trailing in her wake. Up ahead and to port, a concentration of gulls caught Matt's eye. Swinging the glasses and focusing to a mile or so, he could see hundreds of birds on and above the water.

"Steer a heading of 270 degrees, helm." Matt ordered. He punched a button on the intercom calling his first mate, Lieutenant Ernie Daniels, "Ernie, break off what you're doing and get up here fast."

"On my way, Skipper."

Minutes later Matt ordered, "Stop engines." The second mate swung the engine controls to the order and both pulsing

Alco 251B diesel engines came to a slow halt. The cutter's momentum carried her toward the gathering of birds.

Ernie appeared at the starboard bridge door. "What's up, Skipper?"

"Have a look ahead," Matt said, pointing with the glasses. "See that flock of birds? What do you make of it?"

Ernie didn't need the glasses to follow Matt's gesture. "I see an awful lot of gulls. Hey, I also see a lot of fish on the surface, a big patch of them. It's not a school of herring either, they're not moving at all. They look dead. Boy, are those gulls having a feed. They won't have to eat again for a week."

"I think you're right. Next question Ernie, what killed them?"

"Hard to say, Skipper, I haven't seen that many dead fish since Vietnam."

The drifting cutter now slowed silently to a stop, slicing the middle of the patch in two. Only the noise of angry gulls and the ship's radios broke the quiet. The gulls, irate at the intruding ship, had taken to the air, circling and darting around the cutter, squawking angrily, impatient to get back to the food.

In the background, radios chattered. A network of stations ashore and on ships dotted this coast, looking after occasionally heavy marine traffic. Operators talking to other ships and shore stations seemed at times to be talking to themselves. No one appeared to listen.

"Get down to the main deck and net some of those fish. Take some water in sample bottles, Ernie. I'd like to take them in for analysis. I want to find out what killed them. If there's something toxic in the water, we'll have more work to do."

Ernie went quickly out the door and down the ladder, calling to a couple of his deck hands on the way. Two crewmen threw out a dip net, quickly hauling in a dozen or more fish. Ernie picked a variety, dumping them into plastic bags. He saw Matt's six-foot-two frame scurry down the ladder and calling, "They're not all dead, some are flopping around."

The gills on one codfish moved and the tail quivered on another. Stepping forward, Matt flipped a couple. "Look at that. You can tell the ones that are dead; they've been attacked by gulls. Look at this snapper; the eyes and a good part of his back are gone. The live ones aren't touched, and look; they're not all snappers, either."

Matt poked at the pile of fish. "Some cod, flounder, snapper. Look over there . . . a mud shark, Ernie."

"No salmon or herring?"

"Seems strange, Ernie. These are all bottom feeding fish. Maybe there was some seismic activity on the sea bed. You mentioned seeing something similar in 'Nam?"

"Sure, when the navy used to lay depth charges. The explosions always brought up fish. We also got the same results when we were mine sweeping. We'd pop a few mines to the surface with the sweep, then standoff and fire at them with rifles or deck guns. They'd go off with a big roar and a spectacular fountain of water. Any fish in the area were killed by the concussion, they'd float to the surface just like these and the gulls went after them the same way."

"Let's go back up to the bridge. We'll dig out the charts and print a sonar plot of this area."

Matt had grown up near Bremerton, Washington. Even as a boy he'd had awareness beyond the initial pleasures of the sea and considered the very future of mankind depended on the ocean. From an early age he formed a bond with the sea. During his younger years he spent as much time as possible on the water.

As a youngster, he began basic training in the ways of the sea. Holding no fear of the water, he swam well, learned to sail when he was ten. He won the yacht club junior championship at twelve, and went on to take the overall title at sixteen, besting many of the older boys in the club to do it. Yet he had a healthy respect for the sea. His girlfriend had died on a fishing trip. It was a needless death. If he had taken time to put on her life vest she'd be alive today. Matt never forgot that. Her death brought home just how tenuous life and friendships are. He never got close to a relationship with another girl after that.

At seventeen, Matt joined the Coast Guard as a cadet. Their primary mission, to protect life and property at sea, fit right in with his career goals. He tried to live up to their motto, 'Semper Paratus', always ready. Matt's knowledge of the sea and ships smoothed the way for rapid promotions through the ranks to his present position. He now captained the cutter Confidence. Life was good for Matt. He had almost everything he wanted. With a square jaw, dark wavy hair and trim a trim, fit body he was a catch for any woman, yet he had none. He did his best to avoid entanglements. He'd just turned thirty-two last week and even though he was single, he had neatly tucked away most of the loose ends in his life.

"Dig out the charts, Ernie. I'll check the sonar. There might be a clue there."

Matt instructed the helmsman to bring the cutter about and line up for a sonar plot directly over the area where the fish floated. In his head, Matt calculated the tidal drift and picked a course to where the fish came from. "Engines ahead slow."

Bells chimed again as Ernie swung the telegraph handles and the engine room responded to his order. The cutter, making a quick half circle in the water, headed back, paralleling its wake as Matt set up the sonar chart scale and began recording. The gulls weren't happy with this second intrusion and set to screaming loudly. Matt ignored them.

"Here are the charts, Skipper." Ernie laid the charts out on the table beside the sonar set. Matt studied them "I'd place us about here," he said, pointing to a spot three miles from shore and ten miles west of the Coast Guard base at Port Angeles.

Looking thoughtful, he said, "Good. Now get a GIS fix on our position." Matt moved over to the video display and read off the longitude and latitude co-ordinates from the video screen. "The chart shows thirty fathoms below our keel."

Matt rejoined Ernie and checked the chart for any clue to what had killed the fish. "I'd be more inclined to think of seismic activity if the bottom were more irregular," Matt said, looking at the charts. "What's the sonar saying now?"

Ernie moved over to the plotter, watching it produce squiggly lines. "The plot coming out verifies the chart we're looking at. One hundred and eighty-six feet and fairly flat."

Matt pushed the cap to the back of his head thoughtfully rubbing his brow. "If there's a chemical spill in the area, we'd better find it in a hurry." Too many lives could be at stake, particularly the sea life. Matt thought about a large local fishing industry; it depended on having a wholesome supply of fish and shellfish. Harmful chemicals in the water would be disastrous. His mind raced ahead.

"If this is from some fisherman using explosives, we should have seen surface activity like a boat or skiff. Is there anything close by?"

Ernie checked the area. To the west, the strait led directly out to the open Pacific, sixty miles away. A large bulk carrier was a long way off, inbound. "No small ships to the west." Slowly swinging the glasses to the north, he could see the mountains of Vancouver Island with low hills of the southern island barely visible through the haze. Victoria, Canada, twenty miles to the north, was difficult to see during most summer days because of an ever-present haze. At night, though, its lights could sparkle, casting bright glows on any clouds.

"No small ships in sight to the north either."

To the east, a container ship silently coursed outbound from an American port, probably Seattle or Tacoma. A commercial fishing vessel was also outbound. A small sport fishing boat bobbed in the waves about two miles to the south. Bracing himself against the cutter's gentle movement, Matt peered out to the south, squinting against the glare of the summer sun reflecting on the water. He spotted a divers flag on the boat. Three men could be seen aboard. "I don't think scuba divers would be foolish enough to be fishing with explosives" Matt noted. "Maybe we'd better check them out anyway. They may have seen or heard whatever it was that caused this mess. Helm, steer 240 degrees."

"Aye Sir. Steer two-four-zero degrees."

He ordered Ernie to increase speed to twenty knots. The engine room telegraph bells clanged again.

Leaning into a turn and gathering speed, the cutter headed toward the scuba divers' boat at full tilt. Halfway there, the ship's radio squawked, "MAYDAY! MAYDAY! MAYDAY! Cruiser Sundancer on fire! Require immediate assistance, Mayday! Mayday! Mayday!"

Matt grabbed the radio mike, keying the transmit switch on the distress frequency. "This is Coast Guard cutter Confidence, receiving you loud and clear. What is your location?" Why, he thought, don't these guys ever tell us their location when seconds count?

"Sundancer is ten miles northeast of Port Angeles! Hurry!" The panic in the voice was obvious.

Matt knew his helmsman would anticipate the next order but he make no move to swing the wheel until he heard it. "Helm, new heading 095 degrees."

"Aye Sir, zero-nine-five degrees." The cutter responded immediately.

"Roger, Sundancer. Cutter Confidence on the way. How many people on board and what type of craft are you?"

"Coast Guard, Sundancer has six people aboard. We're a thirty-eight foot Berman."

"Roger, Sundancer." Matt knew Berman hulls were fiberglass. Quickly estimating her burning speed, he switched the radio to the frequency of the base. "Port Angeles, cutter Confidence responding to an emergency aboard cruiser Sundancer ten miles northeast of the base, six people aboard. Report from vessel indicates fire. Alert chopper crew."

"Roger, Roger cutter Confidence. We are listening to your transmissions and are standing by, chopper ready."

Matt had control of the situation and the base stood by to assist as necessary. He changed back to emergency frequency while doing some quick mental calculations.

"Cruiser Sundancer, this is Coast Guard cutter. Our estimated time to reach you is sixteen minutes. Can you hold on that long?" Matt could now see smoke on the horizon.

"Negative! We can't last. Fire out of control. We're going into dinghy and life jackets!"

"Roger, Sundancer, stand clear as quickly as possible in case your fuel tanks blow. I'll dispatch a helicopter to you immediately."

He switched back to base frequency requesting chopper support. Base acknowledged and Matt returned to the emergency frequency, listening for activity. The cruiser likely had no portable radio and Matt assumed there'd be no more transmissions once the crew had abandoned her. It would take minutes to get to the cruiser and Matt had time to reflect on the dead fish. He wondered if the boat with the scuba divers had a radio and if they were listening as this little drama unfolded. Probably not. Stepping over to the chart table and opening the ship's log, Matt entered details of the dead fish as best he could. The thoughts were soon crowded out of his mind as he and his crew made plans to extinguish the fire.

Drawing closer, Matt watched the chopper lifting people off the dingy then departing as he approached. Luckily, there was a helipad at the Olympic Medical Center in Port Angeles, where the survivors would get medical treatment.

Fire and smoke billowing out of the cruiser's cabin and cockpit area kept the cutter back some distance. "We'll stand off upwind, to the port side Ernie."

Matt maneuvered the cutter alongside as close as safety allowed bringing his one, big fire monitor to bear, playing it up and down the length of the cruiser, its heavy stream blanketing the cruiser. The fire fell quickly under control, and the cutter moved closer, allowing her deck crew to board the still-smoldering hull. Three men jumped aboard with hand extinguishers, spraying the few remaining hot spots. Now, with the smoke disappearing, Matt could see the gutted interior of the cabin and deck-head above almost completely burned away. His crew made fast a tow line and the slow haul back to shore began. They circled around and captured the now empty dingy.

Confidence towed the charred hull to the Yacht Haven marina in Port Angeles, where its owners would have to decide its fate. Matt made the necessary entries in his log while returning to the Coast Guard base half a mile west. On arrival he had the crew secure the cutter then went ashore, walking to the base commander's office to report.

A paved road ran the full length of the Hook and a wire fence with a guardhouse half way to the tip of the Hook marked the start of the base proper. Ediz Hook had once been a major coaling station. Outbound steamships would put in to fill their bunkers with local coal. What was left of an old lighthouse was still visible at the tip of the Hook. The Coast Guard had been using the spit since 1935; it was the oldest of their Pacific Coast stations. At one time an aircraft landing strip covered the final four thousand feet of spit, and during the Second World War it had been a bustling air station of six hundred men. The strip was still there, but had been downgraded so that only the east portion was used and then only for search and rescue helicopters. Without maintenance, the concrete runway surface was spalling and cracking, weeds were growing everywhere along its main length. Two large hangers stood at the east end of the spit as mute evidence to what had once been. These were now used for helicopter storage and maintenance. Some of the bases' smaller boats were also stored here, and training rooms now filled spaces that once held aircraft parts bins and repair shops.

A two-story administration building, too large for the present staff, contained the operations center on the main floor. The second floor was not used. Another two story building, a barracks block, stood unused. Smaller buildings housed the meteorology and weather station, radio equipment and base maintenance equipment. Commodore Frank Coulter commanded this base of one hundred and fifty men and five vessels. Matt knocked on his door.

"Come." he ordered brusquely.

Matt entered and the two exchanged greetings as Matt tucked his hat under his arm and stood in front of the desk.

"Bit of action today, Matt?" said the Commodore not looking up from the papers he shuffled. A swarthy, balding man in his early fifties, he stood a little less than six feet and was about twenty pounds heavier than he should be.

"Just a little. We were lucky the cutter was in position to save those people. It could have been tragic. Have you heard how they are? I lost touch with them after the helicopter took them away."

"Oh, they're fine. Captain has minor burns, nothing serious. One passenger singed a little. They were treated at the hospital and released not too long ago. Doc Johnson wanted you to know."

"Is anyone going to be talking to them, to find out how the fire started?"

"Doc asked questions. Apparently they had been fishing for a couple of hours and were just going to cook lunch. From what he could make out, nobody purged the cabin before lighting the stove. Stupid. Looks like your safety course is sorely needed."

"I guess so. I'll have to put more time into that course. It's almost ready, a few loose ends, some slides to prepare, then I'll be set to present it".

"Don't take too long."

"I think the first place I should give it is at the local yacht club," Matt said, rubbing his chin pensively, "if today's accident is any indication. Oh! Say, Frank, we saw something strange out there about fifteen miles west of here and three miles north of Agate Bay. Our patrol took us into a mess of dead fish floating over a circle about half a mile in diameter. I'm still at a loss to explain it." Matt paused, then went on, "Are you aware of any underwater seismic activity or the navy testing shells or underwater explosives?"

"Not to my knowledge." The Commodore was suddenly more interested. "I don't know of any activity that would kill fish. What about a chemical spill of some sort? Did you pick up any samples so we could have them tested?"

"Yes, we got some. Ernie is taking them to the lab."

"Anything unusual about them?"

"Not that I could see. I will say, though, I've never seen so many fish killed in one area before. Ernie said he'd seen similar kills in Vietnam."

"The navy's submarine test range is right about where you were. It could be them."

"I'll check the navy and then the environmental protection agency. They're both pretty quick to pick up on this sort of thing. Other than that, I don't know what else we can do right now."

"Do you have a fix on the location?"

"Yes, it's in the log. If we want, we can go back to the exact spot. I even took a sonar print of the bottom and GIS position." Matt glanced at the big military clock on the commodore's wall. It showed 19:00 hours, seven o'clock.

"Well, Frank, I'm going to get something to eat, and then head home."

"I don't think I'll be far behind you. Oh, say Doc wanted to see you at the hospital when you have time, Matt, but stay handy for a while, a scuba diver's missing. We'll be mounting a search if he doesn't show up by tomorrow morning. I'd like to send you out right away, but there's not much sense going now, with darkness almost here, too dangerous. Are your underwater men ready if necessary?"

"Sure. They all still have some time left out of this month's dive quota. In fact, I'm still current if it comes to an extended search. Give me a call as soon as you get anything definite."

Matt left the commodore's office, walking across the parking lot to his car. Getting in, he drove along the spit toward town, then onto the main road toward the hospital. This morning's disaster and thoughts of dead fish were racing through his active mind.

Marine Drive ran a short distance from the spit then you had a choice of paralleling the beach a hundred yards away on Front Street or 1st street. The beach area itself was bordered by park land with green grass and trees.

On the way to see Doc, Matt began wondering if the missing scuba diver belonged to the boat he had seen out by the dead fish. He had nothing to tie them together except the fact there were three of them in the boat and divers, safe divers that is, usually travel in pairs, using the buddy system.

Parking in the hospital visitor's lot, Matt entered through the emergency doors. He asked the duty nurse, "Is Doctor Johnson still in emergency?"

"Yes, he is. Would you like to wait? He might be a while."

"I'm Matt Reynolds. He wants to see me when he's free."

"Fine. If you'll have a seat in the waiting room down that hall," she said, indicating the corridor behind him, "I'll tell him as soon as I can."

Matt found a room with some hard wooden bench seats and a few armchairs. A couple of low tables held magazines, old magazines, for visitors. Harsh, fluorescent lights added a cold, uncomfortable atmosphere to the room. There were no other people around that Matt could see. Picking the top magazine from the table nearest him, he sat on a bench and began flipping through pages.

The nurse entered. "I told the Doctor you were here. He asked that you wait. He'll be out as soon as he can. Would you like some coffee?"

"No thanks, I'll just read a bit until he gets here."

The nurse went back about her work and Matt sat staring at the pages of an out-dated Time magazine. He suddenly realized he was tired. He closed his eyes to clear his vision and was startled by a hand shaking his shoulder. He woke with a jolt.

"Matt, sorry to have taken so long but this guy's in rougher shape than I had thought. It took a long time just getting him stabilized."

"What time is it Doc?"

"One thirty. Let's go to the cafeteria and have a cup of coffee while we talk."

"Sure, Doc, I've had quite a day, how's yours?"

"Like a one armed paperhanger. I guessed you were busy, too."

"A little. Understand you patched up the burn victims from that cruiser fire."

"Yep. Only two of them needed treatment. Second degree burns on one, the other isn't bad at all, minor scrapes and light burns. More shock than injury. They were lucky you people were close enough to help."

Matt's brow furrowed as he heard this. It distressed him when accidents happened at sea. Needless accidents at that.

"Just part of the service, Doc." He felt some pride. He enjoyed the role of shepherd, tending to his flock of boats and sailors. This was his ocean and he felt responsible for what happened on it.

Walking slowly down the dimly lit corridor they emerged at the eating area near the far end of the hospital. It had the sterile smell typical of hospital cafeterias. Picking up coffee, they walked to a table near a window looking out over the harbor.

"How's the patient?"

"Not very good, I'm afraid. His internal problems are giving us most of our trouble, punctured lung and liver, ruptured spleen. The standard injuries you'd expect from an explosion. I saw this type of damage many times in Vietnam. Our first problem was to get him stabilized. He also has a concussion to add to the problem."

"Has he been conscious at all?"

"No. He seems to be drifting close to it now and then but we've had him well sedated to minimize shock when we were inside repairing his torn organs. We've taken some x-rays. He doesn't seem to have too many broken bones. Ribs, of course, took the brunt of the blast but his arms and legs aren't broken. He's lucky in that regard. Had quite a knock on his head though. I'm worried about that."

"What's the prognosis?"

"I'd say 50/50."

"That doesn't sound too good."

"Can I get you some more coffee, Matt?"

"Sure. I'm wide awake now. A little more coffee's not going to keep me any more awake."

Doc walked over to the counter and came back with fresh coffee.

"You know, Doc, I've been trying to visualize what the hell happened. Things just don't add up somehow."

"In what way?"

"Well, if those guys were cutting firewood, and I have no doubt they were, what caused the explosion? The gas can of spare fuel for the saws could have blown up, even gathering some assistance from the fuel in the van, if it blew up. But even with this help it doesn't add up to such a heavy blast. Did you see that hole on the beach?"

"No. I didn't have time."

"Well, the van was torn apart and the men were thrown a good distance up the beach. That took a considerable amount of energy. More, I think, than was available from all the gasoline available in the area at the time. There was a trench blown in the beach, too. That's another puzzle. I'm going to have closer look at that."

"You never know what these guys carry in their vans these days. They might have had dynamite or stumping powder. Who knows?"

"I guess you're right. I'll have a talk with the Deputy tomorrow and see if he found anything. I looked all over for a gas can or chain saw earlier. I found neither. Maybe the man you've got here can shed some light. I'd like to talk to him if I could."

"We'll have to wait a while, probably a day or two. While you're surmising all these things, here's something you may as well add to your bag of pieces. The police have identified the two men as George Walker and Walter Parker. Parker is the patient now in intensive care. He lives in Seattle, and we've sent word to his family. Walker, the dead man, lived here in Port Angeles. The Deputy was over to the man's home a short time ago to break the news to his family. Now I'm coming to the strange part Matt. Parker has some unusual cuts along his left side; the upper part of his left thigh is all peppered with shrapnel. I've dug out some brown plastic material, copper bits and a few fiberglass chunks. The location and positioning of these wounds indicate he was leaning over with his left side toward the explosion at time zero."

"Christ. Maybe that's what happened to the chain saw and why I couldn't find any trace of it. It could have been blown to pieces. They have parts like that in them. But then the damage sounds more like an anti-personnel mine, not a chain saw. What was the other guy . . . what's his name?"

"Walker."

"Yeah. What was Walker's wound pattern like?"

"I don't know, Matt. I haven't had a chance to examine him yet. When we got to him on the beach he was dead. I'll get a chance to see tomorrow when I do the autopsy. I'll let you know what I find."

"Okay. I'd appreciate that."

"I guess there's not too much more I can do here tonight, so I'm going home to get some sleep. See you tomorrow."

"Fine. I'm going to stay for a while to make sure our survivor is looked after, and then hit the hay myself. Good night."

Matt drove home to his house on the bluff, changed from his uniform into a bathrobe, poured a drink and sat down to read the paper. After ten minutes he lost his concentration, deciding to shower and then sack out. Turning the shower to 'hot', he stripped. Running his fingers through his wavy hair, he made a mental note to get it cut soon and stepped into the shower. He reached up, adjusting the head to needle pulse, letting the sharp spears sting his back and shoulders. Toweling dry, he walked into the bedroom, pulled the covers back, hit the bed and fell sound asleep almost when his head hit the pillow.

CHAPTER 2

Matt woke at the crack of dawn with puzzling thoughts still going around in his head. There was obviously more to this beach thing than he could see. As he shaved, he couldn't help wondering what had blown up. Something Doc said had him going, the bit about shrapnel. What the hell could that have been? Then it occurred to him, of course, it must have been the chainsaw. It had plastic parts and the ignition includes copper parts, these were probably the chunks Doc found in the body of Walt Parker. Things were beginning to fit into place. That's why he couldn't find the chainsaw. It had been blown to smithereens. The fuel tank on the saw would hold enough gas to cause quite an explosion. Matt was pleased with this bit of deduction. How simple. But, what about the van? What caused it to blow? And was there enough energy in one chainsaw to fling two men half way up the beach? Something was still missing. Maybe a trip back to the beach would be beneficial now that he knew a little more, or thought he did. After breakfast he'd go down and look around again. He dressed quickly and drove to the Castaway's Restaurant near Yacht Haven. The view out its large picture windows overlooked small boats in the Haven and out towards the Coast Guard Base on the spit. Vancouver Island was visable in the distance. The tables were empty except for a lone fisherman. Matt was not the type to eat alone so, after picking up his breakfast order he walked over to the man by the window

"Mind if I join you?" Matt introduced himself.

"Sure, sit down" said the fisherman. "I'm always glad to have you people around, both ashore and on the water. My name's Jed Walters."

"Nice to meet you Jed, you from around this area?"

"No, I'm from a little town called Shine. It's on the Hood Canal, North of Bremerton. Do you know the where that is?"

"Actually, I grew up in that area. I've been to Shine many times. What are you doing up this way, Jed?"

"Just came up to see if I could tie into one of your big salmon."

"Have any success this morning?"

"Not a nibble, Matt. Don't know what's wrong. Maybe I'm using the wrong bait or maybe I'm down too deep. I've tried it all ways. Who knows what the fish want? I'll do better tomorrow."

"I'm sure you will, Jed, I've seen some good size fish come out of these waters this week. Up until yesterday, very few sport fishermen were skunked. They always got something."

"We'll keep trying," said Jed, "that's why most of us fish. It's not the catching, but the fishing. It's one of the most relaxing sports available."

"Talking about relaxing, Matt, I guess you people aren't going to be able to relax until that sub gets into its base next week."

"Oh, you mean the refitted Trident going down to Bangor. You know about that?"

"Yeah, that's the one. I understand the nuclear nuts are going to cause trouble."

"God, I hope not," said Matt," I don't think they realize what they're playing around with. Those things aren't like little powerboats. They can't stop and turn at will. It takes a long distance, sometimes miles to maneuver or turn them."

"Will your outfit be involved with escort duty, Matt?"

"Yep, we're finalizing routines and strategies now. The Government has been asked to lay down the law though to have civilians keep a safe distance from her. I'm hoping we don't have any trouble. It could be disastrous. If they don't do anything silly, we should be okay."

Matt finished his breakfast, downing the last of his coffee. As he was standing up he said, "Well, I've got to be going, Jed. Good luck with your fishing. They're out there. It may take some time and patience but you'll get them!"

"Thanks Matt, we'll do our best and let them come to us. Good luck to you on that sub deal."

Matt left the cafeteria and drove north on Marine Drive then 3rd Avenue to the beach. Walking along the sand, he tried again to put pieces together. They still didn't fit.

The hulk of the van was still on the beach and at this time, early in the morning, there were no people around. Just as well he thought, most of the area would be undisturbed. The first thing to do, he felt, was to figure out what fed the explosion. It seemed like too much damage to have been done with a pint of gasoline. He looked for pieces of the chainsaw. It seemed the best way to start. Trying to disturb as little as possible, he worked his way around the center of the blast area in ever enlarging circles. Fifty feet from the center he had still not found the saw. It occurred to him that it could have been blown to pieces, but even then he should have found some parts of it. A blade, the handle, even a spark plug. There was nothing. He walked slowly back to the van. The gas tank was located in the back part of the van and after Matt cleared away some of the debris he could see that the gas tank was more or less in place. It was dented and partially flattened which didn't make sense at all. If it had exploded, it should be been obvious, a jagged hole torn into it. Any explosion this tank had gone through had to have been from the exterior of the tank. It was flattened and any fuel forced out fed the fire, not the explosion. Matt was now fairly sure this was the tank's only contribution. So, now, if the gas didn't cause the blast, what did? He was back to square one.

Doc had mentioned last night that it was possible there was some stumping powder or dynamite in the van. Matt surveyed the wreck from a distance. If this were the case, the van would have exploded outward like a burst balloon. Here again this was not the case. The side toward the sea was caved in from the outside and the side away from the sea was also ragged and torn but it had been blown toward the beach road. No, Matt deduced, the explosion could only have come from a spot between the sea and the van. God. If he could only find the chainsaw it might be the key he needed.

The only place he hadn't looked at closely was the crater itself. It wasn't really 'that' large but a lot of sand and wood had been moved. Matt picked up a stick from the beach and began to carefully prod the sand at the side of the crater. Toward one end he dug up a short piece of brown plastic material. Putting it aside he continued to dig along the seaward side of the trough. His probe came up with a piece of copper wire hanging on a chunk of phenolic material like the stuff used to make electronic printed circuits boards. Digging further he came up with another chunk of brown plastic similar to the first except that it contained an actual segment of printed circuit board, with what looked like transistors and logic chips still attached. This was more like what he expected. These must be the pieces of the chainsaw ignition system he was looking for, but where were the rest of the parts?

These were the most promising pieces he had found, so he kept on digging along the crater side. His stick ran into something solid. He probed a little further and found it was much larger than the previous bits he'd found. In fact it was more in the shape of a box, about eight inches long four inches wide and two inches high. There was some writing on the long surface, but Matt couldn't distinguish what it said. He anticipated it was the name of the saw manufacturer or whomever it was that made the electronic parts. One end of the box had been ripped off and Matt could see a stack of printed circuit boards inside. There were three layers with small black and multicolored bits mounted on them. "Christ," he thought, "either this is part of the most sophisticated chainsaw in the world or it's not from a chainsaw at all." Maybe the guys had a small radio with them when they were cutting wood. That didn't make much sense either. Who can hear a radio with a chainsaw running? He kept on digging and continued to find more electronic bits and pieces along with some ribbon wire, like that usually found in computers. He was now looking at an electronic connector and trying desperately to make some sense out of the markings along its edge. He couldn't recognize the letters on it. Matt thought they looked like Greek, but he knew they were not. He dug some more and came up with a plastic door about six inches square, complete with hinges. It looked to Matt like an access door you'd normally find on an aircraft but was a little thicker than that and made of plastic. It was curved slightly as though it formed part of a cylinder and the edges were melted or burned. There were some more of the Greek-like letters on it. Matt added it to the pile that was growing by the minute. Whatever it had been was broken into many pieces and completely destroyed. 'Too bad,' Matt thought, 'whatever it was, it must have been expensive.'

Matt stood back now to survey the parts he had found, studying the crater and re-thinking the whole incident. It was obvious this was no chainsaw or radio he was digging out of the sand. It was also obvious that, whatever it was, it contained a considerable amount of an extremely powerful explosive material to have created this much destruction.

He picked up the brown plastic pieces again to study them a little more closely. Was this the stuff that Doc mentioned he had pulled out of the survivor?

'I wonder what Doc is finding in the dead man?' he thought. Doc was going to do an autopsy this morning. 'I'll bet he finds some of this material imbedded in the guys. I'd better get up there and find out.'

He didn't know what it was that he had found but he realized it was too important to leave lying around. He dug a shallow hole and reburied all the parts he had found, except the door piece, this he would take with him.

Walking back along the beach to the cafe where he had parked his car, he kept turning the plastic part over and over in his hands. The edges were shiny and smooth, but irregular in surface detail. It was fairly hard plastic. One side was curved and rough, looking like the bark of a tree while the other side was smooth and flat. The rough surface showed signs of short-term exposure to salt water. It couldn't have been too long though, as the marine growth had not had an opportunity to cover it too well.

Matt got into his car and drove to the hospital near-by. He checked at the reception desk, asking if Doc Johnson was available. "Are you Matt Reynolds?" the nurse questioned.

"That's right," Matt replied.

"He's expecting you. He's in his office, the first door on your right just down that hall." Matt knew the way. He walked to the door the nurse had pointed out, stopped, rapped on it, then opened it and walked in.

"Good morning, Matt, I've just finished the autopsy on Walker. You wouldn't believe what I found."

Matt held up the short piece of brown plastic," Was it anything like this?"

"Hey. How'd you know? Yes, there was a lot of that type material, along with some larger parts I couldn't identify. Where did you get that?"

"Down on the beach. This thing bothered me all night, so this morning I went down to see what I could find. I found more than I bargained for, but I'm no further ahead in determining what happened than I was last night."

Matt explained to Doc about the Greek writing he had discovered and Doc showed some interest. He also told him about the other parts that he had dug up and how he had buried them again.

"None of this makes any sense, Matt. Can you remember what the letters looked like?"

"Sure, this chunk of plastic I brought along has some of the writing on it. See here?" He showed Doc the smooth side of the plastic "door."

"These aren't Greek Matt, they're Russian. They're Cyrillic."

"Are you sure?"

"Of course I'm sure. We use Greek and Latin to write prescriptions. I'd recognize either of them in an instant. This is Russian."

"Geez, what have we got here, Doc?"

"I don't know. Maybe it's a fishing marker of some sort or some other type of equipment. Whatever it is it has killed one man and possibly another, depending on how Parker responds in the next day or so. Where do we go from here?"

"Fishing markers don't blow up, Doc. I guess we've got to find someone who knows what the hell this thing is. I'll contact the Navy and see if they can help. See you later, Doc."

"OK, Matt, let me know what it is when you find out."

"Sure Doc."

Matt drove back to the base and called his Commander. He filled in Commodore Coulter with what he knew and the two of them discussed the possible courses of action. The decision was that the Navy should be brought into the picture. They may have run into this type of electronic equipment before or they would at least know what to do with it. Beyond this the whole matter was in the hands of the town authorities.

"I don't want you spending too much time on this thing, Matt, we've got the Trident escort exercise to finalize and I'd prefer you give it your top priority. This beach explosion can best be left to the locals". Have you got your basic ship deployment worked out and your crew briefed on where to draw the line if push comes to shove? I don't want to give the anti-nukes any grounds for legal action. I guess what I'm saying is do what must be done, but make sure it's done with considerable forethought. You'll be working with Mike Chambers; he's the officer in charge of base security at Bangor."

"I know him Frank; I've worked with him before." Mat had mixed feelings about Chambers. He was just a little too gung-ho for the way Matt operated.

"Good. He'll provide you with necessary information about route and timing. There was also a chance that the Navy might bring her in underwater, but to the best of my knowledge that idea has been abandoned. I think they want to get all confrontations out of the way as early as possible in the Trident program."

"That would make good sense to me," said Matt. "If they were to sneak the sub in, anti-nukes would only prolong their protest activities to take in the arrival of subsequent boats. Once they get the publicity coverage they thrive on, they'll likely move on."

"Okay, Matt you've a pretty good grasp of the situation, just see that the whole thing runs smoothly and isn't allowed to get out of hand. We don't want to attract any more attention than necessary. By the way, Matt, remember the missing scuba diver?"

"Oh, yes. Do you have any news?"

"The report I've got says the group stayed at the diving site for three hours looking for the missing man. They all ran out of air before returning to shore. Once they got back to shore they contacted the Sheriff's office. The Sheriff contacted us right away and asked us to keep an eye out in case the body of the missing man turned up in the ocean. A fisherman spotted the body this morning. I dispatched a cutter to retrieve it. They should be tying up at City Pier in about ten minutes. The other divers who were out with him have been notified and asked to come down to identify the body. You wanted to talk to them, didn't you?"

"I did. I was on my way to their boat when the cruiser fire call came in. I'd like to know if they saw anything or were involved in that dead fish thing we ran into."

"Well, you'd better get down to the City Pier. You can catch them all together if you want. The Sheriff is bringing them there to identify the body. If this diver died because of poor safety practices we'd like to know. If he was diving beyond his depth we should be able to tell fairly quickly. Talk to his buddies and see what you can find out. This may indicate an area we should be emphasizing in our safety seminars."

"Good enough," Matt said and left for the pier.

Matt drove down West Railroad Avenue, approaching the Red Lion Hotel, City Pier came into view and Matt could see the cutter had made fast and her crew were off-loading a body bag. He would have to look after the beach problem later.

A police car and an ambulance were waiting on the pier when Matt arrived and the cutter was slowly approaching the pier. A small knot of curious bystanders gathered by the observation tower on the pier, straining to see what was going on. There wasn't much to see. Matt walked down the pier to where a small group of 'official' people was waiting. There were six people, a Deputy, two ambulance attendants and three other people Matt assumed to be the friends of the missing scuba diver.

"Good morning," Matt said to no one in particular, "I'm Matt Reynolds."

The Deputy took the initiative, "Good morning, Commander, I'm Deputy Petrie. These three men are friends of the missing man. I think I met you last night on the beach, didn't I?"

"That's right," Matt answered.

"I understand you followed up this morning on the survivor with Doc Johnson. Do you know how he is?"

"I talked to the Doctor just after breakfast. The injured man is still in critical condition. The next couple of days should tell the tale."

"Say, Deputy, while we're on this subject, did you find out any background on those men? Like, were they cutting firewood as we seem to think, had they done this sort of thing before?"

"We did establish that they'd been down a few times before the accident, but I don't think you could call them regulars. They came from that new subdivision just north of the city, at least one of them did. The other was from Sequim, along the coast."

"Do you know if they'd have any reason to be carrying explosives in their van?" Matt was now fishing for some material that could have provided the energy for the blast.

"No, not that I know. One of them worked for the telephone company here in town. I'm not sure where the other one worked, but he was from out-of-town. They might have had a hobby farm up the valley, so many of the townspeople do. Farmers sometimes use dynamite to remove stumps and rocks. I guess that's not impossible. Why?"

"Oh, I was just trying to figure out what caused the explosion. There doesn't seem to be too much around the wreck that would create such a large amount of damage."

"That had occurred to me last night but I didn't have much time to think about it. There was a lot of torn metal. That would take a lot of force. What do you make of it?"

"I don't have any good answers. The Coast Guard is not really too involved. They look on this as a local matter I guess. Mine is just a passing interest." Matt didn't know whether or not to tell him about the pieces that he had found this morning. He decided not to, at least until he had talked to the Navy people.

The three divers were talking among themselves as Matt approached. "Good morning. I understand you were diving to the north-west yesterday."

"Hi, Commander. Yes, we were practicing some deep dives and also doing a little sightseeing on the bottom along the shelf about three miles out."

"How deep were you going?"

"We were down to eighty or ninety five feet most of the time, with some excursions to a hundred for brief periods."

"How was visibility down at that level?"

"Not too good. We had lights with us but they weren't much help. The water's bad for this time of year."

"Have all of you been down that far before?"

"No, only Harry and Bill. Marv and I have only been qualified to ninety feet so far. Oh! Sorry," said the talkative diver, "I'm Barry Swift, this is Harry Forbes and this is Marv Franklin."

"Hi, gentlemen." Matt greeted them. "What training and preparation had you fellows to go that deep?"

"Harry and Bill have made simulated dives in the chamber to a hundred and fifty feet. Marv and I acted as backup for them if needed," said Barry.

"Harry", said Matt, "do you have any idea what happened to Bill?"

"No. We were swimming along the bottom at eighty-five feet when we came to a log sticking out of the mud. Bill stopped to grapple with it and I swam on. I was following a flounder at the time and I guess I got more interested in it than I was in Bill and his log. It must have been about five minutes before I noticed Bill was no longer with me. Just about that time I felt a strong concussion and heard an explosion. It really shook me. I began my ascent right away. My ears are still in bad shape."

"An explosion?" it was Matt's turn to be shaken. "Are you sure? Did you other men hear or feel this explosion?"

"Sure!" It was Marv; "It shook us pretty badly. We thought it was the Navy or something. It was like what I'd imagine a depth charge to be like from underwater. The shock almost blew the air out of my lungs. My ears are still ringing. It must have been quite a ways away from us though or we wouldn't be here now."

"Say, you don't think that's what got Bill do you? I never thought about the connection until now." It was Marv asking the question of Harry.

"I don't know, Marv, now that you mention it. The direction the shock wave came from is difficult to pinpoint. If I had to give any direction I'd say it came from somewhere to the north of where we were. It could have been what got Bill. I didn't think at the time it was close enough, but yes. That's where you and Bill were diving," he looked at Barry.

"The shock wave was pretty strong. It could have been fairly close. I know I was really stunned by it."

"You said Bill was poking around a log stuck in the mud," said Matt, "why would he do that?"

"It was the only thing we had come across all morning. The bottom is really clean and flat where we were. The log was the only thing of any interest. I guess Bill had to have a closer look at it; maybe he wanted to make sure it wasn't part of a wreck or something. I don't know of any wrecks in this area so I kept on swimming."

Matt's interest was now aroused." Can you describe this log?"

"It was just a log," began Harry, "nothing out of the ordinary. What I saw sticking out of the mud was about six inches in diameter and three feet long"

"Did you see what color it was?"

"I'd say it was sort of a brown, although at that depth colors can be distorted. It must have gotten stuck there recently because there weren't many barnacles on it. That alone indicated to me that it couldn't be a wreck. It hadn't been around long enough. I guess Bill didn't think of that."

"Try to remember now, can you think of anything else? Was it crooked? Was the surface rough or smooth? What did the end look like, was it broken off or sawn?"

"Now that you mention it, it was square cut, like it was cut with a saw. It was straight with no branches sticking out of it, and the bark looked like cedar or spruce."

Matt had a sinking feeling in the pit of his stomach. He wasn't sure but he thought he knew now what had blown up on the beach last night. If he were right, the body the Cutter was bringing in would not be a pretty sight. If he was right he also knew what had happened to kill the fish. If he was right the blast area on the beach had better be cordoned off to keep the area undisturbed for any investigations that would surely follow. There was no time now to worry about the security of the beach. The ambulance attendants were parked on City Pier and had carried a stretcher down to the cutter. They held a brief discussion with Lieutenant Ted Bracken, Captain of the Cutter, then loaded the bag onto the stretcher and brought it up to the ambulance where the diver's buddies were waiting. The top of the bag was unzipped and the divers moved reluctantly over to identify the contents.

It was Bill Watson the three divers agreed. This was duly noted in the Cutters log and by Deputy Petrie. There was a silence, seeming eternal. Deputy Petrie was the first to speak. "I'd like some details on his next of kin, if one of you can help me."

"That should be easy," said Marv. "He's single. His parents are both dead. He has a brother living in California. There should be some correspondence from his brother in his apartment. I'll take you there if you like, Deputy."

"Fine. If we could go in about a half an hour, I'd appreciate it."

The gathering was now beginning to disperse. Matt went over to talk with Lieutenant Bracken. The Lieutenant was Matt's assistant with the sea safety program and knew Matt was concerned about the death of this diver. He thought Matt would feel somehow responsible if the drowning were related to lack of training or carelessness. He had seen the body though and was aware that the death was due to more than drowning.

"Hi, Ted, What did you make of the condition of the diver?"

"Not a nice sight, Matt. It's obvious that there's more to this than a diver exceeding his ability. I didn't want to say too much while the others were around. The fish had just started on the body but he was pretty badly torn up before they got to him. His wet suit protected him from scavengers except in the frontal area around his waist and chest. The suit was ripped off in these areas. I don't know what would do this. The police are going to have to consider foul play. It's possible that his friends wanted him out of the way but the circumstances don't point to that. We'll know better once the coroner has had a chance to look at him."

"Ted, I think I know what killed him but I'm not sure. Did you haul the body in?"

"Yes. We picked him up from a fisherman in an outboard boat. He found the man floating and secured him with a rope once he had determined that the man was dead, and that wasn't very difficult as he was already in the later stages of rigor mortise. The fisherman didn't want to take him aboard because he was too heavy and felt that just getting him up and over the side could have swamped the boat. The body was floating face down so the fisherman still doesn't know what the gruesome underside looks like. I suppose it's just as well, as you saw it's not nice. We didn't know ourselves until we hauled him aboard."

"I'd like to have another look before they take him to the morgue."

The two of them walked up the float to where the attendants waited with the body. Ted opened the bag. He was right. It was a sickening sight. The wet suit was torn off the chest area and ragged, raw flesh was exposed everywhere. Matt's eye caught a flash of reflected sunlight from something in the wound. Matt moved over to the body and picked the piece out of the flesh. It was a piece of brown plastic material and stuck into it was a part of what was left of a small electronic type condenser.

"My God," exhaled Matt, "another one."

"Another what?" asked Ted.

"Oh, we had an accident on the beach last night."

"You mean the explosion?"

"What did you hear about it?"

"A couple of guys were hurt, is there more?"

"Quite a bit Ted, one man was killed and another is in hospital now. He's not in very good shape. He may live, he may not." Matt filled him in as quickly as he could with what he knew. The damage seemed to be caused by something that looked like a log. Only it was no ordinary log. It had electronic parts and explosives inside. It wasn't to be tampered with under any circumstances.

"What are these things and what are they doing around here?" Ted asked.

"I don't know yet Ted, but if there are any more of them around we could be in for some real trouble. I'd better get back to the Commodore right away."

The thought of more of the bombs around the Strait area gave him a chill right up the spine.

CHAPTER 3

Sunday, Day 2, 08:30 hours.

The pilot boat departed its berth, slipping quietly out to sea. Aboard, a lone passenger is heading out to pick up his charge. Pilot, Captain Sam Sawchuck was assigned to guide a Russian factory ship along the Strait and down Puget Sound into a Seattle shipyard. She had been tending her fleet of trawlers off the coast of Washington and British Columbia. Sam knew she had been on station only a month and wondered why she had to visit the repair yard so soon. The usual duty duration for a ship this size was over six months and it had the capability of staying at sea much longer if necessary.

Sam knew the game Russian skippers played with their government, sometimes with government approval. Each vessel was allocated so many rubles for operating costs. If these were not fully spent, the remainder went back to the Kremlin. Each captain would therefore make sure there was as little as possible left over. Their method was to go into Canada or the States for minor repairs and make sure the value of the estimate of work to be done was larger than that actually done. An inflated payment for the work was made to the shipyard for the estimated sum. The work done would, of course, never equal the estimate and the remainder was returned to the captain. This money became his to use as he saw fit. He had no problem using it. 'Perhaps,' thought Sam, 'the captain was building his bank account.'

As the pilot boat drew near the Russian ship, Andrey Popovitch, she slowed down, allowing the pilot to clamber aboard. Sam easily made the transfer, jumping off the pilot boat onto the undulating Russian boarding ladder as he had done many, many times before. He ascended carefully to the main deck. Sam looked up at the standard Russian porcupine array of electronic antennae covering most of her topside. He noticed a few of a type he had never seen before. They weren't radar, nor were they the standard radio whip or wire. More like a cross between them. Round dishes with short wires protruded from their perimeters. He could only guess they were something to do with some form of spy communications.

A large, barrel-chested man greeted him, clenching a stiff-tubed Russian cigarette between smiling lips. A thick, black beard framed his round face. "Goot mornink Captain. Velcome aboard my ship." Captain Yuri Propolov greeted him in coarse English, "Please follow to bridge."

"Thank you Captain. Nice ship you have here." Although Sam had guided many Russian ships through the strait it was the first time he had been aboard this particular vessel. Looking around as they made their way to the bridge, he could see she'd not been long out of the builder's yard. He couldn't remember ever seeing any Russian fishing vessel as clean and rust free as this one.

"Dhank you." he said widening his grin. "Ve try keep clean. Hard job."

To get to the bridge, the captain took Sam forward, along the deck to the 'midship-house companionway then up three decks. Aft of the bridge they passed the radio room, protected by an armed guard as usual. The guarded radio room was standard practice for the Russians. Sam always wondered why they had to post a guard, couldn't they trust their own crew? An exception here was a second guard at the door. This wasn't standard practice. He pondered what they could possibly have in there that needed two men to protect?

They walked quickly past the radio room and entered the bridge. The equipment visible to Sam was normal. Gyrocompass, magnetic compass periscope, two radar sets, two sonar sets, (one for navigation the other for fish finding), various radio sets and a rather large and complex intercom base station. Standard engine control dials and levers were contained in a central console.

Captain Propolov introduced Sam to his first mate and the helmsman as they entered the bridge. The captain then asked what course Sam wished.

"Steer a heading of 080 degrees magnetic," Sam instructed. "We'll head on down toward Port Angeles on this course then change to 055 degrees magnetic to go past the spit at Port Dungeness"

"Dank you," the captain answered Sam in his halting English, then barked order to the helmsman in Russian. The ship turned slightly. The captain spoke again in Russian, this time to his first mate and Sam could hear the rhythm of the engines increase, the ship gathering speed.

They had traveled no more than thirty minutes when the engine sounds changed. The ship slowed rapidly, barely making headway. The captain jabbered in Russian to his people then came over to where Sam was standing.

"I sorry," he said, Ve having trouble with gearbox. Ve make repair, then go. Not long."

"Okay," Sam answered, "we have a rising tide. There shouldn't be any problem."

The engines were idling now and Sam could hear at least two large auxiliaries start up. Sam had no idea what they were for, but they had piqued his curiosity. He asked the captain.

"Oh, da," he chuckled, "They are ship generator" Sam knew he was lying and wondered why. He had no reason to press the matter and so, let it drop.

Picking up a little speed now, the ship began to slew to starboard. Sam watched this with some concern. Two minutes later the slew was corrected.

"What's the problem, Captain?"

"Is problem with steering gear. Ve fix".

Strange mechanical sounds were now filtering through from the 'midship section (at least that's where Sam thought they were coming from). The high pitched whine of hydraulic machinery was easily detected while a lot of metal striking metal noises were evident as well.

Sam walked out onto the bridge wing while all this was going on. Looking aft, he saw a string of bubbles moving out from the starboard side of the ship. He sauntered over to the port side and casually gazed to the aft section. There were bubbles spreading away from the ship on this side too. 'What the hell's going on'? he wondered.

Sam called Captain Popolov out to the wing. "Have you got an underwater problem?" he questioned.

"Nyet, nyet", the captain shook his head.

"Well," Sam went on, "if you have any discharge, the port authorities will be on to you in a hurry. They're dead serious about pollution."

The Russian looked at the disappearing bubbles. "Not from this ship. Someone else," he lied.

The bubbles were now well off the stern and almost gone from sight. The ship began to pick up speed and the captain said," It look like gearbox fix. It take us little farther now. We go inside?"

Walking into the wheelhouse Sam distinguished the new main engine noise gradually dominating the other noises the captain said were auxiliary generators. The sound of hydraulics seemed to disappear at the same time.

"Maintain the present course, Captain." Sam went back into his thoughts for a couple of minutes. Something was happening. He couldn't put his finger on it, but it was more than the Russian was letting on. The ship was now making good time. They had been dead in the water for close to half an hour and at dead slow for another fifteen minutes. They seemed to be all right now.

Passing Dungeness Spit, there is a set of measured mile markers, and Sam had nonchalantly taken a reading on his watch as they went by. He multiplied the time and distance for a rough speed check. They were making eighteen knots. Not bad for a ship with gearbox problems. He made a mental note.

They traveled the fifteen nautical miles between Dungeness and Point Wilson in quick time. Turning south, southeast down Admiralty Channel heading for Puget Sound, the engines again slowed. It was almost a repeat of the last time. Captain Popolov appeared nervous. Main engines were idling and the sound of the auxiliaries got louder.

The sound of hydraulics was again clearly heard Sam glanced over at the captain. He knew what was coming.

"Gear box." was all he said.

Sam checked the view from the bridge wings. The same bubbles again, rising this time almost alongside but only on the port side. The whole action took half as much time. Then they were under way again. He considered discussing this with some of the other pilots when he got back.

The responsibility of navigation now occupied all of Sam's attention and he put the incidents out of his mind. The remaining trip was routine. After tying up at McCormack's shipyard, Sam went ashore. On his way down to the port manager's office he again tried to puzzle out what was going on with the Russians. He didn't for one minute believe they had gear trouble.

John Billingsly, the port manager, was a very conscientious man.

When Sam told him about this morning's happenings, he wanted to know more.

"Sam," he asked, "did you see any oil or garbage during these stops?"

"No. Just the bubbles. Not the sort of thing you'd expect from a discharge. There's got to be something more."

"Okay, I think I'd better get in touch with the Coast Guard. It's a little out of my jurisdiction but it should be looked into by someone. If the Russians are in fact dumping anything, we want to know about it. The beaches are fouled up badly enough as it is. If we don't keep on top of these irresponsible ships, the beaches will get worse. How was the trip otherwise, Sam?

"No problems. Other than the two stops, it was routine."

"It might be a good idea to nose around the dockyard and see how bad their gear boxes actually are."

"That's a good idea. Let me know what you find out. It may be interesting."

Sam left the office and John picked up the phone.

*   *   *

Commander Mike Chambers, U S Navy, was in charge of security for the Trident Nuclear Ballistic Missile Submarine Base at Bangor, Washington: a very difficult task, made a little easier because of the base's remote location. Intrusion by land was fairly easy to detect and control. The roads, of course, were gated and guarded. The perimeter fence was augmented with various intrusion detection devices. Vibration, capacitance and visual observations were continuous. TV cameras, infra red and other sophisticated sensors were used in strategic locations. Nothing entered the base from the land side without detection. The water side, however, was a different matter. Without prohibiting all civilian water traffic on the Hood Canal, it was impossible to prevent sightseers, or anyone else for that matter, from getting within yards of America's newest and most powerful nuclear missile submarines. For that reason, the objective was to detect, not prevent intrusion. Once detected, the intruders could be dealt with in the normal manner.

Mike had established a series of underwater sensors in a fan shape around the water perimeter of the base, sensors having a range and sensitivity capable of detecting anything moving within 2000 feet of them. Their placement was such that at least three sensors would pick up the same target moving toward the base. This not only provided confirmation that a target was actually in the area but also permitted a check to insure the sensors were functioning properly. Sensor signals were transmitted to the security command center computers, which provided visual displays on electronic action boards. Security personnel continuously monitored the boards. The system was set up so that disturbance of any signal caused an alarm. Technicians then had to determine what caused the alarm and take appropriate action. A sensor malfunction, a large fish or a school of smaller fish, scuba divers or surface craft could all affect the system. Anything that moved in or on the water within two miles of the base was monitored and displayed on the electronic boards.

In most cases, watching the screens and boards was a boring assignment. To break the tedium, operators developed and often played a game of watching the course of fish moving in the area to see if they coincided with sport fishing boats. The betting was whether or not the fisherman could hook them. Considerable money changed hands through this game, but more importantly the operators become highly skilled at interpreting sensor reports. They could tell not only whether the image was a single fish or a school, but also the size of the fish, thereby making an educated guess as to what species it was. Boat size and make were also part of the game.

Mike's assignment was to detect, not protect. He was not involved with the attack craft, which were at the ready at all times in the water, although when an alarm sounded, it was his job to vector the craft to the target. This exercise was carried out on a regular basis. The attack craft were also used for routine maintenance of the sensors and to patrol base water boundaries. They carried armed personnel, trained in underwater combat. The same men were also in charge of installing and maintaining the sensors. All alarms were treated as serious intrusions whether caused by a malfunctioning sensor, harbor seals, killer whales or an enemy underwater demolition team. You were never sure what the target was, so you geared for the worst case. The command center operators were getting pretty good however, and in most cases knew what the attack craft crew would find when they got to a target. Surface craft of course were easy to identify visually. Killer whales were also easy as they were almost always near the surface. Seals and larger fish were more difficult to identify, and because of this, their swimming patterns and actions were noted and catalogued. The staff, after a while were able to identify individual seals inhabiting the area. They even gave names to some of them.

Mike Chambers walked into the command center on Sunday morning. He worked all hours of the day and all days of the week, much to the annoyance of his pretty, young wife, Sandra. She wanted him home more. Feeling at times like she had no husband.

A 'white train', approaching the south railway gate with a shipment of spare parts for the Trident missiles, was being harassed by group of protestors doing everything possible to prevent its entry to the site. Watching on the video monitor, Mike could see the local police gathering the group together and herding them into paddy wagons. The last of the protestors were put into the police vans with the train coming into view. This type of protest was by now routine and, so long as they were peaceful, the navy tolerated them.

A call came in for Mike, from the naval base at Pearl Harbor.

"Yes, this is Chambers, and this is a secure line." Mike answered.

"Good morning, Commander, I'm Lieutenant Tanya Andrushyn. I'm with the space surveillance team at Pearl. Perhaps you are aware of our operation here?"

"Yes," said Mike, automatically trying to visualize the shape of the woman on the other end of the line. Her pretty voice promised all sorts of things. She sounded quite young. "I have heard about you and what you are doing. In fact one of my old schoolmates is down there I think. Bill Mathews. He's working with the electronics section. Do you know him?"

"Yes, Commander. In fact, it's as a result of what he's doing that I'm calling you now. Briefly, our responsibility is to establish the purpose of foreign satellites and monitor all transmissions to and from them. We've been following a Soviet satellite, Cosmos 987 for quite a while. It's deviated from its normal routine and we're still trying to determine why. There is only so much I can discuss over the phone, Commander, even with scramblers, and we would appreciate it if you could come down here to go over some points with us."

"Well, you couldn't have picked a worse time. You know we're about to receive our first up-graded Trident sub in a couple of weeks. Things are getting a bit hectic just now. What kind of priority do you put on this problem of yours? There are plenty of good men here who could give you what you want." He immediately regretted snapping at her.

"Commander, we know you're busy, but with what we know now, we feel this trip is of the utmost urgency to your base security. I have to consider priority very high."

"Okay, Lieutenant. I'll clear with my superior and see if there is a flight I can catch today. I'll let you know as soon as plans firm up."

"Thank you, Commander. I'll be waiting."

Mike called his secretary and had her make arrangements on the earliest Military Air Transport flight to Hawaii. Going into his office he made a couple of phone calls. He also made arrangements for his assistant to 'watch the shop' for a few days. Checking the time, he called his aide. "I'm going home now. Call me when you have a handle on that MAT flight time."

Driving home he mulled over how to broach the trip to Sandra. He hoped she would have supper ready. They could have a drink after dinner. He would tell her then.

At eight o'clock the phone rang. Sandra answered. Bangor had a seat for him on the two o'clock flight tomorrow from Paine Field to Oahu. She took the message, temper rising.

"What's this Hawaii bit?" she asked through clenched teeth.

"Sorry, I was going to tell you later, when the time was right." He had delayed too long, knowing what the response would be. It always created a scene.

"What's so important this time? Why can't you send Peter or Dick? Why you?"

"This is highly classified. I'm the only one that's cleared."

"Isn't anyone else qualified?" she yelled.

"I'm sorry, no. Not at this time. I'm trying to bring more men into the classification, but they just aren't cleared yet."

"Well, when are they?"

"Look, there's no use carrying on now. I've got to go and that's that."

He phoned back to Bangor and told them to have a helicopter ready in the afternoon to take him over to the airport.

Sandra wouldn't talk to him for the rest of the evening.

CHAPTER 4

Monday, Day 3, 16:00 hours.

The flying across the Pacific was uneventful. Mike could not help feeling it was a waste of his time particularly now with the arrival of the USS OHIO and things were coming to a head at the Trident Base.

What could a malfunctioning Russian satellite possibly have to do with his base security?

The big Starlifter landed at Oahu's reef runway and began its long taxi to the military terminal. Minutes ticked off as they continued weaving a circuitous route that seemed to take it all over the airport in order to get to the loading gate of Hickam Air Force Base.

Lieutenant Andrushyn was to meet him at the arrivals counter. He wondered what she looked like he knew what she sounded like from the phone call. Climbing down the gangway, Mike got his first smell of Hawaii. Even with the occasional whiff of jet exhaust, the warm breeze had a delightfully sweet odor, softness, characteristic of the Islands. The sun had gone down but the temperature was still a balmy 74 degrees. This part of the trip Mike liked.

Glaring floodlights made it difficult for him to distinguish much detail as he walked across the tarmac to the terminal building. Military aircraft of all shapes and sizes were spotted along the hard-stand as men and machines busied themselves servicing them with fuel and supplies. Once inside, he became one of the many passengers milling around waiting for transportation. Mike walked over to the counter.

About 60 people were on Mike's flight and about as many again were in the terminal waiting to meet them.

Out of all of these people Mike had to identify Lieutenant Andrushyn. He stood by the baggage transporter waiting impatiently, fidgeting with the ID tag on his two-suiter. A svelte brunette officer approached.

Tanya, was 28 years old, a trim five foot eight, well built, good looking blue eyed brunette. She had been in Hawaii now for 18 months and hadn't wasted much sunshine. She had a dark even tan and fairly radiated the hospitality of the Islands. Her father, the son of Russian immigrants, had been in the US Army during the Second World War, stationed for a while in Berlin. It had been there that he had met and married Tanya's mother, an interpreter for the Soviet government. Tanya was born and grew up in the Midwest where her father had a small farm and was also lecturing in philosophy at the University of Wisconsin in Madison.

She had never met Commander Chambers but his school chum Bill Mathews had described him to her.

Bill was right. Tall, clean cut, Navy all the way. He also mentioned that Mike could be pushy.

He was a borderline bully at school, used to getting his own way.

"Commander Chambers?" Tanya asked.

"Yes. You must be Lieutenant Andrushyn!" Mike nodded an acknowledgement, stunned. She was beautiful, he thought. The trip was looking better all the time.

"Have you got your baggage yet, Commander?"

"Yes." He picked up his one-suiter bag and they began to walk to the exit where Tanya led toward the parking lot and over to the service car.

"Have you had supper yet, Commander?" she asked.

"No. They had coffee and sandwiches on the plane, but I'm pretty hungry."

"Good enough. I didn't know exactly when you'd get in. I thought the next MAT flight came in at 20:00 hours, so I waited. There's a nice spot just off Nimitz Highway on the way to Honolulu, if that's all right with you."

"Anywhere you say is fine with me."

Tanya started the car and they wheeled out past the gatehouse, turning right toward Honolulu.

"Have you been to Pearl before, Commander?"

"No, Lieutenant, and please call me Mike."

"Fine, Mike, and I'm Tanya."

"I can see what I've been missing."

Tanya let the remark go unanswered. "Well, after we've had something to eat I'll take you to Schofield Barracks. We stay at Schofield, but our station is nearby, on a mountaintop in the Waianae Range to the northwest of Oahu. The station is in the shadow of Mount Kaala, one of the higher peaks on the island and the only way to get there is by helicopter or cable car. We'd rather go up during daylight, so we'll wait 'till tomorrow morning. This location gives us the kind of isolation we need from just about everything. City lights and electronic noise are things we'd rather do without. We spend all of our time watching the sky and listening. It's amazing what you can pick up if you're patient."

"I'll bet," thought Mike. His mind was on earthly bodies, not the heavenly type.

They had a relaxed dinner, and then drove up through Pearl City to the valley and Schofield Barracks.

The sentry at the gate knew Tanya and checked Mike's identification then passed them through.

Tanya took him to the Bachelor Officer's Quarters.

Mike checked into his assigned room and sacked out almost immediately. Tanya was to pick him up at 07:00 hours and that would come early. Mike lay awake for a long time, wondering what he'd find out tomorrow.

*   *   *

Tuesday, day 4, 06:30 hours.

Dawn broke Tuesday morning at about 06:45 finding Mike already up. Tanya picked him up and they drove to the officers' mess for breakfast.

"While we have some time, I'd better begin filling you in on what we think is happening and why you're here. "In routine surveillance work we've come across some strange things and are trying to make some sense out of them. We feel that the new Trident subs are posing a problem for the Russians.

The methods we use to hide them are very effective. So much so that Ivan is having great trouble spotting them.

"Russian intelligence uses many inputs: trawlers, as you are aware, and cargo ships, naval vessels aircraft and satellites plus a lot of land based listening posts. We here in Hawaii look after some of the satellite details.

"Each sub, as it passes through the water makes noises peculiar to that sub, and only that sub. I'm not telling you anything new, but it is relevant to the overall picture. Every sub makes noise. It comes from the propulsion gear, props, shafts, turbines, everything else on board that moves.

Surface ships can be identified by sight, but they make noises too and we catalog them as well but with underwater craft the only way we can identify them is by their noise. Nuclear powered subs make considerably less noise than conventional subs because more attention has been paid to noise reduction on them. They have fewer moving parts and their hulls are thicker. Mass is still the best known medium to prevent transmission of noise. However when you put all of them into water, you find them even more difficult to suppress. All of this, of course, you already know. What you probably don't know, and this is extremely sensitive information, is that the Trident class submarines have been made almost invisible, noise wise by the addition of a new creation which absorbs sound in a special way. It works on the natural frequency of large masses. This has driven the Russians wild.

"They've watched our rebuilt Trident, USS OHIO, going through sea trials and attempted to obtain her noise signature. They got it easily because the special silencing equipment was not installed by the shipbuilder in fact he doesn't even know it exists. That's how secret this is. The Russians tracked OHIO during trials on the surface and underwater. No attempt was made to shield her from them. The boat was then commissioned and put into a navy yard to have this special equipment added.

"Soviet trawler activity was normal for the first few days after OHIO went to sea. Then they must have realized I guess that their detection gear wasn't working properly. All of a sudden we had a flurry of Russian electronic activity. Surveillance aircraft from Cuba and more than double the electronic Surveillance ships off the east coast.

"This increased activity went on for a few days then we began to notice some changes in the orbits of some Cosmos satellites. They were going into low passes over the area they had last seen OHIO. We didn't know at that time what was going on with all this electronic activity but the communications began to heat up at the same time. Our intelligence people, who knew of OHIO's new stealth ability were able to figure it out. They watched with glee as the Soviets scurried all over the ocean trying to find her."

"Just out of curiosity," asked Mike, "do the Russians have a similar capability?"

"No, not yet, but it probably won't be long before they do. They have other problems to clear up first, before they go into this level of sophistication. For instance, their nuclear subs are notoriously dirty. In a lot of cases we don't even have to rely on acoustic or thermographic equipment. All we need is a radiation detector. They spread a trail of radioactive iodine behind their subs as big as a jet plane's vapor trail. We can see it for hours after a sub has gone. We've no problem following them at present but once they get that reactor problem licked we'll have to modify our tracking methods.

"This brings you up to date on our work. Now I'll get to the reason you were brought into the picture.

You see, the Soviets need to know why they can't detect our subs. We feel your base may provide some data to them. Bangor is on a piece of water that is fairly restricted in width and depth.

The subs based at Bangor will likely be travelling on the surface from the entrance of the Strait of Juan de Fuca right to the base. The Soviets would like nothing better than to be able to follow these boats for an extended distance from the air and underwater. This way they can cross check what their equipment is telling them. They can then follow the subs right out to sea, watching all the way through during both on-surface or under-surface travel. Finding some way to calibrate their instruments is a prerequisite to accurate tracking. The confining Hood Canal and Strait of Juan de Fuca are ideal for this."

Tanya had talked almost continually through breakfast. "Well," she said, "let's get over to the car and head up to our station."

They got into the car and Tanya drove. Pointing to the west she explained to Mike, "Our cable car base platform is over to the west of Schofield." She headed toward it.

CHAPTER 5

Tuesday, Day 4, 08:00 hours.

A dirt road ran the four miles from Schofield Barracks to the base of Mount Akaala. From there a small gondola, similar to those Mike had seen at ski resorts, took them up to a crest, just below the mountain peak. Once at the top station, Mike could see the full extent of the installation. He knew it was a satellite tracking station, but he was not prepared for the amount of equipment he was now looking at. Tanya sensed his surprise.

"From here we track every object within fifty thousand miles of the surface of the earth," she said almost apologetically.

Mike saw tracking dishes from four feet in diameter to some that must have been over fifty feet. They were all pointed in different directions. Mike could also see more than fifteen large dishes and many more phased array antennae. A few of the smaller dishes appeared to be moving slowly. Mike thought he could detect motion in the one closest to him. He had often watched satellites with his naked eye or field glasses from his back yard. An hour or so after sunset when the sky was clear, if you waited long enough, you might see a star or what you thought was a star slowly moving across the heaven. Some were blinking, some shone with a steady brilliance. Once you spotted one you could usually follow it right across the sky. At that time

Mike had not stopped to consider what the bright speck was doing or who it belonged to. He was about to find out now.

The two stood for almost a full minute taking in the panorama. To the West they could see the ridges of the Waianae Mountains with their big white inverted mushroom like scanner-speckled peaks strung out in a daisy-chain. Each daisy's head was turned skyward. In the distance they could make out the island of Kauai. To the South stood the fortress of Diamond Head and its crater center. To the east was the Koolau Mountain Range, separating the island into East and West. To the North were a couple of coastal villages, after that there was enough ocean to fill the space between Hawaii and Alaska.

Walking over toward a cluster of buildings at the base of one of the large dishes Tanya told Mike, "We'll be meeting Morgan Snellert of Military Intelligence. He's been working with us for the past four months since this situation arose. Morgan will brief you on what has happened and explain what we think it is all about."

"Sounds good to me. Maybe I'll be able to understand a little more clearly how it all concerns me and my base," answered Mike.

"One of the reasons we brought you to Hawaii, rather than talk to you on the phone, is because of the extreme sensitivity of the subject. We've made considerable headway in our knowledge of Russian space hardware and the electronics connected with it. We don't know if they know what we know about these things, if you know what I mean." Tanya chuckled to herself after that statement. It sounded like it was right out of a comedy routine. It's going to take just about a day to bring you fully into this operation, but I doubt if you'll see the end of it for some time."

They entered a white, one story building. A Naval rating at the reception desk requested Mike's identification and made a phone call while examining it. A man dressed in civilian clothes entered the room from a long corridor.

"Good morning, Lieutenant, how are you today?" He was a tall, thin man in his mid thirties, Mike guessed. He wore glasses and his hair line had receded. What was left of his fair hair was cut short in the military manner.

Tanya introduced them. "Commander Mike Chambers, this is Captain Morgan Snellert of Military Intelligence. Captain Snellert, this is Commander Chambers, in charge of security at the Trident Base in Bangor."

"Commander, if you'll follow me, I'll take you down to our briefing room."

As they walked down the corridor Mike could see small offices on each side, some with electronic equipment, some with only computer terminals. Each of them had people sitting at a desk or machine; head down in what Mike thought was deep concentration.

"I guess Lieutenant Andrushyn has filled you in on the basics and what goes on at this station?"

"She did give me a brief run-down but we haven't had time for too much detail."

"The scanning dishes you saw are directed from a central control room at the discretion of the site commander. The men and equipment in this building are working on data produced by selected dishes." He indicated the scattered dishes covering the mountaintop. "Programs from many countries are going on here all the time. We take on some civilian contracts but most of our work is devoted to military requirements."

They entered a large room at the end of the building.

"This is our briefing room. It contains some audio-visual equipment and that large electronic screen. We often hold meetings here when we want to brainstorm happenings we can't understand. The problem we'll deal with today is a good example. Most of the information and display facilities are available to us in this room. You'll see as we go along. Please sit down." Morgan pointed to the upholstered bucket chairs . . . Tanya, Mike and Morgan each took a seat around a large horseshoe shaped table. Some positions around it had computer terminals and other electrical controls in front of them. Captain Snellert pushed a button and a screen dropped from the ceiling at the open end of the horseshoe.

CHAPTER 6

Tuesday, Day 4, 09:00 hours.

Captain Snellert began his presentation. "Satellites, or birds, as you already know, can be launched into polar or equatorial orbit or combinations of the two."

The screen flashed a picture of a globe with first a polar orbit depicted then the equatorial orbit.

"They can be relatively low, down to less than one hundred miles or right up to twenty-two thousand five hundred miles, where they are stationary in respect to positioning above the earth." These descriptive orbits flashed on the screen. "There are also high inclination orbits and transfer orbits. High inclination orbits are polar orbits, transfer orbits are used to reposition a satellite. Communication satellites are usually at high or parking orbits while the lower orbits are usually used for a variety of other purposes, not the least of which is gathering information. If we want to take good clear pictures of earth facilities, the lower we can get, the better the pictures will be. The resolution of our cameras and computer enhancement can do wonders, but distance does distort. We try to keep as low as possible for photo missions. By the way, Mike, feel free to ask questions as we go. I don't know how much of this you've seen before, so if I go too slow or too fast, tell me and I'll adjust."

"Thanks, Morgan. I will."

"At lower altitudes, we are getting close to the earth's atmosphere where the satellite, passing through the air, even thin air, will be slowed and begin to drop. Once they are caught in the friction effect of the air, they won't live long. An orbit of less than one hundred miles will decay rapidly and the bird will plunge to a fiery death. This makes it undesirable to remain in low orbit for any length of time. There is a way to overcome this problem and it's by altering the orbit from a circle to an oval. What this does, essentially, is bring the bird down to less than the critical one hundred miles, get our pictures then climb it back to a safe altitude. We do this. So do the Russians. By watching the orbits of the birds we can determine their mission from where the perigee or low point of the orbit falls. We can surmise what the bird wants to see. We haven't been wrong too often.

"Our attention lately has been attracted to a couple of Russian birds. One is a high geostationary communication satellite that you now see on the screen. There are three others, two of which are in a medium orbit of 550 to 525 miles; one is in low orbit of 95 to 105 miles."

The screen showed the birds and the shapes of their orbits.

"We suspect, and are reasonably sure that the low bird is photographing naval operations. The two at mid level orbit are primarily data receiver/transmitters. All three are dedicated military birds which means they don't share time or circuitry with scientific exploration agencies as most of our satellites do.

"Our tracking facilities 'observe' all satellites. We can recall information on any bird up there. Each of these birds is rigged for a multi-purpose role. If a control or command satellite is required today, they can establish a high orbit. If, tomorrow they want to take pictures of the cover of a book of matches being held by a sailor in Pearl Harbor, all they have to do is bring the bird down to a lower altitude and activate the camera as it passes over the base. The 'picture' is not what you would normally get from your Kodak Instamatic. It is an electronic picture, much like a video picture . . . "I won't go into great detail here and now but basically what it does is 'read' the target area and convert what it 'sees' into millions of bits of data. These are transmitted back to earth where a computer 'reconstructs' it into the exact image 'seen' by the camera."

"During the years you were building the Bangor Base, Mike, we noticed a photo bird would dip down over your Base area. We assumed they were interested in the Navy yard at Bremerton. We knew what activities were going on at the yard during each recon pass of this bird, and there was nothing we felt was in any way sensitive so we passed it off as Russian curiosity. This is no longer the case. We've established that what they were interested in was your base. From the frequency of their scans, we assume they now know everything about the base. The details probably include where every piece of reinforcing bar, pipe and conduit is located, how much concrete is in each floor and ceiling, even what color paint is used in each room."

"That seems a little far-fetched," Mike injected, "How could they know for instance the color of paint?"

"Simple," said Morgan, "As material is delivered it is easy for the satellite to read what is on each box. Paint cans and boxes are marked with the color of the contents. This can be verified by watching the garbage as it comes out for disposal. Brushes, rollers and rags will all show paint colors.

"The types of paint thinner used will help in establishing the type and purpose of paint used. Special rooms may require a particular paint. The stage of construction will also provide a clue as to where the paint is used. Verification can be made in many ways. Individual workmen can be identified and a record made of what area they work in. The paint on a painters overalls will tell volumes. Not that the paint in a room is important, it only shows what can be deduced from satellite data."

"Good Christ!" Mike said with shock, "How much do they know about my security and the vulnerability of the various systems?"

"They know as much as they want to know. This may give you something to think about, Mike, but it is not the reason you were brought to Hawaii."

"We have discovered recently that one of their photo/com. birds was acting in a strange way, not physically but electronically. You see, while we monitor positions of satellites we also keep close tabs on what they are saying. We listen to them, too. Keeping up to date with this technology is a lifetime career. Lieutenant Andrushyn here is an expert in this field. She spotted some anomalies in the transmissions of Cosmos 964 which we felt were worth further investigation."

"Let's see now, it's about 11:45. Perhaps this is a good time to break for lunch, Commander. I think we've given you enough data to start your wheels turning at high speed. You'll need some time to digest this before we go on to the next part. We'd like to see you back here about 13:00 hours please. Lieutenant, would you take Mike to the mess hall? I'll prepare some slides for this afternoon then join you for lunch."

On their way to lunch Tanya explained the various antennae they had seen exposed on the ridges. The large dishes were used for broad search and lower frequency work while the smaller ones were for higher frequencies. All had the capability to receive and transmit. In fact most of the military communications worldwide were handled on similar antennae spotted around the world. This station however was not limited to dish antennae. There were also many rhomboidal antennae for low frequency work and many large tower-type whips.

Tanya went on, "Our computers are programmed to anticipate the passing of each known satellite and announce via the printout, which ones are due, what they are, whose they are and many more valuable tidbits. With this anticipation comes verification so that if the computer says that Spacelab, for instance, is due at 17:46.25 GMT, then at that time it should pass overhead. If it doesn't, then something is wrong and an alert would be printed. We watch this sort of thing carefully. In most cases we find an altered orbit. If an orbit is changed, then we ask ourselves, 'why'?"

"This is how we detected the fact that Cosmos 954 was giving your area the once-over. Changing orbit is not the sort of thing you do lightly. It's costly. Each bird can carry only so much maneuvering fuel. You don't waste it. Each move is made with extreme precision. To get a bird to reach its perigee or lowest point of orbit, at the exact spot you want to take pictures, requires a very fine touch. If you go into an elliptical orbit you can maintain the same orbit time past a fixed earth point similar to a circular orbit. This allows your bird to get down lower briefly then soar back past your original altitude then drop again. This is preferable to reducing a high orbit to a low orbit as it uses less fuel. It will also allow you a greater margin of error in case your bird gets too low and atmospheric drag increases. You can lose a bird easily that way. With an elliptical orbit you can make your low pass then get the bird back up to a safe altitude. Sensors in the bird will tell more quickly than our computers if the orbit is dangerously low and the orbit can be adjusted from earth."

Mike was amazed, both by the state of this science and by Tanya's grasp of the technology.

"Where in hell did you learn all this high-tech stuff?"

Tanya laughed, "I did some work for one of our bird manufacturers on loan from the Navy. The equipment we had to design was given various parameters. Included was a course in how the satellites work. It was very interesting."

"I'll bet it was," said Mike. "Tell me then, what has all this got to do with my Trident base?"

"Don't hurry it, Mike. What we are going to disclose to you is complex and very sophisticated. You'll have to keep an open mind until you have most of the details. Then it will be obvious to you.

CHAPTER 7

Tuesday, Day 4, 13:00 hours.

When they returned to the conference room, Major Snellert began the afternoon briefing by explaining some basic satellite technology.

"The Cosmos series of satellites is used mostly for surveillance. If you wish you can read 'spying' for surveillance. In reality, there are over 45,000 various satellites roaming around earth right now. Of course we have our own information networks both in space and on the ground from which we receive fairly good information on Russian space intelligence. However, it was only after the crashed Cosmos 954 recovery in Northern Canada that we were really able to determine what scope these birds have."

"The incident, if you remember, was in the winter of 1979 when the crippled 954 descended too far into the atmosphere to enable recovery. Its remains were spread over a large area of frozen tundra."

"The Canadian government and our own team of specialists recovered a good portion of the burned and broken bird, enough to reconstruct both the nuclear power supply and the electronic imaging systems. Published information releases were designed to let the public know that we had recovered parts of the nuclear reactor, and with this, our office of disinformation set about to embarrass the Russians to the fullest extent possible. We even, to a degree, overdramatized the radiation hazard, to keep everyone's attention off the other, and which to us was the more important parts we had to examine, the working or intelligence end of the bird, the eyes and transmitter section of it. These were recovered in pretty bad shape. We did, however, get enough to assess what its capabilities were."

"The Russians have been using this type of bird for a long time, and I must admit we were caught a little unaware of the total capability of each one. We were able to monitor all frequencies transmitted from the Cosmos series and were collecting a lot of good stuff. At least that's what we thought.

"To fully appreciate what I'm going to tell you, you must try to imagine the sheer volume of radio transmissions emanating from Russian sources alone, and then multiply this by ten. This will give you an idea of everyday airwave clutter we have to wade through.

"Out of all this clutter, perhaps only once or twice a day, a command signal is transmitted to a specific satellite. The signal is meaningless to all but the selected bird. A code is used to open the receiver in the bird, and just like a key and lock, only specified birds will respond. Once the bird is alerted, it prepares its electronics to receive the command.

"This command message may be sent immediately or delayed for a specified time period, milliseconds, seconds, minutes or even hours. Only the Russians know how long the delay will be. The bird will only accept commands that fit into preset parameters, ignoring all others. In this way it is unlikely to be triggered by extraneous sources and very difficult for another nation to access a bird not belonging to them.

"The satellite that came down in Canada was recovered by Canadian and U.S. military forces under a joint operation called, 'Operation Morning Light' and provided our first clues of the advanced state of the Russian space program. This was valuable information. Subsequent data however were considerably more valuable. We were not prepared for some of the surprises we were given."

"Are you familiar with flash data delivery, Mike?" Tanya asked.

"I've read about it, but I've never used it in my work"

"You've probably used it in some form, but were not aware that it was anything special. Well, it has been developed into an extremely effective tool for space weaponry. Imagine the telegraph clicking away, transmitting Morse code. Each letter has to be sent at what we now consider a laboriously slow speed, dot by dot. It takes a long time to send even a short message."

"The telephone improved the speed considerably. You could talk as fast as you wanted, so long as your listener could understand. Then radio and television came along. It would take hours to transmit one television picture using the old telegraph method of one dot at a time. Today we are able to transmit millions of 'dots' a second. Our technology is growing so rapidly that even the high speed TV transmissions are too slow. Our space program requires that large masses of telemetry be transmitted to and from space vehicles quickly. Scientists came up with a way to multiply the delivery speed phenomenally. They took the string of data, squeezed it together and spit it out in a short burst." Morgan paused then went on, "It's really the same as you taking your tape recorder and playing a three minute song in three seconds. You wouldn't be able to make any sense out of the 'noise' it produced, but take another tape recorder and record at the same speed as the sending set, then replay at the normal speed what it recorded and it will again be distinguishable.

"This is the method we use to communicate with our unmanned spacecraft. There are computer interfaces at the earth stations and on board the craft which look after all data transmissions. This flash, or burst transmission time can be held to millionths of a second. The benefits are many; less time is needed to talk to birds; more information can be given within a specific time as a bird passes overhead; and it's almost impossible to intercept a message. This last point has great significance to intelligence birds. Not only do you have to know when a transmission will take place, you must also know what 'speed' and radio frequency are being used. It's more difficult than the needle in the haystack. Using this method, a bird can be controlled in total secrecy."

"We discovered that Cosmos 954 was run in this manner, but what was more important, we were able to determine how it was controlled. Frequencies, modes of operation and capabilities were determined. Once we knew how it was done we were able to follow all Russian birds to better advantage. We no longer had to guess what they were doing. We knew not only what, but when and why. We could receive the same reports the Russians were getting. Now we come back to you, Mike.

"We had been watching 954 for some time doing its thing over your area but were not able to correctly guess what it was up to. We surmised that it was following the construction of the Trident base. We were not aware, back then, that it had many other capabilities."

"The Russians don't have tracking signatures for Trident subs. Cosmos 954 is supposed to get them as our submarines come and go through the Hood Canal and Strait of Juan de Fuca. Satellites can't get a signature by themselves though, they must have input from special sono-buoys. Sono-buoys are usually placed on the sea bed and have the ability to record every noise they hear. I'm sure you use them in your base security net, and are familiar with them. You'll know they can hear and record all noises and have a range of over two miles. Everything passing within this distance is recorded; whales, fish, ships, everything."

"That's right. I do use them." Mike's interest grew.

"The data recorded is stored in the buoy until a radio signal triggers its transmitter, then it begins sending all the stored data. This clears its memory, preparing it for the next recording period."

"The trigger signal is given from the Cosmos 954 satellite as it is passing overhead, and here is the giveaway. The bird can't hear too well. In order to pick up a message it has to be positioned as close to the transmitter as possible. The birds orbit must be at perigee just when it passes over the sono-buoy. The buoy is interrogated and fires off a 'burst' of data at just the right time for pickup. From what we can put together, there are probably a dozen or more of these buoys strategically placed to cover the routes to your base. We've not been able to find any of them yet. They could be anywhere on the ocean floor. We don't know where to start looking.

"If the buoys transmitted for any length of time, we could get a fix on them, but with flash transmissions we can't get to them fast enough. They are almost impossible to find. This is where we want some help from you. We'll get to this in more detail later, Mike. Right now, what do you know about the new stealth equipment being up-dated into the Trident Class sub?"

"Not very much." Mike admitted. "When we were formulating security plans for the base a few years ago we were told that some system was being created but I've lost touch with it. Was it perfected?"

"Well, maybe not perfected but improved, certainly. What's designed is a combination of extra silent gear together with an electronic field around the sub. This combination permits the sub to become all but invisible from sonar, acoustic and thermal detection methods. Virtually undetectable!"

"Keep going," said Mike, "I sense we've not come to the main points yet, have we?"

"No," stated Morgan. "As all our new subs are produced they are cataloged by ourselves and, of course, by the Russians as to their capability and tracking signatures. Are you aware of what has gone on regarding these subs during sea trials?"

"Yes, Tanya has filled me in on some of the details, particularly the frustrations experienced by our shadow navy, the Russians. Is this what you mean?"

"Partly. We want the Russians to think they have been successful in establishing the signature of the prototype USS OHIO and all future production models while they are still on builder's sea trials. This way we hope they won't catch on to the fact that we have the stealth capability. While we are able to successfully carry on this charade, we'll have a tremendous power advantage."

"In order to confirm the data they obtain in the Atlantic, they must check them against data obtained in the Pacific. We know they are anxiously waiting for USS OHIO to arrive and start working out of your base. Our intelligence tells us they have seeded choke points in the Hood Canal and the Strait of Juan de Fuca with sono-buoys specifically to detect and record Trident subs. As our boats enter and leave the base area they have to pass over these sono-buoys. Their acoustic signatures will be recorded and sent to the Cosmos birds by the methods we just went over."

Mike was puzzled. "If the subs have their special gear turned on, the sono-buoys won't detect them. Is that right?"

"That's right"

Mike thought about this. "Our base is built so that at no time can we completely hide a Trident sub. The pens were built deliberately so the sub couldn't get entirely into them. A bow or stern must be visible at all times. This was done as part of our Strategic Arms Limitation Talk agreement. The Russians know when there are subs in the pens. They can also see when they aren't in the pens. When a sub is there one day and gone the next, it's likely that it's out on patrol, right?"

"That's right! And that's why it's so important that we get our hands on one of their sono-buoys. The buoys will blow the whole game for us if they send back correct data. We've got to get to those buoys to determine how they work. Then we can fill them with the disinformation. We'd like to be in a position to be able to tell the buoys only what we want them to know. This way the Russians will know when our boats are in port, but as soon as they get to green water, they're essentially invisible."

"This is where you come in, Mike. We'd like you to take an underwater team and find one of these sono-buoys and dissect it. You know the area and are experienced in underwater work.

We feel you are in the best position of anyone to find a buoy for us."

"That would take some time to arrange. There are a lot of things I have to do in preparation for the USS OHIO' arrival and the regular base security before I could take on an assignment like this."

"That's already been taken care of. We have obtained the necessary clearances right from your base commander. The urgency and importance to national security were stressed to him. He agreed to let you go for whatever time is required. Lieutenant Andrushyn will go with you, to assist any way she can. She has more details and will fill you in on the way back to Bangor. And, Mike, I can't impress too much on you just how important the success of this mission is. National security is at stake here. We MUST get one of those buoys!"

"I understand. I'll get one for you." Mike offered without knowing exactly how he would do it.

Tanya and Mike said their goodbyes and left the briefing room, taking a side door leading directly out of the building.

At their feet lay the splendor of Hawaii. Directly in front of them to the East were the sugar cane and pineapple fields while to the Southeast lay Honolulu, Waikiki and Diamond head. Most of the view to the South was blocked by the continuation of the Waianae Mountain Range which ran in a huge crescent shape from Kaena Point to the Northwest almost down to the beach at Nanakuli directly to the South. The Range was the highest on Oahu and it was here that Mount Kaala thrust its tip upward to be the highest point on the island.

As Tanya and Mike walked toward the gondola for the descent, Tanya continued the intelligence story which was by now completely gripping Mike.

"The reason we were at all suspicious about Cosmos 954 beyond our original deduction that it was photographing your base, was purely a bit of luck. I happened to be listening to transmissions from Salud, the Russian space lab one day when I noticed a string of rapid fire noise set in a pattern. Normally this noise accompanies most high frequency transmissions, but it's very random. Because it was so fixed in its pattern I decided to take a closer look at it. There was some substantiation that it might be the 'flash' or 'burst' data Morgan described in the briefing today.

"We record everything we pick up here so we can look at it any time in the future if we wish. I isolated the bursts and began to play with them on the computer. You can tell pretty quickly if what you have is man-made or just interference from external sources. We made note of the time of transmission and established which of the satellites were in range at that time and could have originated the signals. There were about thirty that could have sent it. We then asked the computers to see if there had been any similar signals from previous data. It found some. We cross-referenced this again with satellites which were overhead. It was easy from there. Only one satellite was in the right position at each of the times."

"Don't tell me," said Mike," let me guess. Cosmos 954, right?"

"Right. We then made a study of Cosmos 954 to find out all we could. It was in a circular orbit about 150 miles up but once a day it dipped down to about 90 miles. That's about as low as it could get and still stay in orbit. This placed it right over your base at its perigee or low point."

"We then began to break down any transmissions it made and determined where they were directed. We noted there were two types of transmission: one to command and one to carry data. The command signal appeared to be directed to a ground station. We thought at first it was to a Russian trawler but there were times when there were no ships in the area and the transmissions continued. Yet, it had to be to some fixed point."

The gondola arrived at the top station and they got aboard to make their way to the valley below. Tanya continued her story on the way down. "The fact that it was asking for data from the ground confused us at first, until we realized that the Russians use underwater sensors in many areas of their strategic ports and they monitor them with satellites. Here then was a logical explanation for what was happening. Once we understood this, our investigations could be narrowed down. If in fact the Russians have planted these buoys in our water, they have broken International law and it could start a lot of nasty action, possibly leading to war. If we found any of these buoys and confronted them with the information, they would deny it. They don't want us to find them and will likely go to any extent to cover up."

"How would they set them in place?"

"We don't know that. The type of electronics they would have to use is not very robust. It would have to be set in place very carefully and accurately. This rules out an air drop. We monitor all of their submarine activity in the Pacific and we know they've not been close enough to lay them from subs."

"How about underwater sleds?"

"The range of a sled isn't great enough to do the job from an off shore sub or ship."

"Well, that may be something I'll have to find out."

By this time their gondola had reached the lower station. They drove back to Schofield Barracks in relative silence. Many thoughts were going through Mike's head. How best to attack the problem? Who should be informed? Who knew about these buoys, Naval Intelligence? If they did, why wasn't Bangor informed? He would make some inquiries when he got back. Maybe raise some shit if they knew, and kept him in the dark.

Tanya dropped him off at his quarters. "I'll make arrangements for a flight out. See you in half an hour and we can go for supper."

"Fine, Tanya."

She continued around the barracks, to the single officer's quarters and parked in front of her building.

Tanya required a more time to pack, having difficulty deciding what to take. Would she be away for a week or a month? She figured on the month. What is the weather like in

Bangor this time of year? She'd take clothes for warm. Toiletries and uniforms of course. Shorts or swim suit? Why not?

When she finished packing, she had stuffed a rather large suitcase. She called the air base making travel arrangements. Military Air Transport offered her two seats on a flight leaving at 20:30 hours. Looking at the time she calculated how long they would have for the drive into the town, have supper, then to the airfield. Two hours should do it. Seemed okay. So she took the seats.

Picking up Mike, who had packed in minutes and hauled his baggage out onto the lanai, she picked him up and drove to Honolulu. "There's a Chinese place I know, feel like Chinese food?" she asked.

"That's okay, how much time before our flight?" Mike had difficulty hiding his eagerness to leave.

"The plane leaves at 20:30. They want us there by eight. We've got over an hour to eat."

Tanya deftly wove her way through the narrow streets of old Honolulu and parked at the famous On Woo's restaurant.

Half the tables were occupied. The late evening crowd would soon swell the numbers. They ate traditional Chinese food: wonton soup, fried rice and almond chicken. Over Chinese tea they opened fortune cookies. Mike's said 'a man's happiness is his wealth'. "I'd feel a lot happier with more wealth," he commented more in truth than jest.

Tanya's read, 'Take care around friends in the water.' "I wonder what that means?" she asked, "maybe I shouldn't have brought my bathing suit." They laughed.

Finishing their tea, they left for Henderson Field. Bags checked, they boarded the DC-10 and were soon airborne for Seattle.

CHAPTER 8

Wednesday, Day 5, 07:30 hours.

When Mike and Tanya arrived at Bangor a message waited. Mike was to call the Coast Guard Station in Port Angeles. 'Probably the Coast Guard wanting to know something about the Trident arrival, he thought. There was supposed to be a protest group at the top of Hood Canal when she arrived. The Coast Guard likely wanted some further details. The satellite problem had a higher priority; it gave him more serious concerns. Port Angeles could wait until tomorrow.

He had his secretary call his wife, Sandra to let her know he was back from Hawaii and ask her to get a baby-sitter for tonight so the two of them could go out for supper and a few drinks.

Mike took Tanya to the base cafeteria for brunch, then a base tour. He proudly went over the security facilities he'd designed and installed, explaining the perimeter security and the special I.D. badges they all had to wear. She was particularly impressed with the entry control monitors that identified a person by their fingerprints or the iris of their eyes. They also saw the radiation control and monitoring system in the missile preparation building. It could detect minute amounts of radiation passing within ten feet of it. There was one at each door of every building housing nuclear warheads.

After the tour they went back to Mike's office. A lot was going around in his mind. What Tanya had told them in Hawaii could turn a security man's hair grey. Any security system was penetrable, he knew that, but it shook him to realize the Russians knew exactly what was in every room of the base. What else did they know? Better still what didn't they know?

Mike had his secretary gather his staff for a short meeting that afternoon so that he and Tanya could brief them on some of the points he had learned in Hawaii. There were of course, some items such as the satellite electronic capability which he couldn't tell them. What he had to do was of necessity, top secret and the fewer people knowing about it, the easier to maintain secrecy. Approved for general dissemination was the fact they were under constant surveillance by satellite, and any move they made was monitored.

Complacency was a major problem with any security operation. When your systems and routines were in place and working well, the staff tended to relax. Practice drills helped to keep people sharp, but even drills had a tendency to become routine. Some new and important threat was required to snap the organization to attention. Mike used this crisis to shock his people. After a very animated question period, Mike closed the briefing with a pep talk he hoped would bring the security people up to a high level of concern. He wanted this information to spark new efficiency in their everyday work. He was pleased with the result. The briefing had gone very well.

Tanya needed a ride to her quarters and Mike offered to take her on his way home. He looked at his watch. Four o'clock. Sandra should be home from her afternoon with the girls by now. As they had to pass his office on the way out, Mike took advantage of the opportunity and called to find out if she had been able to get a sitter. She had. Tanya and Mike left the base a little after 4:15. Mike dropped her off at the lodging and continued home arriving at 4:30. Sandra was in the bath when he walked into the bedroom. "Hi, I'm home."

"I'm in here, Mike." she yelled. The anger of two days ago had disappeared with Mike's return. Although she complained every time he had to travel, she was always glad to have him home. He heard the splashes. As he walked in, he bent over and kissed her, slipping one hand over her soapy breast. She responded with her tongue. Mike's pulse quickened and she cooled him off with a wet face cloth to the side of his head.

"Where are the kids?" They had a boy, eight and a girl four.

"Over at Betty's. She's going to feed them supper and 'sit' them 'till we get home."

A devilish look appeared in his eyes. "You mean we're alone?" He thought about this for all of two seconds then kissed her, this time with more passion, removing his clothes while caressing her. She giggled as he joined her in the tub.

Later, they went out to supper and then to a play. The local playhouse theater presented Gagnon's play 'The Birds in the Trees', a light comedy about a young girl's coming of age. For local players, they did a good job. Sandra had read the book and felt the play followed it quite closely. The audience enjoyed it. Home again, they went next door to collect their two children. Betty insisted they stay for coffee. All Mike could think of was bed. Tired from the flight home then the day at the base, he needed rest. They stayed a respectable time, telling Betty and her husband Jim, all about the play, then took the kids home to bed.

Thursday, day 6, 07:00 hours.

Mike arrived at the base early the next morning. There was another message from the Port Angeles Coast Guard Station. A Commander Reynolds wanted him to call. Said it was urgent. Mike felt he may as well look after this call before he went to pick up Tanya at 08:00 hours. He asked the base operator to place the call to Port Angeles and contact him when it was connected.

His phone rang. "Commander Chambers, the Admiral would like to see you immediately in his office". It was the Admiral's aide.

"Okay, Georgia, cancel my call to Port Angeles until I get back."

Mike and the admiral discussed the security problem in great depth.

Matt had wasted no time getting to the Commodore. He hurried right into his office and told him as quickly as possible, all he could put together about the whole affair. He was halfway through his explanation when the Commodore picked up the phone.

"Betty, get me naval intelligence at Bangor, quickly please."

Seconds passed. "Bangor on the phone, Sir," came the secretary's quick response.

"Who'm I talking to?" the Commodore inquired.

"Admiral Blake, Base Commander. What can I do for you Commodore?"

""We've had some strange things happening up here, Admiral. Last night we had two men blown up on the beach, one is dead, the other is just about dead as well. This morning we fished out a dead scuba diver. He appears to have been killed by an explosion also. We aren't sure if the deaths were caused by the same devices, but all indications point to that. We found some bits of what look like electronic equipment scattered around the beach and imbedded in both dead men, some parts with Russian writing on them. We thought you people may be able to help us make sense out of all this."

"We've got some peculiar activity going on down here, too, Commodore. The two may be tied together. My base security officer is involved, and I think he had better talk to you right away. I'll contact him as soon as I hang up, and have him up in Port Angeles within the hour. And Commodore, don't let any of this information out to anyone. This could be extremely sensitive to the defense of the nation. What you've accidentally become involved with could be a part of the arrival of the first refitted Trident."

"I understand, Admiral. We'll wait for your security man. Thanks for your candor."

"Good, Commodore. Commander Chambers will be up there shortly."

The Commodore's phone rang within minutes of the Admiral's hanging up.

"Commodore Coulter?"

"This is Coulter."

"Commodore, this is Commander Chambers at Bangor. Admiral Blake told me a little about your incidents. I'm sufficiently concerned that I would like you to do some things for me while I'm on my way up there."

"Certainly Commander, what would you like?"

"Seal off the beach area where the explosion took place. Use the local police if possible. Gather and put a guard on all the parts of the exploded device you have managed to find and don't probe the sand any more. I think the precise location where they are found may be extremely important to our investigation team if we decide an investigation is warranted. Put a guard on the bodies in the morgue and restrict access to the injured man in the hospital."

"Okay, Commander, we'll look after those details. How long will it take you to get here?"

"I'm going to hop an aircraft now. I'll be there within forty five minutes."

He hung up then dialed the transportation pool. "This is Commander Chambers; I want a chopper ready to go to Port Angeles immediately. There'll be three passengers. We'll be down at the heli-pad in less than 15 minutes. Have the chopper ready."

He next called Tanya, and told her to take a taxi and get to the base as quickly as possible. He filled her in about the call to the Coast Guard and thought they had better get up there right away. She concurred and was on her way.

He then called base ordnance. "Lieutenant Bob Bjorn please.

"Bjorn," came the answer.

"Bob, Mike Chambers here. Can you spare some time for a short trip?"

"Sure, when?"

"Right now. There'll be a chopper at the pad. We leave in twenty minutes. Sooner if possible."

"Why the rush?"

"I'll explain on the way. Don't be late."

"See you there."

At the heli-pad, Mike told Bob what they were going for and what he thought they would find. Tanya arrived at the same time as the chopper crew. They all piled aboard and the pilot fired up the machine.

The flight north was uneventful. A short half hour trip. Tanya had not seen this area before except on maps. The massive mountain ranges and rugged terrain impressed her; much higher than those in Hawaii. There were snow capped peaks to the west. Visibility was unlimited and she knew from her maps that if the aircraft had been flying a little higher, she would have been able to see the Pacific Ocean over the ranges to the west. To the north was the Strait of Juan de Fuca with its myriad vacation islands strung out toward the eastern end. They landed at Tucker Airport on Ediz Hook, right at the Coast Guard Base.

Commander Matt Reynolds met them. While they walked to the operations room, they introduced themselves. Matt couldn't take his eyes off Tanya. The trim body, properly shaped in the right places, brunette hair curled under just at her uniform collar, high Slavic cheekbone structure and blue eyes that betrayed a hint of imp in her. He stood motionless for a moment then shook himself back to reality. This display hadn't been missed by Tanya. She flushed ever so slightly. The start of a smile played on her lips.

Matt broke the mood before it really began. "Where would you like to start, Commander?"

"I think we should start with the area on the beach and play it from there. I particularly want Bob to see it to assess the explosion. Maybe you can show Tanya the electronic bits you found while we do that."

On the way Matt went over the events in more detail, from the incident with the fish, right up to the present. As they approached the beach, they noticed the area was roped off with police ribbons.

"The whole situation is out of my jurisdiction," offered Matt, "but because Doctor Johnson and I were the first ones to arrive after the explosion, we carried on with the job that had to be done. It was just a bit of luck that the Doc was along."

"You mentioned the two men appeared to have been cutting firewood." Mike queried.

"That's right, it's not unusual for area residents to come down and cut driftwood. Now that the price of wood delivered from the mills has gotten so high, more and more people are cutting their own firewood where possible."

"From the sound of it they cut into more than driftwood." said Bob, "What do you think they hit, Matt?"

"As near as I can figure out, it was something that looked like a log but wasn't."

"Why do you say that?" asked Tanya. Their eyes met.

"Because of the bits of plastic we found, Tanya," Matt swallowed hard and stood uncomfortably gazing along the sand. "Chunks that were apparently wrapped around a cylinder or something in the shape of a cylinder. I found some bits buried in the sand here on the beach and Doc Johnson found more in each of the victims. He also dug a chunk of it out of the dead scuba diver. The same brown plastic material and, from what we can determine, the diver was fooling around with a log on the sea bottom."

"You also mentioned some electronic parts you found."

"There were bits embedded in the bodies of the two men involved here. At first Doc and I had no reason to believe they weren't any more than the ignition system from chainsaws. Then yesterday I was poking around on the beach and dug up some large electronic printed circuit board pieces. Much more complex than any chain saw would need. That's when I realized we had something more than a chainsaw explosion. The clincher was when we found the same type of material driven into the dead scuba diver. We called you people."

"If you found parts in the sand near the impact area," said Tanya, "there must be more of them scattered around. Have you checked the surrounding area?"

"I did that yesterday morning."

"What did you find?"

"I poked around in the crater and came up with some large chunks."

"What did you do with them?"

"I reburied them. I thought they could be important."

"They may be. Can you find them again?"

"Sure. They'll still be where I put them."

"They could provide considerable information to our intelligence people. Have you looked further away from the crater?"

"No, once I saw these parts, enough of the picture began to come together for me to realize I was in over my head. That's one reason you people were called in. We feel we are dealing with the tip of the iceberg and we're in no position to explore it to the point of understanding its implications. I've had a nagging suspicion in the back of my mind that it's somehow tied into the arrival next week of USS OHIO. Does this seem plausible to any of you?" Matt threw that last part up to see if there was any reaction from the navy types.

There was. It was immediate and guarded. Everybody looked at everybody else, and then they all looked at the ground. Matt knew he had struck something.

"It could," said Mike rather nonchalantly. "How do you think it would tie in, Matt?"

"I'm not sure, but this could be a marker-buoy. It's got Russian writing on it and it's obviously expensive. It could have drifted in from the open sea or it could have been planted in this area. It's obvious the Russians tried to disguise it as a log. This means they expected it could be observed but hoped no one would examine it too closely. It wasn't supposed to be washed up on any beach. The selection of this particular spot to plant them and the arrival of the Trident sub could be a coincidence, but I doubt it. How'd I doing so far?"

"You could be right," said Mike, "then again it could be something entirely different."

The more Matt thought about it, the more convinced he became that he was right.

A long silence was broken by Bob, "We've long suspected the Russians fishing fleet has been planting sono-buoys in this area but we've never found any. Perhaps we've been looking for the wrong shaped buoy. It's quite possible they've been disguising them to look like logs. They've eluded us so far. This could be how it was done."

They arrived at the beach and were immediately challenged by two men from the Sheriff's office wanting to know who they were and what they wanted. Each of them in turn produced identification for the officers. Once satisfied, they were allowed access to the beach area that had been roped off. As they walked toward the burned out van, Matt pointed out where they had found the two men.

Tanya had walked ahead of them and was scanning the surrounding area for debris which may have been overlooked. She found something and excitedly called Matt and Bob over. They went to see what she'd found. It was a matchbox sized piece of printed circuit board. A couple of integrated circuit chips were still mounted on it.

"Is this the sort of thing you found?" She held it up.

"That's similar to the ones I found," Matt said, "only that one seems to have some of the brown plastic still attached. What do you make of it, Bob?"

"There's not much to go on, we'll have to identify the chips and determine their normal function before we know what it is. Off hand, I'd say it's part of a signal sequencing circuit. Let's see if we can find some more."

The three of them walked back and forth around the area, finding quite a few small pieces. Some were larger than the first one Tanya had found. While they were searching the outlying sections of the beach, the others were standing beside the burned out van and the crater in the sand.

"Bob, if you were to deliberately create this much damage, how much explosive would it take?" asked Mike.

Bob stood back and looked from the crater to the van then over to where Matt had shown them the two men had been tossed.

"To disintegrate its own container, rip the van apart this way and throw two average sized men that far up the beach would probably take about twenty five or more pounds of high energy explosive." Bob continued, drawing Mike's attention to the side of the crater, pointing out that the sides were blown almost flat.

Mike studied the edges, "You mean the fact that the sides are not sharply defined has some significance?"

"It has. Remember Commander Reynolds told us that he had been poking at the crater but stopped when he realized it might not be a good idea. That would account for this flattened edge here, but the rest of the edge hasn't been touched. To make such a depression requires a very fast oxidizing fuel, explosive to you. We will be able to determine the type after a lab analysis of the sand from the wall area. There will also be a good portion of the buoy, if that's what it is, buried throughout the bottom portion of the crater. The blast will have driven it deep into the sand."

With that thought, Bob yelled at Tanya and Matt," Hold on, you two. Come over here for a minute."

"What's up?" Matt said as they joined them.

"Where you find each piece will likely be important to the Intelligence people. They'll want to know exact locations so whatever you disturb make note of what it is and where you got it. In fact we probably should get out of here right now before we inadvertently screw up something vital."

They paced off the distances from the crater to the parts that they found and identified what they were. The group then headed back to the car. Bob Bjorn continued, "We'll want every scrap of this unit we can find to take back to the lab at Bangor. It sure would be a lot easier to have the real thing to examine."

"You're dreaming, Bob."

On the way to the car they informed the Sheriff's men that the Navy would send personnel up from the Bangor Base later in the day to investigate the incident. In the meantime no one was to be allowed to enter the roped off area. The men acknowledged.

Mike got into the car. "Okay Bob, we'll get an investigation crew up here right away. I'd like Eric Cassidy to be a part of that crew. I've worked with him before. He really knows his stuff. While we're at it we'll need security. At least three men at this site at all times. I also want a twenty four hour guard on the man in the hospital and the body in the morgue. No one sees them without our permission.

"Matt, have you put a guard on the injured man?"

"Yes. Right after our telephone conversation. The local police are doing it."

Good. We'll have Navy men replace them."

"Sure, Mike, what else do you think you'll need?"

"Some people to sweep this area. Metal detectors, radiation detectors and sifting gear as well as someone from the electronics section to identify parts and note their location."

Bob was ahead of them. "We'll get whatever you need." He was away.

As the others got into the car Mike went on, "What I would like to do now, Matt, with your permission, is go back to your base and re-hash what we have learned so far. I think it's time we brought you up to date with what is going on."

"Suits me fine. I feel like the only one here who doesn't know."

"Not really." Tanya could detect the frustration in his voice, "You have part of the story; we have another part. When we get them together, we'll all have a better idea."

"We've a conference room at the base we could use."

"That will do fine, Matt. Is there a blackboard in it?" Mike was already going through the details he'd have to elaborate on. Sometimes working on the board can save many words.

"Yes, there is. There's also an overhead projector if you need it."

"Good, let's go."

Matt drove and Tanya sat next to him. He was not oblivious to her proximity nor her perfume. Maybe, if she were to be here for a few days he could show her some of the town, who knows? Matt hadn't had much to do with women since his teen years when he lost his sweetheart Ruth in a boating accident. He blamed himself for her death. His thoughts drifted to some of those happier days. Come to think of it Tanya looked a little like Ruth.

Mike brought him back to reality, "Where was the scuba diver found?"

"He was about three miles from shore to the northwest of town."

"Can you locate the spot with any precision?"

"We can likely get it to within about a 30 foot radius. Is that close enough?"

Mike said, "Well, if he was killed the same way as the man on the beach, we want to locate the exact spot. There is a lot of seabed to cover."

"Not really, except the tide has changed twice since he was found. He could have drifted back and forth over the spot." Matt cautioned. "Maybe we could be a little more precise. I logged the spot where we ran across the dead fish. We should be able to use that as a fix point."

"We'll have a look at that later, Matt. I think I'd better bring some of my underwater men up to give the area a thorough going over. If we assume the diver was killed by the same device, there should be similar bits and pieces down there."

"The Coast Guard can put a cutter at your disposal if you want."

"That will be appreciated. It'll also help to keep the navy profile as low as possible. We don't want any publicity at all, if possible."

When they arrived at the Coast Guard base guard house, Matt met then and took them directly to the conference room. Mike spotted a phone immediately and was on the line almost before everyone was in the room.

"Admiral, I'd like Commander Cassidy up here and I'd also like George Hammerdyne with his dolphins. Do you think that can be arranged?" There was a pause.

"No, Admiral, I don't think so. If my guess is right, there'd have to be at least six of these buoys in a string to relay the type of information we suspect 'they' want"

"No, that's fine, sir. Just as soon as possible. ___ We don't have much time. Oh, one more thing, sir. If we are right and we do manage to locate a live one, I want to bring it back to our remote control cells at the base. I would like your approval. ___ Yes, sir, it has been estimated to contain about twenty five pounds of explosives. ___ Yes, sir, I'm sure it will be fully booby-trapped. Yes, sir, I know, sir. Yes, but that's the only way we'll be able to dissect it. ___ Yes, sir, if we're going to reprogram it, it's necessary. Yes, sir. Fine, Sir. Goodbye."

The others in the room had only been able to hear one side of the conversation but were able to piece together the gist of it.

Mike apologized and explained, "I'd better fill you in on what I have in mind. Each of you will have a key part to play."

"I want to retrieve a working sono-buoy and bring it in for reprogramming. Once we are sure we know how it works we can feed it any information we want and it will tell its owners exactly what we want them to know."

Mike then explained to Bob and Matt, the situation of the satellites and submarines. He cautioned both of them that what they had just learned was extremely sensitive information, specifically the part about the electronic masking equipment aboard the re-fitted Trident class subs.

Bob was puzzled. "Why don't you just eliminate the buoys?"

"We could, and we may have to yet, but the way we can achieve the most benefit is to feed the buoys disinformation. To do this we are going to have to be very lucky. It means not only do we have to, to locate another buoy, if indeed there is another one, but also take it apart, even though it may be booby-trapped, decipher its workings and put it back where we found it. All this has to be done without the owners finding out that we even know the buoys exist."

"That's a tall order," Matt said trying to comprehend the implications.

"It sure is. If the Russians even suspect we are tampering, they'll abandon these buoys and replace them with something else in a different area and with a new operating system. It's better if we let them think they are getting good information. We know where these buoys are. We may not know where the replacements go."

"I see what you mean, but how are you going to find more buoys?"

"There's a lot of ocean to search, Bob. That's why I've asked the Admiral to bring in a Captain Hammerdyne. He's in charge of the Navy's dolphin program."

"Dolphins? Did I hear you talking about dolphins?" Bob thought Mike was joking.

"I don't know if you're aware of what we've been able to do with these mammals Bob, but we've come a long way in the last ten years. Dolphins can swim deeper and much faster than a scuba or hard hat diver. They're used for many tasks not the least of which is recovering practice torpedoes and rockets. They have the ability to understand and obey what I'll call 'requests'. I'm reluctant to call them 'orders' and I don't think the term 'command' fits here. We 'request' that they do certain things and in most cases they will comply."

"That's well and good," Bob was incredulous now, "but what we think we have here is a sono-buoy that looks like a log and may explode when you touch it. What the hell can a dolphin do with something like that, assuming that he finds one?"

"The very fact that we assume there are more out there is even more reason to use dolphins. You've done a lot of diving in the area, Matt, what's the visibility like?"

"Not bad down to fifty feet, worse to one hundred feet. Terrible below that."

"Well, dolphins have no problem finding things in complete darkness. If the buoys are going to be located, men will have a tough time, even with strong lights. Dolphins can do it easily. They can cover more territory than men and do it faster. Time is short. We've got to make the best possible use of it."

Mike detailed the rest of the plan to them.

"Once we find a live sono-buoy we are still a long way from finished. I want to move it down to Bangor and dissect it. We'll have to do that by remote control in case it blows up. We've facilities at the base to do all of this. We'll study its electronics and verify what it's supposed to do. Then we'll have to determine the best way to swing it over to our side. Once all this is done we'll try to set it back exactly where we found it."

"Basically that's what we are about to do. Are there any questions?"

Silence.

"No? Then I suggest we shut her down for today and think about the task ahead of us. We're going to be very busy for the next few days, so prepare yourselves. We'll meet back here tomorrow morning at 07:00 hours if that's all right with your people, Matt?"

"Sure, that's fine. We've been instructed to assist wherever possible. I'll take some time to fill in my C.O. He requested he be kept abreast of what is going on."

"I can understand that," said Mike, "my C.O. made the same request. No one likes surprises when they're dealing with things of this nature. I want to caution you though, be careful what you tell him. You can tell him what we are doing but you don't have to tell him about the sensitive parts as yet. The special submarine electronics and reprogramming of the sono-buoy are best known by as few people as possible."

"I understand."

Matt informed them of the billeting arrangements he had made for them and explained where they could find a reasonable supper. As they left the building Matt walked with Tanya.

"If you'd like, I know a nice spot along the coast where they serve a terrific seafood dinner."

"Sounds like the best offer so far today, Matt. Suppose you pick me up a little later."

"Fine. I'll see you about 19:00 hours?"

"That'll be good. I'll have some time to freshen up and change out of this uniform."

Matt was watching the backside of the well-proportioned woman disappearing down the road toward the staff car when she wheeled and said, "You don't know where I'm staying. How're you going to pick me up?"

"Oh yes I do," Matt flushed a little. "I had a word with the duty officer. In fact, I suggested a place I thought deserving of a woman with your class."

Tanya blushed.

CHAPTER 9

Thursday, Day 6, 18:50 hours.

Matt had made sure the navy billeted Tanya in the Midtown Hotel. One of the most modern in town, it had the more popular lounge and Matt had been there many times to enjoy the quality entertainment. Matt, however, wasn't thinking of the lounge tonight as he strode through the lobby toward the elevator.

Leaving the elevator and walking down the hall to her room, various things he had planned for tonight tumbled through his mind. She had moved him as no other woman. He wanted this night to be memorable. He carried flowers and had arranged with the hotel to put a chilled bottle of cooled, fine Mumms Cordon Rouge champagne in her room around 11:00 o'clock. If he could maintain the schedule he had worked out, they should return just after that.

He strode up to her door, looking clean and sharp in a three piece civilian suit and crisp white shirt. At exactly 7:00 o'clock, he straightened his tie and knocked firmly.

The door opened and Matt backed up a step, able only to stare. He was not prepared for the transformation from naval uniform to evening dress. She was beautiful, Matt knew, but he had not realized just how beautiful. She wore a black, strapless gown, held up by two firm, rounded breasts straining to escape confinement. The skin-tight sheath followed the smooth contours of her body, over a slim waist, curved gently past well rounded hips, then tapered to the floor over what Matt already knew were well shaped legs and trim ankles.

She wore little make-up. She needed little. Light eye shadow accented deep blue eyes, a touch of red on her bow-shaped lips highlighted a very pretty face. A single-strand pearl choker and matching pearl earrings completed the aura. She sparkled. Matt stood, mesmerized.

Tanya's, "come in," broke the spell.

Slowly entering the room, he offered her the gardenia corsage he carried and a dozen roses for her room. She closed the door slowly.

"They're beautiful," she said, obviously moved.

"I can say the same about you. It's a shame I've got to take you out. I don't want to share you with other people."

Their hands touched as he handed her the flowers, and they both felt the electricity of the moment.

"I love the fragrance," she said, taking the flowers. "It reminds me of the Islands. I'll put them in water right away." Looking at the corsage, she said, "Gardenias are my favorite. How'd you know?"

"A little intelligence work," he lied.

The only container she could find was an ice bucket. "Not very elegant but I guess it'll have to do." She added water and set the roses on the little table by the sofa then returned to stand near Matt. A passing hint of her perfume sent his mind racing. She quickly picked up on it.

"Thank you," she said as their eyes met, "for what you're thinking."

His arms went around her and he drew her toward him. This perfume was not the same as she wore during the daytime. This had seductive powers he'd not known before. His pulse raced. He kissed her slowly and gently. She responded, returning tenderness. The promise of more to come raged in each of them as they parted. He picked up her coat at the same time, taking a deep breath. "We'd better go now, or we'll never go. We've got reservations for 7:45 and it's a short drive from here."

On the way to the car Tanya asked, "Where are we going, or is it a secret?"

"No, it's not a secret," he laughed at her little 'in' joke. Everything they had been doing lately was top secret, or so it seemed. "It's a little place a few miles east of here, and I've saved it just for you." They both laughed. "They serve terrific seafood."

The road wound along the tree covered coast, small clusters of houses appeared at irregular intervals. After a few miles, Matt turned off the main highway onto Deer Park Road, continuing up the narrow road heading away from the shore. Half a mile later a low building emerged from the forest. A small, half filled parking lot, spilled out from the wide entrance driveway. There were no signs to say what it was, prompting Tanya to ask, "Is this where we're having dinner, or have you brought me to a remote lodge for debauchery? I don't know whether or not to trust you!"

"Not a bad idea at all." he said, thinking it over as he parked the car.

"How do people know what this place is? There are no signs anywhere."

"Word of mouth. Once you've been here you're not likely to forget it."

"That good, is it?"

"You'll find out! It's called The Bell Buoy Inn. It's owned by Ian Bell, a retired navy man."

Before getting out he reached over, touched her hand, then leaned over to kiss her gently. She closed her eyes and responded. They broke, short of breath and Matt got out, opened her door, and they walked slowly to the entrance.

Matt had reserved a special table away from the main floor area, in a nook providing considerable privacy. A three piece combo played softly creating an atmosphere of calm elegance. They had time for a glass of wine before ordering dinner.

Starting with Dungeness crab salad they worked up to the house specialty, Darne de Saumon Grillee ou Pochee, Salmon steak poached with a special house sauce. They topped off a filling meal with Spanish coffee flambe, providing a spectacular show with the flaming mix tossing back and forth between bowls, blending it. The taste was spectacular too!

The soft candlelight glistening in Tanya's hair did beautiful things with shadows across her face and bare shoulders. Flickering fingers of light, casting a spell, isolating them within a shroud covering the two of them. Sitting quietly in their own little world they talked, each probing backgrounds to learn more about the other.

Soothing mood music penetrated their mystical canopy inviting them to dance. Accepting, they made their way through the tables to the dance floor. Light in his arms, she followed the rhythm beautifully. Holding her close he felt his impatience growing. She was ethereal, moving , . . no, floating without resistance. Her shimmering hair falling to the nape of her neck inflamed him. Her perfume strengthening her hold on him. He fought for control. A losing battle.

They danced 'till 10:30, had one last drink, then left. "What a shame it has to end." Tanya's eyes sparkled.

Matt smiled.

For Matt, the drive back to the hotel seemed to take forever. Small talk kept their minds off each other during the drive. Walking to her room, she handed Matt the door key. He opened it, stepping back to let Tanya enter.

"How about a nightcap?" she asked.

"I think I can handle that," was Matt's quick response.

He had laid his ground work well! Soft music played on the stereo. Perfect, he thought to himself and there on the table, an ice bucket stood cooling a bottle of champagne. Beside it, two glasses.

"What's this?" Tanya spotted it, too. "Pretty sure of yourself, mister"

The grin on Matt's face told it all. He said nothing.

A card lay on the table beside the bucket; she picked it up and read it. She flushed. "Oh Matt. How thoughtful."

He went behind her and took the coat off her shoulders, kissing a bare shoulder as he did so. She trembled ever so slightly. Tossing the coat over the back of the sofa, he gently turned her around, cupping her head in his large hands, kissed her delicately on the mouth, passion mounting. Tanya broke the spell, drawing away slightly, looking into his eyes almost pleadingly. Both were short of breath.

"We'd better open the wine," she murmured as they drew apart.

Matt stood transfixed as she went to the table, watching her fluid body motion carry her across the room and lift the Champagne from the ice. Sure, there had been times when lightning struck and thunder rolled, but not like this. Here he was moved by some force he didn't understand. It was a new situation. He sensed Tanya felt the same way and that probably helped escalate the mood. She brought the wine and glasses back, handing Matt the bottle. They sat together on the sofa. Matt worked the cork out of the bottle. The loud pop, followed by a rush of foam, was always a satisfying display, if not a little sexual.

"I'd like you to tell me a little more about yourself." It was her way of slowing a situation fast getting out of control. Not that she minded, it was just that she didn't quite believe what was happening. It would take a little time for her to assess the strange way she felt.

Matt filled two glasses. Giving one to Tanya, he raised his and said, "To a special woman I know." Her eyes crinkled as they sipped. Bubbles dancing on top of the wine tickled her nose.

"I don't know what you slipped onto my drinks at supper but I'm feeling a bit strange. Nice feeling. It's something I haven't felt since high school."

"I feel the same way, I thought it was you," Matt countered.

Drinking slowly, they spent a good hour discussing their younger lives, then drifted into deeper thoughts about hopes and dreams for the future. There were some minor areas of difference, but all in all, they'd had similar up-bringing. Matt had a love for the sea, where Tanya's was for animals. She had a way about her, allowing her to relate to animals. She had trained almost anything in her younger days, even her pet cat. Matt's interests centered around the outdoors, particularly the ocean.

As they talked, it was all Matt could do to keep his hands off her. He didn't realize she felt the same urges, but controlled them better. Neither had to worry about it too long.

Matt put his arms around her slender body and kissed her with growing passion, his hands moving over the soft, dark skin of her shoulder. She trembled, heart pounding. He kissed the tip of her button nose, then her cheek. She returned his tenderness with kind, hungrily searching for more. Breathing became difficult as his lips reached the lobe of her left ear. Matt caressed the underside of her chin and eased his trembling fingers, slowly down, brushing the sensitive skin between her firm, white breasts.

Breathing heavily herself now, Tanya firmly held the back of his head, lowering hers to catch the tip of his ear, her tongue tracing each curl and depression.

Matt eased his hand around her back and caressed the nape of her neck. Response was immediate. Gently, he undid the clasp at the top of her dress. The zipper ran smoothly down with little help needed. Opening, the dress fell slowly down to her waist.

Matt sat back, absorbing this stunning moment. The allusion of a beautiful butterfly, emerging from its cocoon, struck Matt as she stood up to shed her dress. From the chrysalis emerged a vision. Smooth, soft skin, firm breasts, rounded in the classic shape, each crowned with a delicate rose nipple, now standing erect. Matt stood beside her and marveled at these sensitive, provocative shapes, caressing first one then the other. He kissed each in turn, rolling his tongue around each rose tip, feeling it get harder as he teased it.

Tanya's dress had fallen to the floor revealing her slim waist and firm, rounded hips. They embraced standing by the sofa, then moved as one, to the large king-size bed. Matt shed his clothes almost in one motion as Tanya watched. She squirmed with pleasure as he lay on top of her, a throaty moan escaping her open mouth. "Yes! Yes! Yes." She could not remain still.

Slow rhythm sent ultimate sensations through the lovers. She joined him now in the dance of Eros, their bodies thrusting, gyrating in unison. They moved as one. Building, crashing, building again. Thrust and counter-thrust, the world of fire and ice gripped them as they matched twist for twist, thrust for thrust, united in the very height of passion. Each tuned to exchange the ultimate gift only lovers possess.

Climaxing with a pleasure so intense, Tanya found her emotion impossible to contain, exploding with a scream. Covering her mouth with his, Matt absorbed her final charge of high passion. She bit uncontrollably catching his lower lip. The pinnacle of love, reached and totally enjoyed, slipped slowly back to earth.

They lay still now, Matt atop this love goddess, for the longest time before he, rising on his elbows straight above her, gazed into her eyes. She understood the silent message and returned his statement. He said nothing aloud, nor did she, yet more communication took place with this eye contact than had been said all evening. Matt had heard the term soul-mates before and thought he knew the meaning. He realized now he'd had no idea until this moment. The twinning into oneness bewildered him a bit. He had always been in total control of his emotions under all situations. This new emotion controlled him.

He moved gently off Tanya and cradled her tenderly in his arms. They kissed once, hard, then Morpheus took control of their exhausted bodies and tucked them away in his arms to dream. They slept, deeply.

Two hours later Tanya shifted ever so slightly in his arms and it roused him. A few soft strokes on her breast and she woke too. The previous passions were soon awakened with a predictable result.

The next time they woke it was the hotel's wake-up service. The phone's ring was an unwelcome interruption. A new day had begun. Matt wondered if there would ever be another night quite like last night?

CHAPTER 10

Friday, Day 7, 07:00 hours.

Matt and Tanya arrived at the Coast Guard Base just before 07:00 hours the next morning. Tanya heading off to the communication room and Matt directly to Commodore Coulter's office, to find out when Captain Hammerdyne and his dolphins would be arriving from San Diego. His aircraft, a C-141 Starlifter, was due to touch down at Port Angeles' Fairchild International airport at 12:00 hours.

This was to be a new experience for Matt. He'd never seen dolphins put to work before except in Marine Land type shows. He talked with the Commodore for a while before going to the briefing room. Tanya and Mike were talking with Bob Bjorn, the explosives expert, when he got there.

Bob was explaining the basics of explosions, or as he called them, rapid oxidizations. "The biggest problem we have," he was saying, "is not in getting the material to make a big bang. On the contrary, what we are looking for is stability. It's always a compromise between explosive force and stability. The most powerful explosive isn't much good to you if you can't handle it. One usually has to be sacrificed for the other. The type I think the Russians have used in the destruct charge for the buoy could be a new type with the ability to incorporate the surrounding material as additional fuel for the explosion.

We have an explosive called PETN, it's a plastic explosive, meaning it's pliable, and can be shaped into any form. But, I think, because it is plastic, it would be difficult to use it as a container for electronic boxes or the buoys that hold them, particularly underwater. What they used must be something new. At least that's what I think, and it's borne out by the condition of the debris we found at the beach. We'll be more positive though when we get our hands on an actual sono-buoy.

Mike gave them some of the details of his plan to recover a buoy intact.

"Just a minute," interjected Matt, "when you do, and only if you do, get one of them, what makes you so sure you can just open it up and look at the insides?"

"If I know Ivan," answered Bob, "the thing will be booby-trapped in a dozen different ways. This is typical of Russian equipment, especially the new or sophisticated stuff. It'll be our job to get it open without killing anyone. This will be very difficult."

"I've asked the Bangor Base Commander to get hold of a weapons man who has a lot of knowledge in this area, Commander Eric Cassidy. He learned most of his Russian knowledge in Vietnam. If anyone can successfully open these buoys it'll be him."

Matt began to worry about his ship and the base. There will be a danger to his cutter and crew. The law of averages dictates that the longer a danger is present the more chance you have of being affected by it. He wanted it off his hands as quickly as possible.

Mike was next to add his input. "I've asked Commodore Coulter to assign a cutter and crew to this project. The cutter will recover a buoy and bring it ashore here, where a helicopter will airlift it to Bangor base. It'll be put into one of our remote manipulator cells. The opening will be done there, in an environment set up to cater to this kind of operation."

"The Captain agreed to assign a cutter and suggested that the crew be selected as soon as possible. What we are about to do is extremely dangerous and all the men will be volunteers. Because we're playing this by ear, each man's job becomes more important and to make the right decision, each must be totally aware of what we are dealing with. When Captain Hammerdyne arrives at noon we'll all assemble here for briefing. I also want to stress that time is of the essence. If we are to accomplish our objective in time to be of any value to National Defense we can't dawdle. I'd suggest you get lunch out of the way prior to noon and be ready to get going right after the plane arrives. Are there any questions?"

"Yes," Matt began, "out of curiosity, which cutter and crew did the Commodore assign?"

"Hope you don't mind, Matt. It was your cutter. Your crew volunteered, to a man."

"Oh, I don't mind. In fact, I wouldn't want it any other way."

"Until noon then, get done what each of you has to do and bear in mind that we might have to leave at the drop of a hat and may be at sea for an extended time, maybe a week or so. Pack what you'll need for this time frame and make the necessary arrangements. Just one reminder, this is a mission of extreme importance and utmost secrecy. Let's break now and I'd like to have all of you back in this conference room as soon as Captain Hammerdyne can get his end of things set up. And Matt, I'd like the members of your crew to take part in the briefing."

"Certainly, Mike, I'll have them all here."

Tanya and Matt walked down to the pier where his ship was berthed. The crew was busy provisioning her and doing some touch-up paint work. At the top of the gangway, Matt and Tanya saluted the flag as they went aboard. Ernie Daniels, Matt's first mate, met them as they stepped on deck. Matt asked him to muster the crew at the base conference room as soon as the dolphin crew arrived.

Matt took Tanya on a tour of the cutter and explained the role played by the Coast Guard with regard to water safety. He detailed the programs available to all who used the water, and subsequent enforcement of the rules and laws of the sea. The Coast Guard was responsible for the integrity of the International boundary on the water. The surveillance and apprehension of sea-based smugglers also fell under their umbrella.

They went ashore and caught a jeep ride back along the long narrow spit from the Coast Guard base, into town. When they reached mid-town they got out and walked a short block to the cafe. Over lunch, they made small talk, discussing their childhood days, favorite flavor ice cream and many other important facts. It contented Matt to just gaze into Tanya's eyes. He could sense that she felt the same way. They had finished lunch and sat talking. Reaching across the table he took her hand. Turning it palm-up he pointed out her life line and predicted a long life.

She gave him a sly smile, "Does it say anything about where it will be spent?"

"Not right down to the address, but it's pretty close to Paradise." he turned her hand over and covered it with his other hand. "You've got a small hand, with slender fingers. Are you musical?"

"A little."

"Piano?"

"Right again, how'd you know?"

"Swami Reynolds sees all," he laughed, stroking her fingers. "Do you still play?"

"When I can. There's not always an opportunity in the Navy. If there's a piano on the base, it's usually in the mess. I might play, but I get rusty quickly and I'm embarrassed to practice in the mess."

"I'll bet you play beautifully. Play for me sometime?"

"Sometime".

Time passed too quickly and they had to return to base.

They weren't the first to arrive at the briefing room. Matt's crew was already there as was Morgan Snellert, the electronics man from Hawaii. Tanya was surprised to see him. There was also one man Matt hadn't seen before. He wasn't in uniform, so Matt couldn't guess where he fit in.

Mike Chambers arrived at 11:55 hours with another stranger in tow. He began. "I see just about everyone is here so we won't waste time getting started. I've asked Commodore Coulter to attend also, but he is presently tied up. He will be here as soon as he can break free. I'd like each of you to stand up in turn and identify yourselves and your area of expertise."

One by one they went through their short speech. Matt found out the first stranger, the one in civilian clothes was Eric Cassidy, the weapons man from Bangor. The other man, the one Mike brought in, was Captain George Hammerdyne, the man in charge of the dolphins."

Mike continued, "What you are about to hear is classified information, vital to the defense of the United States and the western world. It's top secret. Remember that. We have known for a long time that the Russian fishing fleet has been deploying highly specialized and sophisticated ordnance along our coasts, and in fact at strategic locations around the world's oceans. We have discovered, through some clever sleuthing and sometimes good luck, a few of these planted devices. When they are found, we attempt to determine what they are for and how they work. All of this information gives our intelligence people some insight into the direction and intention of the Russian military machine. With every bit of information we dig up, we are better able to assess their capability and react accordingly. What we think we have discovered here is a new wrinkle in Russian detection methods. A new type of monitoring device, deployed to gather information on the Trident submarines."

Mike went on explaining that, "Some of the events that have taken place over the past few days are directly tied together and are part of the Russian attempt to obtain Trident data. The dead scuba diver, the explosion on the beach, and the malfunctioning

Cosmos satellites are all related. If what we surmise is true, there will be more sono-buoys 'seeded' across the Strait of Juan de Fuca in 'picket fence' fashion. The exact number we aren't sure, but to cover the area as we think they want it covered, would require a buoy positioned about every two miles across the known path of the submarines."

"If we were doing the 'seeding' we would address three factors: first, the most probable course of the sub, second, the best area to obtain the most effective coverage with the least number of buoys, and third, planting the buoys at the most strategic location under the satellite orbital path."

Pointing to the large nautical chart on the wall, Mike carried on, "The best location is right here," he said, waving the pointer at the chart around the narrowing of the channel at the Hood Canal Bridge. "One buoy would be enough to monitor all traffic passing through the Hood Canal. For many reasons, which I'll not go into here, we can almost rule out this location. We'll not ignore it, but we'll leave it 'till the other areas have been investigated."

"The second area is right here, where Point Wilson and Admiralty Head narrow the channel. Tridents will have to pass through this channel and it's only two and a half nautical miles wide at its widest part. Water depth at this narrows averages 35 to 40 fathoms, or 210 to 240 feet. The third possible site is here, about seven miles west of Port Angeles, between Angeles Point on the U.S. side and Race Rocks on the Canadian side. The dead scuba diver and the beach incident almost confirm this location. Water depth is 70 to 80 fathoms or 420 to 580 feet. The fourth and last site we think the Russians would deploy the buoys is here, across the entrance to the Strait of Juan de Fuca, somewhere here between Koitlah Point on the U.S. side and San Juan Point on the Canadian side. Water depth here is 120 to 140 fathoms or 720 to 840 feet. This depth is almost to the prohibitive edge of what we feel must be the extreme of the satellite/buoy operating envelope. The electronics needed to communicate with the buoys won't penetrate that deep. At least none of the methods we have will. Perhaps the Russians have discovered a way to do this. If that's true we've got our hands full."

"What lies ahead is a monumental task. We've got to locate one of these buoys, remove it to be examined, then put it back exactly where it was found. Then we've got to locate all the rest of the buoys and mark their locations."

Mike deliberately left out the parts about reprograming the buoys and replacing their memories with misinformation. The fewer people who knew, the easier it would be to maintain secrecy.

"Any questions?"

One of Matt's seamen was the first to respond. "Would it be possible to speed up the process by covering the three most likely areas at the same time?"

"It would if we had more ships, however, we have only one cutter to work with," Matt answered him.

"We've got smaller craft here. One of them could look after the narrowest area north of Admiralty Bay," piped another man.

"A good idea. If we can have it properly equipped, it would speed things up considerably, Matt. Would you look after that?" Mike asked.

"Certainly, consider it done."

"How many buoys do you think there are out there?" asked another seaman.

"We can't be sure until we have a look inside one of them," Mike said. "If they work the way we think they do, then each will cover a circle about two miles in diameter. If we assume there are three 'picket fences', as I just indicated, there will likely be about eight in each string across the Strait and three or four across Admiralty Channel. A total of 18 to 22 in all."

"The exact number and locations must be discovered. That's where you men in the Coast Guard play the most important role. Initially we must find a buoy. Once we have it, we'll show it to the dolphins so they'll know what to look for. They'll then go out with Captain Hammerdyne and his handlers to locate more.

I think at this time the Captain could carry on with the briefing and take you through what the dolphins can do and tell you a little about their location exercise. Captain?"

"Thanks Mike." Captain Hammerdyne strode to the front of the room and picked up the wooden pointer.

"The aircraft that brought me also brought my dolphins, their handlers and holding pens. These pens are now being set up in the water alongside the pier behind the cutter. Each is thirty five feet long by twenty five feet wide, with a five foot wide Styrofoam float along one side. That's where the dolphins will stay during this operation. The pens will be towed alongside the cutter when we're searching.

A question came from the crowd, "Why dolphins?

"Before I left San Diego, I picked up some charts of the waters in the area. I'd been given an initial briefing on the problem and with the charts was able to make good use of the flying time getting here. The areas Mike just mentioned are the most logical places to begin a search. They're deep and cover a large area. Dolphins can speed the search over this area." He pulled a clear plastic overlay down on top of the map Mike had used and proceeded to draw horizontal and vertical lines across the Strait. "If we discount the area between the beach and two miles off shore, we can narrow our search considerably."

"Why discount those," asked a seaman. He was sorry he had asked before thinking. It was obvious.

"These buoys are expensive even for the Russians. They will want to make as few as possible go as far as possible. Tridents will keep to the center of the channel to make sure they don't run aground, besides, the bottom close to shore is too shallow for subs."

"Now, we'll be getting into some fairly deep water toward the west end of the Strait and as we want to locate the first buoy with men and diving gear, we'll begin the search up channel in the more shallow water off Angeles Point. This is why the dolphins are here. They can locate the buoys much faster than men, particularly in the poor visibility of this area. They can search the deep water after they have found the shallow buoys and know what to look for. As we are pressed for time, the first buoy must be located by tomorrow morning. Remember, and this is directed particularly at those of you who'll do the actual diving, before we disturb any buoy we find, we've got to get the dolphins to look it over. If they're to be successful later on, they have to see the buoys just as they are, lying on the bottom.

"Going back to the grid I drew, we have an indication where the first buoy was located. Matt had the presence of mind to make an entry in his ship's log exactly where he was when he spotted the dead fish. The dead scuba diver was also in the same area. This should establish the site for the first post Ivan planted in his 'fence'. Just about here." He marked the spot on the grid. "Then if Mike's assumptions are correct, we should find the next one about here." Again he marked the map. "If we search a zone about one mile north of this point, fanning out to the northeast and northwest we should encounter the next buoy. Once we have found it and have done the preliminary work with it, we can go on across the Strait locating the other 'probable' fence posts. That all sounds so simple, doesn't it? Well, to complicate matters, we have less than a week to complete the whole job. The updated USS OHIO, the first Trident, is due in here in nine days. At the same time, don't forget the Cosmos satellite is still there and if they spot us doing anything suspicious, it could blow the whole effort. We'll have to be on guard the entire time we are over the possible buoy positions, covering our actions so they don't get wise."

"It doesn't seem right, George, that we should have to sneak around in our own backyard." This bothered Matt. The fact that not even a man's home ground was safe from espionage

"No, I agree, it doesn't, I just hope we're not wasting our time with this whole operation. It could be that there are no more buoys out there. Did you ever think about that?" George asked.

"I guess we'll soon know," Matt said.

"To make sure Ivan doesn't see us when we don't want him to, Lieutenant Andrushyn and Captain Snellert will be in constant contact once the Captain goes back to Hawaii.

He and his satellite trackers in Hawaii and will inform us if any of their birds deviate from routine patterns. We'll have to stand ready to halt our work at a moment's notice if she gives us the word. Until then, we'll cover the operation as a practice for the arrival of the Trident." Mike turned to the group and waited. "Are there any more questions," he asked. "Does each of you know what is expected of you?"

A murmur ran through the room. Mike assumed this to mean 'yes'.

"What's to stop the Russians from finding out about the dolphins? They'll surely see them, or the pens with their satellites."

"They likely will," Mike nodded his head.

"You're all aware of the large holding pens along the spit to the east of the Coast Guard base. They're part of a commercial farming venture growing salt water fish. We're hoping the Russians will think our dolphin pens are part of that fish farm."

"More questions . . . ? Good then. We still have considerable daylight left today. I'd suggest we all prepare our equipment and make ready to go to sea at 06:30 hours tomorrow. Thank you for your attention and I want to remind you that what you have just heard is top secret. I repeat, top secret. If there are no more questions, this briefing is over. We'll see all of you tomorrow, bright and early." Mike walked over to Matt to discuss equipment needs for the morning.

The remainder of that evening was spent making preparations. Matt with his crew and cutter; Mike with his specialists and George with his dolphins and divers.

CHAPTER 11

Saturday, Day 8, 06:00 hours.

Dawn comes early at this time of the year and Matt was up, shaved and showered as the first faint rays of the sun began to spill over the eastern mountains. Thoughts of their lovemaking the night before coursed through his mind as he drove to Tanya's hotel. His life, up until now, had been relatively uncomplicated. All that had been tossed into disarray by last night's events. His thinking was now confused. He had to consider an emotional sensation, totally new to him. He couldn't wait to see her this morning, and admonished himself for not accepting her invitation to stay the night. Oh, well, there'd be other nights he assured himself.

He greeted her, with a good morning kiss that threatened to expand into the unbridled passion, so fresh in both their memories. Tanya contained it with a breathless, "Let's have breakfast."

"Or maybe a cold shower?" Matt added reluctantly. They had breakfast at the hotel then headed for the base.

*   *   *

Navy support teams had installed retaining nets or pens for the dolphins off the west end of the pier. Tanya and Mat walked down to where Captain Hammerdyne was fussing around his charges.

"Good Morning, George, how're your dolphins this morning?"

"Hi, Matt, Tanya. They all seem to be okay. We humans suffer from jet lag in all our running around the world; the dolphins have their own kind of jet lag. Until they get used to the salinity and temperature of the water, they're a bit off their pace. It'll take maybe a day or two, then they'll be up to their usual antics."

"How does the water around here suit them?" Tanya was now curious.

"It's a bit on the cold side but otherwise they seem to be adjusting well. Give me a hand with this gate, Matt?"

They swung a large dividing gate open and four of the dolphins were able to get together in what was now one large pen. While they were swimming around, Tanya could hear squeals as they 'talked' to one another.

George told them a little of the history behind the use of dolphins. There were over 80 different species of dolphin and whales. Arthur McBride, the first curator of Marine Studios in Florida in the 1940s, discovered that dolphins could echo-locate. Woods Hole Oceanographic Institute published a lot of McBride's work. This remained a scientific curiosity until a decade later when a man named Adolph Frohn, also at Marine Studios, trained a dolphin called Flippy, to do tricks. Scientific knowledge and training of dolphins took a giant step with the Korean war and another with the war in Vietnam. They were suddenly a hot item, doing things in the water that men couldn't, or wouldn't do.

Matt had never had too much to do with dolphins, and listened in fascination as George talked.

"We first recognized that dolphins might have something to offer, half way through the Korean War. You remember the TV show, 'Flipper'? The things he did were a result of the navy's experiments. If we hadn't been working with dolphins at that time, they would never have known he could be trained to do the tricks he did. We made it possible for his trainers to advance rapidly from the primary swimming and jumping tricks to the more complex actions of following given directions."

"Vietnam really made it possible for us to upgrade their training to a much more sophisticated level. Not only can they retrieve practice torpedoes and mines, they were also used in a combat role. Quite a few Viet Cong frogmen were attacked and killed by trained dolphins. Mine fields were located and cleared by them as well, so you see we've come a long way since 'Flipper'."

Matt could have listened for hours, but the cutter was due to shove off at 06:30. Big engines throbbing, she was provisioned and ready, sitting at the pier waiting for the remaining crew and specialists to board. Matt and Tanya climbed the gangway just ahead of three navy men. Tanya headed aft to where the navy had loaded most of their equipment and Matt went directly to the bridge. Ernie Daniels was there attending to some final details as Matt entered.

"Ernie, check with the deck officer and make sure our passengers are all aboard."

"I've done that, Skipper. The group behind you was the last to board. Everyone's here now. We'll be ready to get under way in two minutes, right on time, 06:30 hours."

Lines were cast off, and Matt backed his ship away from the pier, out into the Strait and took a northeast heading.

It promised to be a good day for the kind of work they had to do. The wind was almost calm and there was little wave action. A high overcast was forming. Just enough screen to prevent satellites from getting a good look with their optical cameras. The other cameras, with infra red, thermal and electronic sensors would not be hindered by any clouds. The key, of course, was the optical camera, as the Russians would be more likely to use it to spot subjects, then turn on the other cameras if there was something interesting to look at.

Even if they did happen to be scanning today, there was nothing unusual that might draw their attention. A cutter heading out on an exercise was a daily occurrence. Matt took his ship directly to the spot where he remembered seeing the diver's boat a few days before. The navy underwater teams had suited up during the trip out and were ready to go as soon as Matt gave the word.

They knew their jobs well. Matt admired their efficiency as he brought the ship to a stop. He had decided to drop the anchor while looking for this initial buoy position.

It would be difficult to hold the ship still for any length of time with engines alone. Besides, having the propellers thrashing around with divers down was a dangerous hazard. He wouldn't be allowed that luxury later on in the exercise. When they were over live buoys, the dropping anchor could trigger the buoy's destruct explosives. The risk of losing a buoy would be far too great.

Heavy chain rattled through the hawse pipe, sending a cloud of rust into the wind as the anchor plummeted to the bottom. Matt, easing the cutter's engines into slow astern, took up slack in the chain. Biting into the soft bottom, the anchor held firm. An outgoing tide would hold the cutter in place. Matt signaled 'finished with engines' to the engine room.

Turning control over to his first mate, Matt strode aft, along the upper deck, right back to the aft rail. Looking down on the fantail, he announced, "Okay men, we're ready for your underwater work. You can go over anytime you want.

Looking back toward the bridge, Matt watched the signalman put a diver's flag up on the flag yardarm.

The first two men were over the side almost immediately with the remaining six following quickly after them.

"How long can they stay down Mike?" Matt yelled down to the fantail.

"These are good men in top physical shape, breathing a special mixture. The maximum for this dive is about 65 to 70 minutes.

Matt knew they started with this site rather than going out searching for a non-exploded buoy, because they wanted to establish a known point to start the search. Once this is done, they should be able to find the rest of the buoys very quickly. Remembering the buoys have to be set precisely, Matt realized once the pattern was determined, locations should come quickly. Establishing the position of the first one would save them a lot of time down the line.

There wasn't much for the Coast Guard crew to do while the navy frogmen were underwater. Any assistance topside was provided by the navy support men on the fantail. Matt returned to the bridge to have Ernie keep the crew busy. They were put to work doing general shipboard chores.

Matt left the bridge, walking aft to talk to Captain Hammerdyne. "Well, George, is there any special equipment you want aboard for your dolphins once we locate a buoy?"

"No, Matt. What we will need when we bring the dolphins out is a place to secure the cages to the ship."

"Are you going to use the cages the dolphins are in now?"

"Yes. We'll tow them on each side of the cutter."

"How about the mooring cleats back toward the stern. Will they do?"

"They'll do for the cables at the back of the cages, but we'll need a couple of solid points for the cables further forward."

"You can use the cleats up there, half way along the helicopter deck, see over there?" Matt pointed foreward, along the deck.

"Okay, that's fine."

"Do you want us to travel at a reduced speed when the dolphins are in the cages?

"No, not really. They can easily out-distance your ship if they want to. If you'll maintain fifteen knots, that should be about right."

"Will the pens take that?"

"We've done it before. We'll keep an eye on them, just in case . . ."

"What will they do once we find a buoy?"

"They've been trained to carry a collar or special clamp to an object we show them. They'll put the collar or clamp around the object. They're used to going after torpedoes or rockets, but they aren't confused by size or shape. What we tried to do in their training is prepare them for any job, not just locating torpedoes. For example, they're able to carry a telephone cable down to a submarine, remove a receptacle cap, then insert the connector into the receptacle. They can also go down, remove the connector and replace the cap. We have trained them for multi-mission roles. They're too smart and too valuable to waste on a one task existence."

"Can they do as good a job as frogmen?"

"They can dive to greater depths and do it faster than men. They've got a wider working radius, a longer dive duration and they don't need lights. We never have to worry about one of them getting the bends the way we do our men. All in all, they perform very well."

"They sound very practical. What happens after they find a buoy and slip a collar on it?"

"We're not sure at this stage of the game. It's possible we'll then have them hook on a short line flotation bladder in preparation for raising it or we may just want to mark the location. We won't know until we've got one and have a chance to open it up at Bangor. Once we know what has to be done to it, we may find we can alter it where it sits. If we can program it from the outside, then we won't have to move it at all. This would be the best way for us."

"I agree. I don't relish the thought of bringing each of them on board my ship." quipped Matt.

"No, I don't blame you! They could be a little unstable if not handled in the prescribed manner. You could lose part of the back of your ship!"

While they were talking, a diver appeared at the transom platform.

"Commander Chambers, we've located the area where the buoy exploded. We're sending up a marker now!"

"Good work! Call in the other divers, will you?"

"The rest have been called, Sir. They're coming back now."

The divers were scattered over a wide area. How did the one diver know that the others had been called? Or for that matter how had they been called?

"Mike, what are you using for communication underwater?"

"They're using special computer controlled radios, Matt. Broadcasting over a frequency range similar to the range the dolphins use. The dolphins hear it at the transmitted frequencies, while the divers have to have it modified to hear it. Works out well. All the men and dolphins know what's happening. We also have our diver's video system."

Sure enough, the rest of the divers began to surface at scattered points up to a quarter mile away from the stern of the cutter. They snorkeled back to the cutter, rested for a minute or two on the transom grid then clambered up the ladder to the fantail. As the last diver came aboard, Mike began to map out the next job on the chart table Matt had put on the after deck.

"Okay, we've located this point." He held a pencil on a map close to where they were anchored. "Our next move is to locate another buoy site. The most likely spot is about here. He jabbed his pencil into the map a mile to the north. If we draw a line from this site toward the Canadian shore, it should be the line on which the buoys were planted. If we draw a diverging pair of lines from this site, to a point about a quarter mile on each side of the base line we should have our most likely site location. Does every one agree?"

"That's possible," Matt clarified, more for his own satisfaction than anything else, "but if the buoys were planted by an underwater team being dragged by a trawler, are they going to be accurately spotted?"

"I think they'll be pretty accurate, Matt. The Soviets certainly have the technology and equipment to do so. Don't forget, the underwater teams will most likely be in touch at all times with the trawler. They'll control the placement. Besides, we're not sure the trawlers do the placing"

"You're right." Matt conceded.

Mike circled the spot on the map where they had determined the buoy should be.

"There's your next target, men. Remember, if you do find a buoy, do not, and I repeat, do not touch it. We still don't know how they're rigged. They could explode if we jiggle them the wrong way. We don't want anyone getting killed. Is that clear to everyone?"

The men acknowledged and headed for the two Zodiacs lowered from the stern.

They were gone no more than half an hour when the first boat returned. "Right on target, Commander. It's sitting there as large as life."

"Good job, men we were watching on video, but couldn't identify much."

The divers and the first boat had been taken aboard when the second returned.

Matt was over to the lead diver as his foot hit the deck. "What does it look like?"

"It's about six feet long and eight to ten inches in diameter. It's got a rough brown cover. It looks for all the world like a log. If it was among a pile of logs you'd be hard pressed to pick it out from the rest. The spot where it's sitting is clean of debris and not too many rocks around. The bottom is almost flat."

"That's part one, men. Now we'll have to figure out the best way to bring the dolphins into the act. Matt, can you take your ship over to the buoy?"

"Right away, Mike."

Matt made for the bridge while Mike and George began discussion on which gear to use for recovery.

On the bridge Matt barked orders. The cutter weighed anchor and headed for a point in the water over the first buoy.

While the cutter was under way, George Hammerdyne and Bob Bjorn got into their diving gear. They'd go down for a close inspection and determine the best way to have the dolphins attach a line to the buoy.

"Not too close," Matt instructed his number one. "The tide is ebbing just now so we'll stay to the west. Don't drop anchor. We'll maintain slight headway with the engines. I'll go aft and tell the diving party to watch the screws."

George and Bob were suited up when Matt arrived at the stern. On deck beside them were an underwater camera and a sea sled. They would go down with the chief diver and take pictures of the buoy. Matt warned them again about staying clear of the ship's propellers and wished them luck. He noticed the gear they were wearing. Heated suits and hard helmets. He'd seen this new type of suit in one of the diving magazines.

As the cutter drifted to a halt, three divers and their equipment were in the water. They had been down about twenty minutes when Matt saw their heads surface a hundred yards off the port side. They disappeared only to reappear moments later directly off the stern. The men and equipment were brought aboard. Matt got under way immediately.

George and Bob joined Matt on the bridge.

"No real problem, Matt," George was saying, "we brought along a variety of hooks and collars just in case. There are a couple that should do nicely."

"Good," said Mike. "When can we get started?"

"Well it's just 10:25 hours now," George said. "We can pick up the cages and bring the dolphins back out right away."

"Let's do that. The sooner the better." Mike was pleased how well things were going.

The cutter returned to Ediz Hook in less than twenty minutes and the crews were ready to handle the dolphin cages.

The dolphin handling crew had unloaded their charges and equipment from the Starlifter as quickly as possible the previous afternoon. The portable cages were in the water and the dolphins were in the cages less than ten minutes after the plane had landed. Because moving from one area to another is a shock to the big grey mammals and it's necessary to get them into their new environment with little delay, they took a lot of special care after every move.

The mechanical equipment they brought with them was sitting in crates on the pier where the cutter berthed.

The returning cutter indicated to the men ashore that a buoy had been located and the dolphins were going to be needed. They prepared the lashing for the cages even before the cutter had docked. Little time was wasted and within fifteen minutes the cutter was heading out to sea flanked by two cages and their swimming passengers. They had brought all four dolphins, to show each of them what they were to look for.

While travelling back to base, and now going back to sea, George and Bob were discussing the best ways to attach the recovery ring to the buoy. They had brought two types from the packing cases on the pier. One was a circular band with a ratchet lightener. It was designed to be slipped over the end of small missiles then tightened until it wouldn't slide off. A hoisting cable could be attached to the ring.

The other ring was split in two halves which opened and closed like handcuffs. It was meant to be placed on the target object then the two halves swung around till they met on the other side enclosing the object. The two halves would automatically couple when they came together.

This type was more difficult for the dolphins to handle. The position of the buoy also played a part in this selection process.

If the buoy was flat on the bottom, it would be hard to slip a ring over the end. The handcuff type would be better. If the buoy was partly buried in the mud with an end sticking up, the ring would be easier to place. The buoy they had located was flat on the bottom. The handcuff type was chosen. The other type might be the one to use on some of the other buoys. They would know better after they had located each one.

George was concerned about the pressure the ring may put on the buoy as it was being ratcheted tight. Too much pressure could set off the explosives. Too little could allow the buoy to slip out as it was being raised and it would fall back to the bottom with the same result. They adjusted a slip clutch on the ratchet to prevent over-tightening. They were using dolphins because of this very danger. They had an unknown device which could, and indeed had, exploded on two occasions when it was handled the wrong way. It would be terrible to kill a dolphin. It would be disastrous if human divers were killed instead. No, they had to be very careful.

As they reached the position over the buoy site, George and his crew were in wet suits, ready to go. They jumped into the cages with the dolphins. Gates were swung open and the cages emptied.

Using special gear they communicated with the dolphins. They called them to follow and started their dive down the marker cable. The dolphins followed, talking excitedly as they swam.

On the bottom, visibility was less than five feet and the buoy was difficult to spot even with the marker cable attached. George moved over to it and began a closer examination. There were no protruding spikes that looked like they were there to detonate the buoy like a mine or something. It was fairly smooth skinned. No bolt heads screw slots, or cover plates. It looked, for all intent and purpose, exactly like a log. The bark was supposed to resemble cedar. It did. Bark-like plastic covered the sides. The ends even had the growth rings of a tree. 'Clever these Russians', George thought. 'They haven't missed a trick'. This part of America was known for its cedar production. What would be more natural than a cedar log?

He signaled the dolphins over to the buoy. All four came chirping over. He showed them the buoy. He patted it gently and made some noises. The dolphins looked on with interest. You could almost hear the wheels turning inside the dolphins' heads. The level of squealing increased as they began to chatter to each other. They saw what George did and knew exactly what was expected of them.

Next George sent two of them to the surface with a crisp order. They took off like a shot. Back they came, in no time at all, with a recovery ring.

Now was probably the most dangerous time of the exercise, putting the ring on the buoy. If the buoy was going to explode it would be more likely now, than any other time. It was necessary for the divers to show the dolphins how to set the ring on this particular target.

They had done it many times before, but never on one as sensitive as this. After this demonstration the dolphins would be on their own handling other buoys.

George and the trainers moved in and gently patted the buoy at its middle. The dolphins brought the ring and slid it onto the buoy. They next closed the two halves and brought the ends together on the bottom side. There was a dull 'clunk' as the ends met. George sent two dolphins topside for the lifting cable. When they came back he signaled them to attach it to the ring eye. They needed little direction to complete this move. They were experts at attaching cables to recovery apparatus. At the same time they fixed a marker on the seabed so they could replace the buoy with some precision.

The hair on the back of George's neck was standing on end as they went through this operation. Even underwater the sweat was pouring off his forehead. An operation with an unknown device always made him nervous. The hook safety snapped into place with a crack, as it went through the eye. Men could have set the hook faster than the dolphins and been away from the danger by now, but this was a learning time. The dolphins had to do it themselves. This training time was important!

The next signal was for all of them. Clear the area. They began the ascent. Slowly for the men, quickly for the dolphins. Darkness of the bottom being replaced gradually by sunlight filtering down from above as they ascended. Boarding the cutter, the divers sat down to rest while the topside trainers took care of the dolphins.

"Okay, we're all set below." George yelled up to Mike on the flight deck.

Mike was at the winch position on the flight deck with Matt. Matt signaled the crane operator to begin slowly taking up slack. With the cutter rolling slightly it would be necessary to prevent the buoy from bouncing on the bottom once the slack had been taken up. The operator knew this and was prepared to increase the hoisting speed as soon as the slack was gone. This was one of the more critical phases.

"Careful on the winch," Matt yelled as the pull on the cable began to tighten. The trick was to begin the lift on a down swell and once the weight of the buoy was on the cable, increase the lift speed to keep the buoy off the bottom. The drone of the winch changed as the slack was taken up, then changed again as it took the weight of the buoy.

"Now." shouted Matt, and the winch went into a high speed whine.

"Bring it up to twenty five feet from the surface." he instructed.

The winch stopped, and the seaman marked, "Twenty five feet, sir"

"I want everyone but the landing crew off the fantail, now" Matt directed. "Landing crew, prepare your cradle."

There was a scurry of people moving to their appointed posts. Chocks had been prepared the day before in the shape they thought the buoy might take. They were lined with foam rubber and Styrofoam to make a soft bed so that the buoy would settle into its soft hollow, whatever shape or weight it might be. It was brought into place under the swing of the crane boom.

Once the area had cleared, the winch began its low whine again, and before long the hook, and then its load broke the surface. The crane operator raised it up and swung it over the bulwark and lowered it ever so gently onto the chocks. The landing crew quickly secured the buoy and removed the retrieval ring.

That part was now over and Matt was glad he still had the fantail of his ship in one piece but the worst was yet to come. It was like having a tiger by the tail. Once you had it, you dare not let go.

When Matt was sure the buoy was secure, he bounded up to the bridge and gave the order to get under way. Mike and Bob Bjorn came back to the fantail to study the buoy. How it was to be handled from here would be critical. They had decided the night before to transport it dry. If the booby traps were water sensitive this could be a problem.

They had decided that the buoy on the beach had been there long enough to become very dry and felt this indicated water wasn't that important. Even if it was, they would likely have a day or so. By that time they should have had time to open it up and find out what made it tick. It was a risk they were willing to take.

As time was of the essence, they decided it must be transported as quickly as possible. A Coast Guard helicopter would be waiting at Ediz Hook to take it to Bangor for examination. A second chopper would take the necessary personnel, following at a safe distance, of course.

Mike and George studied the buoy. They couldn't see any access ports anywhere. There was no obvious means of entry. They didn't want to get right down to poking it or even touching it, so any means of entry would have to be found at Bangor.

The cutter slid up to the pier and shed the starboard dolphin cage. The cage was made fast to the pier. Then, the cutter moved ahead and tied up as well, with the port cage still attached.

Transporting the buoy to the helicopter went smoothly. They decided to off load it onto the pier and truck it to the heli-pad.

Mike called to Matt from the pier, "We'll get down to how this thing works as fast as we can. Once we know, we'll get back to you, so we can fix the rest of them. While we are doing our bit, see if you can locate the other buoys. If my thinking is correct, we'll be able to reprogram the others where they lie. If I'm wrong, we may have to take each one of them to Bangor. I hope that's not going to be required.

"So do I." Matt shuddered at the thought of a dozen or more dangerous buoys being carted onto his ship. "We'll get started locating the rest. Whether we rework them as they lie or take them to Bangor, we'll have to find them all. Good luck with your probing." Matt was thankful he wasn't involved with Mike's part of the operation. A slip could be the end.

Mike smiled, "Yeh, you too Matt. You know the next ones might not be as stable as this one. Each of them will likely react at a different sensitivity level. You be careful too. We'll get back to you soon, see ya later."

CHAPTER 12

Saturday, Day 8, 16:00 hours.

The Coast Guard helicopters pilots had two choices: either fly the long way, low, around the mountains, and accept the turbulence set up by convection currents coming off the rough terrain; or take a shorter route, high, over the mountains in what was usually more stable air. The high route will take less time, but what about the sensitivity of their cargo? Mike had explained the delicate nature of the buoy to the pilots, along with the fact that the detonators, and there was probably more than one, were unknown. Altitude might trigger them. Exercising extreme caution throughout the trip is the order of the day, avoiding rough air and particularly rough landings, went without saying.

As far as the pilots are concerned, they want to get rid of this potential bomb as fast as possible. While discussing routes and altitudes available, they had to talk with the FAA flight service.

They checked to find out about winds. "Winds aloft are from 120 degrees at 3000 feet. Strength 15 knots. From 90 degrees at 6000 feet, 20 knots and 80 degrees at 9000 feet and 30 knots." A complete report on weather was offered, but they were on a half hour trip and declined it, reasoning that the weather would likely change before they could reach Bangor anyway.

They had a crosswind or a headwind no matter what altitude they took. Mountain turbulence would be moderate, at 15 knots, if they flew low. At higher altitude, the higher speed air would make it worse.

The turbulence they were likely to encounter at low altitude bothered them. They'd rather fly higher, but what if the buoy was pressure sensitive? They'd have to climb above 7000 feet if they wanted to go over the tops of the mountains. They compromised, chose 4500 feet and a somewhat circuitous route to the north and east through the low passes and valleys. It was just 43 miles from Ediz Hook to Bangor as the crow flies but their course was a little more round about. Even so, the trip would take less than 30 minutes.

"I'll be Blue One and fly lead: you're Blue Two with the buoy, okay?" The other pilot agreed and they were off.

The two helicopters lifted off cautiously, one after the other, pilots nudging their big machines up and forward. The lead machine carried personnel, acting as a pathfinder for the second, which carried the buoy. The lead pilot contacted Fairchild International airport on the radio and declared his intentions, thus alerting other pilots in the area. Rising above Ediz Hook, they could see for miles along the coast to the east and west. The mountains to the south rose to almost 8000 feet like a large green-grey wall. The taller peaks were snow-capped all year long, and the Indians called them, 'the white haired old men. Magnificent, if you just want to look, dangerous, to fly over. Wind currents stirred up by these peaks were unstable, to say the least. Climbing east, the pilots hoped to get clear of this area as quickly as possible.

Cruise-climbing to their 4500 foot altitude and turning southeast, they began threading their way between the lower mountains of the first range. Turbulence was minimal at first. Establishing their ground speed, they found they had a 15 knot head wind. The unwelcome hindrance meant an increased flight time to Bangor. They'd have their delicate cargo with them a little longer.

Once over the first series of peaks, the two pilots discussed on the radio whether or not to descend a bit. The lead chopper tried the air at 2500 feet. "Seems calm here. Come on down."

The second machine joined him. "How about that," he said reading his instruments, "we've picked up a tail wind.

"I don't like it. It could mean we're in a huge back eddy. Wait 'till we hit the other side of it."

Passing out of the low mountains they were in view of the Hood Canal when it hit. Severe turbulence and wind shears.

"You take that bomb up higher right away. I'll try a lower altitude!"

Both choppers reacted instantly, one going up, the other down.

"Getting worse the higher I go, can't handle much more."

Moments seemed like hours. The two pilots had time to reflect on the decision to drop to a lower altitude. Maybe it was a bad error in judgment. The choppers were being tossed all over the sky as the pilots fought to control them.

"Can't stabilize," the pilot with the buoy had panic in his voice. His shoulders cutting from the safety harness. Two men in the rear compartment were having a rough time keeping their lunch down. The buoy shook each time the chopper lurched. They sat helpless, as one of the straps holding the buoy, tore loose from the deck.

"Christ! This thing's almost loose!" one man yelled into the intercom. "Can't you hold this God damn machine still?"

"Doing my best, see if you can secure the buoy."

"No fucking way! I can't even stand up! Get us out of this fucking air! Fast!"

Over the radio came, "What's your situation, Blue two?"

"We're being tossed all over the air. What about you?"

"Turbulence here almost nil, come on down."

"Don't know if we can survive another trip through the rough air. The buoy has torn loose. I'm still climbing and the turbulence is abating. I'll see if we can refasten the hold-downs."

The man aft managed to cinch the buoy in two other spots and told the pilot, "I think that will hold her, but no more of that rough stuff or you'll be in this bird alone."

The pilot knew he was joking, or was he. "When did you last jump without a parachute?"

"I figure I'll have a better chance on my own than with this Bouncing Betty back here." The pilot could almost feel the tension in his crewman's voice.

"What's your altitude, Blue One?"

"I'm at 2000 feet."

Blue Two headed down as fast as he dared. A descent rate of 500 feet per minute was all he would chance. The chopper again danced all over the sky. The descent rate varying from 50 to 1000 feet per minute, very difficult maintaining stability. The pilot feared he would get caught in a down draft and be smashed into the ground.

"If you can't keep this thing more stable, I'm going to toss the cargo out!"

"Hold your horses. We should be through the worst part in about three minutes. Don't do anything foolish."

Severe buffeting continued until the chopper reached Blue One at 2500 feet. The air smoothed out then and they all breathed easier. They could see the sub base now, and swept down out of the mountains toward it.

Descending as they crossed the Hood Canal, the two helicopters landed at Bangor, one with a deadly cargo, one with a human cargo. Bangor's handling crew, instructed by Tom Wiser, head of the assembly cells at the base, was waiting with special equipment to unload the touchy buoy. They had been alerted to the explosive nature of the buoy and had prepared a special cradle resting on air cushions, carried by a soft tired cart. Once off-loaded from the helicopter, they were to hurry it over to the missile preparation complex. This complex contained six isolation cells, each with thick, solid concrete walls and remote handling manipulators. It was built especially for working on nuclear warheads of the Trident's Poseidon missiles. The warheads which had been in the cells this morning had been removed to their storage blocks. Tom took this precaution as soon as he had learned about the impending dissection of the buoy. He couldn't risk damaging warheads in storage, with an accidentally detonated buoy.

Remote handling equipment inside the cells was provided to protect the experts while they worked on warheads. It would now protect this crew while they tried to open the Russian sono-buoy.

The buoy was loaded very gently onto its cart and very carefully towed from the heli-pad along a back road to a large building at the east end of the base. As they approached, a large concrete door on the end of the building swung open to expose a cavernous access chamber, 100 feet wide and 300 feet long. Inside, they could see the smaller doors of the six assembly cells, spaced at even intervals along the left wall. Wheeling through the doorway the crew were instructed to place the cart beside the entrance to cell #2. Three nervous experts waited expectantly.

Bob Bjorn—explosives and materials. Bob, a medium height man of thirty nine, with thinning blond hair and jovial attitude, possibly the top explosives man in the navy. A career man, his work had taken him all over the world. He knew his job well.

Eric Cassidy—electronics and weapons. Eric, younger than Bob also lived for the navy. Slight, with dark complexion, he worked in weapons development. His specialty, down-link control of missiles.

Brian Sommers—ordnance—booby traps and metalography. Brian had spent six years in Vietnam, most of it defusing the best man-traps the VC and Russians could deploy. His steel nerves had been tested more than once. Calm, cool and collected described him; at least he appeared that way.

Tom Wiser, in charge of the cells, ran a tight ship. Nothing moved in or out of his cells without his knowledge and approval. The complex was kept squeaky clean and as sterile as an operating room.

Tom directed the crew to open the heavy door of cell #2 and run the buoy inside. No one on the base except the gathering of experts knew what they were looking at. Not even the handling crew. They were told it was fragile and could explode if given a heavy jolt. No one explained what 'heavy' meant, so they were particularly careful. Tom told the others to wait at the front of the cell in case things went sour. No need to kill or injure everyone. The three of them walked to the viewing room entrance door, next to the main access door, along a corridor and out into the viewing area, which stretched the full length of the complex. Tom stood outside the cell, giving directions. Stopping in front of cell #2, they watched as Tom had the crew transfer the buoy to the cell. The handling crew were the only ones inside the cell while it was gently moved from the cart to the examination table.

With that done the crew moved the cart out of the cell, parked it in the access area and went about their normal duties. Tom started the big cell door-closing motor and the concrete slab swung slowly inward, sealing the buoy in the silent inner sanctum. Tom joined the experts at the large viewing window in front of the cell, and they all stood silently for a long time, looking at the 'log' on the table.

Inside the cell, Tom had collected tools and equipment. X-ray gear, electronic gear, video equipment and an array of tools; wrenches, hammers, socket sets, whatever the team thought they might need for dismembering the buoy. The buoy itself sat on a cradle which allowed it to be rolled and turned. The cradle in turn sat on a rotating plate which permitted the cradle to be turned in either direction. The buoy itself could be viewed from any angle.

Outside, at the front of the cell, where the team was standing, were two sets of remote handling arms called manipulators. Tom had told them, "With these a man is able to duplicate inside the cell every move his hands can make outside the cells. With manipulators you can reach anywhere inside the cell, use tools, even pour liquid from one container to another."

Outside the cell Tom kept a pair of binoculars as well as a telescope. These were sometimes necessary for the close work they were required to perform on some of the missile trigger mechanisms.

A video camera inside the cell could be picked up by the manipulators and used to see into areas not visible from the front of the cell. It was controlled from a unit to the right of the cell viewing window, and had full zoom and wide angle capability. Camera coverage of the cell interior was almost total. Lighting levels within the cell could be varied to accommodate the camera. Because the viewing window was 3 feet thick and filled with an oily, liquid radiation shielding, it had a tendency to darken the view of the cell. In order to see well in the cells, high intensity lights were used, brilliant lighting, too bright for a man to work under without eye protection. There was an interlock switch on the access door at the back of the cell. When the door was opened, the bright lights were automatically extinguished. When the door was closed, the lights were back on. Camera images were clear and crisp because of this special lighting.

Outside the cell, and connected to the camera was a high resolution video screen, along with a video recorder. Every move they made inside the cell could be recorded on tape, and they could go over it again and again, that way if anything went wrong they would at least know what not to do the next time.

The choice of using these cells for the examination was based partly on the fact they were best equipped, and partly on the fact that if the buoy did blow up, the cell could sustain the blast without killing the examiners.

The four men stood now, looking through the yellowish viewing window, "Let's begin by giving the buoy a complete once over," Tom said as he explained the various examination tools to the gathering. "This handle controls the cradle drive. This is how it's done." He moved the handle and the cradle moved back and forth following the command of the handle. "The table can be trained with this control dial." He moved the dial and the table followed. "Let's have a look now at the buoy, from end to end." The camera was turned on and Tom began to slowly turn the table.

Four pairs of eyes strained to be the first to spot some access to the inside.

"The only thing they missed is the worm holes. It looks more like a log than some of the logs I've seen," Tom quipped.

"Did you notice the growth rings on the end?"

"Yeh, I'll bet you could tell its age from them."

They all laughed.

"Okay gentlemen, we haven't spotted anything on the outside. Suppose we try to find a way to get inside".

Tom moved the x-ray scanner into position at the right hand end of the buoy. The scanner had a monitor beside the video screen and what was viewed by the head was recorded the same way as the video system. The depth of penetration could be varied to expose any part of the specimen being examined.

All eyes were now glued to the monitor as Tom began to pass the scanner head along the surface of the buoy. Its 'guts' lay exposed as clearly as if they had cut it open. The plastic skin was no barrier to the powerful beam of the x-ray.

They could see a collection of boxes, stacked tightly together from one end to the other. There were few voids. Definition was excellent. They were able to determine what each section held. Eric Cassidy, the electronics man was the only one excited with the exposure. The rest were intent on finding a door or access plate so they could gain entry. They could see none.

Bob Bjorn looked for the containment used to hold the explosives. This failed to appear also. The power supply was evidently a battery pack visible at the extreme right end of the buoy.

Tom reduced the scanner power to a minimum level and began a slow pass over the skin. They could see what appeared to be an opening over the battery pack. There were breaks in the shell, in the shape of a door, about 9 inches by 9 inches. Also visible was a wire which appeared to run from the door to some point in the interior of the buoy.

Brian Sommers was the first to recognize it as a trip wire. This panel was the most obvious way to gain entry and the Russians had made sure their device would be destroyed if the door was tampered with. Brian pointed out the danger and suggested they look for another entry.

They continued to scan for half an hour. Back and forth, rolling the buoy around, they checked it from every angle. The video recorder, running all the time created valuable footage for later use. They failed to find any other entry.

"We're obviously not looking for the right thing," Brian stated. "We've probably seen the entry but failed to recognize it. Let's stop for a few minutes and go over the way we would do it if we were designing the device."

The access door was held closed by some means they still couldn't identify. The wire attached was obviously a trigger. If they were to gain entry through this door, they would have to solve the closure method. They ran the video tape back to where the door was pictured.

Bob spotted what looked like a dark shadow running the length of the buoy. It went by the battery compartment, then on to the opposite end.

"The strip we can see here," he said, pointing to the monitor screen, "could be a securing bar. It appears to have clips or keepers along one edge. See here and here."

They agreed. The area would need a more detailed examination. They went back to trying to find out how to open the door.

"It must be made so that you can open it without breaking anything." Eric Cassidy said. "Their technicians must be able to repair and adjust it from time to time."

It also has to be protected from unauthorized intrusion, like we're now attempting," Brian Sommers said. "We still haven't been able to detect any explosive pack. We should look specifically for that." If we can find the explosives, we should be able to follow the triggering mechanism back to the triggers."

They went back to the video tapes. Re-ran them from one end to the other and found nothing. They decided to have another look inside the cell.

While they were in the cell, they dared not touch anything. Only when safely behind the protective walls and viewing glass, could they prod and pry. Close examination showed nothing new. There didn't appear to be any crack or fracture in the surface anywhere on the buoy. Even looking at the door, knowing it was there, they had difficulty defining its edges. The plastic of its skin was the same reddish brown material they had brought back from Port Angeles. Mike Chambers had taken a sample of it directly to the Bangor chemical lab when the helicopter had landed. He had not yet returned.

"Everyone seen enough?" Tom asked.

"Just a minute more Tom." Bob was examining the butt end of the log. "The ends of this log look just the way a log would look, with concentric growth rings on it. They're even a different color than the bark, but they seem to have a clear demarcation point between a few of the sets. Look here!"

They all hurried to look.

"Sure enough, there's what looks like a mechanical fit. Here, here and here." Tom said, pointing to spots just visible on the end. "We'd better take a closer look at these ends with the scanner. Everyone, out of the cell."

Tom stood at the cell controls and moved the log around to give the video scanner a good look at the end of the buoy. What they saw was the same thing they had seen from inside the cell. Maybe a little more magnified, but certainly not the answer they were looking for.

Tom brought the x-ray scanner into play. With power at the low setting, they were able to see three separate rings on the end of the buoy. Adjusting the scanner to a higher power, Tom began to make out a cluster of gears and discs. The end section was only about an inch thick and there were wires leading from it to somewhere inside the body.

"It looks like a drive train, or a combination lock."

"It could be a buoyancy mechanism. Some control for positioning the unit on the seabed."

"We'll look at this later," Tom said," right now maybe we should have a look at the other end."

They all agreed.

When the buoy was turned end for end, the scanner went to work again. This end was clear of rings and gears.

"Okay. Now we know the ends are different. The other end seems to hold more promise than this end." Tom commented.

"I'd like to go back to the other end and try to trace those wires we saw," Cassidy thought he was beginning to figure it out and was anxious to see if he was on the right track. "When you people are through with this end I'd like to turn it around a bit."

"Okay Eric," Tom said. "Everyone through with this end?"

Everyone agreed and Tom swung the table to expose the first end again.

As Tom adjusted the x-ray penetration they could see some switches located in the end section attached to the disc pieces. They were obviously operated by the gear drive. This was clearly shown in the x-ray monitor as Eric watched. Wires led from the switches to some circuitry back beside the battery cell.

The end section appeared to be a combination lock which provided access to the interior of the buoy, but how did it work?

"The best person to open this would be a safe cracker! Where are we going to get someone with that capability?"

"I'll get on the phone to Chambers and see if he has any ideas," Bob Bjorn muttered as he hurried out to the main office next door.

"Could the discs be used to adjust the radio frequency or timer?" Tom asked.

Eric answered, "No, not likely. The type of transmission this unit has to make, has to be controlled by crystal. It's possible, but not likely to have a tuner circuit. I still think the end is going to be the way we get into the workings."

"Suppose it is the way inside, Brian. Do you think it'll be booby trapped like the door?"

"I'm almost certain of it. For the uninitiated, the door would be the most logical place to try first. They've tried to camouflage the door pretty well but we found it. Maybe it was designed so that we were expected to think we had found the access and start to open it. We know now that would be fatal. Maybe we weren't expected to have access to this facility and all this equipment so that we could see inside. Who knows?"

Tom began to vary the x-ray scanner power and moved it back and forth along the first six inches of the end. What looked like screw threads began to appear along the first two inches as he varied the power. "There's how the end comes off." He was getting excited now as the scanner divulged the opening method. "It screws."

"Looks like you're right, Tom." Brian was now being caught up in Tom's enthusiasm. "That's the first of the steps. We've got to find out where the booby traps are. If I was going to design it, I'd make sure you couldn't back off the end plug unless you somehow shut off the trigger. Look for an arm or lever sticking out near the geared discs . . . . possibly in a position to strike one of the switches we saw earlier."

Brian went on to explain, "There are two ways to set a trip, either active or passive." An active is where it is armed at all times, and an electrical path must be maintained at all times through a closed circuit. If it's broken, the bomb detonates. The passive is where something has to be introduced to trigger, like removing a pin or allowing contacts to mate."

"Which would you use in a device like this?" Bob was now getting more interested.

"I'd go for the active method and I'll tell you why. With the active there has to be power available to set it off. That means if the batteries fail, the device is rendered inoperative, while in the passive mode if they fail, the whole thing will go up. This could happen easily if salt water got into the innards. I'd back this up with a setup of tensioned trip wires. Either one would make it difficult to gain entry."

"That sounds logical," Bob offered, "why don't we have a look specifically for the switches and trip wires?"

"Tom, can we roll the buoy over," Brian asked, "slowly, with the x-ray on the screw end."

He did, and by varying the beam intensity, they were able to distinguish both the switches and trip wires.

"Right there," Bob pointed, "See that dark block? There's a faint line attached to it. See right there." He pointed at the screen. "Good guess, Brian."

"We'll have to be extremely careful when we remove the end block. If we disturb this wire, it could be game over." Brian made a mental note to watch the wire as the end block came out.

"It's being held by a clip there," he pointed to a shadow on the screen.

"What about the switches?" Tom asked.

"There's one over here, Tom. It's connected to this box just behind the battery. There should be an arm or actuator somehow attached to the end plug".

"Okay, Brian. Let's see if we can find that arm." The scanner moved back and forth as the buoy was rolled to new positions. "Here, this looks like it, right by the disc."

"Good! Now we've got to find a way to immobilize the switch. There must be some way to block it. Look for a pin or something that can be moved into the path of the arm." Bob's brow began to perspire.

"There's a catch over to the left of the arm, Bob, see it?"

"Yeh. What moves it?"

"It could be something on one of the discs. There's a stack of three discs here, almost the same as a combination lock."

"Let's see if we can find the way to turn the end of the log and make the discs move."

"There must be some way to grip the end. It could be that you just push on the end and turn with your hand. We'll have to go inside the cell again and try that to find out."

"Before we go any further we'd better try to locate the explosives."

"Let me have a go." Bob took over now. "Move the scanner along from end to end. Let's see if there is an obvious pack of plastic or something similar."

Tom moved slowly to the end and was starting back.

"Hold it there. Now roll back a bit. What's that empty space?"

Tom brought the beam strength down a bit and moved the scanner closer to the buoy.

"It's not empty."

"Tom, roll the buoy over about 90 degrees."

The buoy began to roll slowly.

"Hold that. Now come back, just a smidge. There, do you see that long cylinder running toward the ends of the buoy? It seems to be coming out of the center of that empty space."

"That empty space is really two spaces. See the divider in the middle? There also seems to be a cylinder running out of each one of them, Bob"

"Right. Tom, follow one of the cylinders along to the end of the buoy."

"There's something that looks like a donut on the end of the cylinder, see there?"

"Right, I see it. There are wires attached to it."

"This could be a ballast device and sensor used to establish negative buoyancy for the buoy."

"Not likely. They wouldn't need the cylinders attached to the space in the middle like they are. Unless the buoy can only work when it's flat on the seabed. If that's the case, there should be some form of level detector on each end of the cylinders. Scan down to find the other end of the cylinders, Tom."

The scanner began to move along the length of the buoy. It became difficult to follow the cylinders when they passed through the electronics packages but they appeared again next to the battery pack."

"Can't see any wires on the sensor, Bob, but I did see a ribbon wire along the bottom of the buoy."

"Probably an antenna," injected Eric

"Did you notice? The cylinders run from one end of the buoy to the other."

Tom moved the scanner from end to end as Bob was talking. They did run from end to end, right through the instrument package.

Bob stopped talking and stood contemplating the screen. "I've got it! They're using a liquid explosive. Actually it's two liquids. It's called a binary explosive!"

"What the hell's that?" Tom asked.

"Each liquid, by itself, is quite stable but when you put them together, Wham. That's all she wrote. The donuts we saw are the detonators. I'll bet you'll find the cylinders have been scored to fracture at specific points so that the liquid can come together faster when the detonator goes off. When they mix, they react violently. Anything in the vicinity is partially absorbed by the liquid then included in the explosion. I'll bet we find the materials they used to make the electronic boxes won't be your regular materials. They'll likely be selected to feed the explosion. That way they'd not only be destroyed beyond recognition, they would also insure more complete destruction of the buoy." Bob walked excitedly up to the viewing glass.

"What did you find at the blast area at Port Angeles, Bob?"

"Not much, Eric. Only some small bits." Bob had his face tight to the window, peering into the cell. "We've got to get the lab report on the skin material. It may give us some clue as to how this thing is sealed."

"Clever, these guys. There's not much to study after an explosion." Tom observed.

"Okay, we know how they blow up, how do we get into them without setting them off?" Eric asked. "That's the big question!"

"The detonator is the type that needs power to trigger it. If we can interrupt the power it will be rendered safe." Brian told him.

"How do we do that?" Eric wanted to know.

"Follow the wires back to the power source and the trigger mechanism, Eric."

Tom was given the tricky task of using the x-ray scanner to follow the wires. He had to manipulate the power of the beam in several places in order to penetrate various densities of material. They ran from the battery pack up through a couple of electronic boxes then out to the end plug.

This group of experts could say with some certainty, which switch on the plug controlled the detonator. How to get to it was another problem. They discussed various strategies for a few minutes then decided on a plan of action.

First Bob and Eric tried in the cell to see if they could move the end plug. They could. It moved ever so slowly, a little right then a little left. After this success, they went out of the cell to the viewing area and repeated the action using the manipulator, only this time following the movement with the x-ray scanner, watching what was happening inside the plug. If Tom moved the plug clockwise the actuating arm moved closer to one of the switches. It was obvious this was not the way to get onto the workings. If he moved the plug too far the detonator would be energized. There must be a way to prevent the arm from moving to touch the switch.

"Look for another switch in the detonator circuit." Brian directed.

Back they went to scanning with the x-ray, moving over the full length of the buoy, rolling and turning it in every direction in order to catch every clue, and altering the scanner penetration repeatedly during the operation.

"One of the wires ran into a black box before continuing to fix itself onto the switch terminal." Brian muttered

"There could be a holding relay in that box," Eric noted. "If there is, how is it operated?"

"Could be by a special signal or even by another switch somewhere," Brian offered.

"There is a second switch on the end plug. Could that be used to cut out the detonator relay?"

"Seems logical, Tom. Scan the plug again."

"Where's the switch, Eric?"

"Over there," he said pointing to a dark spot on the screen.

"Can anyone see how it's activated?"

"It seems to be in line with the middle disc. Let's turn the plug back to where we started Tom, and then go back a little in the other direction."

He turned the plug back then went through the same operation only this time in the opposite direction.

As the discs got closer to the second switch, nerves became edgy. If they were right, when this switch was operated, the detonator switch would be rendered inoperative. If they were wrong, they'd have to find another buoy. With one eighth of an inch to go the disc stuck. Now what?

They had a hurried conference and decided to force the disc a little to see what would happen.

Everyone held their breaths while Tom exerted pressure turning the disc with the manipulators. It gave with a jerk. No explosion. Tom's heart skipped a beat. There were beads of perspiration on his brow. All eyes watched the screen to see in the x-ray view what had happened to the arm.

"Good work Tom, I thought we had bought the farm that time!"

"So did I, Bob."

"So far so good, you guys. Now we have to keep that switch operated while we try to remove the plug." Brian was excited. "Try turning the plug back again and see if the second disc turns with it."

Tom slowly began to turn the plug. The second disc didn't move.

"Good. All the way back now, to a point just short of the detonator switch." Brian instructed. The plug returned to its original position.

"Is everyone satisfied this will disarm the system? Tom asked. There was a long silence as no one spoke.

"Then I take it we're in agreement?" Tom began slowly turning the plug. The detonator arm got closer and closer to the detonator switch. He stopped with the arm almost touching. "One last chance to comment. Everyone still agree to continue?"

The tension mounted. If they had guessed wrong, it would be the end of the buoy. It would also be difficult to assume the Russians would not become suspicious with three buoys missing. The two they'd already lost was bad enough.

"Okay, Tom. Keep turning. We'll see if the third ring turns now or is locked in with the second ring."

It moved! Tom kept turning and when he had a half turn on the plug they all heard a dull clunk from the cell speaker. All discs were now locked together.

"Keep on turning, Tom." The plug was beginning to back out. Tom gentled it away from the buoy. As it came out two attached wires were exposed. Tom laid the plug on the table very gently, being careful not to jerk the wires. Breathing resumed.

They all went into the cell. Brian Sommers disconnected the wires.

"Look inside the end," he said. There's a plate and lifting eye in there.

I'll bet once we remove the power pack, we'll be able to yank all the guts out."

The battery was directly behind the lifting plate. Eric was about to cut the wires connected to the plug, when Bob discovered a connector on each wire. He thought about this for a while then stated, "If the discs are sitting in the right spot, we should be able to disconnect these connectors. Any arguments?"

No one spoke.

"Okay, let's try it with the manipulators, just in case. Everyone, out of the cell." Tom was last to leave the cell, closing the big door behind

Once outside, Tom maneuvered the plug to where he could get the manipulators into position to disconnect the connectors.

He worked off the connector retainer ring and exerting a gentle pressure on the wires. They parted. There was no explosion.

"Next step, gentlemen?" Tom asked.

"While we're here, see if you can snag the end of the lifting eye and start to remove the inner core."

"There's a hook on the back of the cell wall that fits into the manipulator 'hand', I'll bring it up front." Tom moved the arms to the back and picked up the hook attaching it to the 'hand', then moved into position to grab the eye. He set it in place and began a steady pull. The core began to move. It slid out of the cylinder about ten inches.

"Stop right there, Tom, we'd better scan again before we go too far." Brian worried about hidden trip mechanisms.

They ran the scanner up and down the length of the buoy. There didn't appear to be any further triggers, so Eric suggested they go into the cell and prepare the bench to take the core.

"Have we come to a point where we can lift the core out by hand, Tom?" Bob wanted to know.

"I think so. There don't seem to be any further surprises. Let's give it a try, but only two of us in the cell to do it."

Eric and Tom stayed while Bob and Brian went out to the viewing area to watch.

The core slid easily out and they set it on the bench.

Eric looked at Tom. The perspiration beaded on his brow. "He let out a yell, "Yeowwww! We've done it!"

Tom grabbed and Eric high-fived, then they looked at each other and grinned. Bob and Brian, watching through the viewing window were just as elated. They ran around and through the access door, to wrap their arms around the two in the cell. Pressures, built up over the past hours, released in moments. They had completed the first step.

Once the explosive was rendered harmless, they went to work on the electronic boxes with great haste.

CHAPTER 13

Saturday, Day 8, 16:30.

Matt stayed aboard the cutter after unloading the sono-buoy. He knew they wouldn't be going out again now, until Mike had dissected and studied it. On a ship there was always work to be done and he busied himself with little jobs.

His communications officer handed him a message. 'Presence required immediately, my office'. It was signed Commodore Coulter.

"What's this about? Matt asked.

"I don't know, sir. It was phoned in. They indicated it was urgent."

Matt walked down the gangway wondering what had happened to require such a summons. Arriving at the Commodore's office he was ushered right in. "Matt," the Commodore began, "I'd like you to meet John Billingsly, Manager of the Port of Seattle. John, this is Commander Reynolds"

"John had a visit from one of our coastal pilots who told him about a couple of incidents aboard a Russian factory ship. I'd like him to tell you what he just told me."

"Hello, Matt, well," John began, "I don't know whether or not this is important, but I don't think it should be allowed to go without investigation of some kind. Sam Sawchuck, an experienced pilot came to me today with a story. He's been on this coast since he retired from the navy ten years ago. Doesn't know what to make of this and frankly neither do I."

John brought Matt up to the point where Sam had related his story. "After Sam left I put in a call to the yard manager at McCormack Shipyard where the Russian had gone for repairs. I didn't want to arouse too much curiosity, so I sort of beat around the bush. What I did find out was that the Russians hadn't asked them to look at their gear boxes at all. If they were giving trouble you'd think they would be on their repair list, wouldn't you?"

"What did they do then?" Matt asked.

"Some minor work and they installed a fairly large DC generator. I think it was about an 850 kw machine."

"That's all?

"That's all", John replied.

"When did all this happen?"

"A week ago".

"Where's the ship now?"

"She returned to sea last week."

Matt made a mental note to discuss this with Tanya. He certainly didn't want any Russian ships to see him out there with the dolphins. He also wanted to avoid running into any Russian frogmen at the buoy sites. If his thinking was correct, this business Sam experienced could explain what the factory ship was doing. Tending or setting the buoys.

"Where did these incidents happen?" Matt asked John.

John went over to the big map of the Strait on the wall and indicated two locations, just west of Port Angeles and at Admiralty Channel.

'How about that,' Matt mused, 'bulls-eye.' He didn't say anything to John.

"What did you have in mind for us, John?"

"I thought you could keep an eye open for any pollutants that may wash ashore. If that's what they're doing we should put a stop to it right away."

"No problem with that, John. We'll keep an eye on this area and if we turn up anything we'll be in touch with you. We appreciate your bringing this to our attention."

"Thank you, Matt, good luck and I hope you don't find any surprises."

"So do I," Matt assured him. John had no idea what kind of surprises really were out there. Matt hoped he never would.

After John had gone, Matt began an excited discussion with Commodore Coulter.

CHAPTER 14

Saturday, Day 8, 17:00 hours.

An hour later, Matt returned to his ship from the Commodore's office and immediately began preparations to take the cutter back to sea. The stern edged away from the pilings and cages were again floated to each side. Once secure, Matt cast off and headed toward the probable location of the next buoys.

Two dolphins swam excitedly in each of the two cages. They seemed to sense what was ahead and anticipated the enjoyment, seeming to consider it all a big game. They loved games. Their handlers were on the fantail, laying out the special gear they'd need to mark the buoys that were found.

Matt was on the bridge when a seaman entered. "Sir, there's a message for you, in the radio room."

Matt strode aft and went into the communication center. Radios squawked continually like a group of old ladies gossiping. It would seem to the uninitiated, that no one paid attention to anything being said. This is not the case. Every operator develops a capability to monitor his radio while filtering out extraneous chatter.

Tanya had spent most of her time, aboard the cutter, in the communication center. She set up radios and selected frequencies to maintain contact with Hawaii. She now had the communication center set up to provide the channels to Hawaii. Continuous contact had been established with Naval Intelligence in Bangor and her mountain-top base on Oahu. Bangor in turn was in contact with Cheyenne Mountain in Colorado, NORAD headquarters.

"Matt, we've just had notice the bird is deviating from its parking orbit setting up for a low pass over this area."

Matt stiffened, "How long 'til it gets here?"

"Could be about 45 minutes, give or take five either way."

"That means we shouldn't be too close to the buoy sites for a while."

"We'll be okay after it goes by but we'd better stay away until then. Its next pass will be 1500 miles west of here. It won't bother us from that distance. I'd suggest we cruise over to a spot about 15 miles away from your first search area."

"Right." Tanya added.

Matt went forward to the bridge and gave his 'number one' the necessary orders.

They wanted no surprises and with Tanya and Hawaii in constant touch, they should be aware of any adverse moves from the spy satellites. They were in no position to tip their hand to the Russians at this time. Too much was at stake. They knew the Russians were watching a broad area with their high flying birds and would be quick to pick up any activity they thought interesting. The Trident base and the routes the subs would take to get to it were of special interest.

When Matt returned to the communication center, Tanya was talking to her counterpart in Hawaii. "Give me the apogee again, Bill. Okay, let me know when they fire boosters."

Matt caught the last part about boosters as he entered the room.

"Matt, they'll be over the area in seven minutes. If they want more pictures right after this pass, they'll have to move another bird into position. This bird would use too much fuel if they were to try to reposition it. We'll keep an eye on that."

Time seemed to drag as they waited for the satellite to pass. Minutes took hours. Then Tanya announced, "You can resume search Matt. We're clear now."

"How much time do we have before another bird could be swung down to have a look?"

"I'll check."

After a short wait the word came back from Oahu. "The next possible bird will take two hours to position, Tanya. That is, if they want to have another look."

"Thanks, John." Tanya cleared with Hawaii. "We can go on now, Matt. If the last bird gave them what they wanted they may not send another for days or weeks." The satellite passing over will see only a cutter cruising around the strait, nothing out of the ordinary.

"Okay, Tanya. What kind of warning time are we going to have before another bird could be making its pass?"

"We'll have the same amount of time as this last one, Matt, about 45 minutes."

"I'd better tell the navy men. I don't know if they can retrieve their dolphins within that time. The hour's getting late anyhow. We'll scrub the rest of the mission today, and start again early tomorrow." Matt returned to the bridge and called the crews back to the cutter, then set course for the base.

*   *   *

They were all ready the next morning. Rigging the cutter with the pens went smoothly and they were soon under way. Matt stopped the cutter on signal from his navigation officer when they were between the suspected locations of the next two buoys. Once in position, Matt handed command over to his first officer, instructing him to maintain the present position with the ship's engines rather than anchor.

He strode aft to the fantail to talk with Captain Hammerdyne. The aft area was humming with activity. Captain Hammerdyne was giving last minute instructions to his men as they lowered Zodiacs into the water, each with a load of diving gear and equipment for the dolphins.

Matt yelled down at George from the flight deck, "Instruct the men and dolphins to be sure not to push the buoys around. We don't want to lose any dolphins or divers. Be sure they fasten the collar securely, too. We don't want them slipping off when they inflate the bladders."

Matt climbed down the ladder to where George stood, "We'll have about 45 minutes to gather your flock and make tracks before the Russians can drop a bird down on us. Can you get them back in that time?"

"No problem, Matt. The dolphins will recall almost immediately. The men aren't going too deep so they'll be able to surface quickly. It'll only take a few minutes to run the boats back. I think we can beat that time, Matt"

"Good. We'll keep you posted if there are any threats."

The boats left, one to each side of the cutter. The pens were opened and two dolphins tore away after each boat. Their game had begun.

Matt stood transfixed and watched. The way the dolphins had taken off and headed directly to their designated boat surprised him.

George could see the puzzled look on Matt's face. "They're always assigned to the same boat and always have the same crew. They can recognize both their boats and their handlers in them. They've been trained to do just what they're doing now. They know their jobs well."

Matt continued to be amazed. Here was a part of what he considered his world, the marine environment; with things going on that completely surprised him.

The Zodiac off to starboard was the first to report success, then five minutes later the other boat also signaled a find. Matt's navigation officer was on the bridge watching the Loran and GPS navigation numbers coming up on the video screen. They showed longitude and latitude to an accuracy of plus or minus five feet. He relayed the numbers, over the intercom, to the fantail where Matt and George were plotting.

Once the markers had been fastened to the buoys, the dolphins were called in and the Zodiacs headed back to the cutter.

"That's three we've got now, George. Let's get over to the north side of the channel and see if there are more."

After the dolphins were penned and the Zodiacs lifted aboard, Matt repositioned the cutter along the north search area. The dolphins and men again headed out over the green water, one group to each side of the cutter.

Two more buoys were located in short order. George and Matt plotted their positions on the chart. They formed a 'v' or chevron across the channel.

So far they had located five buoys. The Strait was straddled by buoys set at equal distances except for a gap towards Angeles Point.

"This void must be from the buoy that was washed ashore and exploded on the beach. The other one that killed the diver would have filled this spot here," Matt pointed to the map.

"Right. It would complete the pattern." George answered. "I'd say we've located all the buoys in this 'fence'. We'd better move on to the next suspect site."

"I'll move up there now. Have your men secure their equipment. We'll get under way." Matt moved off to the bridge to get his ship moving. Once things were under control on the bridge, Matt called Tanya on the intercom and asked her to join him in the mess. She said she had one more message to send, then she would join him.

Tanya arrived as Matt was starting through the food line. George Hammerdyne had joined him. "I've just talked to Mike Chambers," she told them, "they've opened the buoy and are trying to establish its operating envelope."

What's that?"

"The frequencies it uses. What triggers the transmitters and everything else that may be useful to our intelligence people.

They should have it pretty well diagnosed sometime later today."

"That's good news. With the number of buoys we've found so far, we know the Russians must be serious about getting information. When we bring them up to reprogram them, we'll have to be awfully careful, both from the explosive danger as well as having the Russians spot us dragging them up."

"Mike said we may be in luck there. It may be possible to 'adjust' them in place."

"Christ, that's even better news. We won't have to expose our men or equipment to the danger."

"I thought you'd like that, Matt," Tanya grinned.

"That's all right for the buoys we've found, George, and any more may be in shallower spots but what if there are some at the western entrance to the Strait, off Cape Flattery?"

"You're right, Matt. The depth out there can go to 900 feet! We'll need the whole deep diving outfit if we're to look there. Somehow I don't think they're out there. If there are any more, I'd be inclined to believe they'd be across Admiralty Head."

"Why none at the entrance, George?"

"I don't think the Russians would be anxious to go that deep either to plant them or service them."

"You may be right. Once we've checked out Admiralty Head though, I feel we should take a sweep all the way back along the Strait right out to the entrance."

"I agree with you, Matt. The dolphins can be used to do that. If they find any, maybe then we'll worry about deep diving gear."

The three continued their leisurely lunch while the cutter made her way to Admiralty Head, a distance of about 35 nautical miles along the strait from Angeles Point, east of where they had found the first row of buoys.

Two hours later, when they had arrived, they began the same routine with the dolphins they had used that morning.

The dolphins located three buoys. This perplexed Matt and George. The narrows were only three miles wide. Why would the Russians use three buoys? One in the center of the channel would have been enough to cover the area. They discussed this apparent anomaly at great length. Finding no satisfactory answer, they agreed to leave it up to Mike to solve. They would tell him when they got back to base.

George and Matt discussed their next move.

"We've got to return to the base anyway, so why don't we have the dolphins search ahead of and to each side of the cutter on the way?"

"How can they do that, George?"

"We've taught them a routine for finding lost missiles. Starting from a fixed point, the dolphins swim in ever increasing circles to a radius of two miles. They have an uncanny accuracy for navigation. The circles, even at two miles are almost perfect."

"What about tidal currents?"

"They compensate for that, too."

"That's really a phenomenal accomplishment." Matt was impressed.

"It's not likely there are any more between here and the base but we should look. Just to satisfy ourselves if for no other reason. If we overlook only one buoy, the Russians will get conflicting reports from the buoys and want to know why. Then we'll have wasted all this time because they'll come in and repair or replace them."

"You're right, George. I'll get started after you deploy your dolphins."

Once the Zodiacs were away Matt turned the cutter and started back toward the base, dolphins leading the way. The real test of the dolphins ability would come when they reached the buoys they had already found. If they rediscovered them on this next pass, it would verify their thoroughness. And find them they did. Matt was relieved. George took it casually. He had faith in the dolphins.

An hour later they tied up at the base. Today's mission was successful. Tomorrow they would sweep the western portion of the strait. Matt made sure the dolphin pens were secure, before going ashore. Tanya, already on shore, watched the activity at the pens.

"I'm going down to the float to talk to George Hammerdyne about his dolphins. Want to come along?"

"Sure!" She was pleased he had asked her.

They walked down the ramp and along the float to where George was giving instructions to his crew. They waited for him to finish.

Matt waved his arm toward the dolphins, "I'm amazed at the way these fish, animals or whatever they are," he corrected himself, "can respond to directions".

George pushed his hat to the back of his head took a deep breath and began to explain, "They're actually Cetaceans. They come from a large group of mammals. They're animals in the zoological sense. This particular one is from the species Odontoceti, the eleventh family, Delphinidas. Its proper name is Tersiops truncatus, more commonly known as the Bottlenose dolphin. How's that little spiel for impressing the natives?"

"Top marks as far as I'm concerned," the corners of Matt's eyes crinkled as he laughed.

"They're special among the animal kingdom. They possess attributes we've been able to make good use of in our work. They easily learn signs and signals and are very co-operative."

"Are they the only sea creatures you use, or is that a military secret?' Matt asked.

"No, it's no secret. They're not the only ones we've been able to work with, but they have the ability to understand what we want and are really excited to be able to do it. Their brain and seeming intelligence continually amaze us. We don't know some of the time if we are using them or they're using us."

"Why do you say that, George?" Tanya was curious.

"They learn very quickly when we teach them various things. We start them off with the old standby reward and punishment. They get fresh fish when they do what we expect them to do. They seem to enjoy doing this at first, then after a bit the fish are incidental. If they're going to do the assignment, it doesn't matter if they get fish or not. In fact, sometimes they ignore the fish. We've determined that if they want to do the particular chore it's because they want to do it, not because there's a reward. They seem to like working with man and the more we get to know them, the more we think they're studying us."

"To go back to your last question, Matt, they're not the only animals we work with. Some scientists believe the size and complexity of the brain in relation to human brains and body length or weight has a lot to do with intelligence. If this is the case, there are a lot of marine mammals that could be very smart. The sperm whale is the mammal with the largest brain of any on the planet."

"If that's the case, why don't we train them?"

"We would if we could find a way to contain them. We'd have to keep them for a period of time. This has been impossible so far."

"What about the smaller whales," Tanya suggested.

"We've had some success with the pilot whale. The scientific name for it is globicephala macrorhynchus, a real tongue twister. Loosely translated it means globe head. You've probably seen them, Tanya; they're the big black whales with the round head. There's one in Marine land Park on Oahu."

"Yes, I have. Funny, at the time I wasn't properly impressed. It was just another act. I can better appreciate now what I saw then."

"Their brain is almost equal in size to the bottlenose dolphin. We use them to perform in a manner similar to the dolphin. Larger whales are probably as intelligent as these two, but they are a lot harder to work with. The dolphin and pilot whale are relatively easy to pen up and even hold in shallow water. With the larger whales this is impossible."

"Maybe they're too smart to have anything to do with man." Matt added.

"Could be," George agreed.

"What things can they do and how do you train them?" Tanya asked.

"You mean navy-wise or scientifically?"

"Navy-wise first," Tanya told him.

"Well, the navy started with them about 25 years ago locating practice torpedoes. They did a good job of that and someone figured dolphins could be used to retrieve other things, so they got them to work with divers. When a diver wanted a particular tool they'd write it on a slate, give the slate to a dolphin that'd swim to the tender at the surface. The man on the tender would read the slate and send the dolphin back with the tool. That worked fine. They began to run other errands next and did that very well, too."

"It sounds like they could be really helpful."

"Right, Matt. Dolphins can go up and down hundreds of feet and not suffer from the bends. Not only that, they can do it very quickly. Working with dolphins, a diver can more than double his production rate. Once dolphins got used to doing these errands the next step was to have them perform relatively easy tasks without divers. Special tools and collars were designed. A collar was used to mark practice torpedoes. Once a dolphin located a torpedo, a diver would go down and attach a cable to it. The next step was a natural. The dolphins were taught to attach the cable. Soon we didn't have to send divers down at all. The dolphins could do it for us."

"Surely the work we saw them doing today was more complex than that," Tanya injected.

"True. The identification and location required much more instruction than recovering a torpedo."

"How do you tell them what you want done?"

"There are two ways to teach, Tanya. One is called bridging stimulus. It is simply a repetition. When a dolphin hears a whistle, sees an arm move a certain way or recognizes a specific object, it responds by acting in a pre-learned way. If it performs correctly, it gets a reward. That could be a pat on the snout or a handful of fish. Sort of like Pavlov's dog."

"The other way is what is called the process of multiple approximations, which means if you want it to perform a difficult task; you start slowly with the simple part and build gradually, adding more things until ultimately the whole task is done. The biggest problem with this is to divide the task into parts that are easily understood by the dolphin, starting with the easiest and finishing with the hardest. We sometimes have trouble determining the degree of difficulty for the dolphin. Things we think are easy for them turn out to be most difficult, while other hard tasks they pick up automatically. It takes a long time to get to know what each dolphin can do."

"Are they all different?"

"Just like people, Tanya. Some are smarter than others. Some are smarter than we are at times. They can convince us they can't do something and we believe them. We work for weeks on a task and the dolphin just can't seem to grasp what we're trying to tell him. We abandon that one and go on to another and the next thing we know the dolphin, on its own, completes the first task with ease. What makes it worse is he'll swim to his trainer and tease him."

"It must be frustrating," Matt observed.

"It is. The only thing that keeps trainers on the job is the satisfaction of learning about each dolphin."

"Who does your training, navy men?"

"No, mostly civilians. Most of the time there is a mix of marine biology, psychology and psychiatry students and post grads. Sometimes the training will be directed by a psychology grad, a biologist or any other behavioral scientist wishing to explore the mind. To work with a dolphin requires that the trainer must at all times be 'at one' with the dolphin."

"What does that mean, George?"

"Really what it means is that if you can't empathize with the animal you may as well forget about training it. It'll never do what you want it to do. I mentioned that sometimes they'll work without reward. The reason they do this, we believe, is because dolphins want to please their trainer. The key word here is 'want'. If they sense any bad feelings from their trainer, no amount of reward will get them to do anything!"

"That sounds almost human, George."

"It is, Tanya. That's exactly the comparison I apply. The more you work with them, the more involved you get. Some scientists studying dolphins have gone off the deep end because of just that, and what they feel dolphins really are almost human. There's a term used to describe it. Anthropomorphizing. Applying human personality to them and expecting them to react like people. It can creep up even if you are alert for it. If it gets hold of you, it can be dangerous to anything you might want to do in relation to the dolphins. You forget you are working with dolphins and start to think you are getting human responses. You can imagine how you would feel subjecting a human to some of the examinations and experiments we are putting the dolphin through."

"You make it sound like a crime, George." Tanya was bothered by this.

"Your reaction is exactly the response of some of the people who have worked with them. They develop an attachment to their pupils that is on a human plane. It makes it rough on them if anything happens to the dolphin, as sometimes it does. We have to be able to step back frequently and say to ourselves, 'this is what we are doing, this is how we are doing it and this is the result we expect.' If we find we can't look at it in an objective way, then maybe it's time to look for another line of work."

"Have you ever gotten carried away, George?"

"I did once, Matt. We were working out of San Diego, preparing a class of dolphins for Vietnam."

"We used dolphins in Vietnam?" Tanya was shocked.

"Yes. We had 50 or 60 in service along the coast."

"What were they used for?"

"Mostly mine detection and location, Matt. We used them early on in the war to detect patrol boats approaching."

"What happened to your radar?"

"Radar wasn't the best method to use. The boats would work close in to the shore line where radar had trouble picking them up. Dolphins were able to hear the engines long before we could spot the boats with radar. Our radar couldn't even come close to the sensitivity of the dolphin hearing."

"Their hearing is that good?" Tanya asked.

"It's phenomenal! We've only begun to understand how perfect it is. Their hearing range runs from 4000 Hertz up to 200,000 Hertz. Human hearing ranges from a few Hertz to about 16,000 Hertz. They can communicate and hear things far outside of our capability. If you think about it, they're underwater as well. Sound travels four and a half times faster in seawater than it does in air. Their hearing is so sensitive they can transmit and receive signals over distances of almost 700 miles. We believe they can also calculate how far away the sound originated."

"That's almost scary." Matt's mind considered the ramifications of this. They could talk to each other with one off the Strait of Juan de Fuca and the other off San Francisco. He found this hard to accept.

"Could they tell our boats from the enemy boats?"

"They could at the beginning, Matt. The Viet Cong and North Vietnamese were using Russian equipment. Their engines were larger and slower revving. The dolphins could distinguish between the faster units we used and the Russians units most of the time. We'd get plenty of warning from the dolphins. Sometimes up to ten or fifteen minutes ahead of an attack. Long enough for us to prepare a welcome, with radar we had no more than a few minutes."

"Did the enemy ever catch on?"

"It took a couple of years. We don't know if he figured it out or was told, but he began to run his engines at higher speeds. This had us confused for a long time. It didn't matter much because by then we had listening devices planted in most of the water around his bases. We knew his every move. We even knew when individual soldiers were in for a swim. So the role of the dolphin changed."

"What did they do then?"

"It was about that time both Charlie and our forces began to mine every bit of water that might be used for shipping. The dolphins were used to locate enemy mines."

"Were they able to tell ours from theirs?"

"Yes, they're able to distinguish not only shape but they can tell what material the mine is made of."

"What the mine is made of?" Tanya was puzzled.

"Yes! That's one way they recognize which zodiac belongs to their handlers when we're out in the Strait"

"By the material the boat's made of?"

"Even better than that, Tanya, they can recognize the difference between a six inch square copper plate and one the same size of aluminum or steel fixed on the boat"

"That's incredible. How do they do that?"

"It's really very complex, but to simplify it, they send out a pulse and assess the echo. Metals resonate at their own frequency. The dolphin strikes it with sound and listens for the ring. They can distinguish minute differences in the returning frequencies. They match this up with a certain frequency they have in their memory and know what the material is. Each boat has a small plate fastened to its bottom. The dolphins use that to identify their boat."

"That's a pretty sensitive sound system," Matt added.

"It sure is, Matt. Really they don't need the plates for identification though. They're able to recognize not only the metal but after working for a while with a crew they can even recognize the way each man handles the engine controls. They can even identify individual engines."

Tanya couldn't believe it. Working with electronic systems and understanding the small variations in radio frequencies and the difficulty humans have coping with them, she was having a hard time digesting all this. The ability of the dolphin seemed so incredible.

"What else did they do in 'Nam?" she pressed.

"They were used in combat."

"We never heard of dolphins being used at all, let alone in combat," Matt's curiosity was aroused."

"It wasn't talked about much. Top secret stuff."

"How could they be used in combat? I think of combat as firing a rifle or such." Tanya asked.

"Against enemy frogmen and shipping. They were sent into enemy harbors with limpet mines. They were taught to select the largest hull in the harbor and place the mine on her belly and get out. The mines were timed to explode 30 minutes after they were attached the the hull. This gave the dolphin plenty of time to clear the area."

"How did they know which ships were whose?"

"They didn't and this posed a problem. They took the largest hull, no matter what nation it belonged to. We had to know what ships were in harbor and not send the dolphins in if there were ships there we didn't want sunk. We hadn't explained to the dolphins how to be selective or what to look for. We got into a couple of jackpots over that. Some neutral ships were sunk and there was hell to pay. We discontinued this type of operation after one of our excursions sank a Swedish medical ship."

"I never heard about that either." Tanya injected.

"We kept it pretty well hushed up, but it wasn't long after this we changed the dolphin's role."

"What did they do next?"

We went after enemy divers, Tanya. The Cong couldn't get close to our capital ships. They were always on the move but our supply ships were in constant danger when unloading."

"How were the dolphins used?"

"They were used to constantly patrol around the ships unloading. At first they let us know if there were any frogmen in the area. Then we devised ways for them to attack the divers."

"I thought they wouldn't hurt anything. I thought in fact they'd help each other when they were in trouble."

"That's true, Tanya, and this presented a real problem for our trainers. They had to come up with ways to get the dolphins to disable the divers, a technique where the dolphins were taught to strip the scuba air line from the diver. This was made into a game the dolphins seemed to think was okay. Divers would either surface or drown. The dolphins were able to sense this and would try to help the divers to the surface. It took a long time before we could get them to leave the divers alone. Once they were able to handle this, we came up with the carbon dioxide harpoon."

"A special harness was made to secure a rod to the dolphins. This was similar to a stun-gun we use as protection against sharks but tied to the dolphin. All they had to do was drive the tip into the diver. That released the gas and the diver was finished."

"That's horrible! What a cruel way to fight!" Tanya was shocked.

"It seems pretty bad, I'll agree, but you have to assess it with other circumstances. When we had trained the dolphins to sever the air supplies, the divers who made it to the surface still had their explosives intact. It was easy for them to wait until a rescue boat or a dolphin got near them and blow up the whole works. We lost too many dolphins and sailors to allow that to happen. After an explosion and loss of a dolphin it would take days before the others would patrol again."

"I can't say I blame them," Tanya sympathized.

"No, I can't either but that's why the harpoon was used, to save the lives of our men and dolphins. We had a lot of this type of activity toward the latter part of the war. Then for no apparent reason we were withdrawn from action and shipped home to San Diego."

"Now that we're out of Vietnam, we're still training dolphins. Are they being trained to do the same things?" Matt's curiosity had gotten the better of him.

"No, not the same things, we've advanced in our level of training and are able to teach them more sophisticated routines. The intensity of training has been reduced. The immediate need is to learn more about these animals rather than having them perform work for us."

"How many dolphins are you working with?"

"All together, Tanya, there are 36 in San Diego with another 30 in Florida. A few are scattered in various places around the country. Nowhere near the numbers we had in the seventies. Commercial fishermen on the US east coast use them. They can locate schools of fish sooner and more accurately than most of the electronic gear available."

"How are they being used by the navy now?" Tanya showed concern.

"Much the way we started out. Retrieving torpedos and such. There is a special group trained for submarine rescue work."

"What can they do there?" Matt asked.

"Carry hoses and cables down to a disabled sub. We've got connections on hulls of our subs, spotted in strategic locations and the dolphins can make the connections."

"They're trained to connect plugs?" Matt knew the complexities of making connections underwater.

"Not the kind you're thinking of. We've developed special fittings so the dolphins can handle them. We could probably teach them to use regular fittings but it was easier to design them to suit the dolphins."

Matt checked his watch. "Well, we could talk to you for hours, George, but we're on our way to get something to eat. Want to come along?"

"No, thanks, Matt, you go ahead. I've got more work to do here before I break off for the day. I'll see you in the morning."

"I'd sure like to meet your dolphins, George. Could I come down tomorrow, early in the morning?"

"Sure Tanya. I have a feeling they'll be happy to meet you, you too, Matt. Really, I'd like both of you to see them."

"Okay, George, We'll be here in the morning. I'll check with Mike Chambers at Bangor on the way past the office to see if he will be ready to go after the rest of the buoys tomorrow."

Fine, Matt. Let me know as soon as you find out, so I can prepare the dolphins and crews."

"Right! See you tomorrow."

Matt and Tanya walked along the float to the ramp and up onto shore.

"Let's go over to the office now," Matt suggested, "then we can have the rest of the night off."

"Sounds good to me, you check Bangor and see how Mike's doing and I'll check with Oahu to see if there's any action with the birds."

Each went a different direction. Matt watched Tanya as she walked away. Trim waist, nicely rounded hips, well shaped legs. A fleeting wisp of her perfume carried past on the light breeze. His mind drifted back to the night in the Bell Buoy Inn, soft candle light dancing in her eyes, the warm glow of the wine, then her hotel room and the ecstasy that followed. He closed his eyes and could almost touch the memory. He felt good, having her close.

He opened his eyes slowly and watched. 'Nice view, nice action', he thought, as she went into the communication center. He went to his office where he called Mike to inform him about the three buoys they had found at Admiralty Head. Mike also felt there should have been only one. Two at the most.

"It's beyond me, Matt. Maybe we'll find a clue later."

Matt left his office heading for the communication center. He and Tanya had the night ahead of them.

CHAPTER 15

Saturday, Day 8, 18:00 hours.

Bob Bjorn called into the cell over the intercom, "Better not disturb anything until Brian and I've had a look at the explosive set-up."

Tom Wiser agreed, he and Tom came out of the cell as Bob and Brian entered.

"She's all yours," Tom said, "just don't wreck my shop," he added with a chuckle.

Bob and Brian stood back, looking over the core from one end to the other before touching it.

"Look at this ring of mirrors," Bob was peering at a spot close to the end of the core. There was a band of shining material ringing the core about 6 inches from the end.

"And over here. It's a ring in the shell in a matching position. Only they aren't mirrors in the shell, they're clear glass. It looks like they're meant to let light in."

"Wonder what they're for?"

With the power source removed the buoy should have been rendered harmless, but they took no chances. Working slowly and methodically, they examined the core from one end to the other. They were extra cautious to make sure there were no hidden triggers. Checking the buoy from every angle while it was sitting on the table, they found no apparent booby traps.

"I think we can roll it over a bit, Bob. Are you ready?"

"Okay, just a quarter turn for now. We've got to find the filler holes for the tubes holding the explosive liquid. We'll empty one of the two as quickly as we can, both if we can find two fillers!"

"What are they likely to look like?"

"They should be a short piece of metal or plastic tube with some form of clamp or plug on the end. They're not likely to be hidden or disguised. The Russians wouldn't likely have expected anyone to get this far without blowing the whole thing to pieces."

"What's this?" He held his fingers beside a small black tube. "Something like this?"

"Right idea, wrong area, Brian. It should be more over to this end, where the two cylinders get near the end. What we're looking for should be exactly like that. Let's roll the thing around a little further."

"How much?"

Another 90 degrees, then we'll be looking at the back of it."

It rolled easily on the bench and they found the back side more solidly filled with boxes than the side they had been looking at.

"Over here, see this screw?"

"Where?"

"Right on that small box."

"That looks promising. Hand me the large screwdriver, the one with the wide blade."

Bob gently slid the driver into the screw slot and eased pressure onto it in a normal counter clockwise direction. Nothing happened. He twisted harder. Still nothing. Brian was staring at this action and the sweat beads were forming rapidly on his forehead. "Hold it!" he cautioned sharply.

Bob went rigid. Holding the screwdriver where it was, he slowly turned his head to look at Brian. His eyes were wide open. Startled he blurted, "What the hell . . ."

"That's not the filler. It's a trap! Take the screwdriver away carefully. We'll go out to the scanner and have a look."

Bob removed the driver. When it was clear he began to shake. How close had they come, he wondered? They would see in a minute. "Let's get out of here! We'll have a look on the x-ray."

Walking out of the cell they went straight to the scanner.

"What happened, Brian?" Tom asked in wonder.

"It may be nothing, it may be a trigger. Let's look at it with the scanner. I should also mention to you guys, while you're out on the viewing area, until we get this skunk de-scented, I'd suggest you stand clear of the viewing window. If the buoy blows up, it may or may not have enough force to penetrate the window. No sense taking a chance. If it has the power, you wouldn't want to be standing in the way of flying glass. You can watch in the monitor."

The scanner was turned on and positioned over the tube they were working on. They were looking for some kind of anomaly inside the box. Wire, chain, tubes or anything you wouldn't expect to find in an electronic box. Brian explained.

"The plug should go into the tube about half an inch. Any more and it's likely not what we're after."

Tom moved the scanner back and forth while varying the power.

"Hold it right there. There's an interesting shadow," he pointed to the screen. "Bring the power down a bit Tom."

An image formed on the screen. Directly below the plug was a cylindrical shape about an inch long running down to the opposite side of the box.

"I don't like the look of that!"

"It may only be a filler tube" Tom commented.

"I think the box is a reservoir, Tom. If it is, why would they put a tube down the middle of it?"

"Good point! If we remove the plug, the tube fractures or opens allowing the two liquids to mix and . . . . that's all she wrote."

"I'd like to go back into the cell and see if we can find another place that could be the filling tube.

Bob and Brian went back into the cell and began to examine the main explosive tubes for the elusive filler.

"I just thought of something, Bob. One of these cylinders may be pressurized considerably above the other. If we open the low pressure one first, the other one could go off and shatter the divider between them."

"Good Christ, Brian. How're we to know?"

"If the pressure's critical there'd have to be a pressure gauge somewhere. Look for a gauge."

They looked from one end to the other and found none. "Let's go back to the scanner, Bob."

Once again the two walked out through the thick, heavy access door at the back of the cell, along the corridor behind the cell complex and through the massive end door into the viewing room. The others were waiting.

Mike walked in at the same time. "What's the problem?"

"We've got some trouble finding the filler. I think I'd feel happier if we have another look with the x-ray." Bob explained about the reluctant screw.

Tom ran the scanner up and down over the one box they were trying to open. "Either we've missed it or the cylinders aren't pressurized," Tom observed.

"All of the boxes may not be filled with electronics. Let's check every box that's close to the cylinders to see if there are any tubes leading away from them. Tom ran the scanner up and down the body. No joy!

"Maybe it's not pressurized," Bob had to admit. "Go back to the filler box we were looking at, and we'll see if there are any other boxes near it that could be what we're looking for."

With the scanner sitting over the filler box, Tom varied the power settings. Visible on the screen, the box outline clearly appeared. As the power increased the outside of the box slowly faded being replaced with the innards. They studied the image, but saw nothing to indicate a pressure set-up.

"What's in the box next to it?"

Tom moved the scanner over to the right. "Over here?"

"Yeh."

"Another box Bob, there's a cover on it with eight screws fastening it on. It seems to be casketed as well."

Bob was now more intent, "The buoy is watertight. Why would they have to make this box watertight with a gasket?" Bob asked of no one in particular. "And why do they need eight screws when four would do?"

"Hey! I think you've got something, Bob." Brian now entered the speculation. "Tom, scan deeper inside."

The scanner moved. The heavily sealed box showed itself to be void. The one next to it showed what appeared to be a round one inch drum with a short piece of tubing at the bottom.

"That must be the filler!"

"How is the lid attached to it?" Brian asked.

"Four screws."

"All right, let's open it up and see what's inside." Brian was excited.

"What do you think, Bob?" Tom was concerned about his facility as well as the safety of the men.

"I think he's right. Let's open it up." Bob agreed.

He and Brian walked back into the cell. Brian, so convinced he had the answer, took a half-gallon plastic bottle with him. "We'll drain it into this jug," he told Bob.

The intercom interrupted them. "Commander Chambers, there's a call for you."

"That must be the lab. Boy, are those guys fast!"

Mike walked over to the phone in the viewing room. It wasn't the lab, it was Matt Reynolds, in Port Angeles, wanting to know how they were progressing. Mike filled him in on what they had accomplished so far. "If all goes well the rest of the day, we should be ready to put the buoy in the water sometime tomorrow. Can you have things ready at your end?"

"Will you need anything special in the way of tools or equipment on board my cutter?"

"We'll bring most of the gear we need. I don't think we'll need anything from your end. Give me a call at noon if you haven't heard from me by then."

"We'll be ready and waiting, Mike. See you tomorrow then."

Mike returned to the cell and they examined what was left of the buoy.

Back in the cell, Bob and Brian removed the cover of the box with four screws. Underneath, was a pressure gauge showing numbers and Russian lettering. They'd have to get that translated later. Alongside, was a standard hydraulic connector. Bob called over the intercom for someone to bring in a short piece of half inch tubing and a compression fitting for it. Tom sent a man to the tool crib for the parts.

"What're you going to do?" he asked.

"We're going to try to open this connector. If we're right, the pressure should express the liquid. Take a close look at this pressure gauge with the camera. We'll have to make sure we bring the pressure up to this point when we put everything back together."

"Okay Bob, I've got it." Tom moved the camera back out of the way. What's next?"

"When the tubing gets here, we'll try to open the connector and drain the liquid." Bob answered.

Tom sent the connector and tubing into the cell and Brian fastened the tube onto the hydraulic fitting and tightened the hose clamp around it.

"That should do it, ready Bob?"

"Ready."

He slipped the end of the tube into the plastic bottle, twisting the sheath of the connector as he did. A loud whoosh of air sped along the tube blowing a streak of liquid into the bottom of the bottle.

Bob and Brian glanced at each other. Each had sweat on his brow. They grinned. Another hurdle had been successfully overcome. Bob tipped the buoy on end. Rapidly now, the liquid drained from the tube into the plastic bottle. The last drops ran out as the bottle was half filled.

"Just about a pint Brian, let's see if we can get the other cylinder, too." They marked the first container for later reinsertion into the same vial and sent it to their lab for identification.

With both tubes drained the buoy became harmless. Brian and Bob excitedly started opening the boxes looking for the one holding the tuning circuits. All boxes now lay open. Some held one printed circuit board, others had four or five. Most held stacks of them.

"Look at this. This whole board's made with American IC chips."

"I'll be damned! We supply this stuff to them?"

"No. Not strategic materials. Someone has smuggled these out of the States and into Russia."

Runners stood by to rush each part to the electronic lab as soon as Brian had them identified and the position recorded on video tape. Each must be returned precisely to the same spot.

Mike's experts were waiting for each part and quickly set about establishing its make-up and function. Each bit was photographed from every angle then spent time plugged into the central computer where the assessment of its function took place. Bob's task included determining where the cables at the back of each box led. How they interacted with other boxes could help in determining their function.

While the boxes were being removed, Mike came in with a lab report on the material from the buoy's skin. It proved to be a long chain, synthetic polymer, similar to wood cellulose. The lab established that it would have the explosive yield of low power dynamite when augmented with another explosive. Harmless by itself, stable was the term the lab had used, but combined with a high energy explosive, it would rapidly become unstable and add to the strength of the initiating explosive. Like using a detonator to set off a bomb, only the plastic skin was part of the bomb.

Mike could now understand how the buoy on the beach had done so much damage.

Brian pointed out the mirrors to Mike. "I'd like to do some poking around these babies. If they're what I think they are, we may have stumbled onto one of the Russian's top secrets."

"What's that?"

"Laser communication, Mike."

"My God, Brian. We've barely gotten into that. Our submarine communication system is so new; only the Trident class will have it."

"I know Mike. But if I'm right, this may be the most significant find in this exercise with the buoy."

"What do you want to start with, the mirrors or the skin of the buoy?"

"Let's have a look at the skin."

They set the hollow tube of skin on the bench where they could get a close look at the slotted section at the open end. They were the part that would sit over the mirrors on the plug end when the guts were inserted into it.

They could see now what had eluded them during the initial examination. Slits, in a ring around the buoy, were matching the positions of the mirrors with the buoy assembled. Each slit was about an inch long, running lengthwise along the buoy. They weren't visible on the scanner because the glass and skin thickness, even though different, had the same density for the x-rays. Small as slivers they looked like splits in a real log. They understood now why they had been missed. There were slits on each end of the buoy, so that no matter how the log sat on the bottom, there would always be a mirror exposed to the surface of the water.

"Each one of these slits is directly over the flat face of a mirror inside the buoy. Let's have a look at the mirrors now, Bob"

They went back to the core and examined the flat, dark mirrors.

"These aren't mirrors, Brian! They're prisms!"

"Christ, I was afraid of this. I'll bet if we open the rig up, we'll find a ring of fiber optic conductors leading away from the bottom of each prism."

"I'll see if I can extract some of them and we'll take a look."

Taking a screw driver, he worked on the screws holding the clamp retainer on one of the prisms. Parts separated easily, exposing a clear disc about a quarter inch in diameter.

"That's the magnetic interface, Bob. There should be two of them to each prism."

"Yeh. There's another over here."

"I thought so! One is for transmitting and the other is for receiving. This will make our job of identifying the black boxes easier. The fiber optic conductors on one side will lead to transmitting equipment while the other will lead to receivers."

"I'd better get Mike in here right away. He'll likely want to bring some of his specialists in to see this."

"You go ahead with what you're doing, Bob, I'll get him."

"Send Tom in on your way out. I'd like to take some of these mounting braces off so we can get down to the backbone of the buoy. Tom will have to get some other tools and some of those little round tags."

"The kind with the strings on them?"

"The same, Brian."

Brian went out the back of the cell and 'round to the viewing area, talked briefly to Tom, then carried on to locate a phone to call Mike.

Tom and Bob began to remove bits and pieces from the buoy. They marked each one with a tag and showed it to the camera to record the location as each came out of the buoy. They were concerned that a box might fit in more than one place. If they got one box wrong, they'd probably never know, but the Russians sure would. It could blow the whole operation. They were extra careful. Tom pulling gently on one box, found it came loose in his hands, a connector tied it into the frame. The connector was secured with screws. He undid the screws and the connector parted into two halves. Brian took one and tied a tag to it. Another tag went onto the half remaining on the buoy. He showed both to the video camera. Once they had removed half a dozen boxes, Tom brought back a small cart. The loose units were moved to it and wheeled out of the cell by a seaman. Another cart replacing it, filled up quickly.

Brian phoned Mike and related their findings to him.

The revelation stunned Mike. He had recently returned from a seminar at the War College where they were supposedly brought up to date on the newest Soviet weapons and methods. They hadn't mentioned these buoys nor had they suggested that the Soviets had sufficiently developed laser technology to have working systems in the field. The Pentagon were about to have their sox knocked off if Brian was right.

"I'll be right there, Brian said, this could be worth relaying to Washington immediately. I'm sure they'll want to know all about it."

We'll hold up on putting things back together until you get here, but don't be too long. We've got to get this thing back in the water as soon as possible."

"I'll be there within ten minutes," Mike assured him. Bob went back to the cell and Mike phoned Navy Intelligence in Washington. A woman's voice answered.

Mike identified himself. "Give me Commander Stoddard please . . . ."

"Are you aware of the time, Commander?" It was late night in Bangor, early morning in Washington, D.C.

"I am. This is of the utmost importance."

"I'll have to try to raise him at home. Please stand by," she said reluctantly.

A gravelly male voice grated, "Hello."

"Harry, it's Mike Chambers in Bangor."

"Mike Chambers? Great to hear from you. What's up?"

"Is this a secure line?"

"Why, yes. Why do you ask?'

Turn your scrambler on, Harry."

"It's on, Mike, go ahead."

Mike began with the discovery of the buoys and told him what they were doing now with the one they had retrieved. To qualify what he was about to tell Harry, he mentioned the seminar and the state-of-the-art laser work they had been informed about then gave Harry the zinger, "The buoy is fitted with laser receivers."

Silence.

"You there, Harry?"

"I'm trying to digest what you're saying, Mike. Are you sure it's not one of ours?"

"Not unless we're putting Russian writing on our equipment now, Harry."

"Jesus, Mike." Silence again. "The navy has underwater blue light laser transmission systems for submarine communications, but it's only been deployed within the past year." They thought the Soviets were at least a year behind them. If what Mike said is true, they're way ahead of us.

Mike described the windows and prism set up to Harry as best he could. He also told him that the buoy locations formed two fences across the route Trident subs must take to and from Bangor. Harry couldn't believe what he heard. At least, he didn't WANT to believe it. Mike went on to describe the fiber optic cables feeding the prisms. "Are you still with me, Harry?"

"My God, yes, Mike. Go on!"

"If we're on the right track, the sono-buoy will record data for months, then on command, transmit it back to the satellites."

"And you think the Russians are using lasers to interrogate it, Mike?"

"Yes!"

"This could be even more embarrassing than Sputnik. Jesus, if you're right we may have been caught flat-footed again."

Harry's reference to the world's first man made satellite and, how Intelligence community ignorance of the research Russians had to have done to create it, sent shivers along Mike's spine. They said, at that time that the U.S. couldn't afford to allow the country to be so badly outfoxed again.

"That's why I called you, Harry. I know we only recently put our own laser communications system into operation. In fact the Trident submarines are the first operational users we have. We thought we had a few year's head start on the Russians. Now it looks like that lead is non-existent."

"That's true, Mike. If they're using a similar principle, we've got to know about it. What are you doing with this buoy?"

"We're dissecting it right now. It's got to go back where we found it as soon as possible. In fact it's got to go back before the Russians discover we even know about it."

"Don't put it back before I've had a chance to get one of my scientists to check it out!"

"I can't wait for that, Harry. It has to go back as soon as we're finished with it. If you want to see it, you'd better get someone out here fast, or you can look at the videos we're making."

"Okay, I'll have a man out there tomorrow morning. I'll call him as soon as I hang up. You delay for a bit will you?"

"No way, Harry. We don't have that kind of time. Better hustle your man!"

"We're wasting time on this call, Mike. Talk to ya."

The phone went silent. Mike hung up wondering where his responsibility lay. Getting the buoy back or up-dating the Intelligence fraternity. He felt convinced he had made the right decision. It must go back right away. The intelligence people could examine it if they had a man on site in time. If not, he'd have access to any data they got from it. The video tape and computer work-ups are very comprehensive. That should be enough. Mike reasoned, it's imperative the Ruissians not know we have one of their buoys. If they were the least suspicious, Mike wouldn't be successful at reprogramming them to produce misinformation. The whole exercise would be wasted; the Russians would abandon this snooping method. Lord knows where their next probe would be. No. It's critical that they not twig to the tampering, the hell with the intelligence people.

Mike had arranged to have a staff of electronic engineers available at the lab. They were waiting when the first cart arrived from the manipulator cell, and immediately began to distribute the boxes among themselves. Each man had a test bench holding myriad electronic test instruments. They were well trained in what they had to do and got right to it. They were still working on the first load when another came through the door.

The last of the boxes was being removed from the buoy as Mike entered the viewing room. The men were suddenly tired, stress and urgency finally taking their toll. The buoy looked like a stripped Christmas turkey; a few bones on a platter and bits of meat scattered all over.

"It's almost midnight. Why don't we knock off for something to eat?" Mike offered.

"Best offer I've heard for a long time," Brian agreed.

Three very tired men walked out of the confines of the cell, called to Mike, then all went to the base mess hall.

*   *   *

After eating, Mike, Tom, Bob and Brian returned to the cell. "Bob, we've got to find the way this bouy is tuned. Any ideas?" Mike asked.

"There are a few parts left on the carcass that don't seem to be black boxes. They may give us a clue," Bob ventured.

"Somehow I don't think this baby has to be taken apart to be tuned."

"Why do you say that, Mike"

"Well, the way the buoy is put together for one, too much chance for an accidental explosion. I don't think the Russians would be too anxious to open the plug any more often than they absolutely had to."

That makes sense, Mike. How do you suggest they get inside then?"

"Maybe we've missed a connector somewhere."

"If there was a connector through the skin, we'd have found wires attached to it somewhere. There were none when we pulled the core out of the skin."

"You're right, Bob. How's it done then?"

"We haven't found any penetrations in the skin except for the windows at each end. Could they be the point of entry?"

"I don't think so. Let's go over the core again."

There were few unexposed areas after removal of the black boxes. A central core, or skeleton ran the length of the buoy. There were five, two inch wide bands evenly spaced between the boxes along the buoy. The full diameter of the buoy, they were metal and appeared to support the shape of the buoy. The two at the ends of the buoy were cast metal. There were no wires anywhere around them. The second one in from each end was used to hold the prisms for the fiber optics. The center one now took their attention.

"This could be cabling underneath the plate on this side." Bob noted.

"Let's give the buoy a bit of a turn," Mike suggested.

A screw came into view as the buoy rolled on the table. Bob removed it but nothing happened. The plate held firm. They tried to pry it off but couldn't get underneath. Brian spotted scratch marks along the outer edge of the plate where it mated with the band. Feeling with his fingernail, he discovered sharp rings on the underside of the band. He put his fingertips on the plate on opposite sides of the plate and exerted twisting pressure. The plate began to turn.

"I've got it!" he exclaimed.

The plate spun all the way off revealing a cable yoke similar to the fiber optic setup.

"Now that's more interesting!" Bob observed. "Where do the cables go?"

"Here, out the bottom over here." Brian pointed to the first empty section where the black box had been removed.

"They end in this connector."

The next step required information from the lab.

"I'll call and see what's in that box. What's the tag number?"

Checking the tag tied onto the connector, Tom called, "J 42."

Mike hurried out of the cell to phone the lab. "What else's in there?" Tom couldn't see the rest of the band.

"Some heavy looking parts strung around the back side." Bob answered. "Like pearls in a necklace."

"Can you get one out?"

"I think so, Tom. Hand me that small probe."

Bob inserted the probe behind the closest block and applied a slight pressure. The block eased out and fell heavily into Tom's waiting hand. To Tom it looked like a piece of laminated steel wound with wire. It had a polished top about one inch square and slightly rounded to tightly mate with the curve of the inside of the band. Wires led from the block into the yoke they had just traced.

"Looks like a magnet, Bob." Tom observed.

"I think it is, Tom. It appears to be a magnetic sensor. I'll bet the others are the same." They looked at the rest which duplicated the first one. Bob counted the blocks in the band. There were eighteen all together.

The wheels turned in Bob's head. They were turning in Mike's at the same time. They both exclaimed, "These are programing pick-up heads!"

"They're magnetic pick-ups." Bob echoed.

Mike continued, "They use a band clamped around the outside of the buoy to access the tuner."

"Right. They set it over the internal heads and feed information through the skin." Brian injected. "Of course . . . . That way they don't have to compromise the watertight integrity of the buoy."

"Right. They can even reprogram it underwater. Really smart."

"How're we going to duplicate their tuning band?" Tom wanted to know.

"I don't know at the moment," Mike answered, "But I'll bet my engineers can come up with something before morning."

"Try to imagine working underwater, tuning it." Brian said.

"What're you getting at?" Mike wanted to know.

"Just this. At one hundred and fifty feet, it's pretty dark. There must be some way to make sure the tuning collar's over the right part on the buoy."

That's a good point. It brings up another one, too. How do the Russians find the buoys after they place them?"

"Right. There must be a locating spot somewhere on the skin to locate the band." Brian said.

"Okay, and there must also be some kind of low power beacon to locate the buoy in the deep water." Mike added.

"Why low power?" Tom asked.

"So that it can't be picked up accidentally," Mike told him. 'The FCC would have a fine time trying to charge them with operating an illegal transmitter."

Mike went back to the phone in the viewing room and called the lab. He explained the tuning pick-up heads and asked the boys to see if they could isolate a marker beacon and get back to him at the cell as quickly as possible. He returned to the cell.

Those in the cell gathered around the imitation bark skin to find some bump or flat spot that might be used to enable accurate placement of the tuning band. If the reprogramming had to be done underwater, the method had to be simple. They checked the buoy where the other bands would be located to see if there was a difference between them. The tuning band had fewer rough spots, and in fact, a single ridge showed up along one part of the skin.

"That looks like the mark we're after, Bob said. "You could set the band on with your eyes closed."

"I think you're right," Mike agreed.

Mike called to the crew in the cell, telling them he was going over to the lab to see how they were doing. He also wanted to direct their construction of a tuning unit they could use on submerged buoys.

Entering the lab, Mike met the engineers, explaining the bands in greater detail than he had on the phone. The lab couldn't duplicate the Russian equipment, but could come up with a workable substitute. They had determined that all tuner magnets did not have to be energized at once, one or two would do the trick. The important thing, they said, is to have at least two magnets under the interfacing band at the same time. For this reason, they would build a collar to cover at least four.

Mike wanted to know what they had found out about the type of laser that would have to be used to interrogate the buoy. They had no positive answers as yet but should have something before morning. "They must have powerful receivers in their satellites. The output of this transmitter is pretty low. I guess that's why they have to bring their birds down so low."

"Something to think about, don't let that hold you up though. We've got to get this buoy back together soon."

"We're working at top speed. We'll give you a call at the earliest."

That satisfied Mike for now, and he decided to return to the cell facility.

CHAPTER 16

Sunday, Day 9, 19:00 hours.

Driving Tanya from the base to her hotel, Matt promised to be back within an hour and a half, to take her to supper. He was.

He knocked at her door. They'd each had time to shower and change. Tonight, they'd agreed, would be more casual than last night.

As the door opened, Matt's eyes took in her slim, black slacks and white sweater. She still maintained her elegant appearance, even in casual clothes. Matt told her so, and she flushed ever so slightly. Matt had enough of a tease in him to notice this, mentally filing it for future reference.

"Is this all right?" she asked.

"Couldn't be better," he assured her.

They were headed for a little seafood restaurant down by the waterfront. "Is that okay, or are you getting tired of salt water proteins."

"I'll never get tired of the seafood here," she said with a little pixie grin, "it does things for a person's stamina."

He noticed the pert turn of her lips and softly touched her left cheek just below the dimple it formed. Her eyes sparkled as she took his hand and softly kissed the palm.

Matt's turn to flush. 'We'd better get going if we're to have any supper tonight."

She agreed. "Will I need a coat?"

"Not tonight."

Driving up Lincoln Street and along 1st Street, Matt turned into a low building's parking lot. This was Michael's Seafood and Steak House.

"Is this where we're going?" Tanya asked.

"Not too fancy, but that's no indication of the food quality," Matt responded.

"That's what you said about The Bell Buoy Inn we were at last night."

"Oh, I guess I did. Well they're all the best."

They both laughed.

The cafe didn't let them down; they ate a superb supper. Matt, partial to escargot, started with half a dozen then tested the oysters while Tanya had a Crab Louis. A bottle of dry white wine complemented the casual atmosphere.

They talked for a while in the restaurant, then drove the short distance to the shoreline. It was intimate, walking along the water's edge, catching the warm sea breeze. With few street lights to screen the sky, the starlit canopy appeared nearer than usual. The sun had set half an hour earlier and there was no moon. Walking along, watching the stars, each talked about hopes and dreams for the future. Matt, a career man with the Coast Guard, could see his direction clearly. Tanya, who had recieved her training from the navy, wasn't committed to it for life. Strolling along the shore, they pulled an imaginary protective cover over themselves, keeping the rest of the world out. Looking up at the sky as they walked, they drifted into fantasy, each deep within thoughts only they knew.

A moving star caught Matt's eye, "Look!"

They followed it for two or three seconds and Tanya recognized it as a satellite. "Probably one of ours."

That broke the mood of the moment and they came back to reality. Walking on, they ended up back at Matt's car and they drove to his house.

"How about a quiet drink," Matt suggested.

"Only if you sit at the opposite end of the sofa." she replied.

"I don't know. That's pretty hard to do."

They laughed and walked up the stairs to Matt's door.

He lived in a one floor house. A typical bachelor pad, the furnishings reflected his way of life, straightforward and functional with few frills. Facing the fireplace in a cozy conversation group, he had arranged an overstuffed sofa and armchair, hinting at a subconscious desire for comfort. Bookcases, crowded with books from floor to ceiling, flanked the fireplace, spanning the entire wall. Hardbacks and soft covers vied for space. Subjects ranged from boy's stories to more serious tomes on philosophy and maritime law. Tanya browsed through titles ranging from Shakespeare and Michener, to A. A. Milne.

"Have you read all of these?"

"Read maybe, understood, maybe not." he commented.

The adjoining wood-paneled feature wall of light eastern cherry completed a rustic effect. The beige shag rug under foot went well with the decor.

A coffee table sitting in front of the sofa held two current editions of men's magazines. End tables each supporting a lamp flanked the sofa.

The dining room window offered a view to the west and allowed light into a functional table and six chairs. Toward the north, French doors led to a secluded patio overlooking the Strait, all the way to Vancouver Island.

Matt made sure Tanya was comfortable on the sofa, turning on the stereo; he poured a glass of wine for each of them.

"Take your shoes off if you want," he said carrying the glasses over and handing one to her. They sipped quietly and talked about the events of the day. Both were taken with the dolphins. They'd learned more about these animals in the talk with George than most people discovered in a lifetime. The whole concept that there may be another animal with the intelligence of man confused them. They both had trouble handling that thought. Both wanted to learn more. Tomorrow they would make an effort to pay more attention to the activity around the dolphin pens. Tonight they had other things to pay attention to, more important things.

Tanya told him about her youth. Brought up in South Dakota, her family's farm was almost eight miles north of Mitchell. They had raised dairy cattle and planted corn. She had joined 4 H as all the kids did. She had done very well with her animals, winning many ribbons. The other kids used to give her a rough time because she could get dogs and even cats to do tricks in no time at all.

"They were jealous," she said, "I had a cat once that could do more tricks than most dogs. It's all in knowing how to talk to them. I raised a heifer and won a blue ribbon with her. She used to follow me around the pasture."

They talked 'till the small hours of the morning, sipping wine. Each found the other held similar ideas and beliefs. The little cottage with the white picket fence held special meaning to both. Careers were important also. While they talked they held each other and their hands wandered. They enjoyed this 'touch stage' of their relationship and felt comforted, close to each other.

They finished the wine, kissed tenderly at first, then with more emotion and impatience, exploring the memory of their previous passions. The same sensations were there, with the same results. Matt's caressing fingers aroused responsive areas wherever they touched. The heights they had experienced before were still as rewarding. They drifted in a state of oneness, allowing their hunger for each other total freedom. They made love beautifully then slept, soundly.

*   *   *

Monday, day 10, 06:10 hours.

Matt woke first. Carefully easing out of bed he quietly shaved, showered and dressed. Slipping out to the kitchen, he squeezed fresh orange juice, then ground beans and started coffee. By the time Tanya came sleepy-eyed into the kitchen, he had bacon sizzling in the pan, and toast on the go.

"You should have wakened me, I could have helped."

She wore Matt's pajama top looking much sexier than Matt ever looked in it. He absorbed the effect, answering, "No need. Everything's under control."

She walked towards Matt, hips swaying. He put the egg flipper down and made a lunge for her, she waited to be caught.

"What we had last night was good. I've never felt as close to anyone as I do to you."

"I had the same feeling," Matt agreed, "It was almost as though we were one person." He took her in his arms, kissed her tenderly. They stood in silence for a few moments each thinking of last night. He let a hand slip down her backside to rest on a well rounded cheek. "We can put the eggs on hold," he offered. She thrust forward, warm pelvis pressing hard into his abdomen. He responded. Mouths, tight together, tongues darting, the inevitable emotional rollercoaster ride had begun. A billowing column of white smoke rising from the toaster derailed the cars, ending the ride before it could build to the uncontrollable state.

"Quick, Tanya, grab the plug."

Matt held the toaster over the sink and opened the window. Smoke cleared and the two of them started to laugh. "Hot stuff," Matt offered.

"You, me or the toaster?" Tanya wanted to know.

"All three, I guess! Wonder how the bacon's doing?"

"I'll check, Matt . . . . Seems okay. Did the toaster survive?"

"Could be. We'll try again after it's cooled down."

They ate breakfast slowly and deliberately, then dressed and drove down to the base.

*   *   *

George arrived at the dolphin pens an hour before Matt and Tanya to make sure everything was all right with the handlers. He watched the feeding process, satisfied the animals were fit for the duty that lay ahead. He greeted Tanya and Matt as they came down the ramp to the float.

"Hi, you two, How did your supper go?"

"The best", Matt answered. "Too bad you missed it."

"Well, I didn't get clear of this place 'till after nine. One of the dolphins is off her food."

Is it something serious George?"

"Maybe, maybe not. We'll have to wait and see."

"Is it the water or food?" Tanya wanted to know.

"It could be many things. I'm a little worried about that fish farm along the spit. It may be having an effect on the bacteria content of the water inside the harbor."

"Won't the tidal changes flush the area clean?" Matt inquired.

"Not completely. Some bugs and viruses only wash back and forth, never clearing the area completely. A good part of them are trapped inside."

"What about out in the Strait?"

"In most cases they dissipate out in the open. In here they could build to high toxicity levels. Particularly because of that fish farm.

"How can you know?" Tanya asked.

"I've sent water samples to your local lab for analysis. I should have a report sometime this morning."

"Can you do anything for her in the meantime?" Tanya wished there was something she could do.

"We've given her antibiotics for now, we'll see how they affect her."

"Which one's sick?" Tanya looked out over the pens trying to spot one of the dolphins acting different than the rest.

Four animals swam splashing around the pens, clicking and squeaking among each other. Never still, they seemed to have boundless energy. Tanya couldn't identify the sick one.

"Over there Tanya, see the smaller one of the two down at the end of the pen?"

"That's the female, George?"

"Yep. That's Pua. She's the patient. Come on over and I'll introduce you."

Walking to the edge of the float, they waited while George signaled the dolphins. In a flash the two in the nearest pen were by their feet looking up at them.

"Matt and Tanya, I'd like you to meet Pua and Hoku. Pua and Hoku, this is Tanya," he said, waving his hand toward Tanya "and this is Matt."

Two heads bobbed in the water, clicking and whistling excitedly.

"They were both captured in Hawaii," George explained, "hence the names. Pua's Hawaiian for Flower and Hoku means Star."

Tanya stepped back a bit to avoid getting splashed.

Matt squatted down and patted Pua and Hoku.

"Here, Tanya, say hello," Matt invited.

Tanya edged closer to the dolphins. They increased their noises and nodded energetically. This surprised her. It surprised George, too.

"They really like you, Tanya. I haven't seen them this happy to meet anyone as much as they are with you. You should feel honored."

"I do, George, I just don't know what to make of them up close. Yesterday I saw them from a distance. They looked small and friendly. Today, they're right here, and they're pretty large animals. A little overwhelming,"

Tanya said apprehensively. "It's like getting into a stall with a mule the first time. You don't quite know how to act."

"Pat them on the noses," Matt coached her.

She did. Their skin felt so smooth, like wet silk, soft and surprisingly delicate. The dolphins were ecstatic, chirping and whistling with excitement.

"I don't understand their behavior," George said, "I guess they saw you yesterday and were waiting to meet you."

Tanya found this hard to believe. "They couldn't have seen me before. I haven't spent any time near them."

"They could have seen you aboard the cutter," Matt offered.

"Only in passing," She countered.

"That's all it would take," George confirmed.

"Amazing," Matt added.

"These guys are pretty smart. There are many things we still don't know about them. Their ability to recognize people is one of them."

Pua rolled over and dove beside the float. They lost sight of her until, with a tremendous leap she sailed high into the air at the middle of the pen. Falling back into the water, she circled and leaped again.

"She's showing off. I think it's meant to impress you, Tanya. Wait and see if she returns to you."

As George spoke, she came up at Tanya's feet. She squealed with pleasure and grinned.

"That's what it was," George observed. "She sure has taken to you. Here give her a couple of these yellow-fish."

Tanya threw two in the direction of Pua, her mouth opened and the fish disappeared. Pua opened her mouth for more. "She thinks you're an easy mark, Tanya. Don't give her more until she does something for it."

Pua swam out in the pen and returned with a ball. She laid it at Tanya's feet. She got another fish.

"Well, maybe we'd better hire you to look after them, Tanya." George said, only half joking. "You have a positive effect on them."

Matt would have been surprised too if it hadn't been for their talk last night, when she had told him about her ability to train animals.

She talked to Pua and Hoku. They responded with various noises, almost as if they were carrying on a conversation. They acted like playful kids. Matt and George stood back from the edge of the float and watched.

"I've never seen them act like this before, Matt. Tanya has some strange effect on both of them."

"I know what it is, George, I've sensed the same feeling. She has a serenity, a calmness about her. Maybe the dolphins sense the same thing."

"It could be, Matt, they react differently to different people."

"How so?"

"Remember I told you yesterday about trainers having to be mentally very close to the dolphins?"

"Mmm Hmm, yes, I remember. The trainer has to be able to empathize you said."

"Right! We sometimes get trainers that can't seem to get the dolphins to do even simple tasks. For some reason, their, what for a better name, vibrations didn't match. We've found it's best for the trainer and dolphins if we replace them immediately or we're wasting everyone's time. We can tell quickly if a trainer will get along with the animals. A mismatch is bad for all concerned. It frustrates the trainer and makes the dolphins more difficult to deal with. Whatever it is that's required, Tanya has it in spades."

They continued to watch as Tanya got to know the dolphins. George gave her a few things to try, showing her how to signal and what to do. He tossed all their toys into the pen and started Tanya playing 'fetch'. Circling the pen, the two dolphins lept and squealed and charged back to Tanya with various rings or balls. She sometimes didn't even have to signal them and they were off to retrieve a toy.

"George, I never told them I wanted the ball. They just went after it on their own."

"Tell Pua to bring in the large ring, but don't signal." George directed.

Tanya called out, "The big ring, Pua.!"

Pua charged out and retrieved the ring.

"Now think of one of the shapes but don't say it or signal, just think it."

Tanya stood silently beside the pen.

Hoku sped to the middle of the pen and picked up the small ball.

"That's right!" she cried, as Hoku dropped the ball at her feet.

George, surprised at first with these responses, became fascinated. Tanya continued.

"Matt, I think Tanya has the ability to communicate unconsciously with the dolphins. I've heard of such things but haven't run into it before."

"I don't really understand the significance, George."

"It happens sometimes with people who work for a long time with some animals. They know what each other is thinking or can sense it."

"Tanya's always been able to get along with animals, George. She told me a little of her father's farm and some of the pets she had."

"It may be she's signaling with her eyes or a head nod, without knowing it. The dolphins pick that up quickly."

"You mean like the counting horse?"

"You know about the counting horse?"

"Just what they told us in university psychology. As I remember it, the trainer told the horse when to stop counting."

"That's right. He gave it away with his eye movement. The horse continued counting until he saw the trainer's eyes move. Just happened the trainer's eyes moved at the right count. The trainer had no idea he was giving it away. He really thought the horse could count."

"Didn't they prove that by keeping the trainer out of sight of the horse?"

"Right again, Matt. It could be what Tanya's doing now. Sometime I'd like to do some experiments to see."

"Why not now?"

"We couldn't really establish one way or the other, with any degree of certainty. That takes a more controlled environment than we have here. We could try a couple of simple things, though."

"Why not?"

"Okay, let's go! Tanya, come over here for a minute."

She walked to the far side of the float where they were standing. George explained what they wanted to do and she eagerly agreed. They pulled all the toys out of the pen and set them on the float.

"Turn your back to the pen," George directed.

She turned away.

"Now think of a toy . . . . Got it?"

"Yes."

"Now think about which of the two dolphins you want to get it."

"Okay."

"Matt, throw all the toys into the pen."

Matt picked up the toys and as fast as he could, scattered them to all parts of the pen. The dolphins watched anxiously at Matt's feet. He felt they were waiting for him to direct them. George waited 'till they were all in and more or less stable. "Now Tanya, concentrate on the toy, and which dolphin. Don't move at all."

Hoku took off in a flash and brought back the barbell.

"Tell me what you wanted and which dolphin."

"I asked Hoku to get the baton."

Matt and George exchanged glances. "Do it again." George requested.

Pua sped off and returned with the small ring.

"What and who?" Matt asked.

"Pua and the ring; the small one."

"Astounding Tanya. Both times exactly!"

They worked the trick a few more times with the same success rate.

"I don't believe it, Tanya." Matt commented.

"Neither do I," George added.

"I'm not sure I understand either," Tanya looked a little concerned. "It's kind of spooky. They seem to be able to read my mind."

"That's what they are doing, Tanya. You're either very lucky or very privileged, I don't know which."

"Maybe both!" Matt added.

"I'd like you to speak to some of our people in San Diego about this sometime, Tanya. I'm sure when I tell them what I've seen here today they'll want you to visit them at their lab. Could you do that?"

"If it could be set up with my department . . ." The thought pleased Tanya.

"I'll see if I can arrange it then." That pleased George.

"George, it's almost noon. We should get something for lunch and I should check with Bangor again. What do you say?"

"God, is it lunch time already? I had no idea we'd been here for four hours. Lunch sounds good."

"Tanya, how about you?"

"I'll go along with that."

They walked along the float and up the ramp to the pier, then onto the spit. Matt went on ahead to phone Mike. Tanya and George kept on towards Matt's car.

In his office, Matt dialed Bangor. "Mike, how're you coming with the examination?"

"We've got it apart and are in the middle of determining what the different parts do. Analysis of each black box will take some time. We should be in position to start reassembly this afternoon."

"Any idea when it can go back into the water?"

"We're hoping for tomorrow morning, Matt."

"Okay, we'll set up for an early start. Good luck with the rest of it. See you tomorrow."

Matt made another call; this time to Doc Johnson, then joined the others at his car. He filled them in on Mike's progress with the buoy and the fact that it may go back into the water tomorrow.

"I'll have the dolphins ready, Matt. What'd you say we get some chow now?" George looked tired.

Driving away, Matt told them he had invited Doc Johnson to have lunch with them. They drove along the spit and into town to the Castaways Restaurant on Marine Drive

Sitting at a table by the window, they could see the yacht basin and across the water, the Coast Guard base at the end of the long curving Ediz Hook. The burned out hulk of the cruiser Columbine was still tied to the visitor's float in the marina. Matt's thoughts drifted back to the day they brought the cruiser in. Could that have been only eight days ago? It seemed like years. He drifted away mentally as conversation carried on without him.

The dead fish in the water, the cruiser fire, the dead scuba diver and the explosion on the beach all flashed by in his mind as he retraced the events leading up to today. The critical nature of locating the buoys and establishing how they work, sprang to mind. With the Trident sub USS OHIO due to arrive within days, all the buoys must be worked over and replaced quickly. He had no idea the dead fish would be part of a trail leading to international crisis. The thought shocked him. The world of international espionage was not his bag. The whole idea turned him off. The sooner he and his men were clear of the whole rotten mess, the happier he'd be.

There was, however, a good side to all of this. He wouldn't have met Tanya, were it not for the extreme seriousness. And he would certainly not have known about the dolphins either.

The hand on his shoulder brought Matt back to reality. "Matt!" Doc shook him.

"Sorry, I guess I was somewhere else." Matt apologized. "I was going over the events of the past few days."

He introduced Tanya and George with a little background on each of them for Doc's benefit. "Doc's been involved with this from the beginning. I want him to be aboard the cutter as our underwater safety officer when we go out to monkey with the buoys."

"Are you expecting problems, Matt?" George asked.

"We can't be too safe. I'll feel easier with Doc aboard. Replacing the buoy and bringing the others up to reprogram them wouldn't be an easy task."

Until Mike arrived they wouldn't know what had to be done with the buoys. Matt had serious reservations about bringing each one of them up onto his ship. There was no way of knowing what had set the buoys off and he didn't want the back end of his ship blown apart. Nor did he want any more men killed or injured. The group at the table speculated on the arrangements they would have to make when the buoys were retrieved. There wasn't much they could prepare. Mike was the key. They'd have to wait for him.

Tanya mentioned the problem of keeping out of the way of orbiting satellites. This was something they could discuss. The presence of a cutter in the Strait, over their buoys, could attract Russian attention. The whole thing would have to be passed off some way as routine. The less time they spent doing the job, the better off they'd be.

Matt didn't like the requirement to hurry. That's how mistakes happened. Mistakes here could be disastrous. Again they came back to Mike. If he had found a way to turn off the triggers they might have an easy time of it, if not . . . .

Interest turned to the dolphins, and how George would get them to bring the buoys to the cutter. Matt mentioned the first one they'd found and the danger in touching any of them. The stress involved with having it aboard, and during the transfer to the helicopter, was something he could easily do without and he told the rest of them so. He wanted no part of going through the same thing with each of the remaining buoys.

George explained that dolphins would be used again to locate the buoys, and attach a collar and cable to them. The Zodiacs had winches on them and could raise the buoys for transfer to the cutter. The transfer would be the tricky part. They hoped to make electronic adjustments on the fantail of cutter, then put them right back where they came from. This, of course, was pure guess work. They had no idea what Mike would come up with. "It may be that Mike won't be able to find out how to handle them and the only solution would be to destroy them in place. He might also find out how to modify them in place. This last hypothesis had great appeal to Matt. It would be fine with him if they didn't have to come near his ship.

"What about the satellites, Tanya?" George wanted to know.

"We'll keep an eye on the coverage all the time." She explained the coverage, more for Doc's benefit. "Scanners and computers make the job almost routine. We follow all Russian birds, and get special alerts whenever a bird deviates from its regular orbit."

"Why are we concerned about satellites anyway?" Doc asked.

Tanya told him enough about the photographic capabilities of today's satellite technology to answer his question but not enough to compromise security. After all, Doc had no clearance. What he already knew about the buoys was more than he should have known.

*   *   *

After lunch, Matt and Tanya returned to the dolphin pens with George. Doc had to go back to the hospital to gather equipment for tomorrow's trip and to hand off his patients for the day to his partner, Doctor Spees.

They found Pua's behavior almost back to normal, charging around the pen, squeaking and chirping at anyone in sight.

"Seems to be all right now," George observed. "I'll bet it was Tanya."

"Could a person have that kind of effect on a dolphin?" Matt asked.

"Sure can. It's not unusual for them to pick out people they want to be with. If they don't get their way, they have been known to pout and lose their appetites. In a way they're like children."

"Why don't the two of you get your wet suits on and get into the pen with them? I think you'll have an interesting time."

"Can we?" Tanya couldn't hide her excitement.

"I think they'd enjoy your company."

"Great idea George, we'll see if Tanya's able to get close to them."

They hurried up to the cutter and donned their suits, picked up face masks and quickly returned to the pen.

"I don't know if they'll let you wear those masks," George warned.

"Are they that particular?" Tanya asked.

"They may be, they're wary animals. Give it a try, they'll let you know soon enough."

"Okay, George. Maybe Tanya should go in first; they relate to her." Matt was learning quickly how dolphins acted.

"Sure," she said, sitting down, dropping her feet over the side of the float into the pen. The dolphins had moved to the far side of the pool and watched quietly.

"They seem very apprehensive, George, should I go any farther?"

"Take it in slow stages. Let them get used to you for a minute or two."

Tanya moved her feet back and forth in the water, splashing slightly. The dolphins were almost silent, swimming quietly around the far side of the pen. Tanya called softly to them. They responded with clicks and whistles. She called to Pua.

Pua swam closer, and then backed away. Tanya called again. Pua came over to her feet then scurried off again.

"Matt, you get your feet in there too." George directed.

"Are you sure George?" Matt was reluctant, afraid it would foul up Tanya's chances.

"I think it's all right. Give it a try."

He sat beside Tanya and wet his feet. The dolphins continued to circle at the far side.

"Why are they afraid of us now? They've been working with people in the water all along. They weren't scared of us earlier."

"They know their trainers, they don't know you, particularly in wet suits. It could be the masks too."

"Were they as scared of their trainers at first?" Tanya wanted to know.

"They were. It takes time for them to trust strangers."

"They should know us," Matt said, "they were working with us all morning."

"Yes, but you weren't in the water with them and you didn't have the masks then. They may think you could hurt them. They don't know."

"Why don't their trainers make them nervous?" Tanya asked.

"They trust them."

"Can they distinguish us from their trainers, even in these suits?" Matt asked.

"They can identify individuals no matter what they're wearing. They read your body vibrations, not your appearance. They've already identified both of you. They just don't know what to make of you. You haven't been right in the water with them and they're apprehensive. You may be a threat, you may not. They'll decide shortly. Give it a minute."

They sat still while the dolphins swam to and fro.

"They're talking it over with each other. See the way they look over to you, then swim around?"

"I can't hear any talking George. They were making noise before but now they're silent."

"Not silent, Tanya, they're jabbering away. It's just that they're talking in a pitch so high we can't hear it. Call to one of them."

"She did. Hoku broke away and swam over, stopping just short of her feet. His head popped out of the water and he squealed and clicked loudly.

The chatter startled Tanya. "It's almost as though he knew what I said about their not talking. He's showing me he will talk!"

"You're right. That's the sort of thing we're having happen all the time. It can be spooky." George said. He handed Matt a large fish. "Throw this to him, Matt."

Matt tossed the fish toward the upturned head. Hoku's mouth opened and the fish disappeared. Pua swam over now and waited for her fish. George gave one to Tanya. Pua waited, mouth open. Tanya tossed it and Pua squealed as she caught it.

"Reach down now, Tanya, and pat her gently on the snout. You too, Matt."

Tanya touched her and she backed away.

"Call her again."

She did and Pua edged closer, right between Matt and Tanya. Matt rubbed her head and she stayed this time. Hoku, watching this slowly swam over demanding similar attention. Tanya stroked his nose.

"Tanya, slide gently into the water." George said.

She did and the dolphins stayed close, no longer frightened.

"They're curious now. Matt see if you can slide in there too."

He let himself gently into the water and both dolphins disappeared to the other side of the pen.

"Call to Hoku, Tanya."

"Hoku, come!" she said, and Hoku came.

"Stroke his back if you can. He likes that."

She rubbed the soft skin. "Matt, throw that ball for Pua."

Matt picked up the large ball floating by his elbow, and flipped it to the end of the pen. Pua brought it back to Matt. He threw it again. Pua retrieved it again.

The mood was set. The dolphins and their new friends played together for the rest of the afternoon. They'd not had people to play with since they were first captured over a year earlier. Their days were taken up with training. Dolphins being very playful animals made up games whenever the moods strike. To have two different humans to play with was okay with them. Their trainers seldom had time to play with them. Swim and fetch games, of course, were high on their list of favorites.

CHAPTER 17

Tuesday, Day 11, 05:46 hours.

Slender fingers of the rising sun reached out like wands, touching the mountain peaks. Each peak, bathed in golden light, seemed to glow for a moment. A few scattered clouds dotting the blue sky were highlighted by the illuminated tips. A light, off-shore breeze ruffled the flags along Marine Drive while a morning fog hung low over the Strait, the summer sun, not yet burning holes through it to get to the water. By mid morning the fog would be gone.

The incoming tide caused a rip in the water at the spits tip and whirlpools gathered miscellaneous bits of flotsam and jetsam for deposit on some beach miles away. Seagulls, hungry for their days first meal, screeched overhead.

Matt and Tanya drove by Doc's house to give him a ride to the cutter. Doc, carrying a little black bag, waited in front of his brown, shingled bungalow. Matt stopped at the curb and he got in beside Tanya. They drove silently, each deep in thought. Matt, concerned about today's search; Doc thinking about his patient, Walter Parker; and Tanya's mind on the dolphins. Light traffic allowed them to pass quickly through town, and out along Ediz Hook to the Coast Guard base. They got out at the main building and Matt moved his car to the parking lot.

Tanya went in to check her radio equipment. Matt and Doc headed directly for the cutter: Matt to make ready for sea, and Doc to prepare the equipment he would need. Knowing this part of the job would require underwater work, Matt was cautious, careful enough to make sure the twelve man recompression chamber was put aboard. If there were any accidents, he felt more comfortable when it was close at hand. He had made sure his crew secured it well. He had also asked Doc Johnson to come along as his medical officer. Doc went aft to where Matt had put the recompression chamber.

Tanya, satisfied her communications were working properly, walked to the dolphin pens and was waiting when George arrived. He got his crew going preparing the pens for the day's work then walked back to Tanya.

"Morning."

"Good morning, George. What are your men doing?" Tanya's curiosity showed.

"Feeding their pets. If we feed them before we go we'll have one less break while we're out there." he explained. "Here, toss some of these in."

Tanya took some of the fish and threw them to Pua and Hoku, who thrashed about for the spectators, making a big thing out of a normal feeding.

"Showoffs!" George yelled at them.

"Did you get your lab report on the water samples?"

"Yes, Tanya. The coliform level is high. We've got to watch it for a while. The dolphins will be all right if we can keep them out in the strait more often."

"Won't they catch fish on their own when they're let out of the pens?"

"Probably, Tanya, but they have to be fed fairly often when they're penned up. Not enough fish swim into the pens. We don't have to worry about their overfeeding. They know when they've had enough."

"These should keep them going," she said emptying the bucket.

"That's a good breakfast. They think it's great when you feed them, Tanya. They don't act that way with their trainers. We'll have to start paying you to come on a regular basis." George laughed.

"I'd love that, George, but now I guess I've got to go and make some preparations in the radio room, so if you'll excuse me . . . ?" she turned and walked along the float, heading for the ramp to board the cutter.

She found leaving difficult. After the episode yesterday, the dolphins had really caught her interest. She was totally engrossed in them until the cutter's loudspeaker came to life. "Lieutenant Andrushyn, report to the radio room! Lieutenant Andrushyn to the radio room!" She hurried up the ramp and climbed aboard the cutter, then up the ladders to the bridge deck.

Lieutenant, junior grade, Flannigan had been assigned to assist Doc wherever necessary. Doc knew him from the diving lectures the squadron and Coast Guard had given local divers. A knowledgeable and super-safe diving officer, he was capable of taking charge of the work on the outside of the chamber, if it was needed. Doc wanted him on the inside for this trip though. He would operate the chamber himself on the outside.

"Hello, Doc. I hear you're going on a trip with us."

"Don't know what you guys'd do without me along."

"Well, we hope we won't need you."

"I hope so, too. Is everything ready in the chamber?"

"As far's I can see, Doc. Why don't we go through the checklist together?"

"Good idea!"

"We're going down to a maximum depth of 350 feet, Doc. The navy's using their MK 16 units, breathing helium and oxygen."

Doc was familiar with the breathing apparatus. "What's our worst situation, then?"

"A system failure, with no help available."

"Good. We have the pressure and time charts for that?"

"Everything's right here, Doc."

Doc took the metal plaques the charts were printed on, studying the various ascent rates and stopping depths. "How many men are below at one time?"

"Six at most. Two teams of three. Two underwater at any one time with one man to do the surface work. He'll be suited and ready to go under at any sign of trouble. One non-suited man in each boat to run the gas system and its control computer."

"The most we should have in the water is four, with a maximum of, as you said, six."

"Right. It's not likely, but it could happen, Doc."

"That's no problem; we can get more than six into the chamber if we have to. How about your air and gas supply?"

"All topped off.'

The recompression chamber used compressed air to pressurize its interior, while the occupants breathed mixed gasses or plain air from individual masks, one for each so that the breathing gas mixture could be changed as required to suit an individual's need. Gas, for divers having varying degrees of trouble, could be administered separately through the individual masks. The person tending them inside would be supplied with plain air or a mixed gas, as required. All of the masks exhausted to the outside, to prevent a bad mix forming within the chamber.

The chamber itself stood six feet in diameter and eighteen feet in length. Painted white high gloss enamel, the glare from the bright sun bouncing off it made you squint. Inside there were two chambers, first, the airlock section about five feet long, then the main section. A room in the main section held a maximum of twelve people. Fewer, if a stretcher was needed.

Doc climbed through the entrance hatch on the end of the big cylinder to check the four masks in the airlock. They were all clear. Moving into the main section, he clanged the heavy air tight door shut behind him. While checking the twelve masks inside he and the Lieutenant tested the intercoms.

The chamber held three different units. Two loudspeakers, hands-off types and one telephone type for private conversations.

"All intercoms working, Doc. Do you want to test the door seal?"

"Go ahead. Bring it up to about twenty pounds."

Air slowly hissed into the echoing chamber. Doc's ears popped as he watched the pressure gauge come up to the twenty pound mark. "Good! Bleed that off now."

Doc spun the lock as the gauge dropped back onto the bottom peg. Swinging the pressure hatch open, he stepped out. He picked up his medical bag and checked the contents. Then getting back inside, he put it into the medical locker at the far end of the chamber. Coming back to the open hatch, he stepped out into the sunshine and walked around to the control console at the side of the chamber.

There were seven viewing ports along each side of the chamber so that a constant watch could be maintained from the outside in case of emergency. All the valves to control the inside masks and pressurization of the two chambers themselves were located at a central control console. The whole operation ran from this console.

Having someone inside was necessary so they could be right there if anything went wrong, but they couldn't put the doctor inside as anyone inside could become unreliable, succumbing to the same rapture of the deep as the divers. The man in control had to remain sober. Divers have what they called the Martini Scale. Because drinking and diving pressure have similar effects on the human physiology, every 50 feet of depth simulated in the chamber or underwater has the equivalent effect on the body of one martini. Thus, anyone in the chamber at 150 feet could be in the same shape as someone that'd had three martinis. The medical diving officer controlled gas mixtures to individual masks, the intercoms and the pressure within the chamber. It wouldn't do to have a drunk in the chamber, so he remained outside.

Lieutenant Flannigan went through his checklist for the gas supply bottles reading the pressures and cracking each valve in turn.

Tanya, meanwhile, had made contact with Hawaii and received a status up-date on the spy satellites. There had been no indication from satellite orbits that the Russians were aware of what was going on. The satellites were maintaining their routine orbits. Nothing out of the ordinary to report. She briefed Hawaii on their operation for today and asked that they closely monitor the Cosmos birds. Any extra time they could give her in warning would be invaluable to keep them from being discovered.

Matt contacted Mike again to see what progress he had made and an update on their time of arrival. "It looks like about 10:00 hours Matt. We're putting the buoy back together now. All going well, we should load it on the helicopter about 09:15 hours and we'll fly directly to your ship."

Fears of transporting the ever dangerous buoy from the chopper to his ship sprang into his mind. "What about the explosive?" he asked.

"May not be a problem Matt. We've managed to render it harmless from the tamper triggers. We've still got the problem of rough handling though. It'll still require some respect. I'll explain in more detail when I get there later this morning."

The cutter maneuvered near the pier to attach the dolphin pens then headed out to the Strait. Tanya stood by the aft rail where she could see Hoku and Pua swimming along with the ship, contained in their pens. She felt a little closer to them after yesterday's session playing with them.

Slipping slowly past the end of Ediz Hook, the cutter set a course toward the spot where the buoy had been found. Matt's navigation officer vectored their course with information from satellites and GIS.

The heavy rains of spring had brought a lot of silt down from the mountains, which the streams continued to deposit in the ocean. There was still enough coming down, to create a curtain layer that effectively blocked most of the sunlight from water below about 150 feet. Men working below that depth needed high intensity lights. Dolphins, with their echo-location, weren't bothered by the dark. Complaints of the divers during the previous location of the buoys led Matt to bolster their lighting supplies. He had mustered a large variety of underwater lighting equipment, and the divers were able to select the ones best suited for their work.

Navy crews were going to be diving to a possible 350 feet and would use their Mark 16 re-circulating systems, allowing them to transit down and up more quickly without having to worry about nitrogen narcosis.

Standard compressed air tanks are not much good after a depth of about 100 feet. Even then, descent and ascent had to be made in laborious, waiting stages at various levels. Working time on the bottom would be limited to less than five minutes. Plain air couldn't be considered for the job at hand. Mixed gas as provided by the Mk 16 was required.

Cold water in the Strait also had to be considered. A man's system couldn't stand such low temperatures for any length of time. Hot water heated suits were the only way to survive. The Zodiacs had facilities to support divers with this equipment. There was also a lot of gear scattered on the cutter's fantail.

A thirty minute run put the cutter on station where she now rested, idling to hold position in the water, waiting for the helicopter to arrive with the buoy. Matt, Tanya and Doc were standing at the aft rail of the bridge watching as the navy crews made preparations. Zodiacs were in the water beside the pens and the handlers were busy with the dolphins. An array of diving gear and lighting equipment was spread out on the cutter's deck. Men were transferring some of it to the small boats. Tanya could see Pua and Hoku. swimming excitedly round and round within the pens. Handlers called them to the working platform and put their retrieval collars on them as Tanya, Matt and Doc watched.

"What would happen if one of them wearing a collar decided to take off and not come back?" Doc asked.

"You mean would they have these things on them for the rest of their lives?"

"Yes"

"We wondered about that too, Doc. Matt asked George the same question. George told us the collars have a safety release on them similar to a parachute. One good hit and the whole thing springs loose. The dolphins know how to operate these before George allows any of them outside the pens."

"Why don't they get rid of them themselves? I'd think they'd hate to have them on."

"They seem to enjoy wearing them. George isn't sure, but he thinks they consider them a status symbol among the other dolphins. The ones that have been wearing them haven't given any trouble."

"I'd never thought of it that way, Tanya. I guess I'm thinking it would restrict freedom. If it was me, I'd want to get rid of it as quickly as I could."

George walked over after catching the last part of the conversation.

"That's a typically human reaction, Doc, and it's understandable, particularly from someone in a caring profession. You've got to remember, though, they don't think the same way, or have the same values as us. Freedom to them might have an entirely different meaning. They don't have to worry about where their next meal's coming from or what they must do to keep their family fed and warm the way we humans do. All of this is provided for them."

"It's hard not to think of them as having some human values after yesterday, George." Matt added.

"I know. You've had a limited exposure to them and already you feel that way. How do you think the people who work and live with them feel?"

"Pretty tough to deal with, George." Matt had drifted into the same pitfall as some of those who work closely with dolphins. "I see what you meant yesterday when you told us about, what did you call it . . . ?"

"Anthropomorphosis, thinking of them as having human characteristics."

"Now I can better see what you meant. I don't think I did yesterday."

"No, I can understand that, Matt. I had a difficult time when I started working with them, too. It's something you have to keep reminding yourself of. They become 'family' in no time at all."

Divers in their suits waited at the stern for the helicopter to deliver the first buoy. George had been in contact with Bangor to find out what would be required of the dolphins and underwater teams in re-setting this buoy. Mike told him about the programming band and the special equipment they had hastily thrown together.

George's men would use the dolphins to locate the buoys then guide Mike's men to the markers. They'd reprogram the buoy, and remove the marker. The whole operation should take about half an hour for each buoy. George relayed this information to Matt.

"We should be done before 17:00 hours at that rate George, that is if the men and dolphins can work that long."

"Not a problem with the dolphins, and I think the men can do it, too."

They heard the helicopter long before they saw it. Coming out of the early morning sun, it was almost on them when they spotted it.

The cutter's public address system barked, "Incoming chopper. Prepare to assist. Landing crews to your stations. Non-essential personnel clear the heli-deck." The wind was from the east so they were in the proper position to take the landing. The chopper swung out to the south and began its descending approach from the stern. They watched as the pilot jockeyed the big craft onto the cutter's deck. A clean landing by a well practiced pilot.

Mike Chambers and his crew scrambled out. Mike helped direct the crew unloading their gear, then joined Matt, Tanya and Doc at the port rail.

He explained the method they'd have to use to get to and reprogram the buoys. He told them essentially the same things he had told George earlier that morning.

The underwater crews went to work as soon as the buoy had been placed on the Zodiac. Two dolphins from the starboard pen, Pua and Hoku, were released. They chased after the boat as it skimmed away from the cutter.

Matt's navigation officer stood on the bridge deck, ready to signal the boat crew when they were over the co-ordinates where the buoy was originally picked up. Dolphins weren't needed to replace the buoys, they were along to be reminded of what they were supposed to do with the next ones.

On a signal from the bridge the cutter came to a stop in the water. Two splashes indicated frogmen were in the water and the buoy eased gently off the deck and over the stern into the water to begin its descent to the ocean floor. George had been timing the operation. The dolphins surfaced and returned to the cutter in four and a half minutes, the divers were back in six. Total time elapsed to re-place the buoy, eleven minutes.

This buoy of course took less time than the next ones would need. This one had already been programed. Total time for the others would likely be closer to thirty minutes each. They had to be raised a bit off the bottom so that the programing band could be wrapped around them. The actual transfer of data into the buoys required only about thirty seconds. Mike's men would then remove the band and marker, putting the buoy back where they found it, on the bottom. Getting the cutter into position would take the longest time. If it was not needed to transport the electronic gear and to locate the precise buoy positions, the job would have been simpler and quicker to do with Zodiacs.

George suggested to Matt that as soon as the buoy position had been determined and the boats were on site, the cutter could be positioned at the next site. Matt agreed. It could reduce the time needed by a considerable amount.

With the first buoy in place, the cutter was on its way to site number three. The dolphins were swimming free during this part of the job, and they thoroughly enjoyed themselves.

"Will they stay close by, George?" Tanya asked.

"They're pretty good. They usually return to the Zodiac when their handlers call. Sometimes they're a little slow, like kids. If they're playing or run across something that catches their interest, they can be frustrating. Call as we might, they come when they're ready, not before."

"Have you ever lost any this way?"

"Oh, sure Doc. We can expect one or two a year. We call them 'defectors'," he said with a grin, "they just disappear."

"Ever find them again?"

"None so far, although we think we had one return in San Diego. We weren't sure though. He came back near the pens but never close enough to make a positive identification."

The cutter reached the site of buoy number three against a freshening wind, holding her position with main engines and bow thruster. The first boat and its dolphins, Pua and Hoku, sped off to locate the marker. Tanya stood at the rail watching them go. "When they located the buoys originally, how did they mark them, George?"

"They put a clamp around the buoy and tied on a float with a thin cable. There was enough cable to allow the float to rise to about thirty feet below the surface. Why do you ask?"

"When they monkey with the clamp, is there any chance it might set off the explosives?"

"Possibly. I don't know for sure. You should check with Mike, if you really want to know."

Tanya thought about this for a while, mulling in her mind the hazard to dolphins and, of course to the divers, too.

The Zodiac crew signaled a contact, and the second boat with two dolphins, Frankie and Johnnie, sprinted to join them.

George called Matt on the bridge using the ship's intercom. "We're ready here, Matt. We can head for a spot between sites 4 and 5."

"On our way, George."

The cutter's engines throbbed, kicking out a white froth from the stern. Veering left and gathering speed, Matt set course for an imaginary dot somewhere about four miles ahead. Twelve minutes later they were in position to direct the lead Zodiac with Pua and Hoku, who were circling to the south of the cutter. When they were near the position, the cutter signalled and the dolphins began their search. By the time the second Zodiac had reached the spot, the marker had been located and Mike's men went down immediately. The first boat turned and headed toward the next site two miles north.

"Lt. Andrushyn to the communication center," the PA barked . . .

Tanya hurried across the flight deck and up the ladder to the radio room, saying as she went, "I hope this isn't what I think it is."

Oahu had spotted a bird boosting out of orbit. She called Matt on the intercom. "Captain, stand by for a possible low pass."

"We've got two boats out and divers down. How much time do we have?"

"I'll check, hold on." In the radio room, she returned to the radio.

Matt, on the flight deck, called George over. "Well, George this is likely to set us back a couple of hours. I don't know if we have that kind of time."

"Yeh, we're going to be hard pressed to fix all these buoys in time as it is. We'll probably be out here most of the day."

"Maybe into the night, too." Matt added in a discouraged tone.

Tanya discussed the overhead time with Morgan in Hawaii.

"Maneuvering boosters have just been fired. It'll take a few minutes to determine the power and duration of the 'burn'." Morgan Snellert knew that the satellites position, relative to the earth when the boosters fired, could give an indication of where the perigee would be. He used this knowledge to calculate where this particular bird was headed. However the duration of burn and the power used also had to be factored into the calculations. It takes a computer to handle these data with any speed.

"I understand," Tanya knew what Morgan had to do. She could almost see him sitting at the computer console, watching a bright blip moving across the screen.

"Data are going into the computer now, Tanya."

"Captain, we're still waiting for orbital information, but I'd suggest you alert the boats to be ready to move."

"Will do, Lieutenant."

"Hear that, George?"

"Got it, Matt. Boats one and two make ready to return to the cutter on notice."

Watching the water surface, Matt saw the diver's heads break surface and the divers swimming toward their boats.

"Firing's completed now, Tanya—beginning calculation—. Low pass over Puget Sound in eighty two minutes."

"Is that far enough away to miss us, Morgan?"

"Hold for one—, the scanning swath is over one hundred miles wide and the bird is on a heading of 300 degrees True. The beam spread will take you in. Better cover yourselves."

"Okay, will do. We'll stay in contact until the bird passes over."

She leaned over and pushed the intercom button. "The bird will be in position to see us in—" she checked the large clock on the bulkhead,—" seventy nine minutes. Better clear the area."

"Thank you, Lieutenant." He swung around to face George. "I guess we'd better bring them in."

The divers were already aboard their boats and, on signal from George, they weighed anchor and were soon on their way to the cutter.

"I'll let you know when we're free of the prying eye, George. I'm going to move the cutter a few miles north."

Matt grabbed the rail, swinging himself up the stair to the flight deck then walked along to the deckhouse, stopping by the communication center on his way to the bridge. "Tanya to keep me posted so we can return as soon as possible."

Entering the bridge he had the cutter begin a short excursion toward Victoria, to the north.

Matt returned to the radio room. "Where is it now?" he asked Tanya.

"Probably over India about now, or somewhere in that area. It'll be fairly low. Once it gets over Antarctica, it'll rise to its apogee, and then swoop down right over us. It'll be here in about—let's see—forty two minutes."

"How long do we have to wait after it's passed?"

"Two or three minutes should be enough. Why, are you getting anxious?"

"I guess I am. We've just lost two hours of daylight search time and we're already pushing a tight schedule. I'm afraid if we have to go too fast well are asking for accidents. Besides, the longer we're out here monkeying with these buoys, the more chance the Russians will have to catch us. I'm going aft to the fantail; call me if anything changes with the satellite."

"I will."

Standing at the aft rail, Mike watched the southern shore disappearing in the mid-day haze.

Matt joined him. "What do you think this bird is doing? Can it be working with the buoys?"

"I hope not, Matt. Some of the buoys are reprogrammed, others aren't. If it tries to interrogate all of them, it'll get nothing but confusion. Why don't you check with Tanya and see if she knows the operating envelope of this particular bird?"

Matt returned to the communication center and posed the question to Tanya.

"This is a photo bird, Matt. I don't think it has the capacity to contact the buoys. I'll double check with Morgan. He'll know for sure."

She asked Oahu. "This bird can only see, not talk," came the reply.

"Thank God." Matt keyed the intercom to the fantail. "Mike—, I think we're okay. This bird has only photo capability."

"That's a little easier to take, Matt." Mike breathed a sigh of relief.

The satellite passed and they resumed the search mission.

*   *   *

All of the buoys in this 'fence' had been taken care of by 13:00 hours. Boats and crews were all aboard the cutter and she headed for the smaller second 'fence' some 40 miles to the east.

Matt turned the bridge over to his first officer and made his way aft to the radio room to see what Tanya was up to, and get an update on satellite activity. She was at the control desk talking to Hawaii when he entered the radio room. He watched as she cleared with her tracking station and turned the control desk back to his communications officer.

"Everything's all right so far, Matt. All birds are orbiting normally."

"That's good news. Another couple of hours to go and we'll be finished here. I'll be glad when it's all over."

"Me, too. We've been lucky so far. No more injuries or deaths and best of all, I think, so far we've been able to fool the Russians."

"We're on our way to the next set. It'll take a while, what'd you say about something to eat?"

"Timing's good, mister. I've completed my report. Oahu'll get in touch with us if there's any change. I've got some time off, d'ya know a good spot to eat?"

"I've got a place in mind. If you'll follow me, I'll take you there."

"If you mean the mess deck, I've seen their menu and it has some interesting items. Lead on."

They stopped by sick bay to see if Doc could join them. He could and did.

As lunch finished, Matt noticed the rhythm of the engines change. "We must be at the narrows. I'd better check in at the bridge. If you'll excuse me . . . . ?"

George stood up to leave. "I'd better get back to the fantail, my divers are getting ready."

Tanya stood up, too. "George, mind if I come along with you?"

"No. Come on. Why don't you get into your wetsuit? We'll be finishing the site work with Pua and Hoku earlier than the other two. They'll be back in the pens while the other crew is wrapping up the underwater work. Maybe you can get into the water with your friends."

"Oh, George, could I? I'd like to see if I can do some more things with them."

They left the mess at the same time as Matt and Doc. Tanya detoured to her cabin to change while George walked directly to the dolphin pens at the aft end of the cutter.

Matt cleared his duties on the bridge then strolled aft along the flight deck, one deck above where George worked with his men. He watched the crews placing harnesses on the dolphins. With that chore done, the pen doors opened to free the dolphins. Tanya appeared at the lower rail and disappeared over the side, emerging again on the float of the starboard pen. She arrived just as the pen gate swung open. Pua and Hoku bounced out of the pen and darted about near the Zodiac. They saw Tanya and acknowledged with bobbing heads and a few loud clicks.

Matt noticed that Tanya was prepared. She wore her wrist depth gauge and a sheathed knife on her calf.

The Zodiac took off west to locate the first buoy and the dolphins scrambled after it like children at play. Tanya prepared her tanks but didn't put them on. No sense hanging the heavy tanks on too soon. The dolphins would be a while at each of the three sites before returning.

"Matt yelled down, "Watch the tide. Don't get too far from the ship. You be careful now."

"I'm not going in. I'm going to wait for the dolphins to return and join them in the pen. I don't want to get caught in the current."

"That's a good idea. We don't want you to go missing."

Matt's concern was not with Tanya's diving ability. She'd had plenty of experience. He was concerned about the footing on the float; it could be slippery. He wanted no accidents.

Doc came up from the fantail to see what all the shouting was about. Leaning on the rail beside Matt, asked, "How deep is it here?"

"I'd say close to 200 feet give or take ten. It can go to 250 in places though."

"That's deep enough to get into serious trouble."

"Not for these divers. They're all well trained, besides they're wearing hot suits and breathing mixed gas. They'll be all right."

The Zodiac located the first buoy and on signal, the second Zodiac took off to do its job. The first boat now crossed the cutter's stern heading for site number two. They watched the dolphins bouncing ahead of the boat, obviously enjoying the game. Tanya watched as they leaped and darted around the boat.

Travelling close to half a mile past the cutter and on signal from the bridge, they cut their motors, drifting to a stop. Handlers directed the dolphins to start their search and they disappeared below the water.

It seemed no time at all, when one of the animals surfaced in frenzy, thrashed, head bobbing around the boat for a few seconds then was gone again. The water foamed from the strong agitation. Tanya saw the display and heard the accompanying shrieks from the dolphin.

She asked George, "What was that all about?"

"I don't know. I don't like the look of it though."

The water stilled around the boat. "Where'd he go?"

Seconds passed.

Suddenly, beside the pen, Hoku broke the surface squealing and clicking in panic, startling Tanya. She raced along the float to the end by Hoku. "What is it?" she yelled. "Hoku, tell me what it is!"

Hoku continued to squeal and thrash. Tanya reached out to touch him. He moved closer to the float and calmed down just a bit. Tanya held the harness and rubbed his nose.

"Where's Pua?"

Tanya knew something serious had happened. She had no idea what. There must be trouble with Pua. That's all she could think of. She must help! Quickly she threw the air tanks over her back, snapped the harness straps together and cracked the valve at the same time wetting the mask.

"What are you doing? George yelled.

"Pua's in trouble. Trapped in fishing nets. I've got to help her," she yelled back. "Hoku will take me to her."

"Stop. Don't go . . . ." But George's warning came too late. She had grabbed Hoku's harness and dropped from sight in a flash.

"What are they doing?" Matt called down from the flight deck.

"Christ, Matt, she's gone crazy. Says Pua's in trouble. She's going down to help.

"Oh, my God. Doc. Get the chamber ready. She's only got air in those tanks. She can't stand too much depth. George, get the men over from the boat and have them go down." Matt flew down the ladder to the fandeck.

"They need the dolphins to locate Pua."

"Then get the other Zodiac over here fast."

There was no need to call the other boat. The dolphins were already aware of the situation and were half way to the first boat while Matt talked. Pua's underwater distress calls had travelled to the other dolphins in no time at all. George saw this and contacted the first boat by radio, to tell them what had happened. "We don't know what the problem is, but we think Pua is in trouble. When the dolphins get there, let them take you to Hoku and Tanya. You'll never find them otherwise."

"Roger, we're waiting now," came the reply.

Maintaining his presence of mind, Matt had punched the timer on his watch. Knowing how long Tanya had been down could be important. They'd know how deep she had gone by the tattle-tale marker on her wrist depth gauge. All they could do now was watch and wait. The dolphin's descent rate was more than a scuba diver can take. Tanya knew that. Where was her logic? The pressure build up on her ears would likely burst the drums. Just great. He chastised himself for her actions. He ran across the flight deck and down the access ladder to the fantail where Doc and Lieutenant Flannigan stood by the waiting recompression chamber.

"All ready?"

"All we can do is done, now we wait" Doc answered.

Matt directed his crew to prepare the basket stretcher.

"Hook it onto the crane and drop it over the side by the starboard pen." He went back to Doc.

"What's the worst that could happen?"

"Lung collapse if she goes deep enough, but we don't know how deep Hoku'll take her.

"Jesus, Doc, the deepest water here is 250 feet. She shouldn't go lower than 150 feet on compressed air. Even if she exceeds 100 feet, we'll have problems. The dolphin will take her straight down, too. Her ears may give her trouble. She'd better keep them clear."

"Going down's not what I'm worried about, Matt, it's coming up!"

"I know, Doc, but there's nothing we can do now, except wait."

"Lieutenant, what do your charts say about how much time she can spend at 200 feet?"

"On compressed air, practically none"

Stark reality struck Matt full force. Tanya might die. If she went too deep or stayed too long, it could finish her. The dolphins had no way of knowing this. They could go below 500 feet if they wanted to.

The navy divers, on mixed helium and oxygen, often dive below 600 feet and because of their computer controlled breathing mixture, had no restrictions on how fast they could go down or up. Tanya, with a demand type air supply, would be essentially out of air at 200 feet because the mixture carried too little oxygen content. Nitrogen content became the villain. All this ran at high speed through Matt's mind. It seemed certain that she would have nitrogen narcosis, the dreaded 'bends'. Any other damage, they could only speculate.

"What the hell happened, George?"

"I'm not sure, Matt. She yelled something about nets and dove in. I think Pua's caught in a net."

What's a net doing on the bottom?" Matt found it difficult to stay still. He paced back and forth along the rail.

"They get snagged and the fishermen abandon them. Too expensive to bring them up, besides they'd likely be torn to bits anyway. Not salvageable."

Matt looked at his watch. Six minutes had elapsed. The divers from boat one and dolphins from boat two, only now, got together. The divers splashed onto the water, heading down. Seconds went by like minutes to Matt. They were taking far too long.

"What can she do at that depth, Lieutenant?"

"Not much. If she's strong and in good shape, she may do some work. It's more likely she'll be disoriented or dizzy by the time she reaches 200 feet. I don't know, sir."

George added, "she didn't take a light. She'll have to work in the dark. If Pua is in a net, she could probably free her by feel. She only has to cut the net in a few strategic places, if she has the strength. Besides, she could easily get tangled herself."

Matt didn't want to hear that. "How about the ascent, Doc, will she lose consciousness?"

"Your guess is as good as mine, Matt. It depends on too many factors. How deep. Her physical shape, her experience, how long she's down. All these are unknowns. We'll have to wait and see."

"George, will the dolphins bring her up?" Matt began to show signs of panic, an action unknown to him up to now.

"Probably Matt. In fact we'd better hope so. The divers can't make it as fast as the dolphins."

"What happens if she can't free Pua? Will the dolphins stay down?" Matt struggled to gather himself together.

"Not likely, they'll be running low on air themselves and come up to breathe. The divers will stick with it."

Matt checked his watch. Seven and a half minutes. "Too long, too long," he muttered.

A dolphin broke the surface near the stern of the cutter. It had a diver with it. "Wire cutters." he yelled. George threw him a line with the tool tied onto it. The diver disappeared.

Thirty seconds later a second dolphin burst to the surface near the pen. It had Tanya in tow, barely conscious. They scrambled to the float where anxious hands raised her onto the stretcher. In one sweep the crane operator had her on the way up, landing on the deck beside the recompression chamber.

Tanya did not move. Her breathing shallow, panting. Other than that, nothing. Doc quickly unfastened the mask from her face. Blood appeared on the glass, not a good sign. He mentioned it to Flannigan.

The chamber stood ready, outer door gaping, stretcher slide rail fitted to the chamber ready for the victim. Time now their enemy, Doc unhooked the cables from the stretcher. He and Lt. Flannigan carried her to the slide and pushed her right through the air lock into the large inner chamber. Lieutenant Flannigan scrambled in behind her.

Doc removed the sliding rail for the stretcher. Lt. Flannigan clanged the heavy inner door shut like a steel trap as Doc started compressed air hissing through the pressurization valve into the chamber. Needles began dancing on the control console gauges in front of Doc as he began the pressure sequence.

Inside, the Lieut. covered Tanya with a blanket to retain what body heat she still retained. The increasing pressure elevated the temperature in the chamber as it climbed. He began his assessment examination. Still unconscious, Tanya continued to cough and choke. She moaned, arms and legs twitching in fits. No vomit appeared so she had apparently kept her mask and mouthpiece in place and hadn't swallowed any salt water. No easy task considering the speed at which the dolphin must have transported her down and up. Insuring her throat was clear he slapped the chamber mask over her nose and mouth and yelled into the intercom for oxygen from Doc.

Doc, anticipating the call, had the gas valve open as the mask hit her face. Lieutenant Flannigan donned a mask that gave him normal air.

Outside, Doc asked, "How long did she have at the bottom Matt?"

"Twelve and a half minutes, Doc."

"Hear that, Lieutenant?"

"Yes!" He checked her wrist depth gauge. It showed 198 feet. "Navy table 5, Doc." He referred to the US Navy recompression table for "pain only" decompression sickness. That required a total elapsed time in the chamber of 135 minutes. They were going down to the equivalent of 60 feet at a descent rate of 25 feet per minute, to start. That took 2.4 minutes. It seemed like forever to Matt as he stood, helpless, beside the chamber.

Can't you hurry it up a bit, Doc?"

"There's no way to rush it, Matt. We've got to go through the proper sequence and we've got only one try."

"What the hell do you mean one try?" Matt was shaken.

"I mean if we don't clear her blood of nitrogen on the first sequence she could die before we can re-sequence. We've got one chance to do it right. If we miss . . . ." Doc went back to his gauges

Reaching the 60 foot level, he set his timer to 20 minutes. Tanya would be on pure oxygen for the first period.

The Lieut. inside continued his check, scanning her skin color. The slight blue tinge of cyanosis appeared under her fingernails and around her mouth, (what he could see around the mask). He recognized the early signs of death. As the pure oxygen poured into her body, he watched her color closely, looking for any change. He checked her pulse rate. Her heart raced. He didn't bother to count. Instead, he opened the top of her wet suit and taped a transmitter to her chest, pressing on with the examination. Doc could check her heart rate on the scope outside. Matt continued to pace.

Still on the stretcher, Flannigan rolled her onto her left side, elevated her lower body and removed the scuba tanks. A trickle of blood escaped from her ear. He made a mental note and carried on, flicking the flashlight across her dilated eyes. No response.

A loud commotion over the stern attracted Matt. Three dolphins swam around the starboard pen carrying on loud and continuing conversation. "Where's Pua?" he yelled down to George.

"Over at this end Matt."

He looked down to the float where Pua was being held in the water by two trainers. She had cuts across her back and along her head. Matt tried to imagine what she had gone through. The wounds had bled some but were now sealing and the healing process beginning. She moved in the water very slowly; tail barely swinging from side to side. The handlers, talking to her and stroking her back, calmed her. George prepared a syringe of antibiotics. She'd need the help of his medicine to fight off infection. One problem dolphins in captivity had was a loss of resistance to normal illnesses.

Back at the chamber, Doc called to Matt. "She's coming around."

Matt closed the distance to the chamber in long running strides.

Peering in the viewing port, he could see that Tanya had her eyes open but lay quite still. "Lieutenant, can she talk?"

"Not yet."

Matt heard him asking her questions. Who she was? What day was it? Where was she? There was no response.

"Only been twelve minutes, Matt."

"Shouldn't there be more recovery by now?" Doc felt Matt's distress.

"Not necessarily. She's had a rough time. Give it a few minutes."

"How much longer at this pressure?"

"Eight minutes, then she goes on air for five minutes, then another twenty minutes on oxygen. After that we start to reduce the pressure."

"How long after that?"

"We come down a foot a minute to thirty feet, then onto air again for five minutes. Back onto oxygen for twenty then back to air for five. The final drop at a foot a minute to zero will take thirty minutes."

"When will we know if she's all right?"

"We'll have to do tests over the next couple of days but we should have a good idea in a few hours."

"How can someone so full of life just lie there?" Matt hovered close to the chamber, while the work on the buoys continued. Crews, out with two dolphins located the buoys while Pua and Hoku stayed in the pen. Communicating constantly, Hoku never left Pua's side. Their 'talk' stayed at a frequency level above anything humans could hear but George could tell they were indeed conversing.

There were two buoys left to modify, then this phase would be over. Two fences they had found would now be desensitized.

The two dolphins out working now found their role changed slightly but were able to cope with the new job. They now had to locate the buoys as well as guide Mike's divers to them for reprograming. Their squeaking noises told the handlers they were in touch with Pua all the time.

The last thing anyone wanted was to have another accident with a net. Matt mulled the incident over in his mind. Why didn't the dolphins 'see' the net in the first place? He climbed down the ladder and hurried over to talk with George.

"How did she get tangled in the net in the first place? I thought they had a good sonar system."

"They have, Matt. Unfortunately the net Pua hit was made of monofilament nylon. It has the same density as sea water. Remember I told you about their ability to identify objects by determination of its density?"

"They vibrate it with sound and measure the vibrating frequency. Yes, I remember."

"Well the monofilament vibrates at the same frequency as water. This makes the net essentially invisible to them."

"How can they protect themselves against this danger?"

"They can't."

"My god." Matt had trouble with this. "How long could she last before she drowned?"

"Depends on depth and how the dolphin prepared for the dive. If they know how long they're going to be down and how deep, they can take a full load of air into their diving chambers. If they're going down in a shallow dive they take in less air. It all depends on how they prepare. But the bottom line, if they load to the maximum, is only 15 or 20 minutes"

"How often do they run into nets down there?"

"Too often. You dive and are involved with other divers. You must have had a case where a diver has been trapped in a net."

"Yes, I have, but I guess I had in mind that dolphins could steer clear of the nets."

"Matt." Doc called. "Come up here."

He scampered up the ladder and over to Doc.

"She's coming around. Not completely but she's responding to the oxygen."

Matt stared through the port. All he could see was the back of Lieut. Flannigan. He moved along to the next port. Tanya's eyes were open but staring blankly at some spot in space.

"Tanya. Tanya." Lieut. Flannigan tried to get her attention. "TANYA" he shouted. Her hearing presented a problem.

Slowly she drawled "y e e e s . . . ?"

"Where are you?"

"Hmmm?"

"Tanya, Where are you?"

"Pulse rate still high, breathing slightly above normal."

"Pua?" She gasped.

"Tanya,"

"Wha a a, Where . . . ?" She tried to roll over and sit up. Lieut. Flannigan held her down.

"Hold it there for a minute or two." He didn't want the blood rushing from her head. "Tanya, grab my arm." He held his arm out for her. She put her fingers around his wrist.

"Squeeze as hard as you can." there was little pressure.

"Ease your head up." She sat up on one elbow. "Oh . . . My head. Hurts." she said between clenched teeth. Her eyes blinked uncontrollably as he checked her pupils with the flashlight. The pupils were dilating and contracting in response to the bright white environment inside the chamber.

He moved over to her ears. "Hold still now." The left ear drum appeared ruptured. Blood had been trickling from it, the right ear was still intact. Her breathing gradually stabilized.

"I want to sit up."

"Okay but do it slowly." He helped her up. Her head pounded, she looked around perplexed. "Where am I?" The surroundings were strange to her.

"In the recompression chamber."

"I can't hear you. Speak louder."

He yelled, "You're in the recompression chamber."

"How long have I been here? Pua! Where's Pua?" Her voice showing panic.

"In her pen, thanks to you." it was Doc's voice.

"Doc, that you?"

"Yes, it's me, Matt's here too."

"Matt. I'm glad you're there. I had thoughts of never seeing you again!"

"Hi. How're you feeling?"

"Terrible. Like I've been used for a punching bag. Head hurts, chest tight and sore; feel so weak." She started to cough and there was a show of blood.

"Enough talking for a while." Doc commanded. "Lie down again, Tanya, we've got a ways to go here. You may as well get comfortable," he added, knowing there'd be little comfort for her in the next couple of days.

"Pua.?" she whimpered as she slid down again.

"Pua is recovering, too. We think she'll be okay." Matt informed her. "She's cut up pretty badly and is very subdued. The handlers are attending to her right now.

"Didn't know I'd be going down that deep. Guess I didn't have time to think."

"Your quick action probably saved Pua's life. We were concerned about yours for a time though!"

"Rest for a bit while we bring you back up to 30 feet. It'll take thirty minutes, so you'll have some rest time."

Her head throbbed, and her eyes flickered, barely able to focus. "Things getting fuzzy again," she said and drifted back into unconsciousness.

Matt asked Doc to cut the intercom so they could talk without being heard inside. Doc flipped three switches and asked, "What's up?"

"I want to know how bad she really is."

"From the initial signs, not too good. Although her response is improving and the oxygen seems to be effective."

"That's not what I mean, Doc. Her lungs have been ruptured. What about embolization?"

There it was out in the open. The dreaded air pockets in her system. Quick silent killers. Alive one moment, dead the next. Just that fast and there was nothing they could do. They both knew the danger. They were doing everything they could. Repressurization would hold the threat to a minimum but if the killer bubbles were there, little could be done. Medically they had to take each step in order of criticality, treating the greatest danger first then the next most important and on down the line until everything that could be done was taken care of.

She should have been staged during ascent, but if she had, she would have been out of air and dead before she reached the top. Now that she was on top the next step was to pour in pure oxygen and get rid of the painful and destructive nitrogen. With that taken care of they checked her other problems, trying to bring her to consciousness so she could tell them where she hurt. At any of these levels there was a grave danger of an embolism breaking away and flowing to the brain or heart. If the pleural cavity had ruptured there could be air trapped in her chest. That could spread to her throat and neck area. She had no obvious swelling of the throat, so there was hope the pleural cavity had not burst. Time would tell. Eliminating nitrogen was the main task at hand and they were doing all they could in that area.

Doc hit the intercom switches again and barked, "Time to go onto air, Lieutenant." He valved in the air to Tanya's mask. "We're at thirty feet. Starting the time count for five minutes."

Tanya stirred, tried to sit up.

"How're you feeling now, Tanya?"

"What's that?"

Doc repeated the question, shouting now.

"Sore. My head feels like it has a steel band around it. Can't hear very well."

"Other than that, how's your eyesight?"

To function properly, the eyes require considerable oxygen. If the lungs break down and reduce the amount of oxygen available to the body, the eyes suffer early, as does the brain. That's why Tanya's responses were so significant. They gave an indication of the state of her lung damage.

"Having trouble focusing. Can only see things in front of me."

'Okay, take it easy for now. How does it feel to breathe air?" He was still yelling. Lt. Flannigan's ears were beginning to hurt now from the hollering.

"Different," she said, "feel a bit woozy still."

"That's understandable." Doc noted.

"You've got another minute on air, then back to oxygen for twenty minutes. You're at a thirty foot equivalent."

"She seems to be coming around well, Matt. The internal damage is not obvious. Her faculties are responding as they should. I wouldn't guess at the lung damage though."

"How do you determine the extent of that, Doc?"

"We'll have to do that at the hospital as soon as we're clear of the chamber. That's something you could do. Call the chopper out to transfer us and have them get the two-man chamber over to the hospital." Doc figured that would keep Matt's mind occupied for a while. He didn't want him to be standing around the chamber. It frustrated Doc not to have any answers for Matt, but without special equipment, he could only guess. He'd be glad to get her back to the hospital.

"I'll get on that right away, Doc!" He departed for the communication room.

"Lieutenant, see if you can find out what's going on in her lungs."

The Lieut. dug the stethoscope out of the bag and laid back the blanket. He unzipped the top of Tanya's wetsuit and began probing her back, listening for signs of fluid. Starting with the right side he listened to half a dozen spots then tried a few on her chest

Tanya had drifted back into unconsciousness; still he used the phone rather than the intercom. "Right side is marginal, Doc. I'll try the left."

He repeated the check. This time he took longer at the lower portion of her chest. "Nothing happening here, Doc. Not even gurgling."

"I was afraid of that, probably filled with blood. Elevate her feet some more."

He linked the end of the stretcher chain higher up toward the top of the chamber, and then went back to her left chest. "There's movement now. It's still loose. She'll be able to cough it up later, I'm sure."

"Don't force it now. The tissue's insecure. Probably do more damage."

"Right, Doc, I'll let the feet down a bit."

"How's the skin color?"

"Looking better. Taking on a little color. Oxygen must be getting to her extremities now." He checked her finger and toenails. "Looking real good, Doc. Back to pink."

"Fine. We've got another eight minutes on oxygen then back to air for five minutes. After that it's oxygen for thirty minutes as we bring you both to surface pressure at a rate of one pound per minute. Can you hang on?"

"No sweat, Doc."

Doc called George over. "We've got to get her back to hospital in another thirty five minutes and I've got to go with her."

"I understand, Doc."

"What I'm getting at is Lieutenant Flannigan will be the only medical officer aboard. Your divers will have to be on the surface when we leave."

"US Navy regulations about diving and medical attendants?"

"That's right, George."

"Hopefully we'll be finished by then. The crews are at the last site now. With any luck we'll all be back aboard before you leave. I'll see what's left to do and speed them up if possible." He went back down to the aft deck to radio the Zodiac.

Doc began to think about the regulation that placed him outside the chamber rather than inside where he dearly wanted to be. The man inside could experience the same pressure problems as the victim. He wouldn't know but the effect on him could distort his mental capability. He could be in as much trouble as the person he was trying to help and wouldn't have any idea. He could become irrational. No, the one in control had to be insulated from the pressure. It was a good regulation.

"Going over to air." He announced.

"Roger."

Tanya stirred a bit and her eyes opened. The change to air had shaken her senses. "What're you doing?"

"We're going to begin coming up to surface pressure in five minutes." he said.

"A little louder, please."

He hadn't realized he was back to talking normally. "How do you feel now?" This was louder.

"Head hurts, pain in chest!"

"Okay, got that. How're your knees and shoulders?"

She moved her arms and legs "Seem okay. No pain."

"Good." He checked her eyes. Pupils had returned to normal and response to the flashlight was looking a whole lot better. The temperature in the chamber dropped as the pressure came down. Lt. Flannigan, finding it pretty warm for a while, now became more comfortable.

George's crews returned to the cutter and put the dolphins in their pen. They hurried up onto the deck asking how Tanya was doing. George could only relay what Doc had told him.

They knew what she was going through. Most of them had also suffered to some degree from the water. They busied themselves stowing gear and equipment.

The ship's PA announced, "Helicopter will be here in fifteen minutes, sir." Matt acknowledged from the remote station at the stern.

CHAPTER 18

Tuesday, Day 11, 15:00 hours.

Matt returned to the flight deck as the chopper neared. Anxious to see Tanya safely in the hospital, he made sure everything would go without a hitch.

"All hands prepare for incoming chopper," The PA startled Doc. Landing crews scurried to their stations as the big white machine hovered over the deck. A lot of noise, wind, and the smell of jet fuel wafted through the air. Matt crossed over to the recompression chamber as the chopper touched down.

"Doc, they'll have the small recompression chamber at the hospital before you get there. This chopper's standing by to go any time you say."

"Great, Matt. We've got another four minutes to go here before we're back to surface pressure. Tanya's awake again, if you want to talk to her.

Matt hurried over to a port, looking into the chamber. He could see Tanya's face behind Lieutenant Flannigan, but that was about all he could see. The blanket still covered her.

"How's your head?"

"Oh, Matt, it's sore." She managed a slight grin, or was it a grimace?

"Won't be long now, we'll have you in the hospital for some rest."

"What about monitoring for satellites? Who's going to look after that?"

"Don't you worry about it. Our communications people have that in hand. Anyway we're almost through. We'll be heading in as soon as the underwater crews get everything battened down."

"What are they going to say in Oahu?"

"About what?"

"My being so stupid."

"Well, if they don't give you a medal, you should apply for a transfer to another navy," Matt said, only half joking.

"They'll be mad that I went into the water in the first place."

"When they know the whole story, you'd better receive at least a commendation, not a reprimand."

"Hope you're right."

"You can get ready for transfer in three minutes. You're almost at surface pressure. I've got to get to the bridge now, I'll see you later tonight."

"Bye for now. I'll be waiting."

"Bye,"

"Take care of her, Doc."

"You know I will, Matt. See you when you get in."

Matt crossed the flight deck and climbed the ladder to the bridge deck. Preparations to move included log entries. Matt marked the log, and then walked to the bridge wing to watch the chopper leave. He'd like to have been on it. "All Zodiacs home," barked over the fantail speakers and Matt waited to see them retrieved.

"All ahead one third. Right helm." The cutter eased slowly around and pointed toward Port Angeles. "Take a heading of two-eight-zero degrees, Number One."

"Aye, Sir."

Looking aft from the bridge wing, Matt made sure the port dolphin pen was towing properly then went to the other side to check the second one. They were both fine. The whop, whop,

whop of the chopper gradually faded as it skimmed low over the water, rapidly becoming a speck in the distance. 'She'll be in hospital in another ten minutes' he thought. The damage she had sustained worried Matt. There wasn't much he could do now. He knew Doc would do everything possible. He was the best. The rest was up to Tanya.

Matt returned to the bridge as Mike entered through the 'midship companionway. "Hi, Matt. I just want to thank you for the success of this whole operation. Without you and your crew, we couldn't have pulled it off."

"You people did all the work, Mike, we only provided the transportation."

"More than that, Matt. If the navy had been involved with our own ships, the Russians would have been down to see what we were doing the first day. Because all they saw was the cutter, they obviously thought it was routine."

"Could be. We got away with it so far and it looks like we'll be able to get away clean."

"I sure hope so. How's Tanya?'

"As well as can be expected . . ."

The intercom crackled to life. "Matt, its George. We've got a problem with Pua. Can you stop for a minute or two?"

"You've got it, George. Crash stop?" The thrashing propellers would create a maelstrom at the stern if they went into full reverse. Matt knew this and wanted to avoid it if possible. If George really wanted to stop immediately he would risk it.

"No, just coast will be fine."

"All stop." the engine room telegraph bells rang, and the cutters engine throb stilled. She drifted to a stop.

I'm going aft to see what the problem is, Mike. Want to come along?"

"Sure, Matt, let's go."

They walked aft down the inside stairs and out onto the flight deck, then down to the fan deck. George had gone over the side to the starboard pen. Matt and Mike leaned over the rail. "What's up?"

"Pua's not following too well."

"Is it her injury?'

"Probably. She just doesn't seem to be swimming at all well. It could be that she has some internal damage we're not aware of. There are no outward signs, but she was pretty well wrapped up in the net."

"Is there anything we can do? Do you want her air transported?"

"No, I think we're better off leaving her in the water. We might aggravate any internal problems if we pick her up."

Mike offered, "We can half sink a Zodiac and put her inside and tow it. That way she wouldn't have to swim."

"That sounds like a good idea, Mike. Let's do that."

Mikes crew stripped all the gear off one of the boats and dropped it into the pen. Tying the bow to the leading edge of the pen, they began to deflate the sponsons or side floats of the Zodiac. Removing the transom board they indicated to Pua that she was to come into the boat. She seemed to understand and moved into the half sunk boat.

"Let's try that for a bit, Matt."

Matt crossed the deck to the intercom. "This is the captain, both ahead dead slow, number one." He explained to his exec what they were doing, and that he would stay in touch from the stern. They might have to stop at a moment's notice.

The cutter inched ahead. The Zodiac, being towed now, wanted to lift her bow which would empty the water out of her hull. Two handlers in wetsuits clambered onto the nose of the boat and their weight was enough to hold the bow down far enough to prevent this.

"It looks good, Matt. let's try it at slow speed for a while."

"Increase twenty revs, Number One." Matt's order, over the intercom, prompted instant action. The cutter slowly picked up a couple of knots.

"Still okay at that speed? Matt inquired.

Let's hold it there."

"Right, George."

George checked Pua. She lay still in the boat. Hoku, swimming alongside, was in constant contact with squeals and clicks. Pua appeared to enjoy the ride.

They continued slowly to the base at Ediz Hook. On arrival they slipped the pens and tied the cutter up at its berth. It was a tricky maneuver as Matt had to avoid crushing the pens between the cutter and the pier. He also had to be concerned about the amount of thrust he could safely use without blasting the pens.

It was after 8:00 o'clock when Matt stepped ashore. He had yet to make his report to the Commodore. Mike asked George and Matt to assemble their crews on the flight deck and Matt announced over the ship's PA, 'All hands stand to on the flight deck, all hands to the flight deck."

When they were all present, Mike addressed them. "What you people have accomplished over the past few days is phenomenal. You have completed assignments outside of your normal routines and performed them with speed and efficiency.

"What we have been doing, I must remind you, is TOP SECRET. I want to emphasize the importance of maintaining that secrecy. The security of the United States is in jeopardy here. If information of our project becomes known to the wrong people, it could set our defense capability back at least five years. The longer this operation goes undetected, the longer we will hold the advantage at sea. Because of the extremely sensitive nature of the project, no one person has access to all of the information, but I can tell you this, what we have accomplished will serve to insure peace throughout the world for years to come.

"It has in most instances been a very successful undertaking. You have worked well together and under conditions and time restraints more severe than any we have a right to impose on you. Your response has demonstrated your mettle and indicated that nothing is too tough for good old American ingenuity. However, we have not come away unscathed.

"One of our crew is in hospital and another is recovering in the pen at the aft end of this cutter. Our dolphin members performed admirably, doing work that would be impossible without them. Locating the sono-buoys could have been done by our divers, but certainly not within the time-frame necessary. To them we owe much. To Lieutenant Andrushyn we also owe much. She displayed the type of courage each of us has but seldom has an opportunity to demonstrate. Her injuries are not the result of any accident. Sure, the dolphin getting caught in the net was accidental, but the humanitarian way in which Lieutenant Andrushyn, disregarding her own safety, took responsibility to save the dolphin took enormous courage. The fact that she is still alive is an indication of the determination this officer possesses. Her response was certainly above and beyond the call of duty. If she had not reacted as quickly as she did, I have no doubt our dolphin would have perished.

"Proper recognition must also go to all of you who performed so well. However, because of the nature of the project, we are not allowed to make public announcements about any part of it. What I'm going to do is the best I can do at this time. I'm going to put each of you up for a special award. There will be no fanfare, no parade, but each of you will know what it's for, and how much we all owe to your special skills and abilities given so generously.

"Again, let me remind you of the secrecy which must be maintained and my special thanks to each of you for a job well done. You may go now, but remember, you can hold your heads high. You can be proud of the success of the project. You made that success. Again, I want to thank you all."

Mike dismissed them and walked over to the flight deck rail where George and Matt were listening. He shook hands with both of them. "Thanks to you two as well."

"Quite a speech, Mike." George commented. "and thank you, too."

"Right." Matt added. "That's some way to leave a project. If you're bucking for admiral or senator, I'd vote for you."

Mike laughed. "Neither admiral, nor senator either, I guess. The men did a top class job. They deserved all that and more.

What have you heard from Doc?" He knew Matt would know if anyone did.

"Nothing yet, Mike. I've got a report to make at 'head office' then I'm going up to the hospital."

'Captain to the radio room. Captain to the radio room," the PA interrupted.

"Don't go back to Bangor 'till I've had a chance to talk to you about the Trident, Mike, okay?"

"Okay, Matt. I'll wait here while you take the message."

"George, your work's done now, when're you heading out?"

"It'll be a few days at least, Matt. We've got to make sure Pua's all right before we can carry her around. If she still has internal trouble, we'd like her to have some time to recover."

"Good, I wanted to talk to you, too, before you go."

"No problem." said Matt sprinting up to the communication center. "See both of you later then."

His communications officer greeted him with "Message from Oahu for Lieutenant Andrushyn, Skipper."

He took it. It was from Major Snellert. "We have a bird just kicked out of parking orbit and will make a low pass over your area in fifty eight minutes, what is your condition?"

His instruction was to send, 'Condition green. Project successfully concluded.'

"Roger, Skipper."

Matt smiled to himself. They had pulled it off after all. Got back to base just before the bird came in for a close look. Tanya'd be happy about that when he told her, so would Mike. He hurried aft to tell him.

Mike and George hadn't left the flight deck. They were ecstatic to hear the news.

"There were times when I had my doubts," George said.

"Frankly, me too." Mike added. "You two have no idea how close it was at Bangor. Those men opening up the buoy deserve a citation too. It could have ended right there many times, not just from explosions but from the dead ends we had to contend with in trying to understand the electronics. Those guys were super. It's comforting to know we have that depth of engineering expertise."

"Does that mean there were parts of the buoy you couldnt figure out?" Matt questioned.

"There were a few all right. We only had time to dig into the functions we felt were important. Some other areas, we'll have to go after now."

"How can you do that now?" George couldn't understand. "You've put the thing back in the ocean!"

"True, George, but we have all the necessary data. Each part had an analysis done on it and recorded on tape. Both computer and video tapes."

"Is that enough?"

"We think so. The rest can be examined at our leisure. The big job was to get into its receiving circuits and make sure they heard what we wanted them to hear. This we did."

"I'll be darned," George let out a low whistle, "you can remote control it."

"Right, George." Mike was pleased with this accomplishment. "Well, I've got to get going men. Matt, we'll have to get together shortly to go over the arrival plan for OHIO."

"Any time, Mike. How about next Monday? She's not due 'till Thursday."

"Give me a call. We'll set something up."

Mike left the cutter and headed for the helicopter waiting on the old airstrip beside the admin buildings. George and Matt slowly followed him ashore, talking about the dolphins. They reached Matt's office block as the chopper noisily rose above them. Mike waved from the co-pilots window.

"I'm going to the hospital now. Want to come along?"

"Thanks, Matt, not tonight. I've got my work cut out for me here. Say, I'm going to take the dolphins out for exercise tomorrow and we'll be using the Mark 16 suits. Want to try one?"

"Do I? Sure do. What's the problem with the dolphins? I thought they would want to rest after the past few days."

"We had some problems with their responses to the communicator; we want to run them through the hoops to make sure they will retain the training. We also want to take Pua out for a bit. See you back here tomorrow?"

"Count on it, George. Tanya'll want to know all about Pua, too, so I guess I'll be gathering data for her. She'll be envious of my going."

George walked down to the pens and Matt headed to the administration building.

He entered the Commodore's outer office and knocked on the inner door.

"Come!"

"Oh, Matt. All done with the buoys?"

"All done, Frank! The ones we've discovered are all adapted to our liking. Commander Chambers and his crew have just left for Bangor. George Hammerdyne and his people will be with us for a few more days to allow Pua to recover a bit before they return to San Diego."

"I heard about the problem with the net. Caught bits of information here and there. What happened?"

"One of the dolphins got tangled in an abandoned fishing net snagged on the bottom. Tanya went down to cut it free. She didn't have time to check the critical factors, she just went. A dolphin took her down to 200 feet where Pua was caught.

"She was on compressed air?"

"Yeh, with a standard wetsuit. No heating."

"Why didn't the navy men go instead of her?"

"It all happened too fast. There wasn't time to think. The only way anyone could locate the trapped dolphin was with another dolphin leading the way. Water's so obscure, light can't penetrate more than five or ten feet. The dolphins echo-locate so the condition of the water doesn't bother them. Besides they can descend much faster than a diver. Tanya held onto the dolphin's collar, and he towed her down.

"Over the past few days, Tanya got to know these two dolphins and established a close relationship with them. They took to her straight away. Her ability to understand them made it easier. I think they knew this. That's why Hoku went to her. Anyway Hoku approached Tanya in a panic. Tanya knew there was trouble and dove in to save Pua. Chances are that if he had gone to the navy divers at either of the two boats, they wouldn't have understood as quickly as Tanya. The moments that were saved probably made the difference between life and death for Pua.

"The pair of dolphins working with the other boat knew there was a problem right away. They immediately headed for the first boat at top speed. They passed the stern of the cutter just after Tanya went down. Both of them went directly to the first boat where the divers were waiting. It all ran like clockwork. No time was lost. If the dolphins had waited for their own divers to get the boat over to the right spot, or if Hoku had gone to his divers and tried to tell them what the problem was, I doubt if Pua would be alive today. I'm sure the dolphins knew all this and ran the whole thing themselves."

"Come on, Matt, aren't you putting too much into this? Giving them too much credit?"

"That's the way I might have seen it, too, a couple of days ago. After seeing what the dolphins can do, I think that's exactly how it was. They knew what had to be done and they had to communicate the instructions to the only help they had, humans."

"Sounds incredible to think the dolphins could organize something like that, Matt."

"I know, Frank, as I said, a couple of days ago . . . . They're capable of things beyond my understanding. Even George Hammerdyne has trouble sometimes. We're just beginning to realize their level of intelligence."

"Well, I hope the injured one recovers soon. I guess I've got to get down to their pens before they leave and see some of this for myself."

"You won't be disappointed," Matt assured him.

"How's the Lieutenant?"

"I haven't heard yet. I'm going up to the hospital now, I'll let you know."

"Please do. Say, she's been taking up a lot of your time hasn't she?"

"Fair amount, yes."

"I thought so. Well, they don't come any better looking Matt and the word has it she's got a lot of that grey matter, too. That right?"

"She has that, Frank, and a lot of courage, too."

"Well you'd better get up there and find out how she is."

"Yes, Sir!"

"This will be some report. I can't wait to see it, Matt."

"You're right, Frank. See you tomorrow."

"Okay. But give me a call tonight when you find out. I'll probably be here most of the night."

"Will do, Frank."

Matt headed for the parking lot. There were not many people left on the base at this time of night. He had to go home first to shower and change, and then he was off to the hospital.

He entered the hospital through the large glass double doors of the main entrance and walked along the hall to the nursing station.

"I'm looking for Doctor Johnson."

"He's in the cafeteria; would you like me to page him?"

"No thanks. I'll meet him there."

He had passed along this same hallway only a few days ago when the man from the beach was being repaired. It seemed a long time ago.

Turning into the cafeteria he looked around for Doc. It must have been lunch time for the afternoon shift, the cafeteria was busy. He spotted Doc over by the windows at the same time Doc saw him. Doc waved. Matt drew a coffee and joined him.

"How's Tanya?"

"Still on the critical list. She's resting now."

"What does 'critical' mean, Doc?"

"It means she's had a lot of tissue damage within her lungs. It's always a difficult area to heal. The lungs have to keep on working while the healing process is going on. She carried a considerable amount of blood in the lungs for a while. We removed most of it and the bleeding has stopped. It's up to her own healing processes now. She's a strong woman physically. I think that's a point in her favor."

"Can I talk to her?"

"If she's awake yes but don't wake her. She needs rest now. Remember too, she has one ear drum ruptured, so you'll have to talk a bit louder than normal."

"What room's she in?"

"1025, just past the nurses' station where you came in."

"Oh, by the way, how's Parker?"

"Not good, Matt. We're having trouble keeping him alive. He's fighting hard to survive."

"Has he come out of his coma yet?"

"Off and on. Even when he does he's too mixed up to carry on an intelligent conversation."

"Too bad. I'd still like to talk to him if I could."

"I'll give you a call." Doc offered.

Matt finished his coffee and got up to go to her room.

"Don't wake her," Doc prompted.

"Okay, Doc. See you later."

Walking through the hall Matt checked the room numbers, 1015, 1019, 1021. There it was—1025. Opening the door slowly, he peered into the dimly lit room. A small table on wheels crowded the foot of the single bed standing by the wall, a curtain effectively cloistering the occupant. Matt silently opened the curtain to make sure it was Tanya. It was. Her eyes closed, sleeping. He stood for a while looking at her, willing her to recover. A long time passed while he stood watching, then he quietly left the room and walked down the hall. The hospital PA broke the silence. "Doctor Johnson, I.C.W. stat, Code 21. Doctor Johnson, I.C.W. stat."

Matt was surprised by the scurry of people. The hall, deserted one minute and the next, there were people coming out of rooms all running past him along the corridor. He walked out the main entrance doors and over to the parking lot, heading back to his apartment.

At home he had time to reflect on the activities of the past week. The business of the buoys was not the sort of thing he wanted to deal with. Why must a country be so suspicious about another that it makes this type of spying necessary? Planting spy devices in each other's backyards was a little too much for him. Not that he thought it shouldn't be done, it was probably justified. But he didn't want to be mixed up in it. After all, what could the Russians learn from these buoys that they couldn't find out in some less intimidating way?

The work Mike and his crews had done to make sure the buoys would perform for them by transmitting misinformation seemed to be justified at the time but looking back now he wondered if it was all worth it. They had almost paid with the lives of Tanya and Pua, not to mention the danger to the men in Bangor.

'If I was the Russian intelligence chief, he thought, 'I'd make sure there was some other way to verify what the buoys told me. Anyway, in the first place, I don't think I'd make the satellite my only means to gather data the buoys collected. What would be better? A shore base? Not likely. Too easy for discovery. Aircraft? No commercial routes over this area. Surface craft or submersibles? More likely. Mini-subs? Could be, but they'd need a mother ship. Trawlers were going in and out of the Strait all the time. Didn't they plant the buoys in the first place? What would stop them from bringing in a small manned sub? They could drop it anywhere within the Strait and pick it up a couple of days later. The more he thought about it, the more sense it made to him. What if the trawlers tended something besides the buoys? What was it the pilot said? 'There was a lot of hydraulic machinery noise'. We had assumed that was for sea sleds going to the buoys. Maybe it was to do with more than buoys. Maybe underwater teams have to attend to some other gear. What could that be?'

Matt's spinning head could take no more of the mystery tonight. Picking up the phone, he dialed the base. "Commodore Coulter, please." He related Tanya's status to him, and then bid him good night. He watched the late news on TV showered and went to bed.

CHAPTER 19

Wednesday, Day 12, 06:05 hours.

Matt rose early and ate a hurried breakfast. Driving down streets all but deserted at this early hour, he anticipated the morning's diving. As excited as a kid on Christmas morning. This opportunity to get checked out using the Mk 16 underwater breathing apparatus (UBA) was a rare experience. He hadn't used it yet and looked forward to experiencing the freedom it provided regarding ascent and descent rates. The dolphins were going to be exercised along with them while they were out. He arrived at the base early, even then, he got there after George, who stood, suited up, ready to dive. 'He must sleep here,' Matt thought. The handlers were feeding the dolphins as he approached.

"Which dolphins are you going to take, George?"

"Frankie and Johnnie. Pua's not up to running around yet. We don't want to rush her. Dolphins heal quickly but we're not going to take unnecessary chances."

"I've been over the operation of the Mk 16 UBA and your men have given me general instructions. Is there anything specific that might give me trouble?"

"I don't think so. Just make use of the control lights and respond when required. There's a suit for you on the float there," he said poinitng toward the float beside Pua. "We'll be going out about 09:30, you can put it on when you want to. All the equipment is on the Zodiac, ready to go."

"Where'd you plan to dive?"

"There's a shelf off the Hook about three miles out. I thought it'd be a good starting place. Depth is close to 200 feet, not too deep but a good level for you to get used to the suit."

"Good choice, George! That's a new diving area for me"

"The light'll be poor. I'd like to take some of the gear I saw on your ship, if that's all right."

"Fine, take what you need."

George's men loaded the two Zodiacs, checking the chemicals and other diving support equipment, adding fuel to the tanks for the outboards and electrical generators.

Matt suited up and returned to the float, concerned that the suit would be too cumbersome. That wasn't the case. He had free and complete movement and was quite comfortable.

Everything ready, they climbed aboard the two boats. Engines roared to life. The dolphin pen opened letting Frankie and Johnnie join them. They were off.

A calm sea met them as they rounded the sheltering tip of Ediz Hook. Heading north, they made good time, dropping anchors ten minutes later at the co-ordinates George had selected on the charts. Matt helped them position themselves over the spot, using familiar markers on shore.

Scurrying dolphins were splashing around, chirping as their handlers called them to harnesses up. They couldn't wait. Harnesses snapped into place in no time.

"They know they're going to play games. They love game times. The harnesses usually mean fun." George explained.

The handlers splashed into the water and disappeared below the waves with the dolphins.

"Let's check each other's suits. I'll check you first, and you can see what to do with mine." George pushed, pulled and twisted all parts needing testing. Everything seemed okay. He checked valves and gauges. Indicator lights blinked. "Seems fine. Now check mine."

Matt poked and prodded.

"Now what we'll do, Matt, is go right down to the bottom and once more check that everything is still functioning properly with each part of our suits and equipment, then we'll explore some bottom. Grab your light and set your timer. Stay close. If you have any problems call out. The intercom is one luxury of these UBA units, unlike scuba gear; we'll be able to talk to each other and the Zodiac."

"Sounds terrific. Let's go!"

George rolled off the boat, dropping quickly. Matt followed.

Once they had their bearings, they dove beside the anchor cable. Light grew poor at about fifty feet, and really dimmed at one hundred feet. They turned lights on half way down. The bottom was dark but the lights gave considerable penetration. Shining them on each other, they went through their equipment check.

George pointed to his wrist depth gauge, "Two hundred and seven feet, Matt. How does that feel?"

"I can hardly believe it. I'm impressed with the intercom system too. The fact that I can talk to you here underwater is really great."

"Watch the hot water heating. Sometimes you can get so wrapped up in what you're doing you don't notice the temperature's getting cooler. That could be dangerous. If there's a problem, it's probably the control valve at your waist. Clockwise is colder, counter-clockwise is hotter. Is yours comfortable?"

"Seems good for now."

"Okay, let's move off to the west for a while. Head 245 degrees."

Each checked the compass on his wrist, and then swam off, five feet above the bottom. With the umbilical they didn't have to worry about getting lost, they were attached to 'home'. If they were swimming free they'd have to be concerned as the tidal current here ran at close to two knots. They went west because the tide was running from the west. They'd have an easier time swimming back.

The bottom proved to be flat and granular. Matt had expected more fine silt and mud. This surprised him. They found a few logs, boulders and some discarded soda cans rolling around. There were a couple of small fish, but not much other life.

After wandering around for an hour Matt was tiring. He suggested they go topside. The ascent directly to the surface really impressed him. He was used to time consuming staging on the return. The ability of the Mk 16 to make the necessary changes in the gas ratio allowed the quick ascent.

On top, they propelled themselves over to the boat and pulled themselves aboard.

"Christ, that's the only way to go, George."

"Like that, do you?"

"Wow. If I could do that any time I wanted to, I'd be in the water all day."

"With the mixed gas and heated suit, you probably could, so long as you didn't have to pay for the gas."

"Expensive?"

"Very. We've got to watch the amount of diving we do in the navy. We're like you; we'd stay down forever as long as someone else paid for the gas. Good old Uncle Sam's paying for this, but he has tight purse strings. How'd you like the mobility?"

"Hey. Isn't that something?

"Ready to go again?"

"Sure am. Only this time let's go to the north. There's supposed to be an old ship wrecked in that area. Let's see if we can find it. I've seen it on side scan sonar but never had an opportunity to dive deep enough to get to it. I'd kind of like to have a look."

"These Mk 16 units were made for that type of exploration. If we do find it, keep in mind the umbilical cord can tangle easily. You don't want to spend all your bottom time freeing it."

They could see the other Zodiac about a hundred yards to the east of their position. George radioed them, to let them know that they were heading north about half a mile. Raising anchor, they sped off covering the distance in short time.

Matt studied their position, looking at the shore for reference markings. "Right about here, George."

The tender crew threw out the anchor and set it into the bottom. George and Matt dove again.

"I think we should start toward the north-west, George."

"Okay, let's go." Their lights, poking slim yellow fingers into the murk, led them down.

Swimming close to the bottom, there was certainly more to interest them here than the last area, lush marine growth and rock outcroppings sheltering a large variety of fish.

"Over there, George." Matt pointed toward a huge dark area looming through the murky water.

The angular hull of the long dead ship blocked their progress. Lying at a 45 degree angle, she showed her deck and part of her flank, rigging standing out at a rakish angle. To the tender on top George called, "We've found it, Toni. It's lying east and west. We're going to see if we can get to the north side of it."

"Yes, sir," was the reply.

Moving toward the stern they could make out the large bronze propeller and barn-door sized rudder, leaning at a crazy angle. Barnacles covered almost every part of the hull and long banners of seaweed fluttered in the gentle current like flags on the Fourth of July. Small fish scurried about among the weeds.

Moving up the side of the hull they could see the reason for her demise. Half of the mid-ship hold was torn. Jagged steel protruded like mammoth fingers. She looked like she'd had a bad encounter with a reef or something had exploded in her hold. Ripped and torn, the hull plates lay open as if some giant can opener had been at work. Most of the mid-ship bottom had disappeared. A huge cavern lay in front of them.

"Wonder what she carried?"

"Let's have a look, Matt."

They probed the gaping hole with their lights. Poor penetration hampered their effort. They could see less than five or ten feet.

"Don't see much cargo at all in this hold. Maybe she was empty."

"Looks like it, George. Can we go inside?"

"Yeh, but watch your line."

With most of the bottom missing, no barrier stopped them from getting inside. The lower portion was filled with sedimentary deposits. Nothing visible indicated any cargo.

"You swim to the aft bulkhead. I'll go forward, George. See if there is anything sticking out of the sand."

They swam around, digging in the loose bottom with their hands. There were a few small round cans scattered in the sand on the bottom. No sign of anything large that would give a clue to her cargo. It could have been grain. That would have been eaten or decomposed years ago. It certainly had no big chunks of machinery lying around. Matt swung his light up towards the top of the hold. The hatch covers were still in place and a large air bubble was trapped up there in the corner of the ship where the deck met the hull. The beam of light bounced all over the place, reflected by this captive water surface.

"Matt, over here."

Matt swam over toward the glow of George's light. The two of them moving around had stirred up a lot of the bottom and vision became even more restrictive. George prodded something as Matt approached. Looked like a canvas tarpaulin or net, a camouflage net, the kind they use to cover artillery guns. "Something big under this. Give me a hand."

They hauled the cover off one end of a dark grey cylinder as big as or bigger than the recompression chamber.

"What the hell is that?" Matt wanted to know.

"Looks like a diving chamber. Get that other end."

Matt moved over to the other end and they pulled the cover back. They moved down to the bottom to look at it. Sitting on three stilt like legs, six to eight feet high the cylinder had an entrance hatch out the bottom which caught George's attention. It confirmed his earlier observation that this was a diving chamber.

"Is this one of yours, George?"

"Not that I know of, Matt. Open that lower hatch and we'll have a look inside."

With no marine growth on it, the hatch wheel turned easily. It pulled open effortlessly and George poked his head into the opening.

"There's air in here, Matt." Shining the light around he spotted electrical control panels and lighting fixtures. "Matt, this could hold five or six people easily. There are a bunch of panels up here with writing on them. Can't make out what they say. I'm coming out. You go have a look."

Matt replaced him in the opening, shining his light up onto the panels. He knew right away what the writing was. He had seen it before on the buoy's electronic boxes. "Russian, George. They're all in Russian."

"Holy Christ. What have we stumbled onto?"

"What're you guys into down there?" Toni, who had been listening on top, couldn't stand it. "What have you got?"

"We're not sure, Toni. Looks like a Russian diving station."

"In the Strait?"

"Yeh, right in our back yard." Matt added.

"Get up inside, Matt, I want to come in."

They moved into the chamber. Control panels included air and gas systems as well as the electronic type meters, switches and knobs. All the writing was in Russian script.

"What's in the next room there?"

Matt opened the watertight door leading into the right half of the room. "Sleeping area. Four bunks. What's in the one behind you?"

"Gas bottles."

"Take a good look, George, and then let's get the hell out of here."

"Mike's going to have a hemorrhage when he hears about this."

"Jesus. You aren't kidding."

"Do you think it's got anything to do with the sono-buoys?"

"I'd stake my life on it, George. It's the missing link."

"What missing link?"

"I'll tell you about it topside. Let's get."

They dropped out the bottom and closed the hatch behind them. Outside they put the tarp back the way they had found it, then swam out of the wreck.

"What a place to hide it. No one would normally be anywhere near this wreck. It's too deep for most of the divers in the area. The navy can go this deep but they don't practice dive around here. There's a submarine trial area right here, though. A perfect hiding place."

Clear of the wreck, they ascended as fast as they could. Topside, Toni reeled in their umbilical lines keeping up with their ascent rate, ready to help them aboard.

George and Matt excitedly told Toni they had stumbled onto something extremely important. The sooner they got the news to Mike the better. Toni cleared the hoses and weighed anchor. They headed in at top speed. George radioed the other boat, telling them they had to return to base.

Sliding in next to the dolphin pens, they tied up quickly. Matt, who had stripped the hot suit off during the trip in, jumped onto the float and sprinted toward his office. On the way he stopped by the Commodore's office and asked him to join in a conference call to Mike.

The connection made, Matt spoke. "I think you'll want to scramble this, Mike. I've got Commodore Coulter with me."

"Okay, Matt, it's on. What have you got?"

He could hear Mike catch his breath as the story unfolded.

"Son of a bitch. We thought we had the Russians by the short hairs. They may have us instead. How wrong we were. I'll be up there in less than an hour, Matt, with a couple of my best electronics men. Can we borrow the services of your crew again, Frank?"

"Sure thing, Mike, we'll be ready and waiting."

Matt added, "You had better alert Oahu that we're not finished yet. Have them back on high alert for satellite movement."

The Commodore walked back to the float with Matt. He wanted more details. They joined George and his crew and discussed the discovery.

George asked, "Do you recall any ships going down in this region Commodore?"

"Where did you say you were, exactly?"

"About fifteen miles west of the base, three miles off shore, Frank. I've heard a story from divers, of a liberty ship going down in that area"

"I think there was a ship wreck there about 60 years ago, I'd have to dig the records out. I'll have someone start looking now." He left, heading up the ramp at a fast pace toward the office.

Matt told George about Mike being on the way and asked if everything he would need was ready. They'd have to replenish the chemicals for the Mk 16 units. Other than that, they were ready. "I'll send one of my men out to pick them up."

Mike's helicopter landed on the apron to the north of the old hanger. Mike and three of his men debarked. Matt met and escorted them to the cutter. George had laid out diving suits so they could change aboard ship then go down to the float. They also had underwater cameras to get shots inside the Russian equipment.

Matt explained his 'backup' theory to Mike.

"You could be right, Matt. We were so glad to get the buoys finished we didn't think of looking beyond that. What you say is so obvious. I don't know why I missed it"

"I don't know what else it can be, Mike. What could the Russians do here with that equipment other than the same thing as the buoys?"

"You're right. I just hope we can do something with it in time. Here we go again, working against another tight deadline. Only this one's even shorter"

"You've got the weekend plus a few days before the sub's due.

"Not much time to understand Russia's latest electronic gear. We'll go down and take pictures and try to determine a use for the stuff you described."

"You remember the trawler incident? We thought they placed the buoys."

"Yeh?"

"Suppose they also used the station, dropping men off for it as well as the buoys."

"That could be, we'll know better after we see what the station contains."

"Just knowing may not be enough. Suppose whatever it functions for screws up what you did to the buoys?"

"You sure know how to make a guy feel good, don't you?" Mike laughed, "I guess you're right though. That could be."

"What can you do about it?"

"I don't know yet, Matt. We'll have to wait and see."

"Well you'd better get suited up. I think George is waiting to take you out. He's so excited I think he might go down with you."

"We'd like to have him. Aren't you coming?"

"No, I think you've got enough help out there already. Besides I've got some other things that can't wait. I'm anxious to see what you find though."

"Okay, we'll keep you informed."

The men, now suited up, walked down to the float like a squad of alien beings. George settled them aboard the Zodiacs and the outboard motors roared to life. He waved to Matt and they were off. Matt climbed the ramp from the float and then up to the cutter's bridge. From here he had an unobstructed view over the buildings and out to where the boats would work. He watched with binoculars as the two boats sped out, heading toward the horizon. He could barely make them out half an hour later, as they dropped anchors. Divers splashed into the water. Matt figured they would be down at least an hour. He'd take advantage of the break to see Tanya. He left the cutter, heading to his car. Detouring through the admin. Building to the record's room he found the Commodore.

"Here it is, Matt, the 12,000 ton freighter, Diamond Knot, rammed in 1947 by another freighter, Fenn Victory, sank off Crescent Bay in 200 feet of water. Her cargo was canned salmon, over seven million cans, and herring oil as well as some cannery equipment."

"That's our ship, Commodore, but we only found a few cans scattered in the hold. I wonder what happened to the rest?"

"Says here most of it was salvaged."

"Okay, that makes sense. What amazes me is that the Russians knew about the wreck and were able to make use of it to spy on us. Even though we knew vaguely the thing was there, they knew enough about it to make it work for them. How many more situations are there like this?"

"That's why we have counter espionage agencies, Matt. They worry about that."

"Well, they haven't done too well around here. They didn't even know about the buoys, let alone this wreck. What else have they missed?"

"Kind of scares you, doesn't it?"

"Sure does Frank. I'm going to try to put it out of my mind for a while though."

"Going up to the hospital?"

"Yep."

"Give Tanya my regards will you?"

"Will do, sir." he said, leaving the room.

Driving through town he remembered how stark Tanya's room was. He stopped, picking up a large potted hyacinth in full bloom. The flowers should help to raise her spirits. He'd like to be able to take her down to the wreck and show her their find. He knew at the same time, she'd likely never dive again because of the ruptured ear.

He tried to guess what the underwater station could do and why it was there. Maybe it was used by technicians to program the buoys. How would they find the buoys and how would they travel between the two locations? The distance was too great to just swim. Maybe it was used for other purposes unrelated to the buoys. Pretty coincidental. All sorts of ideas went through his mind but no solutions. The hospital parking lot was nearly empty. Afternoon visiting hours didn't start for another hour.

He wanted to talk to Doc before he went in to see Tanya. He checked at the nurses' station. Doc was in his office, expecting him. Matt knocked at the inner door and opened it.

"Come on in, Matt. I expected you sooner than this. What kept you?"

"A couple of things, Doc. I'll tell you about it after you tell me about Tanya. How is she?"

"Well, she's off the critical list, not out of the woods yet but making satisfactory progress. Parker didn't fare so well, though."

"What happened to him?"

"He died last night, while you were in with Tanya, as it turned out."

"Was that the PA call I heard. Code . . . something?'

"Yes. Code blue. Cardiac arrest. The damage was just too much for him.

"Nobody talked to him then?"

"'Fraid not."

"That's too bad."

"Let's move to a lighter subject, Matt. Tanya's awake now. Do you want to see her?"

"Sure do, Doc." He turned to leave.

"Hey, just a minute, Matt. You said you'd tell me what kept you."

"Later, Doc, we'll have coffee, 'kay?"

"S'pose so . . . ." was all he had time to get out. Matt was gone.

$$* \quad * \quad *$$

Looking out the window, Tanya didn't see him enter. Her hearing, still poor from the injury, didn't pick him up either. He set the flowers on the bedside table, saying, "They're not as beautiful as you, but they're the best they had."

She turned, startled. "Matt. I didn't hear you come in." She gazed at him. "Oh, Matt, I missed you, oh, how I missed you."

He leaned over and kissed her hard. Tears formed in the corners of her eyes.

"Hey now. None of that." He sat down beside her on the bed.

"I'm just so glad to see you," she snuffled.

He took a Kleenex from the box on the table and handed it to her. "I missed you too," he offered. "I came by last night, but you were asleep."

"I know. Doc told me. You should have wakened me."

"Doc threatened me. Told me he'd do nasty things to me if I did."

"Just like him!"

"How are you? How's your ear?" He took her hands and impressed an intimate greeting through them to her.

"Sore and a little hard of hearing. You'll have to talk to my right side."

"What about your chest?"

"Still sore and stiff, hurts when I cough."

"I guess so. Do you feel up to talking about the dive, or would you rather leave it for a while?"

"No, I'll talk about it. First though, how's Pua?"

"Recovering pretty well. She had a bad scare and she's cut up badly, but she's coming around as well as can be expected. How about you? Whatever possessed you to go down?"

"There wasn't much choice. If I hadn't gone, the other divers wouldn't have been able to get to Pua in time, or so I felt at the time. Besides Hoku told me to hurry."

"Hoku told you, did he?" Matt figured she was still a bit delirious.

"Come on, Matt. Not in so many words, but the message was clear. 'Pua's in trouble, hurry', is what I understood."

"I watched as all that happened. I didn't get that. When you dove in you yelled that she was caught in fishing net. How'd you know that?"

"I did, didn't I? I had forgotten that. I don't know. I can't explain. It's just the way I took it. As it turned out I was right."

"Except Hoku didn't tell you he was going to take you down to 200 feet and nearly kill you."

"No, I guess he didn't realize I couldn't take that pressure. He probably thought the other divers do it all the time. Why shouldn't I be able to do it, too?"

"Maybe you're right. You must have gone down in one hell of a hurry. Is that how your ear got hurt?"

"I remember keeping them clear as I went down, and you're right, we went down like a stone. The pressure built up but, I managed to dump it before my ears got hurt. This damage must have happened on the way up or while I was at the bottom. Half way down it started to get dark and I realized I had forgotten to grab a light. There was no turning back at that point so I just hung on. Hoku took me right to Pua. The net that she was caught in, had her fanned out away from us. I think Hoku must have had sense enough to take me to the up-current side so that we wouldn't get caught up too. Pua was thrashing and crying pitifully. When I touched her, she calmed right down. I worked by feel as best I could, cutting the net away from her head area and working back. She was really tangled up. I couldn't see, but I could feel she was watching me. It was an eerie sensation."

"You couldn't have been able to do much at that depth. Your strength should have been down to zero."

"I seemed to function all right. With the darkness though, I had a difficult time equating anything. It seemed like I was cutting a heck of a lot of net and getting nowhere."

"You managed to get most of it. Do you remember the divers getting to you?"

"Hoku was there all the time talking to Pua. I remember a brightening of the light in the water and something touching me. I didn't see anyone. In fact, everything from that point on is blank until I woke up in the recompression chamber."

"You had Pua almost clear. The divers had to use wire cutters to free her completely. Before they did, they sent you and Hoku to the surface. They were up a few minutes later with Pua. What you accomplished saved Pua's life. She was close to being out of air herself."

"I'm happy she survived."

"I'm even happier you survived. It was nip and tuck there for a while. Remind me to give you a serious chewing out after you've recovered enough to take it."

"Don't be too hard on me."

"I'll take into account the fact that you saved a fellow diver's life, but you did a very stupid thing. Broke every rule in the diving book."

"I know, now. But it was the only thing to do at the time."

"I think you acted in the best way possible under the circumstances. I'm proud of you." He kissed her. "I'd have been disappointed if you hadn't gone. You were the only one in the right position to respond in time. But the thought of what could have happened makes me shudder. I could have lost you."

The meaning took a short time to penetrate Tanya's tired mind. When she finally realized what he had said, she burst into tears.

"Hey, hey. Enough of that." His arm went around her and her head found the hollow of his neck. She sobbed uncontrollably. Emotion exposed the terrible stress she had built up over the whole episode.

"Oh, Matt." was all she could manage.

"Relax. Get it all out. From here on it's all downhill. You've been put through the wringer and survived."

She slowly settled down. The sobs stopped and Matt wiped away the tears. Tanya blew her nose and looked into his eyes. A pixie grin wrinkled the corners of her lips. Matt smiled. "Feel better?"

"A little. She spotted the flowers as if for the first time. "Hyacinths. Next to gardenias they're my favorite."

He laughed, "You like all flowers. What'd you mean 'favorite'?"

"You're right. I like them all." She could smell the strong fragrance.

"The room seemed a little cold without flowers. It needed some to perk it up." He added

"Matt . . . How long am I going to be here?"

"I don't know. It's up to Doc. I haven't had a chance to talk to him yet. Oh yes, Major Snellert asked about you and wishes you well."

"That's just like him, always thinking about others. If you're talking to him again, tell him I'll be up and around soon."

"I will." Matt had decided not to tell her about the underwater station until she had recovered for a few more days. He didn't know what effect it might have on her. Besides it wouldn't matter if she didn't know right now. He stayed with her, and they talked for another half an hour.

"Well, I'd better get going. Time for you to rest."

"I'm not tired. Do you have to go right away?"

"Doc says you tire easily, and you need rest. He's the Doctor."

"Will I see you later tonight?"

"Try and keep me away."

He gave her a gentle hug and a peck on the cheek.

"Come on, you can do better than that."

He did . . . .

*   *   *

Matt went to find Doc, to see about Tanya's progress.

"When will she be released?"

"Not for a few more days, Matt. She's been through the grinder. It's a good thing she's a strong healthy woman. It would have killed many others. That doesn't mean we can get careless now though. Just because she seems so well doesn't mean we can forget she's hurting. Outwardly she looks good but she's still running a high temperature. That indicates infection. Her lungs have a long way to go, and so does her ear for that matter. Once her temperature drops and stays down for a day or so we'll consider letting her out. Even then she's going to need special care."

"In what way?" this surprised Matt

"She should have the ear drum repaired and some special exercises for her lungs. She also needs a lot of tender love and care. Know where she can get that?"

"I might have a couple of ideas on that," he grinned, "I just happen to know a dispensary where they've got a sale on."

"That's the news you've been waiting for, now how about mine?"

"Oh, the wreck and underwater station." He told Doc as much as he knew and what they were going to do about it.

"My God, Matt, the pressure's not off then? You've cleaned up the buoys but may still be in trouble?"

"Looks like, Doc. We'll know better after Mike gets back. He's out there now. Matt looked out the window from Doc's office. It overlooked the Strait. He could see two black dots 'way out on the water.

"See the boats out there?" he pointed.

"Northwest?"

"Yes."

"Oh, yah, I see them. Is that Mike?"

"That's him. When he comes in we'll know more. I'd better get down there now. They should be back any time. I'll be back later tonight to see Tanya. Oh, by the way, I didn't tell her about the wreck. Figured she had enough to worry about, but she's doing so well, would it be all right to tell her tonight?"

"I don't know why not, Matt. She's getting more able to cope with each hour that goes by. She shouldn't have any problem with that."

"Good, Doc. Take care of her now, d'ya hear?"

"Will do, Matt. See you later."

Matt drove back to the base and fussed about in his office, waiting for word from Mike and George. He had trouble concentrating on his paperwork. The divers were out longer than he had anticipated.

An hour later he heard motors and walked quickly down to the float. Anxious to know what they had discovered he took the line thrown to him, secured it around a cleat and button-holed Mike.

"You were gone quite a while."

Mike stepped onto the float. "Well Matt, we've got another crisis to handle."

"Christ, no. I was afraid of that. Come on and get out of that suit and tell me about it. How bad is it?"

They both walked toward the cutter, Matt striding and Mike awkwardly trying to keep up in the diving suit. "Bad enough. The station must be used to gather data from the buoys and store it on tape. It has a large tape capacity. It looks like the buoys transmit at very low frequency and the station holds weeks or months of data at a time."

"What does that mean in regards to the work done on the buoys?"

"We'll have to find out how much is on the tapes already. We may have to find a way to alter it."

"What does it transmit to, and how does it get its signal out? The whole thing's wrapped inside a steel hull. We looked for some kind of antenna. We saw none."

"We thought of the same thing and looked for cables out of the station. We found them. They're there all right, disguised like part of the ship's rigging."

"Really? No wonder we missed them."

"They're also using a large, low frequency setup to transmit to ships at sea. The antennas on the bottom are spread out in a fan shape from the wreck. The unit will probably reach over two thousand miles!"

"My God. How long has the station been there?"

"That's where we're probably lucky; I don't think it's more than three or four weeks since it was planted. There's very little marine growth on any of its parts. I'd say that in such a short time, they haven't been able to establish signal input patterns from the buoys. What we did to them might be impossible to spot."

"What's to be done to the gear on it?"

"The whole works will have to be reset to be compatible with the buoys."

"If they can access the buoys directly from a satellite, why do they need this station?"

"Remember I told you about the parts of the buoys we didn't have time to examine?"

"Yes, the LF stuff."

"Right. It's used to contact this station and store data on its tapes. The buoys hold about 24 hours of data, the station holds about 60 days. If they want, they can transfer the data from the buoys or the station. Quick updates from the buoys, history from the station.

They entered the after deck change room.

"When the new sub comes in, they'd get data from the buoys?"

"Exactly. When there's activity they want immediately, they ask the buoys. They get it, but it costs."

"You mean the satellite maneuvering costs?"

"Yes. If they can wait, say until they have two or more inputs from subs, like when one comes in and another goes out they can get that right away."

"Why don't they put larger tapes in the buoys and do away with the station?"

"Many reasons. Power and space considerations plus the station has the capability to repair the buoys."

"What's that going to do to the 'fixed' buoys? The first one they repair will destroy your work. They'll have to know there's something wrong."

"That's why getting at this station's critical. We can fix the programming gear aboard to input whatever we want. The Russians will think they're using the programs they put in at the factory. That way we've got the whole ball of wax."

"What if we hadn't found it?"

"Matt, you're a worry-wart, but I'm glad you are. We'd have as long as it took Ivan to come in and check the buoys, however long that might be."

"That could be anytime. I'll see when the next trawler's due."

"How'd you know that, if they only come in when they need repairs Matt?"

"I've been thinking about that. I've checked with the pilots, both US and Canadian. They gave me a list of all the Russian ship movements in the past year. It's in my office now. Maybe you'd like to run a check of related events to see if a pattern emerges?"

Mike finished dressing and they went out to the fantail, continuing the conversation. Mike had no idea what Matt was getting at. "What pattern was there?"

"You have access to movements of the Russian fleet, Mike. Does that include fishing vessels?"

"Yes, it sure does. Most Russian fishing vessels around our coast are spy ships anyway."

"Okay, suppose the arrival of a factory ship or large trawler tied in with the time the buoys and station were put into place?"

"I see what you MEAN Matt. Get me the dates you have. I'll have my people check with central intelligence. If they show up at the right times, they're the ones to watch for.

"What's your next move, Mike?"

"We'll go down after the transmitters. We'll need a couple of offices to use as a base while we're here. Can you help?"

"Sure. We've got a couple of spare spaces. What kind of equipment do you need?"

"Phone, to start. Data link after a bit. We'll play the rest by ear. Most of the gear we'll bring from Bangor will go directly to the station. I wish we could bring the station ashore. It'd make our lives a lot easier. We'll have to make all of our stuff watertight to get it down there. We'll need a power supply and a breathing gas supply."

"Why not use the systems in the station?"

"Can't. The Russians will have the stuff aboard inventoried. If we use it, they'll know right away someone's been into their station.

"Oh, right." Matt thought about all the equipment, the air and power supplies, "you'll never get all that gear on the Zodiacs. You're going to need the cutter."

"We'll probably get away with Zodiacs tomorrow, but from then on the cutter would certainly be better. Can you square it with the Commodore?"

"Already have, Mike. My ship and crew are at your disposal for the duration. I'll pass the word to my men that we're not going out tomorrow but after that we'll be full time."

"Thanks, I appreciate that, Matt."

"After we get through with this Russian thing, we'll have to go over the planning for the arrival of the sub."

"I'd sure like more time to work on one or the other. The Peaceniks are going to give us a bad time. They've been trying to stop our supply trains for six months. They've been more a nuisance than a problem but they're going to be out in full force when the first upgraded Trident comes in."

"We'll give you all the assistance we can, Mike."

"I was kind of hoping the Coast Guard would spearhead the operation, Matt."

"I don't know if we can handle that large a role Mike, we've only so many ships and crews."

"Well if you can use what you have, the navy's prepared to supplement with some of our smaller craft."

"With a little help from you, we might cope."

"Think about it. We'll talk about it again later today."

"I had planned to have this escort business all firmed up by now. The buoys threw a wrench into that."

"I know what you mean, Matt."

"What have your intelligence men gathered regarding the protestors?"

"Call Lieutenant Commander Kingsley, at Bangor. Tell him what we we're discussing and bring him on line. He'll also be able to tell you all about the Russian ship movements. We want the navy to maintain a low profile but we're prepared to assist you every way we can. Kingsley can give you the rundown on what to expect. He'll also fill you in on the types and number of vessels we can offer for escort duty."

"Sounds good."

"While you're talking to him, ask him if a laser man from the Pentagon arrived. They were all excited about the laser aspects of the buoy."

"Will do Mike. Right now, let's see if we can find you some office space."

Mike organized his crew for their next dive, then joined Matt walking to the administration building. Before they had gotten off the pier, the Zodiacs' outboards roared to life propelling them away from the float and out into the harbor. The dolphins, anxious to go with them, kicked up a fuss because they were left behind. The boats left without them. There was much noise and splashing. Handlers calmed them somewhat with a fish treat.

Matt located three offices in a cluster for Mike to use. There were phones and desks as well as a long chart table.

Mike was on the phone immediately arranging for delivery of electronic equipment and a couple of engineers to use it. Matt left him, returning to his own office down the hall. Thoughts of the undersea station were pushed to the back of his mind by concern for the confrontation he knew he was going to have when the sub arrived.

CHAPTER 20

Wednesday, day 12, 16:00 hours.

Matt assembled a list of ships and boats he could call on: six ships in sizes ranging from the Reliance cutter to eighty-five footer, three thirty-six footers, and a handful of Zodiacs in an assortment of sizes.

They would pick up the re-fitted sub at the western entrance to the Strait, off Cape Flattery and escort her all the way to her berth in Bangor. What he was up against in the way of protesters vessels, he had no idea, he would find out from Kingsley in Bangor. Matt phoned and told Kingsley who he was, and what he wanted.

Facts came out of Kingsley in a deluge. There were rumors of a large flotilla of pleasure craft gathering to obstruct passage of the sub. They were prepared to go to any length to interfere.

Matt had seen these people in action before during the first trip of the Arco super tanker to the Cherry Point oil refinery. Foolhardy stunts that could earn them a spot on the nightly news seemed to be their goal. Lucky no one got killed in that fiasco. Getting in the way of a whaling harpoon or cutting across the bow of an aircraft carrier, it made no difference to them. The end justified the means. They were right, and the rest of the world was making a mistake and had to be corrected. They risked their lives to attract the spotlight, and that was all right, but let one of them get hurt or killed and the howls were deafening. They played by two sets of rules: one said they could do no wrong, the other said whatever they did was right.

He, too, felt the fear of a major oil spill catastrophe, but could not see himself giving up his life for that kind of cause. There were proper and more effective ways to deal with matters that you thought were not in the national or international interests.

Kingsley had considerable intelligence compiled on various groups that would be there, from nut fringe groups to misled do-gooders. Matt would have to go to Bangor to see it all. He would leave in the morning.

He gathered his data on Russian ship movements and took it all down to Mike's temporary office. Mike scanned the papers and set the investigative wheels in motion.

"Kingsley should have some new information on these by the time you reach Bangor tomorrow. I've asked him to put all this into our computer, and it'll mix with other data. If there are any coincidences, they'll show up in the analysis"

"Well, there's not much more I can do here today, I'm going for supper. I'm picking George up on the way. Want to join us?"

"Sure. Give me about ten minutes, can you?"

"See you in ten, then."

Matt wanted to check on Pua and let George know he was ready to go, so he strolled over to the pier and down the ramp to the float. With darkness setting in, George was checking the dolphins when Matt arrived. The pier floodlighting was on, making the water in the pens sparkle like a school of herring were milling about in the water.

"How's the patient?"

"Pua's coming along fine, Matt."

Pua heard Matt's voice and swam immediately over to him. Somewhat subdued she poked her head out in front of him, nodding and squeaking. Matt knelt down and patted her snout.

"I don't know what you're thinking, Pua, but I can guess. Tanya's getting better. Not as fast as you, but every day she's a little stronger. I'll bring her down to see you in a day or so." More squeals and clicks. Matt rubbed her chin and she stood still in the water, eyes probing. "I'm sure she wants to know how you are, too. Are you okay?" Pua squealed and as if to show him she was getting better she dashed around the pen, jumping high in the air. She returned to Matt.

"That good, huh?" Matt and George laughed.

Hoku came over to get some attention. Matt patted him, too. "You guys look fine to me. You're getting lazy with all this time off. We'll have to find some work for you."

They both charged off, splashing and jumping. Matt picked up two toys and threw them to opposite ends of the pen. The dolphins tore off and retrieved them. Matt threw them again. Great splashing and 'talking' from the dolphins. They had a game going. They were happy.

George finished what he was doing with the other two dolphins and joined Matt.

"They don't do that for us. You and Tanya have an effect on them that I've rarely seen. They respond to the two of you as if they'd worked with you for years. I'd like to know what it is you've got."

"Good looks, George. The dolphins appreciate the finer things in life." He grinned.

George slugged him on the shoulder, "Can't be that. They'd never go near the likes of you."

They left in high spirits. "We'll go by and pick up Mike. He said he'd join us."

"Good. I've got some questions to run by him."

The three of them drove to the cafe, talking about events of the past week. They had enjoyed working together. They got along well together, working like a well oiled machine. Each had an area of expertise and contributed effectively to the overall scheme and results were satisfying. They had taken on an espionage probe of the most sophisticated kind, the best the enemy had to offer, and had come out on top of it. They had good reason to feel smug.

The waitress took their supper order. No drinks. George seldom drank and definitely not if he was diving. Mike was the same so Matt refrained, too.

"Will you want the dolphins tomorrow, Mike?" George had preparations to make if he did.

"I think so. Just two until we find out what we're up against. Is Pua up to diving yet?"

"I don't think so, Mike. We could send Hoku with the other two if you want though. Give you three."

"No. Let's start with two. There'll be gear to run up and down. They'll be very useful for that. If we get too busy, we'll call on the other two. Are they able to get in and out of the wreck, or are we going to have to meet them at the hull opening?"

"They'll come right in to the station if you want. They're not afraid of the hole. There's room for them to turn around and the only spots that might be dangerous would be the ragged edge of the hull plates. They'll stay clear of them though. I don't see any problem."

"How're you going to work inside the station Mike?"

"How do you mean?"

"What about breathing and light. If you don't use the Russian's system, what are you going to use?"

"Well, we can't work with the suits on. We'll have to have air, heat and light. We'll need power to fire up our test equipment and the Russian stuff, too. If we have to, we'll take air right into the station. Portable lights'll have to do. A dozen or more and an electric heater. About fifteen kilowatts."

"You'd better consider how you're going to keep track of all that equipment. If just one piece is forgotten in the station, it's game over!"

"Good thought, George. We'd better lay everything out on the cutter and take inventory of everything going down and coming up."

Matt observed, "It'd be easy to leave a screwdriver or a probe inside one of the cabinets, for sure."

"A final sweep of the station seems a good idea, too. A little solder on the floor would give the game away."

"You're right. This isn't like the buoys. A different set of circumstances govern here. Super careful. That's the by-word."

"The cutter can supply a mixture of helium-oxygen to the station. We can keep it circulating using the Mk 16 type analyzer and maintain a safe balance." Matt offered.

"What about power?"

"We've got just about anything you require, AC or DC, from 1 to 600 volts. We can also supply limited amounts of 400 Hertz for your electronics."

"May need that if the Russians are using new technology. Have you got all that aboard the cutter?"

"Yep, we've got it all. I'll have to get some longer cables though. How much power are you likely to need?"

"The heaters'll take the biggest slug. Electronics take very little. One kilowatt should do it. What about a data link cable?"

"No problem. I'll get my chief petty officer to scrounge the cables. What times are you going to be working? Daylight hours?"

"I think we'll have to go around the clock, Matt, at least until we find to what extent we have to modify the equipment. We could go for an eight hour day, but we may run out of time. I have no idea as yet how long it'll take to make the changes, and I'd rather be finished early so we can have a couple of days to sit back and relax. We don't want the OHIO coming through while we're still down there."

George understood the problem, "There's no way to buy time. Either you're finished or you're not."

"I agree," Mike added, "Get it done as fast as we can. What about your dolphins, George? Will they work at night?"

"They'll be all right. They don't require light."

"I was thinking more about sleep." Mike added.

"They don't need our eight hours sleep either. They catch short naps all through the day. They're awake all night anyway."

"Is that a fact? Mike was surprised. They don't float and sleep for a couple of hours then?"

"No, the naps they take give them the rest they need."

"Well, we won't have any trouble with the dolphins then, I wish my men could do the same." Mike was dreaming.

They all laughed at this thought.

"Think what a difference it would make to running a ship," Matt added. "I'll get my crew started gathering equipment now. We'll head to sea first thing in the morning.

They finished their meal and sat for a while, going over tomorrow's exercise. Matt told Mike that he would go to Bangor in the morning. If there was anything he needed he was to see his executive officer, Ernie Daniels. Matt planned to be back before noon.

"How was the water sample you sent to the lab, George?"

"The count is getting pretty high. In fact, higher than I like. The less time the dolphins have to spend in the harbor, the better!"

"I guess there's not much we can do about that, except maybe take them out for exercise as often as possible."

"That's about all." George was resigned to the danger.

Matt drove Mike to his hotel and George back to the base then carried on to the hospital. It was getting late for a visit. The nurses got sticky about having visitors wandering in and out at all hours. Matt hoped he had some leverage using Doc to okay it.

Tanya was all smiles as he walked into the room. Neat as a pin, every hair in place. Obviously, she wanted to look her best.

"Doc says my temperature's better and heading lower. If it continues, I may be discharged in a day or so."

That pleased Matt. The fresh air would probably be good for her, and she'd have some time to visit with the dolphins. He knew she could hardly wait to get down to the pens again. He also knew the dolphins would be even happier to see her.

"What have you been doing all day?" Matt was more interested in what Doc had her doing. "You sure look fit. Are you sure you're not malingering? How about jogging around the block?"

"Not quite yet. I'm able to get up and move around now. Still a bit sore, 'you know where', from the needles. Antibiotics, Doc says. He wants me to take deep breaths regularly to help the healing process."

"What about food?"

"Anything's okay. No alcohol though. I'll suffer for a while with an oxygen deficiency until my lungs heal. He says it's a good thing I don't smoke. Probably saved my life. What have you been up to? I've watched the Zodiacs go back and forth but the cutter stays put."

Matt told her about the underwater station and what the implications were.

"I'd like to come out and have a look at it."

"Well not for a day or so. You've had your share of diving for a while." As far as Matt knew, her diving days were probably over, he said nothing about that to her. The damage to her lungs would be enough normally but with the ruptured ear it's unlikely she'd want to risk the other one. Doc would probably want to discuss it with her at the right time.

"You've got your hands full right now just looking after Tanya. Get that job done, and maybe we'll see what else you can handle. The dolphins have been exercised a bit. That's what the Zodiacs were doing the first time you saw them out, taking the dolphins for a 'walk'. That's when we found the station. The next time out, it was Mike on a discovery trip, to assess how much trouble we're in. The dolphins stayed home for that trip."

"How's Pua doing? Her sores bothering her?"

"Not really. I visited the pens and they came right over to me. Both of them wanted to play. You'll have a great time, if they're not out working."

"Are they going to work on the station?"

"Part of the time. They'll run tools and equipment down and up when necessary. Not much more though."

"How long is George going to keep them here?"

"He planned to take Frankie and Johnnie back to San Diego this week. Pua and Hoku next week. All that's changed now of course. Mike has to reprogram the gear in the station pretty quickly. We haven't too much time before OHIO is due."

"What do you have to do when she gets here?"

"Our full complement is assigned to make sure the protestors don't get into trouble."

"Do you think they will?"

"They pull some pretty stupid stunts. I sometimes wonder about their intelligence. They've been known to drive small boats in front of large ships, expecting them to stop. They have no idea how those ships handle. Some of them take miles to stop."

"Will you have to keep them away?"

"Right now we can't even do that. The water is unrestricted. They go where they want."

"Why don't you pass a law to keep them ten miles away from the sub?"

"That's not a bad idea. I've already suggested it through channels. I have my doubts whether or not the government can move fast enough to help us with our sub. I don't know if even the president has enough power."

"I'll bet he has. Call it a matter of national security or something."

"You might have something there. I'll run it by the Commodore. If we could restrict their movement, it would make life a lot easier for all of us. There are rumored to be about fifty boats ready to take part."

"How can you control them all?"

"We can't. It's a futile effort. We're supposed to make sure they don't get hurt. If we can do that we'll consider the operation a success."

"If it's a nice day when you go, can I come with you?"

"I don't see why not, if you're well enough to spend a day at sea. We'll be escorting her right down to Bangor."

"I'd like that. The trip on the water will be good for me. Besides, I'd like to see more of this beautiful country."

"I'll see what Doc says. You'll have to be in uniform if you go. The situation is sticky enough without having to explain why a civilian is aboard at such a time."

"I could always work, maintaining radio contact with Oahu. That's a job that has to be done anyway."

"Feel up to that?"

"It's not that hard, physically. Besides if the birds stay put there's not much to do."

"Okay, you've got a deal, if Doc says it's all right. I'm going down to Bangor tomorrow to check some things with Mike's people so I won't be here until maybe sometime after supper."

"I'll miss you all day."

"I'll come as soon as I can. Meanwhile I'd better be on my way now; I've got work to do for an early start tomorrow. You'd better speed up your recovery, so you can come on the trip."

"I'll do my best. See you tomorrow."

*   *   *

Matt stopped by Doc's office to see if Tanya could go on the trip."

"No problem, if she's not too tired. That's the biggest worry now that we've got her temperature almost back to normal. I think we could release her today but she'd have to do too many things herself. I'd rather hold her for one more day to give her the extra day to rest."

"You're right. I'll be working most of the day so I couldn't spend much time with her and Tanya's not the type to sit around too long."

"Well, each day now is worth two days a week from now. Once she's over this initial period, it's downhill all the way."

"Good. I'll see you tomorrow night, Doc."

Matt returned to the base to finalize preparations, then went home, showered and got ready for bed. He had brought the pilot's report on Russian ship movement home from the office. He looked at the types of ships, dates and destinations. Timing didn't form any pattern nor did the type of ship. Dates were random from what he could see. There must be some thread holding the whole thing together if his thinking was right. He hit the sack with a flurry of facts running through his mind.

Awaking early in the morning he had breakfast then headed directly to the base helicopter hanger. He had laid on a Jet Ranger to ferry him to Bangor. The pilot, a young Lieutenant, was standing beside the machine.

"Pre-flight done?"

"Aye, ready, sir."

"Let's go then."

They climbed aboard and the pilot fired up the turbine. Contacting the tower at Fairchild field he announced where he was and where he was going, before lifting off.

They fought the bright morning sun until they were ten miles east of Port Angeles where they turned south east and entered the valleys. Here they could relax and enjoy the scenery. Bangor from the air is not an impressive sight: a few large buildings and of course the submarine pens with piers for surface ships. Dedicated to missile subs, there were seldom many large surface ships visiting.

They set down on the heli-pad where Lieutenant Commander Kingsley came out to meet them. Matt instructed the pilot to plan for a noon take-off, until then he was on his own. Kingsley pointed him toward a small building near the pad. "If you'd like to see the base, there are some people in there who can take you around. Tell them I've okay'd it."

"Thank you, sir. I'll take that tour and be back at 12:00." He sprinted away.

"Matt, if you'll come with me . . . . ?"

They passed several buildings which were obviously administration, and then a two storey with no windows, its roof covered with antennae of many sizes and shapes.

"This is 'home' to a few of us," Kingsley told him. "We have everything we need here, our own computer plus tie-ins with our major military mainframes and the CRAY 3 and more. We can communicate either by satellite, radio or hard ground lines. We also receive regular information on many items of a national security nature. What we're going to do is try to match your data with data we have on Soviet military shipping. We don't normally keep tabs on commercial shipping. Maybe we should."

"The Russian fishing fleet also acts as an intelligence gathering net to my knowledge. You don't monitor it?"

"No, we don't. Others do though. There's too much going on with the monitoring of regular naval ships. The type of spying the fishing boats do has more interest for other units of our intelligence community. We've got our hands full just watching the navy ships."

They came to Kingsley's office and went in. A desk and computer terminal stood along one wall, filing cabinets and another desk along the other.

"You feel there may be some connection between navy and fishing boats?"

"We know the factory ships are met by navy ships from time to time, Matt. We assume they're exchanging crews and reprovisioning, stuff like that. We don't put much importance on these meetings."

"What if they're doing more than that?"

"Well, we don't like surprises. What do you have in mind?"

"They could be transferring things like sono-buoys and the underwater station. They could even act as cover for attack submarines, bringing them right into our inner coast."

"We'd sure like to know if they were. Where's the data you brought?"

Matt opened his briefcase and extracted a file folder. "This is the Canadian data folder; this is the US data folder." There were half dozen sheets in each folder.

"I'll have these entered in our computer then we can use the terminal to play 'what if'."

"What's 'what if'?"

"We can call up various scenarios and see if there are activities happening which we haven't seen, like meetings of various ships, which ones and when. That sort of thing. The computer is programmed to react to things that might be difficult for us to spot."

He called a data entry clerk in, handed him Matt's Material, and instructed him as to what system to put it onto. "Call me when you've got it all in."

"If there's a common denominator in these ship movements, the computer will find it. Shall we have a coffee, Matt?"

Matt nodded. Kingsley punched the intercom. "Two coffees, please."

"How do you take it?" He asked Matt.

"One sugar, just a little cream."

"Two coffees please Pat, one black, one cream and sugar."

"I understand you grew up in this area Matt?"

"Yes I did, down at Bremerton. I know the waters around here pretty well though."

"You may know the Headland Yacht Club."

"Sure. I used to keep a boat there at one time."

"Well, you'll probably know some of the people who'll be out to greet OHIO. The club is organizing a welcoming flotilla for next Thursday."

"Is that right. Friendly or non-friendly? There were some real patriots in the group. I wonder if they're still there?"

"Probably, Matt. They thought this one up all by themselves. They'll meet OHIO at the Hood Canal Bridge and help escort her down to here. Wanted to do something for their country. You have to be well motivated to do something like that."

"Or pretty bored. I'd better talk to them. Seems to me there are a lot of well to do retired members in that club. Some, as I remember, would get involved just for something to do."

Kingsley's phone rang. "Up now? Thank you!"

"We're ready to play, Matt." He went to his terminal and hit a few keys. The screen came alive interrogating the keyboard. He entered the program number and his password.

DEFINE: came up on the screen.

He pushed a few more keys. "What do we want to see?"

"How about matching the arrival of naval ships to visits of fishing vessels in the Straits."

"Sounds good. When they meet at sea, limited to the past three months." The keyboard clicked.

Six dates appeared on the screen with the names of the navy ships in red and the names of fishing vessels in green.

"Can you make a print of that?"

"Sure, Matt."

More keyboard clicks and the printer began to hum.

"Now see which of the fishing vessels went to Canada and which went to Puget Sound."

The screen flashed. All but one to the US."

Where'd the other one go?" He punched the keys and entered the question.

ESQUIMALT. TO GRAVING DOCK, came back almost instantly.

"What type of ship?"

TRAWLER.

"What's the age of these ships?"

ALL LESS THAN ONE YEAR OLD

"Isn't that interesting, Matt?"

"Yeh. Wonder where they were built?" The keys clicked.

SEVEROMORSK SOVIET SHIPYARDS

"What type of navy ships were involved."

SUBMARINE TENDERS

"How about that. See where they stopped before coming here?"

He keyed it in.

PETROPAVLOVSK

"Looks funny. Let's see what it says about the ships stopping there in the three months previous to today."

The screen produced eight ships names.

"What type were these?"

1 OILER (30,000 TONNE).

1 REFRIGERATOR SHIP (45,000 TONNE).

3 PROVISIONING SHIPS (18,000 TONNE).

2 LIGHT DESTROYERS (3,000 TONNE).

1 SMALL TRAINING SHIP (8,000 TONNE).

"No sub tenders?"

"No! __ Interesting to say the least."

"Sure is. Let's see what port they came from."

"Which ones?"

"The sub tenders."

Click, click, click.

"They all came from the same place, Petropavlovsk."

"Just for the hell of it, where'd the others come from?"

He keyed that in.

"Various places. The reefer came from North Vietnam, provisioning ships from Vladavostok, training ship from the Black Sea."

"So, the only visitors they've had recently have all been from Petropavlovsk."

"Right"

"Let's go back, now and look at which yards they went into."

Mc CORMACK SHIPYARD

"And how long did they stay?"

2 DAYS 3 DAYS 1 DAY 3 DAYS 4 DAYS 2 DAYS

"What repairs were made?" He fingered the keyboard.

MINOR REPAIRS

"At the pier or or drydock?" Matt was getting the hang of it now.

1 DRYDOCK THE ANDREY POPOVITCH

"No bottom painting? Isn't that normal for ships that have been at sea for a while, Matt?"

"Not necessarily. The paint they use will last for longer than a year. The Russians probably wait and have it done at home. Besides, if they had something to hide on their bottoms, they wouldn't want to go up on the dock."

"I guess you're right. Maybe we can see how long the navy ships stayed with the ships at sea."

"What's the significance of that?"

"Not much, unless they stayed until the trawlers returned from the repair yards."

"It's worth looking at. If they waited for the trawlers to return, it's likely they transferred something back to the navy ships. Maybe equipment or personnel."

"Like underwater teams."

"Right."

In all cases but the one where the ship had drydocked, the navy ships waited for the returning trawlers.

"Well, I guess that says something."

"Is there any way you can find out what went on at sea between these ships?"

"There are some things we can do, although they're not too complete. We've got satellite pictures of the areas. We can scan them to see if they show anything special."

"Can you see what passes between ships?"

"Sometimes. If the sea is calm, they usually tie up alongside each other. The only way we can see what's passing back and forth is by watching what they put on the open deck. It's better when the seas run high. They transfer with cables between ships, much the way we do in our own navy. You can see the actual material being transferred, including personnel going back and forth. We see a lot more that way."

"Is there any way we can see what went between the ships that met within the last three months?"

"I can pull the satellite pictures. They may or may not have what we want."

"What about an underwater transfer?"

"Normal pictures won't pick that up. If we were to see anything it would have to be with the infra red. Are you thinking about a submarine?"

"Uh huh, does the infra red see that kind of thing?"

"If it stays within 100 feet of the surface it does, Matt. Below that, things become obscured rather quickly for infra-red."

"Can you get hold of the data for the day we want?"

"Not immediately. I'll have to ask for the data taken on specific dates to be put onto the computer queue. That may take a day or so."

"Why so long?"

"There are so many users wanting data, we have to wait sometimes. If we declare a red priority, we can get it almost immediately but we'd have some tall explaining to do. The paperwork wouldn't stop flying around for months. We don't do that unless we've almost got incoming missiles. It's just not worth it."

"I can see that." Matt checked the time, 11:30 hours. "I guess there's not a whole lot more I can do here and there are things waiting for me back at the base, I'd better head out. When you get the infra red information, give me a call. I'd be interested to know if they show any underwater transfers."

"I'll let you know. Don't forget, any of the material you are talking about could be brought in by submarines."

"That's a pleasant thought. We may be looking at the wrong delivery vessels."

"Could be."

"Can you check the data over the last three months to see if there were any Russian submarines in the area?"

"Will do. You know, the Russians don't usually send submarines in this close to shore here. We haven't thought it was necessary to look for them. Maybe we've been overlooking the obvious. If they've been sending them in, we're going to have a lot of egg on our faces!"

Matt left him interrogating the computer and stepped outside into the bright sunshine. He covered the short distance to the heli-pad in a few minutes. His pilot waited at the aircraft. "Pre-flight check done?"

"Yes, Sir!"

"Well let's get airborne." They climbed aboard and ran through the engine start check."

"Did you get your tour?"

"Sure did. This place is something else. They showed me things I didn't know existed. The workshops here are as up to date as possible and are fully equipped for whatever is needed. They can function totally on their own and I mean totally. The rest of the world could be gone, and these guys could fix their ships in any way necessary. This place is a self contained world."

"I can believe that," Matt agreed. "They sure have the cream of the crop working here. The best men and equipment available."

"Sort of lets you relax. If all the people protecting our country are of this calibre we don't have much to worry about. You know all that can be done is being done."

"You're right. I've got a lot of confidence in our capability just from this one base."

The chopper lifted off into the clear blue sky and headed north west. Climbing to 6500 feet they threading their way through the green valleys of the Olympic mountains. Roads looking like pencil lines wound up and down around the low, eroded peaks. Rivers picked their way along the valley floors tumbling and boiling as they dropped over ledges and cliffs. The air became more turbulent as they approached the coast line of the Strait. Dipping down, they landed at the Coast Guard base. Matt checked in at the office then carried on down the hall to the rooms Mike and his crew occupied. They were still out at the dive site, so Matt drove to town for lunch. After clam chowder and a tuna sandwich, he drove to the hospital. The head nurse directed him to the lounge at the front of the hospital. A large, airy room opening onto a balcony overlooking the town and Strait, provided pleasant R & R for patients. Poolside furniture gave it a relaxing resort type atmosphere, designed to assist in patient recovery. Tanya lay in one of the chaise lounges, almost asleep.

"What are you doing lying around. You're supposed to be exercising."

She stirred.

"How're you feeling, lazybones?"

"A lot better today. Doc says I can get out tomorrow." She took his hand. Pulling him close, she kissed him.

"That's the best news I've had all day."

"I've still got to be careful. He said I'll tire easily."

"We'll, just have to make sure you're properly looked after."

"For instance?"

"Well for instance, you can't stay at the Hotel. They don't know how to look after you."

"Well, if they don't, who does?"

"I do! You'll have to stay at my place at least until you're well. Then we'll have to decide what's best for you."

"WE will, will WE?"

"You just relax and work on getting better, leave all the hard stuff to me."

"Got it all figured out, have you?"

"Just doing what's best." They both laughed. It was good to see her laugh. The sparkle had returned to her eyes. Matt took this as a good sign. They talked for the best part of an hour. They saw the Zodiacs returning to base and Matt thought it best if he was there to meet them.

During the drive down to the Hook, Matt thought about how the Russians had placed the station. How did they know the wreck was there in the first place? Could the scuba divers have been working with the Russians? They were down pretty deep for sport divers. They were slow in reporting the missing diver. Could they have been reluctant to bring any attention to themselves? He wondered if there was some connection that he should maybe have Mike's people look into. The more he thought about it, the more he felt it was worth investigation. He made a mental note to mention it to Mike.

He arrived at the pier just as the Zodiacs were tying up. Crews were on the float by the time he got to them.

"How're you doing out there, Mike?"

"So far so good. No surprises. The equipment is similar to the stuff we found in the buoy, and the men I have here were involved with the examination at Bangor. Things are moving smoothly."

"That's great. When do you think you'll be able to finish?"

"With luck, tomorrow or the day after. We'll need the cutter for our next dive though. We've identified the pieces of equipment we have to modify. Now it's just a matter of getting to it. Are you ready to go?"

"Any time you say."

"We'll give these guys an hour and a half to get something to eat then we'll go right back at it."

"I'll prepare the ship and crew."

"Thanks, Matt. I'll let my men know."

CHAPTER 21

Wednesday, Day 12 19:00 hours.

The cutter eased away from the pier as the Zodiacs skimmed past with Frankie and Johnnie leading the way. Mike joined Matt on the bridge for the short trip out to the wreck. Matt took advantage of the opportunity to bounce a few ideas off him, particularly the one about the scuba divers being part of the Russian spy mission.

"We can run their names through our computers to see if any of them are known spies. If they really are only sport divers, they won't be listed. It's worth a try though."

Matt also explained to Mike his theory on the Russian naval ships making underwater transfers to the fishing fleet.

"I'd be interested to know what Kingsley comes up with. Keep me posted on that one will you Matt?"

"Kingsley should be calling sometime tomorrow, as soon as his request for computer time is granted. I'll let you know."

Watching the sonar plot Matt could see the wreck site coming into view. As they approached, Matt turned the cutter toward the west, pointing into the incoming tide.

"I'll pull half a mile past the wreck, Mike, and then set the anchor. That should put us about 500 yards away from it. Your men will be able to drop the cables and hoses straight down and let the current carry them back to the wreck. The divers in the Zodiacs can moor a long tether to the cutter and dive right over the wreck."

"Okay, Matt. I'll go aft and get them started."

Matt gave the order and the heavy port side anchor plunged into the water with a huge splash. Clouds of rust flew above the bow as the thick chain rattled through the hawse pipe, plummeting to the bottom 200 feet below. Matt let the cutter drift to a stop then eased her slowly astern. The chain pulled at the anchor, dragging it along the bottom until its flukes bit into the bottom, holding fast. Once the cutter was fixed in place Matt went aft to see the lines and hoses deployed. There seemed to be an awful lot of them over the stern.

Matt thought how well the cutter was suited for this kind of operation. The flight deck on top of the back half of the cutter screened the fan deck from view by the satellites. Whatever they did back there, they could do without fear of prying eyes watching. The place was a beehive of activity as the breathing gas hoses and power lines spilled over the rail and down to the underwater station. Small support engines roared to life smothering the voices of the men working to get everything in order.

Zodiacs were close to 500 feet off the stern and Mike's divers were in the water. He watched their umbilical's paying out. The cables and lines from the cutter should be carried to them by the tide as they neared the ocean bottom. Matt joined him at the rail.

"The report of the pilot aboard the Russian ship bothers me a little too, Mike. I don't think the trawlers were used to set the station in place. I don't think they're large enough to handle the equipment required. The factory ships could do it."

"You could be right, Matt, and if that's the case we've got to worry about Russian ships catching us in here as well as their damn satellites."

"Yes. I've checked with the Canadian and US pilotage authorities to see how much lead time notification they need from foreign shipping. Twelve hours is all they get."

"That means we could have Russian ships in here any time."

"That's right. I've asked both authorities to contact the Coast Guard office as soon as a Russian ship notifies them that they're coming in."

"Only Russian ships?"

"Yep. Why?"

"What're they going to think about that? They'll know something's up."

"I covered it by saying we had oil dumping problems with the Russians and wanted to keep an eye on them. It satisfied them. They even wanted to help; told me they'd watch for oil spills, too!"

Noise on the intercom broke their conversation. The divers were calling for equipment. Men on deck packaged it in waterproof bags and sent it down by dolphin express. The Zodiacs hovered directly over the wreck well out from the stern of the cutter and the dolphins swam from it to the cutter to pick up and deliver materiel. Among the lines flowing from the stern Matt had included one for an intercom. The divers in the station would be working with their helmets off so they needed some way to communicate easily, hence the intercom. Breathing gas consisting of a helium/oxygen mixture had to be piped down into the station supplying the men, but a return hose was also necessary in order to analyze the ratio and maintain the proper mix. While the supply for the divers Mk 16 units came from the Zodiacs, the mixture for the station had to come from the cutter. The cutter also supplied power for the station, mostly for heat and lights.

Matt scanned the water around the stern. There were no bubbles rising to the surface as there would have been from regular diving equipment. The mixed gas returned to the cutter for monitoring. Other than the cutter and two Zodiacs, there was no indication of anything going on at all.

"Captain to the radio room Captain to the radio room" The PA was insistent.

"I guess we've got trouble, MIke. I'd better go and see." Matt strode across the after deck and up the ladder to the flight deck then up again to the bridge deck.

In the radio room a message from Oahu waited. BIRD IN TRANSFER ORBIT. EXPECT LOW PASS IN EIGHTY FIVE MINUTES. ACKNOWLEDGE AT ONCE! SIGNED, SNELLERT.

"Send, "Message received and understood. Signed, Reynolds."

Matt instructed Ernie Daniels to haul in and get under way on his signal from the fan deck. He then raced back to tell Mike to clear out. "Mike how fast can you get your men topside?"

"We got trouble?"

"Seems so. There's a bird coming in for a look in eighty minutes."

"We should be able to meet that, let's find out. Mike called down, "Clear out guys. We've got a visitor in no time flat. Leave the gear where it is, but get yourselves topside, right away. Disconnect all lines from the cutter too."

Power and gas cut, the lines were reeled up by the men on deck. The divers were into their gear and on their way up within ten minutes. Matt signaled the bridge and Daniels began to weigh anchor. The cutter's engines throbbed as she moved ahead taking up the slackening anchor cable as she went. The Zodiacs had the umbilical's all aboard. A total of fifteen minutes had passed.

"Not bad." Matt said. "Not bad at all."

"We'll have to do better though. If we had to bring the equipment too, it would have taken much longer."

"Let's hope that will never have to be tested. We'd only have to do that if a ship was due."

"That's right, but if we get caught it's back to square one; we can't afford that."

"I'll contact Oahu again and see how our 'friend' is doing." Matt went back to the radio room to talk to Captain Snellert. "What's the situation now Captain?"

"The bird's half way to perigee now. It'll be over you in about four minutes."

"How long do we have to wait after it goes by?"

"You mean before you can go back to work?"

"Affirmative."

"Ten minutes should do it."

"Copy ten minutes. How about other birds?"

"All others remaining in normal orbit. If any move, we'll give you notice again."

Matt checked his watch. He'd give it another five minutes beyond the ten for a little more safety. 'Why had the Russian brought the bird down?' he wondered. He called Mike to the wardroom.

"We've got more than fifteen minutes before the bird's gone. But I've been wondering, do you think we should go back to the station right away?"

"Why not, Matt?"

"We don't know why the bird was sent down. The Russians must have spotted something very interesting with the Cosmos satellite to send the smaller bird down. They must have really wanted to see whatever it was to have spent the fuel repositioning the little bird."

"Could it be that they wanted to see some other target?"

"What else is going on, Mike?"

"Well, we've got the Nimitz departing Bremerton today. She's due to leave just about now. Maybe they're looking at her, Matt."

"Would it be more prudent to call it a day for now?"

"I don't know. What you say could be right. I'll check with my men and see if we can afford the time. If they're far enough ahead, we could chance some time off. If they figure it can be completed tomorrow we could go home until then. Ivan could suspect something; maybe a rest would do all of us some good."

Mike scrubbed the mission. They'd continue tonight after dark. Matt turned the ship around heading back toward the base. The dolphins came over from the Zodiac and took up positions in the bow wave. Moving just below the surface and slightly ahead of the cutter, they found the pressure wave and rode it like a slide all the way in.

Matt eased the cutter alongside the pier and watched as his deck crew threw out the heavy lines and secured them to pier mooring cleats. He alerted the crew that they'd be departing again at 21:00 hours, then went ashore to his office and phoned the hospital. He wanted Doc to let Tanya know he wouldn't be able to get there tonight. He also wanted to get a report on her progress.

"She's recovering well, Matt. I think she'll be able to leave tomorrow morning. As long as she watches what she does and takes it easy she can resume normal work."

"I'll see that she's well looked after Doc. Talk to you tomorrow."

Matt checked with his clerk to see if there were any messages. He half expected something from the ship pilots. There were none. His concern with Russian ships coming in got the best of him. The more warning they had, the better. If a Russian ship was to send divers down to the station he wanted to be sure the place would be just as they left it. If a ship was due while they had all the equipment down there, it would be a mad scramble to clear it all before the Russians spotted them. The thought occurred to him that the Russians didn't have to announce their intentions to bring a ship in until they were all the way into the Strait as far as Port Angeles where the pilot joined them. They might have to wait for the required twelve hours but at that point that wouldn't bother them, in fact that might be what they want; they could use the time to send divers to the station. It sent a chill down his spine. His thinking was based on the premise that the Russians played the game by the rules. If they came all the way in and anchored, waiting for the pilot, they'd have ample time to work on the buoys.

Matt hurried down the hall to the offices Mike occupied and told him what had occurred to him.

"Where do you get these ideas, Matt? You're going to drive me nuts."

"You don't think that could happen?"

"Yes, I do. That's the problem. I think it's so God damned obvious that it embarrasses me that I overlooked it. If I was Ivan, that's exactly what I would do."

"What can we do about it now?"

"Let's think for a moment. How long will it take us to get the Zodiacs from shore out to the station?"

"At best, half an hour."

"And to clean our gear out of the station, about another half an hour."

"That means, Mike, the warning time we've got to have is an hour."

"Not quite. When the Russian ship is approaching, how far ahead can they see?"

"About twenty miles."

"That means if they steam in at ten knots they'll be able to see us working two hours before they actually arrive over the station."

"Christ, that means we'd need three hours Mike."

"That's right. We can't rely on the pilots to tip us off. We need earlier warning and the only way we can get that kind of time is from closer surveillance of their fleet. I'll contact our reconnaissance arm and have them get on this right away!"

"If any of their ships move toward the coast, have them contact the cutter immediately. I'll give you a standby frequency. That should keep us posted, but what are the Russians going to think when they start getting all that attention?"

"Likely not much. They're used to having planes and ships watching them, particularly this close to the coast. I'll get right on this"

Mike dialed the phone as Matt left the office. The Zodiacs had to be alerted to be ready to go at a moment's notice. He walked out to the pier to see if there was anyone still around the float. George came up the ramp to meet him. Matt filled him in on what he and Mike had discussed. The dolphins would play a pivotal role in any scramble because of the speed at which they could retrieve equipment. George thought the only thing that could give them trouble would be the diving gas. If they ran out, that would be the end. He took the responsibility to ensure they had enough in reserve at all times.

"Maybe, George, if we're not actually at the station. We'd better make sure we've got one Zodiac ready to go at all times."

"A good idea, Matt. We've also got to make sure each crew knows what has to be done inside the station if the scramble is necessary. You know, what has to be cleaned out and making sure we don't leave a scrap of paper or a drop of solder anywhere in the place. We don't want to leave calling cards."

"Yeh, and something else. We want to make sure there's no water on the floor. That'd be so easy to pass up. All signs'll have to be removed. That means we've got to have rags or drying agents available to go with the standby Zodiac. I'll look after that."

Each of them took off to get busy arranging details, George up to the cutter and Matt to the Coast Guard stores to get desiccant, towels and plastic bags.

Matt returned to the cutter at 20:30 hours with his errands completed. His next task, to ready the cutter for sea.

They departed on time and took up their position over the wreck. They worked through the night. Mike went down a couple of times himself to check progress. The going was slow.

Once the equipment and tools were down there wasn't a great need for the dolphins so George sent them back to the cages. They could be recalled in a moment. There wasn't much to do for the others on the cutter and Matt had those not actually involved, stand down. There were five electronics specialists down in the station, and they were working harder than everyone. There was nothing further anyone on the surface could do to help them. The surface team could only wait.

Dawn broke gently with a slight glow in the east. A few minutes later there was enough light to read a newspaper, then the sun broke over the distant Coast Mountains. Rays of warming light spread over the water raising a low layer of fog which drifted along the surface hiding from view all but the antenna rack and diving flag of the Zodiac. The divers came topside to eat. It was easier for them to come up to eat than try to send food down to them. Mike met them at the stern ladder and anxiously gleaned information from each as they reached the deck. They had run into no snags. In fact they had found two spare buoys and containers of the binary explosive used to booby trap them. It appeared the buoys were transported inert, the explosive not in them. They were filled in the station and then programmed to respond to specific signals.

The Russians had felt so sure the station would never be discovered, they left their code books in it. Code books not only for these buoys but all of their buoys throughout the globe. An oversight that compromised their world operation. The books permitted a foreign nation to eavesdrop on all Russian satellite-to-buoy communications anywhere in the world. An espionage coup. The significance was lost on Matt and George but to Mike it was the single most important thing to come from the whole operation. The importance of getting away clean was suddenly magnified tenfold. The need of vigilance became top priority. If they were careful before, they were going to find out what careful really meant. The stakes in this game had just doubled.

Another warning came through from Oahu. A bird had been kicked out of orbit with a low pass due over western Washington at 08:00 hours. Matt discussed with Mike the advisability of leaving the area during the pass, returning when the satellite had passed. Mike concurred. It would be worthwhile. The divers were on top for breakfast, there would be very little time lost. Two divers went down to unfasten the hoses and cables. These were reeled in quickly and the cutter moved to a point five miles North West of the diving site and began to scribe large circles in the calm water. Anyone watching would take these for normal Coast Guard exercises.

Mike took advantage of this rest period to get to the radio room. He contacted navy intelligence to have them find out what the Russian fleet was up to. They had observed no unusual activity. He then checked with Lieutenant Commander Kingsley to tell him about the air surveillance he had ordered. He already knew. His own data gathering network was aware of the increased air activity as soon as it started. He had been watching data coming in and surmised correctly that Mike was responsible. Mike wanted to know if they had detected any submarine visits to the fishing fleet. The only sub in the area was a picket, off San Diego. A Soviet surface electronic snoop ship accompanied her. There were a few others scattered over the Pacific Ocean but none were close to the fishing fleet. There was one that could be headed this way. They lost him for a while but expected to recapture him any time.

"What are you doing to relocate her?"

"We've sent one of our attack subs after her, the Tampa Bay, I think. She's a Los Angeles class carrying the BQQ-9/ towed sonar array. If anyone can find them, she will."

Mike asked to be notified immediately if any even looked like they were headed toward the fleet, particularly the 'lost' sub. He gave Kingsley a radio frequency to use adding, "Any time day or night. We'll keep constant watch on that channel." Mike returned to the bridge.

The communications officer came in with the news that the satellite had passed. They resumed diving.

"If all goes well in the next few hours, Matt, we should be about ready to wrap it up before lunch."

"Can't be too soon, Mike. I get more nervous all the time that a Russian ship could drop in at a moment's notice."

"I know what you mean. I've just had a report from Kingsley that a Soviet 'Foxtrot' class sub may be headed this way. She's primarily a mine layer but she can also carry deck cargo. It wouldn't surprise me if that type of sub brought the underwater station here for the factory ship to set in place."

"Is she a nuclear missile sub?"

"No, she's an older type diesel electric patrol sub. They built them in Sudomekh starting 'way back in '58. They have over 60 of them and use them as workhorses."

"Would they bring them into the Strait underwater?"

"Not likely, although they have more than once taken them up to the Canadian submarine test range at Nanoose Bay. It's about one hundred and twenty five miles north of here. We've tracked them without confronting them. They don't even know that we saw them. We can spot them relatively easily, and use them for practice. No, it may be delivering something."

"Maybe there's some other reason for her to be heading this way. Would they use it to follow the Nimitz when she leaves?"

"No, they have a top speed of only 16-18 knots. The Nimitz is capable of an excess of 35 knots. They'd never keep up. If they wanted to follow her, they'd send an 'Alfa' class. They're nuclear powered attack subs that do better than 45 knots underwater. I think she may be coming here to service the buoys. We'll know soon enough. The Nimitz will be by here later this afternoon. We'll have Intelligence keep a sharp watch on the sub. I'm sure that's not her mission, though."

The divers called for the dolphins about 10:00 hours and began bringing up the equipment. They had done everything they could to the Russian electronics. Now it was only a matter of time until they'd know if they were successful. The first Russian ship that sent divers down to the wreck would tell the tale. Matt thought, 'if they had done their work well, Ivan would never know they had discovered the station. If they had slipped up and tipped their hand, the Russians would quickly know. Mike now had the means to interrogate both the buoys and the station whenever he wanted.' If the Russians found this out they'd alter some frequencies inside the buoys and negate Mike's advantage.

Mike had told Matt he made some changes in the buoys and the station equipment that would warn him if the Russians found they had tampered with their equipment. Mike had not told Matt everything about the modifications made.

"The code books are the most important single espionage breakthrough we have made in years. The discovery has to be protected at all costs and I have every reason to believe that the secret will be preserved." Mike said confidently. He said no more, but Matt wondered what he had done.

"You had the books copied?"

"I wish we could. The books are part writing, part magnetic. They can't be copied. We had to take the books as they are."

"The Russians'll see they're gone."

"We're making arrangements to prevent that, Matt."

The last of the equipment came aboard and the divers clambered up the ladder to the aft deck, then Mike and one of his men went over the side for a final dive to clean up the station.

"Everything's fine. Let the Russians come. There's no way to tell we've ever been down there. We even checked the air pocket at the top of the wreck's hold to make sure nothing had floated up unnoticed. It's as clean as a whistle, Matt." Mike had reason to be pleased.

"Okay, Mike, let's get away from the area. This is the end of a job well done. Congratulations."

"Thanks, Matt, and a special thanks to your crew for all they've done."

"Glad to be of service, Mike."

"Get your men to reel in those cables, Mike; we'll get under way in ten minutes."

"Aye, Sir!" Mike responded.

CHAPTER 22

Wednesday, Day 12, 16:00 hours.

With the cutter secured for the day, Matt attended to some administrative duties in his office and managed to squeeze in a call to the hospital to find out about Tanya.

She waited for his call. "I'm ready to go. Can you get away? I watched your ship returning to the base and figured you might be finished"

"For now. I'll be there in a half an hour. How's that?"

"Fine. I'll check out and wait with Doc in his office."

Matt made some phone calls clearing some pressing paperwork, part of it being a letter to the local boating clubs regarding the arrival of OHIO. They'd have to be hand delivered now as there was no time to get them there in the mail. He explained that they would tolerate no nonsense around the submarine and asked each club commodore to inform all members. He also suggested they post someone on the slips tomorrow to tell each departing boat. He issued it to the print room with instructions that it be delivered right away, today if possible.

Matt had gone through many channels to ask for special procedures to be instituted at the Federal level preventing anyone approaching a buffer zone within five miles of any sub.

Five miles would give his ships room to maneuver and prevent the protesters from getting hurt. Even if they were bent on injury or destruction, Matt was charged with their safety and he would protect them. There was no correspondence in his pile of paper to indicate that this request had gotten to the right place. He didn't like the prospects of escorting the sub without the buffer zone, but it looked like that would be the case.

With the letter to the yacht clubs taken care of and most of the paper pile reduced, he drove to the hospital and walked directly to Doc's office. Doc and Tanya were about to go to the cafeteria for coffee and Matt joined them.

"Has this guy made you one hundred per cent again?" Matt asked pointing at Doc.

"Almost," Tanya replied, "he says I've got to come back in a month or so to have my ear worked on and run some tests on my lungs."

"Is that the best he can do, a conditional warranty?"

"Seems like it." She laughed at his terminology.

"She's made a very satisfactory recovery Matt." Doc added. "She's not back to normal yet though, so don't work her too hard. I'd suggest she take at least three weeks off."

"That means she should stay around here for a while?"

"If she wants to, Matt."

"I want to." Tanya injected with an elfish glint in her eye.

"Well, I don't know . . . . if she can't pull her weight Doc, we may not be able to keep her around."

"You'll think of something, Matt, I'm sure." They all laughed at that.

"I'll contact your commanding officer, Tanya, and recommend that you take medical leave for a month, okay?"

"Thanks, Doc, for everything." Tanya appreciated the attention she had received.

"Well, why don't you two take the rest of the afternoon to get organized? I think you've got some lost time to make up for."

"Sure have, Doc." He turned to Tanya, "Shall we go?"

They left the hospital, driving into town and along to the beach where this whole thing began almost two weeks ago. Getting out of the car, they strolled through the trees, along the parkway between the beach and road. Walking along Matt described what they had found underwater, and what their first impressions were. Tanya had seen the beach disaster the second day and at that time, they were in the midst of discovery. Many details eluded them. This re-visit allowed them to think events through without many of the distractions of their previous visit. How the buoy got there in the first place was still a mystery. It may have somehow lost its negative buoyancy and floated to the surface to be washed ashore by the tide. Matt studied the distance from the water's edge to high water mark and guessed that the spot where it had exploded was a little below spring high tide. The buoy could have been there for a couple of months or it could have washed up only last week. It was hard to tell. The marine growth, or rather the lack of any substantial growth, on the parts they found was all they could go on.

Tanya couldn't wait to see the dolphins so they walked back to the car and headed for the base. She was happy to hear the animals were in their pens, not out working, she'd have a chance to visit with them again. Matt drove along the Hook and parked at the pier. Tanya could see the four dolphins swimming lazily through the calm water, their singing clearly audible above normal background noises of the busy base. As they approached the pier, the two nearest dolphins, Frankie and Johnnie watched. Their vocalization pattern changed, and they began tail standing to see who was coming. Pua and Hoku in the next pen, obviously listening to the chatter, picked up on the activity and tried desperately to see over the float. When this failed they began jumping high, in the middle of the pen. They recognized Tanya and thrashed madly over to the corner of the pen, squealing to show off. Tanya ran the final fifty feet to greet them. She dropped to her knees, reached out and touched them. The two dolphins were beside themselves with excitement. Matt noticed this. He swore they were smiling. He stood back and watched, hard pressed to say who was more excited, Tanya or the dolphins. There were tears in her eyes as she patted Pua. She fed them and tossed their toys, moving ever closer to the edge of the pen. Matt could clearly see she'd dearly love to get into the water with them, but that could not be for quite a while. She'd have to be content to participate from the edge of the float.

The time spent during the rest of the afternoon was good for Tanya, having a greater healing effect than the last few days in the hospital. It pleased Matt to see her so happy. He checked his watch. It was getting late. After five o'clock. "Come on now, leave your playmates for a while, we've got to get something to eat ourselves."

"Okay, Matt, one more fish for each of them." She reluctantly left.

Driving toward town, Matt asked where she'd like to eat. She suddenly realized how tired she was.

"I don't know, nothing fancy, I don't want to have to work at it."

"How be we barbeque a steak at my place?"

"That sounds about the right speed. We'll have to stop by the hotel so I can pick up some things. Have we got time?"

Matt had been avoiding the suggestion that she stay with him but the time had come to broach the subject. "Sure we've got time. While we're there why don't you collect all your gear and register at the hotel up on 3rd Avenue? Doc ordered you to rest."

"Third Avenue. That's your place. Are you asking me to shack up with you?"

"Yes. Call it what you will. I could look after you if you want."

"I know you could, but I wouldn't want to put you out . . . ."

"No problem. We'll collect your stuff, and then have supper. What do you say?"

"Sounds good to me. Do you provide all the comforts of home?"

"More, wait and see. And think how much you'll be saving the navy in lodging costs."

"I knew there must have been a good reason for you to ask."

They enjoyed the humor like two kids getting into trouble. Clearing the hotel, they were soon at Matt's place on 3rd Avenue. He brought food from the fridge and freezer and got everything ready for a typical west coast barbeque. Tanya was tired and while Matt prepared the meal she cat-napped. When everything was ready he gently woke her. She sleepily joined him at the balcony table. They were high on the bluff above the Olympic Discovery Trail and the view took in everything. The Spit, Vancouver Island and, best of all a clear view of the Strait.

"I think I'm going to like staying at this hotel." she said with that impish grin of hers.

"Wait 'till you find out what the dessert is," Matt shot back with a larger grin.

They capped a delicious tossed salad and steak dinner with a bottle of dry red wine, then sat back to watch the summer sun setting like a golden orange over the Strait of Juan de Fuca.

Relaxing on his comfortable deck furniture, they talked for a long time, about one another, their hopes and desires, likes and dislikes, divulging their innermost thoughts. It was therapeutic for both of them, this learning period.

Matt brought up the escort duty for the incoming submarine that they had already discussed a couple of days ago. "She'll be coming in Friday. Are you strong enough to go?"

"I think so."

"We could use a radio officer. You say you handle that?"

"I'll be able to monitor the satellites for you." she said.

"You're on." Matt added as he rose. "I suppose we should think about some rest now. We've got a busy day tomorrow, and we don't want you getting over tired."

"No, I guess not. It's a shame to end this perfect night though."

"We don't have to end it quite yet. How about just changing the tempo."

"Got something in mind?"

"I may have. You head in that way. Take the near side of the bed." he said pointing toward the bedroom, "I'll clean up a bit here and be with you shortly."

Matt tidied up, putting the dishes in the dishwasher and clearing the table. He turned off the stereo and the lights, and then got ready for bed. Entering his bedroom Matt saw that Tanya had curled up on the far side of the bed, his side. 'She's playing games' he thought, I'll slip gently into the other side. He moved around to the other side then noticed she wasn't playing. She was out like a light. Too heavy an evening had taken its toll on a not fully recovered woman. Matt slid into bed and soon, he too, was sound asleep.

*   *   *

Thursday, Day 13, 09:00 hours.

Matt gathered the Coast Guard officers in the base briefing room to discuss tactics for tomorrow's escort operation. Mike had returned to Bangor, and George had things to do at the dolphin pens. Matt would have liked to have had George at this briefing.

"The sub will pass Port Angeles around 13:00 hours tomorrow. My ship will meet her earlier, off Cape Flattery and take our position. Our 82-foot ships will meet us twenty miles west of the base and get into position. All smaller boats will join off Port Angeles. This should give us time to establish ourselves and run with the sub for a while before the protestors have a chance to interfere. We should present a solid barrier they'll find difficult to penetrate."

"How do you want us deployed, Commander?"

"The cutter'll be ahead of and to starboard of the sub. The two 82-foot ships will stay to port, one slightly ahead of and one abeam the sub. The two captains can decide which one will be where. The smaller ship's Zodiacs will form on the flanks and to her stern. Remember to take long range fuel tanks in the Zodiacs.

We'll use the ship's helicopter to monitor, acting as our overhead eyes. A second helicopter has been assigned to spell the first one throughout the day. We'll pick it up as we pass the base. There will always be at least one chopper in the sky at all times."

How close should we be to the sub?" questioned one of the boat skippers.

"She'll maintain a speed of fifteen knots. We'll keep within a mile distance."

Matt had seen the wheels of democracy turn. He was pleased that the recommendation he had made had been acted upon. He was even more pleased at the speed at which it was done. The President had issued a special decree. The five miles he had suggested had been reduced to a mile, and that could always be improved on later. What was important was the fact that law enforcement agencies now had the power to apprehend any violators. Previously, they had to deal from a relatively weak position. Now they had some teeth! This would be the first time they had the authority to seize vessels, using force if necessary.

"To keep all of you up to date, we now are in a position to stop any boat that in our opinion could cause damage or injury to either itself or any federal property. This includes the sub. We can handle this in any way we see fit. I have orders from the White House to make sure the situation isn't allowed to develop into a national headline story."

"How far can we go?"

"We can take the boat in tow and arrest the person in charge of it."

"What happens when we have ten or fifteen boats in tow? How're we going to maintain our positions?"

"A good point. Any suggestions?"

"Take names and boat registrations." piped up one sailor.

"No! The culprits will just make further attempts to harass the sub." rejoined another.

"I think you're right. We've got to protect the sub without getting too far out of position." Matt agreed.

"If we're travelling at fifteen knots, it's not likely any sailboats will be able to keep up. That'll leave only the larger motor powered boats."

"What's the point?" Matt asked.

"Just this. If we take a critical engine part, they'll be dead in the water. We can go back and return the part after the sub is safely in Bangor. This will successfully keep an offending boat out of the way."

Someone suggested, "I can see it now. We'll arrive at Bangor with our boat loaded with all sorts of engine parts and in our wake, the longest string of bobbing boats you ever saw." They all got a good laugh at the thought of this.

"You could be right, but I'll bet it only happens the one time. After that they'll think twice about interfering." Matt brought the group back to the seriousness of their task. "We can't forget that every boat we disable is immediately put in peril. If anything happened to them while we had them shut down, there could be serious problems."

"You mean like drifting ashore or wrecking on rocks?"

"Something like that. While they're lying dead in the water, we've got to insure that no harm comes to them. How can we do that?"

"We could gather them into groups."

"That's a good idea. Let's do that. We'll try to leave them close to where we stop them, so they aren't going to be dragged all over the water. We'll have to let them know we'll be back with their machinery parts or tell them they can pick them up at the base later that day. I want each of you to act in a responsible way. You'll have to be aware of wind and tide direction when you leave them. We don't want to have them carried out to sea so that we have to spend the next week on a search and recover mission. Understood?"

They understood.

My ship will have to leave the base at 04:00 hours tomorrow morning Gentlemen. We'll pick the sub up at Cape Flattery around 09:00 hours. I'd suggest you make your preparations today. We will issue all radio frequencies for this exercise tomorrow." Matt closed the briefing and checked in at his office for messages.

There were no messages but Tanya was waiting for him.

"Ready for something to eat?" she asked.

"God, is it that time already?"

"Sure is."

"Well, we can eat aboard or go into town. Which would you like?"

"Let's go into town."

They drove to the Wayfarer Hotel and found a table in the lounge. Ordering a drink to start, their attention was drawn to the large screen TV where the noon hour news was showing a major oil spill in the Seattle harbor. This type of accident bothered Matt. The damage to the system was difficult to assess, not to mention the mess it made among the pleasure boats. The thick oil stuck to a ship's hull like glue. It was an expensive and dirty job to clean.

The next item on the news was an interview with a spokesman for the protest group who were going to try to prevent the refitted USS OHIO arrival at Bangor tomorrow. Matt showed more interest. The interview finished off with the announcer reading a statement from the Whitehouse. The President had established a new FIVE mile safety area around naval ships. This new law would be tested tomorrow in Bangor Washington, with the arrival of the Trident submarine. All vessels were to remain outside this zone Matt was elated. He was disappointed not to have been notified at the base, but the news was the important thing, not the way it was delivered. Tanya commented on the grin on Matt's face.

"I think that's the best news I've heard today. Let's have a drink to celebrate." They ordered lunch at the same time as the drinks.

*   *   *

Friday Day 14, 04:00 hours.

Matt's ship left the pier at 04:00 hours heading for a 09:00 rendezvous with OHIO at the entrance to the Strait of Juan de Fuca. Travelling the 60 miles of ocean between his base and Cape Flattery would take four hours; he planned to arrive half an hour ahead of the sub. Commodore Coulter came along to observe, but not to direct operations. Matt had gone over the details with him so that he knew what to expect. The larger ships would join them west of the base and smaller craft just off to the north of the base. This way the smaller boats wouldn't be exposed to the rough water of the open ocean at the mouth of the strait.

"That's a good idea, Matt. We can do without someone lost overboard at this stage."

"Right, Frank. Our vessels will maintain a one mile distance from the sub and form a ring around her. (I guess we can now move out to five miles). The larger ships providing a shield will be moving in front."

Matt explained a contingency plan to bring six Zodiacs into the gaps between them if it turned out that the shield was penetrated. The helicopters will watch this area particularly closely.

Matt talked to the OHIO's commander by radio while she was still an hour away from Cape Flattery. He explained their deployment and how the Coast Guard would shepherd them all the way to Bangor. He confirmed they'd run at fifteen knots until approaching the Hood Canal Bridge where they'd have to reduce speed to five knots.

"The smaller protestor's boats shouldn't be a problem as they won't be able to maintain fifteen knots. It'll be a different story after we reach the Hood Canal Bridge though. From the bridge to Bangor we expect trouble. There's a high concentration of pleasure craft resident in the area and a good number of them'll be out. The navy's providing six Zodiacs to reinforce us at the bridge. It's only nine miles from the bridge to Bangor, so I suggest we pick up speed to at least ten knots for the final sprint and we'll do our best to keep small boats out of your path."

Heavy seas rolled the cutter during the last ten miles. Strong winds blowing twenty five knots from the south west whipped the wave crests into spray. Matt thought of the surfaced submarine riding through all this weather. The crew wouldn't like it. Normally they escaped all turbulence by sailing beneath the waves. He assumed she was on the surface.

"Radar contact bearing 214 degrees." Lieutenant Daniels announced.

"Distance?" Matt asked.

"Eighteen miles, closing at twenty two knots."

"Roger."

Matt turned the cutter in a wide circle to begin the intercept course. He wanted to approach her starboard bow and establish his position early.

"Let me know when they're ten miles."

In this rough sea Matt had to rely on his radar to tell him where the sub was. He couldn't depend on spotting her sail. The sub, on the other hand, should be able to make visual contact with the cutter as she was much higher out of the water. The sub also had a lot more electronic detection gear.

"Is the 'scope clear of other targets, Ernie?"

"That's affirmative, Skipper."

"Thank God for that. I don't relish dodging small fishing vessels in this water."

The radio marked first contact. "We have you visual, Confidence. Five miles, bearing 036 degrees magnetic from our position.

Ernie transposed the reading to its reciprocal "Heading 216 degrees Skipper."

Matt scanned with the glasses. "Have a visual contact. Maintain present course. We're right on the money, Ernie."

"Roger, Skipper."

Matt could make out the sail clearly now. This was not the first time he'd seen a sub this large. However, other subs which had visited were all much smaller.

"She's a long sub, Ernie. With the sail so far forward she looks like an eel."

"I see what you mean, Skipper. The rounded nose and tapering stern do produce that look. She cuts the water nicely though. Look at how the bow wave breaks passing up and over the fore deck. It looked almost like hair, parted in the middle, sweeping off to each side."

"Smooth isn't she? Even in this rough sea she's pretty stable." A wide wake of foam suppressed the swells where she cut through the heavy seas. A white bubbling trail spreading out for half a mile behind her.

"How big is she, Skipper?"

"Almost 600 feet long and 16,600 tons."

"Christ, that's bigger than most World War Two cargo ships."

"And she'll dive below 1000 feet, Ernie."

"Very impressive."

"Engines ahead full." Matt ordered.

"Engines ahead full, aye Sir." Ernie swung the handles on the telegraph.

The telegraph's bells rang and the engine room responded. The cutter's speed picked up.

"I hope we can keep up to her," Ernie joked.

"Come around to 060 degrees. We may have trouble 'till we get into the Strait. She's still doing twenty two knots."

Moving into position took a lot of engine and rudder changes. Matt controlled his ship well, soon matching the sub's speed and course.

"Well done, Commander." came over the radio from the sub. The captain was aware of the difficulty and recognized Matt's good seamanship.

"Thank you," Matt responded.

The two vessels entered the Strait on schedule and reduced speed to fifteen knots. They closed the distance to the base in good time. Two 82-foot cutters joined them off Crescent Bay, ten miles west of Port Angeles, taking their positions to port of the sub. Matt's helicopter hung in the sky 2000 feet over him and he watched as the smaller ships positioned themselves to 'run the gauntlet', as it were. An impressive flotilla!

Tanya stood by the radio, talking to Major Snellert. No unusual activity among the satellites. They didn't really expect too much until after the sub had completed the trip.

Matt watched their position closely. By the time they'd passed the first sono-buoy 'fence', there were close to twenty small boats plus all the Coast Guard vessels plowing through the water. 'The noise reaching the buoys must be deafening,' he thought, and wondered how the buoy could extract only the submarine noise from the entire din. He'd have to ask Mike about that.

With the pace beginning to pick up now, a few of the protestor's boats tried to make runs at the sub. Coast Guard boats were on to them immediately, turning them away. Matt asked the spotters in the helicopter to let him know where the faster protest boats were so that he could bolster the protective circle in their area.

"They're more to the south, off your starboard side. They're staying between you and the shore. Your speed's leaving many of them behind already. I'd say only a few can keep up to you."

This made Matt happy. He wasn't sure whether or not the higher speed would prevent trouble or cause it. It looked like the right choice. Matt thought about the easy time they were having now, but he knew the run from the Hood Canal Bridge could be a different story. A larger number of boats would be waiting, and they'd be more aggressive than these here in the Strait. If he closed ranks a little he should be able to keep them away from the sub. The thought of going to jail was not sufficient deterrent to the kind of fanatic this type of event attracted. Perhaps the stiffer penalties laid down just yesterday would make them think. The Coast Guard was armed and directed to fire if necessary.

Passing Dungeness Point they began to gather more small boats and by the time they rounded the point at Point Wilson and entered Admiralty Bay there were over fifty of them.

Matt got more nervous all the time knowing the channel narrowed considerably once into the Hood Canal. There would be less room for all these boats. There were also a lot that were waiting on the other side of the Hood Canal Bridge. There will be a crunch. Five miles north of the bridge he directed his two 82-foot cutters to run ahead and take up positions at each side of the pontoon swing span, the center passage of the bridge. They were to keep all small boats away from the bridge and warn all of them to stay north of the span's narrow opening. This would let Matt's cutter and the sub through followed by the other Coast Guard boats and, more importantly, it should reduce the number of small boats milling around south of the bridge. The helicopter reported close to thirty boats south of the bridge, not counting the boats supplied by the navy. 'Still too many' Matt thought, but there wasn't much he could do about that.

Passing through the bridge opening, they encountered their first real problem. The mass of small boats trying to follow under the bridge crowded one of their number into the bridge pontoon. This, combined with the current of the incoming tide, was enough to overturn it. Six people were dumped unceremoniously into the water. A mad scramble of boats resulted, each trying to pick up survivors. Coast Guard Zodiacs made the rescue: one, bringing all six wet protestors over to the 82-foot cutter on the west side of the bridge; another, getting a line on the hull, towing it to the west shore so that it wouldn't sink.

The two cutters followed the sub through the opened bridge and took up their positions again, now travelling at much reduced speed. Matt radioed the two Zodiacs to clear and rejoin as quickly as possible.

A good majority of the small boats were left on the north side of the bridge, but those already on the south side seemed to be more aggressive. High powered inflatables created a real problem weaving in and out and making dashes toward OHIO. Coast Guard Zodiacs raced after them and shut down their engines. That kept them out of the game altogether. They informed the owners that they'd come back after the sub was tied up and return their engine parts. The usual howls of protest were heard. "You can't do this to me. I'm an American citizen. I demand my rights," and so on. When Matt's men simply told them, over their loudspeakers of course, that they could go to jail and be fined instead if they wished to pursue the matter, most of them fell silent. Other boats witnessed all of this going on and soon there wasn't the same interest in colliding with the sub. The remainder of the trip was without incident. Boats from the Headland Yacht Club joined them.

Matt pulled the cutter up to the pier at Bangor. They had been steaming for over twelve hours and it was now late afternoon, time they had a rest. Mike greeted them at the gangway.

"Fine job, Matt. The whole thing went off pretty well."

"Thanks, Mike. She's all yours now. I'm glad to be finished."

"Come on up to the office, I'll buy you a cup of coffee."

"Just a minute. Tanya's aboard. I think she'd like to come, too. I'll call her." He used the PA to bring her to the pier.

The three of them walked along the huge wharf area to one of the roads leading to the administration building where Mike had his office. Mike wanted to know how Tanya was feeling and all the details of her excursion to cut Pua clear. She explained what had happened.

"You're lucky to be alive after that."

"We've been telling her the same thing, Mike."

They went up the few stairs into the administration building, down the hall and into Mike's office. "Pat, will you bring in some coffee, please?"

"Well, we've had a busy two weeks, Matt. Since your call about the explosion, things have been hopping."

"Looking back on it, I don't think I'd want to do it all over again."

"Me either. Oh. You might be interested to know we used those Russian code books to decipher some messages from their buoys in the Baltic. They are going to be worth their weight in gold to our intelligence people."

"That's good news, Mike. I was going to ask you how the buoys can pick up the noise of a submarine from all the noise set up by the flotilla going by today?"

"I don't think they will, Matt, not the first time anyway. They'll wait until they have the sub all alone, probably when she goes to sea next month."

"I guess that makes more sense. I hope they don't discover we've been into them before that."

Mike's aide, Pat, brought in a pot of coffee. Setting it down on the table he asked if there was anything else they might want. Mike told him no, not for the present.

Matt asked if there had been any developments with the research Kingsley was doing. "He's come up with a couple of things that we're going to follow up on. I think you were right that Russian subs have been transferring something to the ships in the fishing fleet. What it was we don't know yet, but we'll find out."

"Were there some subs among the trawlers?"

"Yes, on several occasions. We'd never have known about them if all this other stuff hadn't happened. We went back over some of our old satellite pictures, checked the infra red scans and there they were, large as life.

"What happens now?" Tanya asked. "If OHIO won't be leaving for a month, the Russians could come in to check their buoys?"

"They could, but we're not as worried about the buoys now as we once were. The buoys are small potatoes now, of course."

"I don't understand, Mike. Why have they lost their importance all of a sudden?"

"Matt, the code books are infinitely more important. The buoys are incidental. Finding the code books has elevated the operation from a theatre status to global status."

Not being familiar with the terms, Matt could only guess. "You mean this is no longer a major incident, is that it?"

"The discovery of the buoys was significant to the locale. That means it had importance for activities around the west coast. The knowledge we gained from the code books has importance on a scale much higher than the buoys. They provide a basis which we can use to formulate national defense tactics. You can see the difference."

The cloak and dagger stuff was a long way outside Matt's understanding. He could see the difference, but he didn't get as excited as Mike about it. Sure it was an edge, but that much?

"What you're saying is that if the Russians do come in to do maintenance on the buoys, and discover they've been tampered with, that's not important?"

"In a way. You're only partly right."

"Now you've confused me, too, Mike." Tanya added.

"What if the Russians find out?"

"They won't find out, Tanya. If they suspect we've tampered with the buoys and send teams in to check, they'll have a surprise waiting."

"How's that? Matt's curiosity was piqued.

"What surprise?" asked Tanya.

"We were prepared to leave things as they were with the buoys until we, rather, until you discovered the underwater station. Even then our plan was to get out, after reworking the electronics in the station."

"There's more?" Matt couldn't believe it.

"Finding the code books changed all that. Once we realized what we had, the Pentagon stepped in. They took the books and decided for us what was to be done with the station."

"Well, what was to be done with the station?"

"The analysis of the situation was done at the War College. They determined that maintaining secret the fact that we had discovered the code books, took precedence over all other considerations. It was my responsibility to guarantee the Russians don't find out."

"Fine, Mike. I can understand their concern but asking you for such a guarantee is a little much. You can't possibly do that. You'd have to stand guard over it day and night."

"That's what I thought, too, Matt, until the solution came to me on your cutter. Do you remember when we were clearing the equipment out of the station I made a final inspection dive?"

"Yes. I remember. You and one of your divers went down for a last look."

"Right. Well, we did the final inspection, but we also rigged a booby trap to the drawer where we had found the code books. Using the binary explosive we found in the station, we wired it so that if the drawer was opened the whole station would destruct. To the people topside it would look like an accident."

"YOU DID WHAT?" Matt, wheeling to face Mike, was yelling. He couldn't believe what he was hearing. "What happens if some of our local divers go in there exploring? There were gallons of that explosive. The whole ship would be blown apart!"

"That could be unfortunate, particularly if they find the station and get into it. If they try to open the drawer . . . ."

"Jesus Christ. How the hell can you justify such a thing?" He didn't speak the words, they tumbled out.

"The national interest . . ."

"National interest. Bullshit, Mike. Innocent Americans could be killed. You think it's all right to lay a trap like that and pass it off as national security? Why. Do you think that 'all's fair'?

"That's right, Matt. It's of vital, I repeat, vital importance that the Russians don't find out."

"At what cost, Mike? Half a dozen innocent divers and who knows what else? What price do you put on the lives of people who might be killed?"

"You know we can't put a price on lives. What was done had to be done for the good of all."

"That's crap, Mike, and you know it. Jesus Christ, how would you feel if your kids happened to be the ones killed?"

"That's a risk we feel is worth taking. Information the code books have provided has already permitted us to take up new defensive positions in regards to both our own and the Russian submarine forces. Matt, you don't appreciate the strategic advantage this gives us militarily."

"You're God damned right I don't. There's no way I can see to make your actions right. I still can't believe you'd do it, Mike. God damn, you think any means is justified by the end? Suppose the Russians did discover you had their code books. What's so God damn crucial? Would the world end?"

"No, of course not—"

"Well, it might for anyone with enough curiosity to be diving around that wreck. It could end very suddenly. Did you or the War College think of that?"

"Those were my orders, directly from the Pentagon. I carried them out."

"Just like a good soldier, Mike?"

"That's right, Matt. Just like a good soldier. I did a job, that's all." Mike scrambled to defend his actions.

"Well, I don't like the job Mike. I couldn't live with myself if I had to do jobs like that."

"I didn't say I liked it. I said I did it." He was reddening in the face.

"Come on, Tanya, I've got to get some fresh air. Good bye, Mike. I just hope the whole thing doesn't blow up on any one I know." Matt motioned to Tanya and headed quickly toward the door.

"I hope so, too Matt. I'm sorry you feel that way. I had my orders and carried them out. I'm not in a position to please everyone."

Matt stormed out of the building with Tanya almost running to keep up.

"Calm down a bit, Matt, you're going to blow a fuse." She put her hand on his arm.

"God damned zealots. That sort of thing scares the hell out of me. They get to a point where the system replaces logic and moral responsibility." He pulled his arm away.

"There's not a lot you can do about it now, so take it easy."

"God damn war machine. Why must it be so impersonal?"

They walked the last half of the distance at a slower pace. Matt was still burned but he slowed down so she could keep up. They boarded the cutter and Matt got under way as fast as he could. He gave control over to Ernie who started home to Port Angeles.

Matt seethed all the way. Tanya had never seen him so furious and tried to placate him.

"After we're docked, can we go somewhere special to eat?"

"Yes." He answered sharply, almost in a shout.

They left the pier immediately on docking. Matt turned the securing chores over to his number one. Tanya, without Matt knowing it had hustled him away to give him time to cool down. She had no idea what he might do. It would be better if he had a drink or two before he made his reports.

They parked and entered the hotel lounge. There was comfort in the dim lighting. Matt's eye was on a back corner booth where they could be isolated from the bustle of the other patrons. He led the way. A pretty waitress took their order, Matt a double whisky and Tanya a spritzer. They sat quietly, saying nothing.

"What happens now," Tanya broke the silence.

"I don't know. One half of me says, go down and make the area safe, the other half wrestles with the moral aspects of national security."

Tanya easily saw his moral conflict, so obvious by the strain on his face.

"I've got to make some kind of recommendation to the Commodore."

Their drinks arrived. Matt picked his up. "To Mike's better world, whatever it is." he said sarcastically.

"What's done, is done, Matt. There's no need to let it extract a heavy toll from you." She was right. There was nothing he could do about any of this. The die had been cast.

"I know that, but knowing doesn't make it any easier. I guess when it comes right down to it, I really have no choice if I want to stay in the Coast Guard."

"That's true. Why don't we look at the good side of the whole project?"

Matt put his glass down. His brow raised. "What might that be?"

"Well, if none of this had happened, we'd never have met."

He smiled. "I guess some good has come out of it after all." He took her hand and squeezed gently. Their eyes met and he gave her a flirtatious wink. They ordered another drink, this time Matt had a single.

"Where do we go from here?" she asked.

"I've got some holidays to use up before the end of the summer. How'd you like to take George up on his offer and go down to San Diego for a visit with Pua?"

"Only if you'll come over to Hawaii with me afterwards."

"You have a deal." Looking at the way her hair fell around her face and the cute tilt she gave her head, he wanted her right at that moment. He'd have to wait, though. "Let's get this report off my mind, and then we'll go over to my place and have a something to eat and then see what develops".

"Let's go!" She sensed his thoughts and grinned her little pixie grin.

CHAPTER 23

Saturday, Day 15, 13:35. Hours

A Russian vessel had called for a pilot at 13:00 hours that Saturday afternoon but not until she had sailed almost to Port Angeles. Waiting now fifteen miles west, she moved only fast enough to maintain headway.

The Pilotage Authority had called the Coast Guard base immediately to inform Commander Reynolds. Captain Sam Sawchuk drew the assignment to take her to a Seattle shipyard and the pilot boat quickly ferried him out to the Russian.

Sawchuck's pilot boat drew alongside the Russian factory ship, Mikhail Stroyny and just as it reached the crest of a wave Captain Sawchuk leaped. His agility carried him from the little boat onto the Russian's accommodation ladder.

Making his way up the ladder, he noticed that like all the other Russian ships he had been aboard lately, this one looked fairly new. Very little rust showed in places exposed to the harsh action of the salt water. The hull, clean and freshly painted. The boot-topping paint below the waterline had no voids or scrapes that he could see. The hull above that was equally free from rust spots. Quite a difference from some of the rust buckets in many other nations's fishing fleets.

Reaching the top of the ladder on the main deck, he was met by the first mate who introduced himself as Yuri Voroshilov, then escorted him to the elevator. "Do you speak English?" Sam asked the officer on their way up.

"Yes, I do." he said. "I have spent some time in your country. Actually I have a degree in oceanography from the University of Washington in Seattle."

"Oh! Then you must know the water around here fairly well."

"Yes. Most of my studies involved salmon of the Pacific Northwest."

The elevator stopped and the doors opened onto the bridge, four decks above the upper deck.

They stepped into a large business-like room scattered with the electronic navigational aids normally seen on naval ships. Sam's glances taking them in didn't go un-noticed. There were three other men on the bridge. Yuri introduced him to the captain, Gregori Prozolivy. He guessed the captain couldn't be more than thirty years old, a young man to be in charge of a ship this size, Sam thought.

"You seem to be surprised at the equipment, Captain." Another one that spoke English. Sam appreciated that. He'd be able to talk to someone during the trip.

"It certainly looks impressive. Do you need all of this in your work?" he asked as he waved his arm from one side of the bridge to the other. Radar, sonar and communications gear, crisp and clean stood on brand new pedestals.

"You must realize that fishing these days is becoming a much more exact science than it was only a few years ago. The successful fisherman not only requires this type of equipment he also needs a lot more luck than in the old days."

"Your ship must be very successful then, Captain."

"We have good and bad days, like everyone else."

"I guess you do. We can get under way now if you wish."

"What heading?"

"Steer 075 degrees magnetic until we get a bit further away from shore."

Captain Prozolivy issued an order to the second officer who swung the ship's telegraph. Bells rang and Sam felt the throb of engines and a slight vibration as the ship began to move. The captain's next order was directed at the helmsman. "A compass heading 075." The helmsman turned the wheel as he verified the order by repeating it to the Captain. The factory ship gradually gathered speed.

"Hold her about twelve knots, Captain."

"Certainly." He gave the order to the second officer who twisted a knob on a control console, watching a needle dance on an electrical gauge. Under way now and on the assigned heading, things settled down to ordered routine.

Yuri entered the bridge from the elevator, walking directly to the Captain, at the opposite side of the bridge to where Sam stood. Talking Russian and in hushed tones to the captain.

To the south, on Ediz Hook, a lone Coast Guard officer and a Navy woman stood in the bright sunshine, with binoculars, watching the Russian factory ship passing eastward in the Strait of Juan de Fuca. Sailing slowly along now over the spot where all their action took place. Matt's anticipation rose.

"How long before any divers could get down to the station?" Tanya asked.

"If they are going down, and I hope they're not, we'll know in about ten minutes."

Time suddenly slowed to a crawl for the two of them. The Russian ship continued sailing eastward until it became a spec on the water.

Tanya broke the silence, "Nothing's happened. It's been over twenty minutes, maybe we got lucky."

"I certainly hope so, but there's a ticking time bomb down there. I hope we never hear about it again."

Tanya added, "We've got better things to look forward to. The dolphins are waiting for us down south and we shouldn't disappoint them, should we? Let's go pack for our trip to San Diego. I can't wait to get away from here for a while."

-    30—
    -